Praise for

The Healer's Heart

"*The Healer's Heart* had me with the first paragraph. It's a warm and intelligent novel of deftly drawn characters that tells a timeless story."

—BILL MYERS, author of *Soul Tracker*

"With beautiful writing and an honest look at the harshness of the world we live in, Diane Komp creates a masterful story of faith and redemption in *The Healer's Heart.* The journey of Luke Tayspill to discover the secret of his grandfather's prophecy is our journey as readers to learn more about what it means to live by faith and sacrifice ourselves for others. This is a rich, meaningful novel that will resonate in your mind and heart long after the final page!"

—DAVE DRAVECKY, former major-league pitcher, and president of Outreach of Hope Ministries

"In *The Healer's Heart,* Dr. Komp skillfully intertwines the lives and unfolds the healing hearts of Yale AIDS physician Dr. Luke and African American Bishop Paul. She brings together the timeless biblical picture of the healer into the modern setting as her real-life characters deal with the devastation of disease, modern epidemics, interethnic and intertribal wars, and human conflicts. She shows how people from other cultures and backgrounds can impact Americans in a positive way. In this fast-paced, thrilling story, courage, faith, and love triumph over prejudice, mistrust, and hate."

—DR. TOM HALE AND DR. CYNTHIA HALE, medical missionaries in Nepal for twenty-five years, and joint authors of *Medical Missions: The Adventure and Challenge*

"Diane Komp brings us a modern-day Luke who finds healing by reaching out to those who are marginalized. The enormity of the HIV epidemic cannot be understood in numbers alone. Komp helps us understand that it can be embraced through individuals who transform our intellectual and spiritual struggles."

—ARTHUR J. AMMANN, MD, president of Global Strategies
for HIV Prevention

"A moving story about finding faith and discovering forgiveness. Komp challenges the reader with the same question presented to her characters: If you have no cause worth dying for, do you have a reason to live? Readers who take this compelling journey from Ohio to London to Sierra Leone will be inspired to answer that question."

—KATRINA KITTLE, author of *Traveling Light* and *The Kindness of Strangers*

"I am very pleased to endorse Diane Komp's *The Healer's Heart*. The reach of the novel is truly global. More specifically, with the shifts from the Gullah islands and Sierra Leone, she has revealed the links among sites of the African diaspora. Her innovative use of the Gullah account of St. Luke, which begins each major section of the book, keeps alive for the reader the blend of the biblical past and the Black diasporan present. I view these structural links and the treatment of the theme of generous, selfless caring as the book's major achievements."

—JOHN A. MCCLUSKEY, professor of African American and African
Diaspora Studies and professor of English at Indiana University, and
author of *Look What They Done to My Song* and *Mr. America's Last
Season Blues*

"In *The Healer's Heart*, we're reminded that the past is never just the past; it resonates through all that follows in sometimes painful, sometimes joyous, often unexpected ways. Diane Komp writes compellingly of secrets guarded and then revealed, of lives transformed when we face them honestly. A graceful book by a talented storyteller."

—ROBERT INMAN, author of *Captain Saturday* and *Dairy Queen Days*

The HEALER'S HEART

DIANE M. KOMP

WATERBROOK
PRESS

THE HEALER'S HEART
PUBLISHED BY WATERBROOK PRESS
12265 Oracle Boulevard, Suite 200
Colorado Springs, Colorado 80921
A division of Random House, Inc.

Scripture quotations and paraphrases are taken from the following versions: A Gullah transla-
tion of the gospel of Luke, *De Good Nyews Bout Jedus Christ Wa Luke Write,* prepared by
The Sea Island Translation and Literacy Team in cooperation with the Summer Institute of
Linguistics and Wycliffe Bible Translators, copyright © 1995 by the American Bible Society.
Used by permission. All rights reserved. The Jewish-English translation of the Masoretic
Text, *The Holy Scriptures According to the Masoretic Text,* copyright © 1917 by the Jewish
Publication Society of America. Public domain. The *King James Version.*

ISBN 1-57856-913-3

Published in association with Yates & Yates, LLP, Attorneys and Counselors, Orange,
California.

Library of Congress Cataloging-in-Publication Data
Komp, Diane M.
The healer's heart : a modern novel of the life of St. Luke / Diane M. Komp.—1st ed.
    p. cm.
  ISBN 1-57856-913-3
  1. Physicians—Fiction. 2. Americans—Sierra Leone—Fiction. 3. AIDS (Disease)—
Treatment—Fiction. 4. Sierra Leone—Fiction. I. Title.
PS3611.O584 H43 2006
813.6—dc22

                                                          2005026173

Printed in the United States of America
2006—First Edition

10 9 8 7 6 5 4 3 2 1

To Brima Bangura and World Hope Sierra Leone

Acknowledgments

"Tayspill" is a Flemish Huguenot name. Like the fictional Luke, I found a genealogy in my father's desk that allowed me to trace the Tayspill branch of my family back to thirteenth-century Flanders. Giles and James Tayspill, Elizabeth Gurney Fry, Thomas Wentworth Higginson, Charlotte Forten, Margaretta Forten, and Dr. York Bailey are authentic historical characters. As much as possible, I have paralleled their genuine roles in history. The Tayspills' role in the Gullah Bible translation is fictional.

I wrote portions of this novel during Antioch Writers' Workshops in Yellow Springs, Ohio, and received their 2004 award for the first work published based on the workshop. Special thanks to Joan Horn who assisted me with research at the Glen Helen Nature Preserve and Friends Care Facility. Although the village of Yellow Springs and Antioch College exist, the town of Hobart Corners is fictional as are the Sierra Leonean villages of Lonko and Kameara.

Thanks to the staff of Penn Center (former Penn School) on St. Helena Island, South Carolina, especially to Veronica Gerald, and a boy named Cedric who befriended me one morning in the graveyard of Brick Baptist Church.

The concept and components of spiritual diagnosis are a modification of a system described by Paul Pruyser in his book *The Minister as Diagnostician*.

Thanks to iron-sharpening-iron friends like Marge, Philip, Juan, Randy, Martha, Renate, Dale, Karen, Mary Ellen, Wilton, Betsy, Hayden, Debra, Matt, and members and staff of the United Methodist Church of Branford, Connecticut, who slugged through the manuscript one chapter at a time to give me their feedback.

Thanks to the Prinsell, Emmett, Shea, and Zikes families and other members of the Wesleyan Medical Fellowship who shared their fond memories of Sierra Leone and their snake stories.

The congregation of St. Stephens AME Zion Church, Branford, may find that Bishop Paul Pinckney bears a suspicious resemblance to their pastor, Rev. Charles Woody. The staff of World Hope Sierra Leone may find that Brima, the nurse, bears a suspicious resemblance to their nurse, Brima L. Bangura, who turned me into a "bush doctor" upcountry in Sierra Leone. Rabbi Hilkiah is modeled after an authentic Jew I met who was living in a Muslim village in Sierra Leone. Captain Cut Hands was the *nom de guerre* of a rebel during Sierra Leone's ten-year civil war. Fortunately, I never had the opportunity to meet him. Also thanks to S. D. Kanu, Saidu Kanu, Jo Anne Lyon, and Anne Meddars. A portion of the income from this book will go to support the work of World Hope Sierra Leone.

So the story of…St. Luke is the story of everyone's pilgrimage through despair and life-darkness, through suffering and anguish, through bitterness and sorrow, through doubt and cynicism, through rebellion and hopelessness to the feet and the understanding of God.

 —Adapted from Taylor Caldwell,
  Dear and Glorious Physician

THE TAYSPILL FAMILY GENEALOGY

Giles Tayspill (1548–1588)—son of Jean Tayspill and Martine van der Fosse Tayspill; Flemish Huguenot cloth maker exiled to England during the Protestant Reformation.

Lucas Tayspill I (1830–1875)—great-great-great-great-grandson of Giles; Quaker sailmaker born in Philadelphia; conscripted by the Federal army during the Civil War to serve in South Carolina.

Lucas Tayspill II (1864–1887)—also known as Junior; son of Lucas Tayspill I and Amoretta Capers Tayspill; born on St. Helena Island, South Carolina; moved to Hobart Corners, Ohio, after his marriage.

Giles Tayspill (1888–1969)—son of Junior Tayspill and Mary Elizabeth Biggs Tayspill; carpenter and painter; born and died in Yellow Springs, Ohio.

Martin Tayspill (b. 1924)—son of Giles Tayspill and Katherine Harrington Tayspill; born in Yellow Springs, Ohio; retired philosophy professor from Antioch College.

Luke Tayspill III, MD (b. 1964)—son of Martin Tayspill and Edith Yancey Tayspill; born in Yellow Springs, Ohio; AIDS specialist at Yale University School of Medicine in New Haven, Connecticut.

PROLOGUE

Jedus…say, "Come folla me!" Bot de man ansa um
say, "Sah, fus leh me go an bury me papa."
—LUKE 9:59, *De Good Nyews Bout Jedus
Christ Wa Luke Write* (Gullah)

Thanksgiving Night

It would be easier to bury my father, he thought, *if he had already died.*
Dr. Luke Tayspill hesitated at the door of his father's study. The
simple act of returning home had reduced a confident doctor to a hesi-
tant child. He reached for Theo's hand—an automatic gesture—but came
up with air. That motion, intended as a spousal embrace, ended in a
clenched fist. *Inhale…exhale…inhale…exhale…* Luke's measured breaths
failed to banish the thousand and one thou-shalt-nots that fixed him in
place. He remained frozen on the threshold.

He had come to the room to find a dying man's living will. As far as
Luke knew, his father had never signed such a document, but now, to
withhold life support, the hospital wanted a clear indication of Martin
Tayspill's wishes. Under most circumstances Luke would have considered
such a request to be quite reasonable. When his own patients were dying,
he wanted clarity in such matters. However, standing at the door to his
father's study, the head of Yale's AIDS Care Program wasn't operating
within the realm of reason. When he entered Martin Tayspill's house,
Luke abdicated the role of eminent scientist and reassumed the posture
of child.

In a hallway looking glass, he caught a glimpse of himself framed by
late Victorian oak. He frowned at the younger specter of his father he saw

reflected back. A few years earlier, when his facial hair began to show specks of silver, Luke had shaved off his mustache. He was thirty-four at the time, too young (in his opinion) to be sporting gray. Just that morning at the nursing home, he had noticed the milky arcs that dulled his father's eyes. Luke hated the betrayal of age that allowed others to prejudge a man. How soon would medical students call him "the old man" behind his back? Most of his patients died too young, but standing in front of the mirror, Luke could think of nothing good to say about growing old.

Framed by a pair of diamond-paned windows, the desk that drew him to his father's study loomed tall against the southeastern wall. Now as in his childhood, Luke felt as welcome in this room as the late-morning sun now flooding in through Belgian-lace curtains. Closing his eyes, he willed himself back to his fifth year of life, when the room and the Queen Anne secretary desk with a thousand secrets had belonged to his grandfather. So had the sunshine.

Inside the room to the left of the door, a longcase clock struck eleven in Whittington chimes. The clock was the last piece of furniture Grandpa Giles had crafted before his death. An easel with half-used tubes of paint stood in the far-right corner of the room, just as it had when Luke was a little boy. Giles's self-portrait, muttonchops camouflaging jowls, remained propped up on the easel, unfinished. *These days,* Luke thought, *Grandpa only comes to me in my dreams.*

Finally Luke found the courage to step into the room. Drawing close enough to the desk to caress its slanted lid, he allowed his fingers to trace the wounds in the wood that had banished him from this room more than thirty years before.

Three years after Giles's death, Luke had yearned for the comfort of his grandfather's lap. The boy came into the room and sat down on the

Chippendale chair. He studied the old familiar desk. Until Grandpa took sick, the two of them would come to the study together after breakfast. Luke's task had been to guess which cubbyhole hid that day's special treat. The desk was rich with concealments, including drawers that only Giles—its designer—could have located. Luke wondered if, before he died, his grandfather had hidden one last treasure for him to find.

He pulled down the desk lid and found a picture card secreted in a niche. Was it Grandpa's final surprise? On one side he saw printed words. On the reverse side a robed man knelt in a painted garden, his face looking as sorrowful as Luke felt that morning. The boy—who had never been in a church—could not explain why that religious picture appealed to him. Nor could he explain why he took a letter opener from a drawer and gouged three words into the folding top of the desk: WHERE ARE YOU?

Martin Tayspill's eyes blazed the day he found the defacement. After Giles's death, the study and the desk had become his property. Luke's father sanded and stained the desk surface but ignored the child's lament carved in the wood. Martin banished the culprit from the room, but scars remained on the barrier that locked the picture in. Grandpa Giles was gone, shut away with Jesus so many years ago.

In vain Luke searched for his father's living will. Then he yanked on a fixture on the bottom drawer. It resisted entry. He frowned, unable to remember his father or grandfather ever opening that drawer. The brass pull, he assumed, accented a false facade. Dropping to his knees, Luke ran his fingers around the rim and slipped a credit card between the drawer and the frame. He found an unexpected gap and continued to explore beneath the desk. A block of wood moved at his touch. As he rotated the knob, a lock gave way. "Sly one, Grandpa," he whispered.

Nothing in the drawer belonged to Martin Tayspill—or to the present. Luke found his grandfather's Marine Corps commission and honorable discharge from the end of World War I. Some mice had left their calling cards on letters from Grandma Kate, addressed to Grandpa Giles at Parris Island.

Luke had completed his search, but a mystery lingered. The drawer containing the mementos was not as deep as the one above it. Pulling it out as far as he could, he stretched his hand to reach the back of the drawer. As if released from a secret it longed to reveal, a panel folded forward, disclosing a second compartment.

The hiding place surrendered a faded packet the mice hadn't reached. Untying the butcher's string that bound it, Luke slipped out a thick black-and-white composition book filled with his grandfather's handwriting. On the cover, in a more calligraphic style, Giles had written a title: *The Deaths of Lucas Tayspill.*

Not death, but *deaths.*

PART I

Deah Theophilus, plenty people beena try fa write down all de ting wa we beliebe fa true, wa done happen mongst us.

    —LUKE 1:1, *De Good Nyews Bout Jedus Christ*
      Wa Luke Write (Gullah)

ONE

Ohio

Hunched over the operative field, the doctor pulled opposing pieces of skin together. The needle curved in and out, closing the gap with 3-0 silk sutures. Satisfied with the results, Luke straightened up and stripped off his apron. As he slipped the turkey into the refrigerator, he told his mother, "This year we won't lose any stuffing."

Edith Tayspill supported herself on the kitchen counter and kept her back to her son. She picked up an onion and cut through its middle to veil her tears. Then she risked speaking. "It's nice to have you home."

Luke bent down to kiss the top of his mother's head, but quickly returned to his chores. He pulled a BlackBerry out of his pocket and consulted a to-do list. He attacked a moment of domesticity the same way he tackled his chores at the hospital.

He read the list aloud. "Day before Thanksgiving: Chop celery, walnuts, and onions. Peel potatoes. Halve and seed butternut squash. Chill wine." He reached into a shopping bag he had brought with him from Connecticut and pulled out two bottles of 1977 Cochemer Nikolausberg Eiswein Riesling. "Can you think of anything I forgot, Mom?"

Edith sniffed and inhaled her tears before she turned around. She looked confused. "Is that an Ohio wine? Father prefers local vineyards."

Luke caught himself before saying how costly the wine was and deflected the choice from himself. "Theo loves Eiswein."

"Theodora's not here."

"When I bought the wine, I thought she would be."

The tears Edith had banished resurfaced. "Father will be so disappointed. I don't understand why Theodora has to be in London on Thanksgiving."

Luke returned to the squash. "The Brits don't celebrate Thanksgiving. It's an American holiday. This assignment is very important to her."

"'Important' isn't a career or a foreign wine. 'Important' is making a family. Anyway, that's what Father always says."

Luke frowned as his mother parroted Martin's opinion. As usual, his father had life figured out on his own terms. *It could have been worse,* Luke thought. Theo could have been there to hear what his mother said about her failure to get pregnant.

He turned from his mother's thoughts to his upcoming sabbatical. "If faculty wives have nothing of their own to do, they can be miserable in a foreign city, even in an exciting place like London. Didn't Dad ever take a sabbatical out of the country?"

His mother, wife of an academician, didn't answer, and Luke was sorry almost as soon as the words escaped his lips. His father had made a career of making his mother's life miserable.

Edith tried to smile. "Father adores Theodora."

"Dad should have had all daughters." Luke wasn't joking. Martin could always find room for improvement in his son, but both Theo and Luke's sister, Johanna, he considered perfect.

Edith reached for a container of milk in the refrigerator and stumbled over a sleeping dog.

"Moose, come!" Luke called as he reached out to prevent his mother's fall. The Yorkshire terrier hobbled toward his master and settled at his feet. Luke petted Moose to console him. "Good boy."

Moose lifted his lip to smile, revealing an Appalachian toothscape.

Edith started crying again. "Moose misses Theodora."

The dog had come into their lives when Luke and Theo had almost divorced. Six years into their marriage, they were fighting about everything, including the breed of dog to share. Luke wanted to recreate the boy-dog palship of his childhood. He would have preferred a bluetick hound like his old Beauregard.

The day Theo walked out on Luke, she bought a Yorkie to take his place in her bed. During a brief reconciliation, she allowed Moose to join Luke on the sofa bed in the living room. When the couple finally reunited and Luke had been welcomed back to Theo's bed, Moose made the definitive decision to sleep between them.

These days Luke made jokes about living with a runt. He even coerced doggy dementia pills out of a drug rep at the hospital to keep Moose going. Moose was a vital link between him and the woman he had adored for most of his life. And Beauregard had left Luke too soon. When words failed, it was better to have a dog do his communicating for him.

In the backyard, not far from the kitchen where Luke and his mother were preparing Thanksgiving dinner, Beauregard lay buried. As Luke peeled potatoes, he looked out on the grave Grandpa Giles had dug for Beau under a weeping cherry tree.

Watching his grandfather shovel dirt, the child reached up and tugged on his father's sleeve. "Can we say a prayer?"

Martin slipped his arm around his son's shoulder and squeezed tight. "No one will hear it."

"When people die, don't the other people talk to God?"

Luke felt his father stiffen and waited for the lecture that would follow.

"Some people pray when they need a crutch to lean on. Intelligent people don't need crutches."

The boy persisted with his questions. "Is God someone you lean on?"

Color rose in Martin's cheeks. "Where did you ever get an idea like that?"

Luke pointed to his chest. "I looked it up in my heart."

Martin lifted his arm from his son's shoulder and poked his index finger into the side of the boy's head. "You look things up here." Then Martin turned to the boy's grandfather, knee-deep in the grave. "You're filling Luke's head with nonsense again."

Giles kept on digging, but Luke was certain his grandfather had heard what his father had said.

Color drained from Martin's face as he turned his attention back to Luke. He collected himself and resumed his lecture. "The heart is a muscle that pumps blood. It's not a magical place to store myths." Martin clenched and pumped his fist to illustrate the propulsion of blood.

The boy was confused. "Is your hand the same as your heart?"

"No, Luke, your heart is inside your chest."

"Then why did you squeeze your hand?"

Martin frowned. "To show you what happens in your chest."

"Is your heart where you hold things tight?"

Luke watched his father turn his attention back to the burial. Lecture over, the boy opened and closed his fist.

Later that evening Luke concealed himself in the hallway shadows outside his grandfather's study. Giles sat at his easel, sketching the beginnings of a landscape in charcoal. Martin came in and stood behind the old man. Luke could see the tension in his father's neck muscles. The old man sensed Martin's presence but didn't stop what he was doing.

Martin's voice faltered as he spoke to his father. "I don't want you teaching the boy mythology. Respect my right to raise him as I see fit."

Giles kept working on his painting, just as he had continued digging in the garden. He might as well have been alone in the room.

Martin grasped his father's shoulders. "Are you listening to me, old man?"

Giles spun around, dislodging his son's grip. "In a world of competing ideas, why shouldn't Luke hear as many ideas as possible? What are you afraid of?"

Hiding in the shadows, the boy watched his father and grandfather contend. He saw tenderness replace the tension around his grand-father's eyes.

Giles spoke to his son in an even voice. "I love you."

Martin bristled. "You're changing the subject."

"That *is* the subject. A man should love his son."

In the safety of the hallway, Luke agreed with his grandfather. His father, however, became defensive. "Are you implying I don't love Luke?"

"No, Martin, but this morning that little boy's doggy died. Instead of comforting him, you lectured him about the way you see the world."

"I could have made my point more readily if you hadn't confused him with all that talk about his heart."

"We both used analogies. What's the difference?"

Martin turned on his heel and marched out of the room. "There's a big difference. He's my son, and I'll raise him my way."

The boy under discussion blended with the hallway shadows as his father stalked out. For a moment, Luke hid and watched his grandfather. Giles clenched callous hands and rested them on his easel. He turned his eyes toward the ceiling. His eyes burned as if he could see through the plaster to the sky. When he picked up the charcoal stick again, Luke entered the room and climbed onto his grandfather's lap.

"Did I do anything wrong?"

"No, child. Of course not."

"Why is Daddy mad?"

"Your father doesn't always know why he feels the way he does."

"Why should that make him mad?"

"It's hard to be a daddy, but your father tries his best."

"Is it hard to be a grandpa?"

Giles laughed. "Sometimes, but most of the time it's a lot easier to be a grandpa than a daddy."

Luke rubbed out tears escaping his eyes. "Where's Beau, Grandpa?"

Giles took Luke's hand, traced the path of one tear that ran all the way from Luke's left eye to his T-shirt, and then made an abrupt stop at chest level just above the letter *r* in YELLOW SPRINGS printed across his chest. He took the boy's hand and let him feel the lingering wetness. Ashamed to be a crybaby, Luke tried to pull his hand away, but his grandfather held Luke's hand so tightly to his chest that it hurt. A torrent escaped Luke's eyes and made its way down to meet his fingers. Grandpa Giles caressed the boy's hand, guiding the tears to find their mark. "That's where Beau is, child. He's swimming from your head to your heart."

Luke closed his eyes to forget the day of Beau's death. He had to focus on the Thanksgiving holiday at hand, with his wife in London and his father in a nursing home.

"What time should I pick up Dad tomorrow?" he asked his mother. He wanted to enter the time in his electronic brain.

Edith stared at him. "Whenever dinner is ready."

Half a mile from the Tayspill homestead in Yellow Springs, Martin Tayspill was recovering from the latest of two strokes. Thanks to the founding Quakers, Friends Care Facility smelled of fresh baked bread rather than unchanged linen. Martin's room looked out on a garden named Planet Earth. There, too, strong, pleasant perfumes prevailed.

Edith leaned against the kitchen counter to keep her balance. "I may just lie down for a while although there's still a lot of work to do for our dinner what time do you think you'd like to eat should we do it after Father takes his morning nap?"

Luke frowned when he heard the confused sentence. If his mother's symptoms repeated themselves, a headache would come next.

When Martin was a younger man, Edith's headaches had been more frequent. He had often stayed away from home overnight and returned the next morning without offering any explanation. With his advanced age and diminished vigor, his wife retired less often to the darkness where she locked the bedroom door.

"You take your nap, Mom. Moose and I will go out for a run."

When Moose saw Luke's running shoes, he roused himself and stomped out a happy dance. If the dog could endure a mile of their run, Luke reckoned it would be a lot, so he grabbed a backpack to tote Moose home. "What else do we need? Some trail mix. Some water." He tossed his BlackBerry into the pack. "The troops are moving out," he called, and the Yorkie soldier ran for the door.

Leaves crunched underfoot as Luke and Moose padded together through Glen Helen Nature Preserve. As the dog's nose pursued scents on the trail, he burst ahead of his master. But he waited when he reached a bend.

At that special place, Luke had first seen Theodora, and the couple and their dog had returned there many times after. Moose knew it as a place where his master and mistress were as happy as they had been when they were children growing up in this small college town.

Like many faculty families, the Tayspills went for Sunday strolls in Glen Helen. That particular day, Martin, chairman of the philosophy department at Antioch College, sauntered ahead with art chairman Harry Jenkins. Their children lagged behind, searching the woods for leaves rumored to take the itch out of poison ivy. When the hikers reached the ruins of an old hotel, they ran into the new owners of the Antioch Diner.

"Is this your daughter?" Martin asked Dimitrios and Eleni Kannoudakis. The girl had knee-length raven hair and hazel eyes flecked with gold.

Her parents smiled as they nodded.

Harry Jenkins looked as if he had seen a glorious ghost. "La Bella Simonetta!"

"No sir," the child answered. "My name is Theodora."

Martin agreed with Harry. "You're right. She's a perfect Botticelli."

Theodora Kannoudakis had no idea who Simonetta and Botticelli were. But Luke was certain that the professors were going to inform them all.

Harry Jenkins gestured as he warmed up his lecture. "Simonetta Vespucci was the most beautiful woman in all of Renaissance Florence. Botticelli used her as a model for all the divine women he painted. She was his Venus. She's the Madonna. She's every man's dream of heaven. All the men in Florence called her 'La Bella Simonetta.'"

While Harry carried forth, Martin knelt in front of the child and turned her face on profile. "You have Simonetta's face, but her hair was reddish gold. All the famous artists of the day wanted to paint her."

That day her future father-in-law dubbed the Kannoudakis girl with the pet name of the Renaissance beauty. Later she became "Theo" to Luke, but Martin always called her "La Bella Simonetta."

A few days after their meeting on the trail, Luke tagged along with Martin and Harry when they took an art book over to the Antioch Diner. The professors showed the Kannoudakis family reprints of the Botticelli paintings. Theodora saw her face on someone the whole world thought of as divinely beautiful.

Eleni Kannoudakis smiled that day. She shared her daughter's eyes and lips, even the shape of her face, as if an artist had charcoaled a preliminary sketch before attempting his final masterpiece. In Theodora, Eleni's features had reached perfection.

From that moment on, Luke found as many excuses as possible to prod his family to eat at the Antioch Diner. The Botticelli book disappeared from Martin's bookshelf and found a new home underneath Luke's mattress. The boy had fallen in love with that face.

Luke was running over a footbridge when his cell phone began to ring. It had to be Theo, so he panted into the device, "Hey, babe."

"Luke, Luke."

Wailing faded in and out, but the connection was too poor for Luke to make out what she was saying. He juggled the phone for better reception. "Theo?"

"Luke? Are you there? Oh, please, Luke, you've got to come!"

Two

London

In Suite 401 of the London Crowne Plaza, Theodora Tayspill piled her waist-length black curls on top of her head and sank into a cloud of fragrant bubbles. Unlike other guests of the establishment, she didn't use the little bottles of hotel bath foam. She floated in suds that smelled of "Theodora."

A decade ago the *New York Times* had assigned Theo to cover the Bosnian War. When she returned home after the war, Luke paid experts in aromatic romance to create a personal scent for his estranged wife. For $275 per quarter ounce, they blended floral extracts with mossy top notes of clary sage, bergamot, and galbanum to come up with "Theodora."

Formulated as an invitation to love, the scent perfumed her neck, sacheted her pillow, and bubbled her bath. "Theodora" celebrated try-again love. You could trace the vigor of the Tayspill's marriage by this scent—until Moose started to sneeze. The dog, of course, was sleeping in the marital bed and was happy with that arrangement.

Luke never told Theo, but he was delighted with Moose's allergy. He expected his wife to banish the dog from bed. Instead, she put away the scent of love.

A few vials of "Theodora" survived. Theo kept some in the master bathroom of their Connecticut home and one vial in a makeup bag she used for overseas travel. But Theo hadn't traveled abroad in recent years. Not at all, in fact, until an invitation drew her back to her private hell. Into the inferno known as Sarajevo, she carried "Theodora."

✠

Theo stretched back into the tub and let her neck sink into the bubbles. She wanted to remember those first days at home with Luke and Moose after the war. The memory was hard to recapture because the moment hadn't lasted very long. She had retired Luke's costly love gift, and the dog had remained in bed.

✠

As Theo lay with her back to Luke, she heard him pick up Moose and deposit the Yorkie at the bottom of the bed. She remained unmoved as her husband nuzzled at her neck. She buried her face in her pillow so he wouldn't see her tears. Then she felt Luke pull away and turn his back to her. Theo listened to hear whether Luke would fall asleep, but all she heard were short puffs of anger that swelled into staccato bursts of words. "I want back the girl I met in Glen Helen."

Theo remained on her side of the bed. "I'm not a little girl. I'm a grown woman."

He reached over and placed a hand on her shoulder. "Why can't you be both?"

Her tears soaked the pillowcase as she spoke again with muffled voice. "I can't."

Luke released the unresponsive flesh. "You can't? You mean you won't!"

"You know what the doctors said—"

He interrupted. "You wouldn't have needed those doctors if you had stayed home."

She turned to face him with tear-stained cheeks. "What home? When I left, we weren't married anymore."

"Yes, we were," Luke said. "The separation was just a formality. We were just having a few problems we could have worked out. We've always loved each other, haven't we?"

Theo turned away again and took a cigarette from the bedside stand. In defiance, she lit up and puffed in the doctor's direction. "Sometimes love isn't enough."

She watched him watch the smoke, his eyes narrowing into a medical lecture. Then he took his eyes off her cigarette and willed them to relax their look of condemnation. He leaned over Theo and took a cigarette out of her pack. As he put it to his lips, she pulled it away. Then she crushed out her own cigarette and kissed him on the cheek. "One of us with a filthy habit is one too many."

They sank back onto the bed and molded to each other, not moving except for stroking each other's arms. Luke was the first one to break the silence. "We live in the same house, but we inhabit separate worlds. I feel as if you're in a witness-protection program, while I'm continuing on with our normal old life."

"There was nothing normal about our old life," she said. She bit her lower lip as if self-mutilation would mitigate the defiance in her voice. "It's going to take time," she whispered.

"Time," he repeated. "Well, I've got plenty of that."

As thoughts of the Bosnian war crowded back into her consciousness, Theo remained silent. So often in those days, she had thought she had no time left.

✠

Theo sat up in her London tub and turned on the faucet to reheat the water. She slipped under the bubbles and remembered the psychiatrist who treated her when she came home, the one who blamed her mood swings on the horrors of war. For the next ten years, she had accepted the diagnosis of post-traumatic stress disorder, but she had her own more personal description for what ailed her. She lived with too many ghosts and too much failure. One day she would have to face both ghosts and failures, but that day had not yet arrived.

When Theo and Luke left New York City for Connecticut, she thought their day had arrived. The move was good for them both. Luke was happy with his new position as chief of the AIDS Care Program at Yale. Theo traded in the overstimulation of the city for the shelter of a country home and a feature column in the Sunday *Times*. Through Luke's connections at Yale, she had access to enough minor luminaries to please her new editor. Then, after so many years of trying to forget Sarajevo, she accepted another assignment there.

Theo climbed out of the tub and pulled the plug on the foamy water and painful memories. Better to think about the reason she was in London, and her meeting with Nathan Green.

The London bureau chief of the *New York Times* kissed Theo on the cheek, but he got right down to business. "How did it feel to go back to Sarajevo?"

Theo knew Nathan was watching her as she answered. Was she ready to jump back into the thick of things? In the old days Theo had been the best war correspondent on staff at the *Times*, but that was before Sarajevo.

As much as she wanted this assignment while Luke was on sabbatical, Theo hesitated to answer and measured her response. She chose a diversion. Better to invite Nathan's personal reflection than to allow the focus to remain on her. "Do you remember the signs on the way into Sarajevo from the airport?"

Nathan was not distracted, even when Theo wove her arm through his. He grunted and frowned. "I remember the bullet-riddled sign on the old Olympic stadium. *Dobrodosli u Sarajevo*. 'Welcome to Sarajevo.' Then you turn the corner and—*poof!*—the dilapidated building with the spray-painted words 'Welcome to hell.'"

Theo nodded. "That was the truth during the war. The truth now is that it still is."

Nathan stopped talking and turned to her. "But you couldn't stay away from that hell."

It bothered Theo that her potential boss was pushing her into the center of peril. She had barely recovered from her first visit to Sarajevo more than a decade before. She tried to smile. "You're right. I had to go back."

Nathan relaxed—slightly. Once Theodora Tayspill was a renowned journalist, and under his tutelage, he hoped she could be again.

"Tell me what happened this week in Sarajevo," Nathan asked, ushering her into his office.

As he settled behind his oak desk, Theo wondered why the setting reminded her so much of a psychiatrist's office.

Nathan's question made her crave a cigarette. After ten years of nicotine abstinence, she had yielded as soon as she got off the plane in Sarajevo. She pulled her last pack of Bosnian *Drinas* out of her purse and lit up. There was no ashtray on his desk, and he didn't look for one to give her. She put out the cigarette in her coffee cup and picked up the story.

"Do you remember Jasmina? She was one of the doctors I interviewed during the war. When she called me recently, she sounded scared to death. She claimed that someone was building a high-level containment lab in the hospital where she was working. She suspected it was being used for germ warfare."

Nathan was skeptical of tips offered by old contacts seeking new dollars. "How could she be so certain?"

Theo lit another cigarette. "None of the hospital staff was allowed in that wing. The guards looked like Arabs rather than Bosnian Muslims. Jasmina wouldn't talk to anyone but me—and only in person. So I agreed to check out her story. If her life was in danger, I wanted to get her out of the country."

Nathan was satisfied with what he had heard so far. It matched what Theo's editor in New York had told him. "What did Jasmina say?"

Theo frowned. "I couldn't find her. The chief of staff at the hospital told me she had gone to visit an uncle in Tuliz. One of the nurses said she was with a lover on vacation. I didn't think either one of them was telling the truth. My whole trip was a waste. To make it worse, the whole international press corps showed up in Sarajevo. They had all heard the same rumor."

Nathan leaned back in his chair. "It wasn't a waste if you were willing to return to Sarajevo. I'd say you're ready for action again."

Theo didn't contradict him, but neither did she smile. She had gone back to Sarajevo to get rid of her ghosts, not to keep them constant company. "I'm all yours for six months, if you want me."

Nathan rose and took her hand. "You've got the job if you want it."

After the interview with Nathan, Theo walked out into the November air and pulled her coat around her. Despite the cold, she chose to walk the mile to Harrods.

Shopping did nothing to improve her mood, so she crossed over Brompton Road toward the Victoria and Albert Museum. A display of sixteenth-century Limoges enamels failed to distract her from what was on her mind. From the museum she wandered toward Hyde Park Corner and threaded her way through the streets of Shepherd's Market. She was about to turn onto Curzon Street when she heard rock music coming from a church. Curious, she tried the door of Good Shepherd's Chapel and found it unlocked.

The sanctuary was bare, except for folding chairs stacked against the walls and a stained-glass window over the altar. A group of young rockers with tattoos on every inch of visible skin, spray-painted hair, and pierced body parts was making music in front of the altar.

We believe in God the Father, Maker of the universe...

The words to their song sounded ancient, but their instruments throbbed with a modern beat.

Theo heard a voice behind her.

"Hello there."

She spun around and faced a gray-haired woman wearing a thin coat over a housedress. "I didn't mean to intrude," Theo said.

"You're not intruding any more than I am. I'm on my break right now."

Theo felt relieved. "I was looking for a place to sit and think."

The woman smiled. "You've come to a good place for that, you have. I come here often."

Theo looked around. "I'm confused. I've never been to church much. I kind of expected..."

The woman laughed with such warmth that Theo relaxed. She took Theo's elbow and guided her toward the altar. "Smells and bells and wounded knees? This church isn't that formal. There's an organ all right, but most of the time we sing to band music—songs like these young people are rehearsing."

The musicians packed up their instruments and departed. The woman pointed to steps leading to the altar. "We can sit here on the steps. On Sunday the little children love to sit here. They feel so safe and welcome."

Theo joined the woman and looked up at the figure of Jesus holding a lamb in his arms. "That's how I need to feel."

"He's searching for lost sheep," her companion said, reading Theo's thoughts about the fragments of colored glass.

"I know how that feels."

"To search or to be found?"

Theo raised an eyebrow but didn't answer. For the next ten minutes, she stared at the window, grateful for the astute charwoman's quiet presence. "Thank you for staying here with me."

"No problem at all."

A half hour later, Theo stood up. "I must go."

The two women walked down the aisle toward the exit. "I'll be praying for you," the stranger said.

"You're very kind."

"When I'm praying, what would you like me to say to God?"

Theo turned toward the altar and gazed at the window. "Tell him not to give up on any lost lambs."

Then she walked back to the hotel and drew her bath.

✠

As Theo climbed out of the bubbles, she breathed in the last whiff of Luke's love. In front of the bathroom mirror, she frowned at herself through the fog on the glass.

"La Bella Simonetta," she mocked. "The feminine divine."

She took a towel from the rack and wiped mist off the mirror. Exaggerating each vowel, she began her nightly facial calisthenics. "I feeeel beee-uuuu-teeee-fuuuul." She exercised each muscle around her mouth. She examined the left and right sides of her face for signs of asymmetry, any hint of a tremor. Her survey complete, she consoled herself. "Not yet. Not yet."

How long would it be before she needed a lip-plumping procedure to keep from drooling? How many months after that would her eyes become forever locked in place? Tomorrow she would pose the same questions to a Harley Street neurologist. How long after she heard his answers would she be able to keep the truth from Luke?

Long after midnight she lay awake. Sometime before dawn she fell asleep, but she woke up crying, "God help me, Luke! I'm locked in!"

THREE

Ohio

Luke sat down under a tree and fiddled with the cell phone, trying to get better reception. The sweat on his forearms started to evaporate and give him a chill. He stood up and tried running in place.

"Luke," the voice repeated. "Luke. Help me."

Moose barked as if he had recognized the caller's voice.

"Hello? Hello?" Luke said.

Finally the voice came through clearly. Edith Tayspill spoke through sobs. "Please come home right away. Father had another stroke."

As he jogged back to his parents' house, Luke saw their Thanksgiving plans dissolve.

As Luke and Edith arrived at Friends Care Facility, an escape attempt was in progress. Luke could hear the alarm from a block away. Someone was determined to run the gauntlet of nurses and aides to make it to freedom. Nurse Nancy Anderson was in pursuit of a wheelchair charging through the front door. Luke heard his father yell, "Let go of me. I want to go home."

"You *are* home, Professor," the nurse said as she stopped him dead in his tracks. She paused when she saw Luke and Edith, and then patted Martin on his shoulder. "We're a little upset this morning, but doctor says it was only a little TIA."

"That's a transient ischemic attack," Luke said, translating for his mother. "A mini-stroke."

Edith took over steering the runaway back to his room as Nancy led Luke to her office.

"Your father doesn't have any new neurological damage, but he is unhappy. The professor doesn't know why we're fussing." She closed the office door and pulled out a chair for Luke. "I need to talk to you about something. Do you know if your father ever made out a living will?"

"I'm not really sure."

"When this happened this morning, I looked through his chart and couldn't find any advance directives. If your dad stops breathing, we will have to call a full code and transfer him to an emergency room."

"We wouldn't want that."

"Has your father ever talked to you about his wishes?"

"No, but he's still competent. I can't make decisions for him without his consent."

"Perhaps you could get him to sign a health-care proxy giving you the power to make his decisions about DNR orders. We'd all rest a lot easier if we had something in writing."

"I'll try, but you know how independent he is."

"But please try."

Nancy knew because she had been dealing with Martin since his first admission, when the professor had gone home more by escape than by medical design.

✠

After his first stroke, when his inpatient benefits had run out, Martin told Edith to bring his car around to the front door of the nursing home. The doctor hadn't discharged him yet, but that didn't hold Martin back.

"I'm not going to pay out of my savings to be kept in jail."

When Luke heard about this escapade, he flew to Ohio, where he found his father in the garage, hobbling around his workbench with the help of a walker.

As Luke got out of his rental car, his father fumbled with the tool belt around his waist until he found the nail he was looking for. Martin held it in place with his weak arm and hammered away. "You startled me," he said to Luke. "I thought you were that nosy social worker from the funny farm."

"Friends Care is for rehabilitation. You know how much you need that, and you know how nice they've been to you."

"Fine. You go sign yourself in and see how friendly you find it."

"Why are you afraid of the social worker?"

"She'd rat me out, and they'd cut off my home therapy if they knew I could drive."

"You can't drive. You just had a stroke."

"Who are you—the DMV?"

Luke panicked as he watched Martin hold down a piece of wood with his paralyzed hand and reach for the power saw. "Can I help you?" he asked, fearing the answer.

"I don't need anybody's help, thank you." The expected answer.

Martin fixed his attention on his project. As he leaned on his walker, he used his nonparalyzed foot to push a wedge of wood toward a place between the house and the garage.

"What are you making?"

"I'm building a handicapped access ramp for my car."

Edith appeared on the front porch, dressed in a summer frock. She seemed more fragile than the last time Luke had seen her. How had the social worker described his parents? *The Brain and the Legs.* Martin and Edith possessed a complementary set of handicaps. On that June day his father's brain seemed to be plotting overtime, but his mother's legs didn't look as if they could hold up her half of the bargain.

"You're just in time," Edith said. "Father and I are going to Glen Helen."

Luke immediately grasped the implications of the plot, and he turned to his father. "Shall I drive your Caddy or do you prefer to come in my car?"

Just a few months before, they had all walked the few blocks to the main entrance and had easily descended more than a hundred steep limestone steps. Luke could just imagine a man negotiating that with a walker.

"I'm driving," Martin said, disengaging further debate.

Now alarmed, Luke said, "I can take you and Mom wherever you need to go."

Martin stared ahead, escalating the confrontation. "I'm driving to Glen Helen."

Luke's alarm turned to anguish. "You shouldn't be driving at all. You had a right-sided stroke that affects your ability to control your emotions. If you get in an accident, you may not be able to think clearly. Other people might get hurt."

Martin set his jaw into his words. "When I'm in the car, I'm in perfect control."

Luke had played his trump card but trailed in the game. "Your pride is interfering with your judgment. You have to think about the welfare of others."

That was a serious miscalculation.

Martin fumed. "Thank you for your diagnosis, Doctor. If you don't trust your father's driving, take your car, and we'll go in ours." *Final.*

Luke turned to his mother. "Dad shouldn't be driving. You can talk him into letting me drive."

"I can drive," said the woman with fainting spells and headaches who always took Martin's orders. "No doctor ever told me I couldn't. If anyone told me that, I would be the first one to give up my driver's license."

Long ago Luke had given up checking on what doctors had advised his parents and then making sure they complied. His meddling had signaled them it was time to change doctors. No law says that competent adults have to stick with doctors who tell them what they don't want to hear. And Luke knew that if he took away their drivers' licenses, his parents would continue to drive anyway.

With Edith beside him and smoking oil trailing behind, Martin wove the mile to Glen Helen in his twelve-year-old Caddy. Unable to negotiate a better compromise, Luke followed a car length behind.

On the garden paths, former colleagues enjoying the summer day welcomed the Tayspill family. The retired college librarian greeted Martin and Edith. "How nice that Luke could bring you this morning."

Edith snapped at her old friend. "Luke's visit had nothing to do with us getting here today."

Like a pimpled teen without honor in his home country, Luke put his hands in his pockets and stared down at the path.

Why does it always come to this with age? he wondered. He didn't want to strip away the last vestiges of his parents' pride, but the village professionals had left it to the son to handle the driver's-license confrontation.

Heading home at a safe distance behind the Cadillac, Luke calculated the final score of their morning jaunt—zero-zero. Everybody lost. His father, however, was using a different scoring system. Martin reached over and patted Edith's thigh. In the rearview mirror, Luke caught his father grinning.

✠

In the months between his strokes, Martin became more cunning than compliant. He suspected he might never make it home from the nursing home again. Until he was certain who was standing by him, he kept his eyes closed. As Edith wheeled him to his room, he whispered, "Bring the car around to the front door."

"Why, Father, you know I can't do that."

When Luke came from Nancy Anderson's office, he found his father sulking. He watched tears form in the old man's closed eyes. Thanks to the stroke, the stoic philosopher could weep over the most trivial thing, then he'd weep over the fact that he had wept.

"Hi, Dad," Luke said.

Quickly the survivor of the real-men-don't-cry generation wiped away the evidence and clicked on the TV remote.

Luke refused to let Martin ignore him. "Nancy asked me to help you with some paperwork."

"There's no paperwork to do," Martin said without looking at his son. "Mother brings everything I need from home, and I tell her what to do."

"Have you ever signed a living will?"

Martin began to fidget and fixed his eyes on a football game. He never watched football at home. He hated the game. "Maybe I did. Maybe I didn't. It's none of your business, sonny. I took care of everything in my will."

Luke fidgeted as much as his father did. To accomplish what he set out to do, he would have to be more explicit with his father than he had hoped to be.

"This isn't about money or inheritance. A living will is about medical decisions. There may be things you won't want to happen in the end. If your situation gets worse, would you want to be on a respirator or be fed by a tube?"

"It's not going to happen."

"What's not going to happen?"

Martin changed the channel to another football game. "Not gonna linger."

Luke had reached his limits for pushing his father. "You've done a great job recovering from your strokes, but you can't always count on that. What will happen if you have a third big stroke, not just a little TIA like this morning?"

"There you go with those doggone abbreviations again. I sent you to medical school speaking perfect English, and you came back speaking gobbledygook."

"You had a mini-stroke this morning."

"Nothing happened this morning. Nothing important."

Luke conceded that point to make a larger one. "What happens if you have another major stroke?"

"That's easy," his father said, staring at the television without looking. "If I have another stroke, I die and my will kicks in. It's very simple. You just make things so dang complicated. Did they teach you that in medical school?"

Luke pressed on. "It's not that simple. What if you have another big stroke and you don't die?"

Martin closed his eyes to shut out the question and the questioner. "That's not going to happen." End of conversation. Then with Edith in pursuit, he took off down the hallway in his wheelchair, grabbing onto the handrail to propel himself along.

Luke stopped at the nurses' station to see Nancy Anderson.

"My father is stubborn, but he's not incompetent," he told the nurse. "No judge or doctor would override his right to make decisions for himself. You know my father's will of steel."

"The professor's steel will isn't what we need. We're after his living will."

"As long as he's fully aware of the implications, I won't do anything to override his wishes."

"Of course not. But could you look through his papers at home and see what you can find?"

At bedtime that evening Luke emptied his pockets onto the top of the dresser. A framed black-and-white snapshot stood there. In it, Grandma Kate and Grandpa Giles sat on a loveseat with children on their laps. Luke's older sister Johanna straddled Kate's knees, and Luke nestled with his head on Giles's shoulder. You could see cancer's toll in the old man's face and a lifetime of carpentry in his hands. Edith sat on the floor in front of her in-laws. Martin was the only family member missing from the portrait.

✠

"Look over here, everybody," Martin said. "On a count of three, everybody say 'cheese.'"

Luke yelled out before his father could start the count. "Cheese!"

Edith felt Giles's legs stiffen behind her. "Are you okay, Dad?"

"It will pass. Just give me a second."

Sitting on Giles's lap, Luke felt his grandfather's back arch and turned to see his face become ashen. "What's wrong, Grandpa?"

"I just got a crick in my back."

"Do you want me to rub your crick for you?"

"That would feel good. Oh my, yes."

Luke stumbled onto a painful point, causing his grandfather to grimace. Giles tried not to react to the pain. Grandma Kate dabbed at her eyes with the lace handkerchief tucked into her sleeve. Edith choked back tears. "Is that better, Grandpa?" Luke asked, missing the cues of the adult drama.

"It surely is. What would I do without my little doctor?"

"We can take the picture another time," Martin said from behind the tripod.

"Let's do it now," Giles answered, forcing a smile. "I want to capture this moment while it still belongs to us."

"On the count of three—one, two—"

"Cheese!"

Luke remembered the sound of everyone laughing at him. Two weeks later Giles was dead.

✠

Luke set the clock radio for 6:00 a.m. and crawled under the covers. Moose climbed on top and blanketed his master with sprawling warmth. The dog's sighs transitioned into soft snores. As stressful as the day had been, Luke's breathing soon synchronized with the dog's gently heaving chest. In a recurrent dream, Luke found his grandfather alone and alive in Flanders fields.

Giles was crawling through rows of white marble crosses bordered by a field of blood red poppies. Rather than delicate blossoms swaying in a Belgian breeze, Luke saw paper buttonhole poppies crushed by the weight of domino-downed doughboys. The flowers had fallen like a little boy's tin soldiers.

"Where are you going, Grandpa?" Luke asked.

Resting on a grave, Giles pointed to the horizon past the town of Ypres. "I'm not really sure, but I think this is the way."

Kneeling on the ground next to his grandfather, Luke moistened the tail of his T-shirt with spit and cleansed the old man's wounds.

"You're the best little doctor in the world," Giles told him.

The child summoned all his strength and hoisted the fallen marine out of the white-manned graves and onto his feet. Giles stood before him, a vigorous young man. "I must go on a mission, but I don't know where it's leading me."

Grasping his grandfather's hand, Luke said, "Please don't go away again." He stretched to his full height and straightened his back like a little marine. As he stared down the rows of crosses, Luke said, "Come on, Grandpa. We'll go there together."

With these words and his small hand, he took his grandfather into his heart.

Four

London

On Thanksgiving morning, Theo woke up alone and afraid. She was tempted to skip her appointment with Sir Nigel Garvey, MB, FRCP, and fly home to Luke, but she knew that wasn't an option. If she arrived home before Luke expected, she'd have to explain why she hadn't gone apartment hunting in London. If she called him, he would ask about Sarajevo and her week in London. *Liars,* she thought, *never act in a vacuum.* For every lie she told, someone stood on the receiving end. Usually it was Luke.

She pulled a telephone directory out of the bedside stand and looked up the number for Marta van der Fosse. Again she hesitated. Her relationship with Luke's cousin had been troubled since their student days at Antioch College. Back then Theo had known the woman as Martha Foster. Sometime later Martha traded her British birth name for something pseudo-Flemish. "Marta" claimed the change had something to do with family heritage, but Theo suspected her motivation. Ever since Theo had known her, Luke's distant relative wanted to be more than his cousin.

Despite her misgivings, she dialed. "Hi there," she said, waiting for Marta to recognize her voice.

"What a surprise to hear from you." The neutral tone didn't betray whether Marta considered the surprise pleasant or disturbing.

Theo waited for Marta to say more, but she didn't. Finally Theo filled in the silence. "I'm in London for a few days."

Marta kept her answer crisp. "I just got back myself."

After another long pause, Theo asked, "Anything interesting?" She wasn't really interested.

"I had an assignment for the Middle East peace process. I was unpacking when the telephone rang."

Although she hated to put herself and Marta on the same level, Theo needed to bridge the gap she felt growing between them. "I guess conflict mediators cover as many wars as foreign correspondents do."

"Are you back to covering wars?"

"I'm on my way back from Sarajevo and have a few days of business in London."

"Sarajevo? I'm surprised to hear you went back."

"So am I," Theo said, but then couldn't think of anything else to say. Again, silence. This time she waited.

"Is Luke with you?"

"He's with his folks."

Theo felt rather than heard the loss of enthusiasm in Marta's voice. "Isn't today your Thanksgiving Day?"

All right, Theo thought. *I'll beg.* "Yes. A tough day for an American to be away from home."

She wondered whether the next painful pause was deliberate. Finally the invitation came.

"Come by this evening around six and share some chicken. It won't be as fancy as your American turkey, but it's the best I can do under the circumstances."

"Thanks. See you soon."

Theo packed her bags and checked out of the Crowne Plaza. Half an hour later, eight hours before Marta expected her dinner guest, Theo and her luggage appeared at the door to the flat.

"What a surprise," Marta said, staring down at Theo's bags. "Welcome to my crumbling edifice." She tried to remember if she had invited Luke's wife for more than a meal.

"I was hoping I could stay with you for a couple of days."

Face to face with Theo, Marta found it harder to inflict silence. "Sure," Marta said but frowned.

Theo hesitated at the door as if considering her alternatives, but then she followed Marta through rooms filled with Penny Lane bargains and Belgian artifacts. Marta put her bags down in the single bedroom.

"You can sleep in here. I'll be fine in the sitting room."

"Oh, I couldn't let you sleep on the couch!"

"Nonsense," said Marta, who tried harder to be a hostess than Theo worked at being a guest. Marta moved into the kitchen and plugged in an electric teakettle. "My digs may not be as fancy as the Crowne Plaza, but I do make a better cup of tea."

When Theo sat down at the breakfast bar, she kept her coat on.

Marta had finished with the small talk. "Okay, Theo, what are you doing here?"

Theo fiddled with her teacup as she thought of an answer. "I just came back from Sarajevo," she said, as if everyone would understand what that meant without further explanation.

"So you said." Marta sat back, remembering what she had heard about Theo's first trip to that city. "Is Sarajevo still hell?"

"How about another cup of tea?"

"Are you changing the subject? You've got to admit that you might owe me an explanation for dropping in like this."

"Can we talk about tea?"

Marta pressed. "It's Earl Grey. Are you still living in hell?"

"I didn't want to be alone this weekend."

Marta raised an eyebrow. "And you thought of me?"

Theo looked down at her cup. "I didn't know where else to turn."

"Tell me about Sarajevo."

Theo stood and paced the length of the kitchen. She held out her right hand as if she had a cigarette.

Marta persisted. "How did it feel to go back?"

Theo sucked air from an imaginary butt. "Do you have any smokes?"

"There's a shop a block away, if you really need fags."

"No, that's okay. It was an automatic thought."

Marta hoped her guest would get on with the story. "What was it like?"

"Smoking?"

"Sarajevo."

Theo talked about her trip, or at least as much of it as she seemed willing to disclose. "I thought I could turn the clock back and start over again. Maybe I could return to Sarajevo and get it right. I thought I might be able to leave town when I finished this assignment and let the ghosts stay behind."

"What were your ghosts up to?"

"Raising hell. When I got to the Holiday Inn, I had to stay outside on the promenade for ten minutes. I just couldn't go inside."

Marta wondered how much trivia she would have to endure before Theo got to the meat of the story. She stood up and started working on the chicken while her guest continued her narration.

"It started snowing lightly, just like my first day in Sarajevo all those years ago." Theo mimicked the motion of drawing snowflakes onto her tongue, and then contorted her lips into a grimace. "I looked across the highway to the UN building. They've only repaired one of its towers since the war. That skyscraper is just like my life—half healed, half still a wreck under repair. Finally I made my way to the reception desk and asked for a room without a view."

Marta remembered the Holiday Inn during the war, full of reporters and relief workers. A view of the Dinaric Alps meant a window facing the snipers' nests. She wanted to speed up the pace of Theo's storytelling. "Did you meet any snipers this time?"

Theo fiddled with her teacup and laughed nervously. "Only a man I knew during the war."

"You know the oddest people."

Theo raised an eyebrow in agreement. "My tip was a dead end. I couldn't even find my informant. I was ready to head home when I ran into him." Theo touched her fingers to her lips and inhaled. "A storm was forming over the mountains, churning up clouds. The weather fit my mood. I left the hotel and set off down the promenade for breakfast. I wanted to find the guys at Café Sarajevo and bum a cigarette. I had been in town for three days and had already smoked nine packs."

Marta didn't want to hear about cloud formations or smoking habits. "Who is this man?"

Theo stared at her teacup. "Someone from the old days I didn't want to see. An Aussie named Shane Callahan. But I was dying for a cigarette, and I knew he'd have some. I told Shane, 'I'd be happy to join you.' Big fat lie."

"He knows your whole story?"

Theo's face clouded. "Some of it. Too much."

Marta waited, hoping for details Theo had never disclosed, but instead Theo seemed to lock away that part of her mind. "What about your assignment—the reason you were there? Did you get the story you were after?"

Theo shook her head. "I couldn't find Jasmina. The chief of Internal Medicine gave me a tour of the new facility. It was full of empty beds. He said they were taking a page from the Israelis' book and were building a hospital wing for victims of bioterrorism."

"But that's not what Jasmina suspected. Did you believe her boss?"

"From what I saw, it appeared to be just what he claimed it was. He gave me a copy of standing orders for patients who would come to that unit. And, to tell the truth, I've never heard anything about biological weapons in Bosnia."

Marta put the chicken in the fridge. "These days, if you have the money, you can rent mass destruction from your friendly street-corner terrorist." She washed her hands. "You'll have to tell me the rest tonight. I'm off to work for a few hours. Divorce mediation today. Personally I'd rather deal with civil wars than uncivil spouses. At least war zones have cease-fire lines. What are you doing today?"

"I have some appointments around town. Then I'm going to find a flat. Luke has a sabbatical coming up in London."

Marta tried to control her surprise, but Theo caught the beginning of a smile.

"I hope we can find something affordable in Mayfair or Bloomsbury."

Marta shrugged. "Keep dreaming, Theo. You're talking about pricey neighborhoods. Well, I'm off to holy deadlocks."

When Marta left, Theo went into the bathroom and examined her face in the mirror. She wondered whether she should put on makeup for her appointment with Dr. Garvey. Finally she just washed her face. Doctors, she decided, prefer to see you naked.

Adjusting her steps to the pace of Londoners, she hurried down to the Underground at Bayswater Station. With time to kill before her appointment, she looked for estate agents.

As Marta had predicted, the rents for flats in Mayfair and Bloomsbury were priced out of reach. None of the agents held out any prospect for a short-term rental in that part of town, either. Theo walked up to Cavendish Square with less spring in her step. On Harley Street, address of the medical superstars, she found a brass plate with Sir Nigel Garvey's name set on a red lacquered door. She hesitated on the steps until she realized she'd be late if she waited a moment longer.

Sir Nigel ushered her into his consultation room. "You're a long way from home, Mrs. Tayspill."

Garvey looked like the type of doctor who, no matter how long you knew him, would never call you by your first name. Even on your deathbed, he would probably address you as Mrs. or Miss, but never Ms.

Theo tried to be cordial. "Thank you for seeing me today."

"Connecticut has many fine neurologists, especially at Yale. At home you have access to some of the top men in their field."

"My husband is one of Yale's 'top men.' He's an infectious-disease specialist. He'll be at University College this spring on sabbatical, so I thought I'd shop for a doctor in the area."

"Considering your symptoms, I'd say that is wise." Sir Nigel's left eyebrow took a northern excursion but promptly returned to a non-judgmental plane. "What you described on the phone could be nothing. On the other hand, I might have some most unpleasant news to report." He left the room to allow her to undress and get lost in her thoughts.

Theo looked into a mirror over a sink. Even without makeup, she saw no clues on her face. She slipped into a gown, climbed onto the examination table, and waited for the doctor to return.

"Is it possible this is all in my mind?" she asked as Garvey examined every muscle group in her body.

He paused from checking her cranial nerves long enough to listen to her question. Patients can't show their teeth and talk simultaneously. "Do you mean conversion hysteria? I don't think so, my dear."

Theo didn't like having her ideas so easily dismissed. "Why not? I told you about my psychological problems."

Garvey shook his head as he resumed his exam. He asked her to grimace, a silencing gesture. "You lack two key elements for that diagnosis. In conversion hysteria, the neurological symptoms solve a psychological problem." He paused in his exam long enough to invite a response. "Wouldn't you say your symptoms have caused anxiety rather than alleviated it?" Without waiting for her answer, he resumed his exam.

Theo moved her eyes on command to the left, to the right, up, and then down. "So I fail 'la belle indifference' test. What's the second key?"

"The subconscious doesn't know its neuroanatomy. When the mind invents symptoms, they don't fit together into one neat disease."

"Just my luck my disease knows its anatomy." She brushed away tears. "Is there anything I can do—diet, vitamins?"

Sir Nigel shrugged and signaled her to stick out her tongue. "Good nutrition and vitamins won't hurt, but they won't cure you."

Theo felt desperation rising in her throat. "I want you to tell me the truth."

Sir Nigel scratched his beard and motioned her to lie back on the exam table. "Well, yes, but one would think one would want the company of the doctor in the family at a time like this."

Theo sat up, interrupting the flow of the exam. She was tired of the "one speaking to one" clinical formalities. "It's my body and my problem. The truth belongs to no one else."

Theo fell silent. The anger left her face as she allowed Garvey to resume his probe. He motioned her to get off the table and stand on the floor with her feet apart. As he signaled her to touch her finger to her nose with her eyes closed, he studied the face before him. If the situation had been different—if he were not her doctor, if she were not his patient—he would steal a moment to trace the line of that face. How often when he admired a Botticelli painting had he longed to have its model come alive. Of all the faces he wanted to see retain their beauty, the one before him was the archetype. But Theodora Tayspill was no more accessible to him than Simonetta Vespucci was. To regain his clinical indifference, he asked her to keep her eyes closed for another neurological trick. His throat dry, he said, "I'll try my best to help you regain your health and maintain your independence." Even as he said the words, Garvey wished it were possible.

Theo had run out of questions. Reluctantly Garvey indicated he was through. "Join me in my office when you finish dressing," he said, walking out of the room.

Theo refused to sit down when she entered his office. She took a pen and a slip of paper from his desk and wrote out her cell-phone number. "Use this number to reach me with any results. I prefer not to have any messages on my home answering machine."

Sir Nigel sat back for a moment, debating whether to rise to face her.

Finally Theo sat down. Garvey wrote out a list of instructions. "These are the tests we need to do. They are not to confirm the diagnosis. We need to determine how advanced your case is." He placed the paper on her side of the desk, but she didn't pick it up. Once again he studied her face. "Are you trying to protect your husband or yourself?"

Theo took the paper and put it in her purse without reading it. "I'm trying to survive."

FIVE

Ohio

J oyful, joyful we adore thee. Marlena Smalls and her Hallelujah Singers
blasted open Luke's Thanksgiving morning. Disoriented, he sat up
in bed and reached for the clock radio to turn down the volume. *Oh, I
want to praise him.* As Luke shook himself conscious, Moose moved over
to claim the whole pillow.

It was midday in London, an ideal time to call Theo, but when he
dialed her number, he heard a computer voice. "Your cellular party is out
of reach." So much for the latest teletrinket the *New York Times* gives its
correspondents. He tried the Crowne Plaza Hotel next but was no more
successful in locating his wife. The desk clerk said she had checked out
that morning. Next came the *Times* London bureau. He hoped that, like
most Brits, their staffers didn't celebrate the American holiday.

"I'm sorry, sir, but Ms. Tayspill isn't here."

"What time are you expecting her today?"

"We're not expecting her. Shall I have her call you if we hear from her?"

"Did she tell you where she'd be staying?"

"She booked right across the street at the Crowne Plaza. Would you
like that number?"

"No thanks."

Luke turned to the sack hound on the bed. "Where's your Mommy
Dog?" As he slipped on his clothes, he heard his parents' telephone ring.
He ran to the kitchen to grab it. "Theo?"

"Sorry, Luke. It's Nancy Anderson. I'm glad you answered instead of
your mother. A few minutes ago the professor had a massive stroke. We're
transferring him to Good Sam. The ambulance just left."

✠

Since Luke's last visit to Good Samaritan Hospital, mammoth white buildings had sprung up to dwarf the familiar faded brick. When he was a little boy, the brick buildings had seemed like giants. But even giants have their predators. He remembered seeing signs everywhere when he was too young to read the words. Quiet Hospital Zone had disappeared, along with the hushed tone it demanded. Ambulances sirened their way to the emergency-room entrance. Doctors yelled to nurses in the hallway. One sign remained—Children Under Sixteen Not Allowed. All those years ago when he visited Grandpa Giles, his mother had served as his passport. The rickety lift was gone, with its clanging gate and the attendant who stared straight ahead. This time Luke was steering his mother, their roles reversed from his last visit. Luke entered the sleek new Otis elevator and closed his eyes just as he had on his way to see his dying grandfather.

Only one person in the corridor was on a child's level the day he visited Giles. A young nun knelt as she scrubbed the floor with the same intensity she might have applied to fighting a spiritual battle. Luke saw the bottom half of another figure, a starched superior of the kneeling novice. Unlike his grandfather, who always stooped to a child's position or lifted him up to his own, the matron loomed over her charge. He pulled his mother along the corridor as quickly as he could to the open charity ward and jumped onto Giles's bed.

"Grandpa, Grandpa! Today's my birthday!"

The child caught his mother off guard. Edith was relying on the strange environment and escalating morphine dose to blur Giles's sense of dates. He was supposed to be home by his grandson's birthday.

The odors of cancer and death had replaced Giles's familiar cologne. Luke held his breath as he clung to the old man. "Grandpa, your hands are so cold."

"That's just my skin, Lukie. I still have a warm heart."

The child took his grandfather's hands in his. "I'll make you all better."

"That's my little doctor," Giles said as he nodded off to sleep.

Luke's grandfather never made it home from Good Sam, but he survived as long as he needed to. He had seen his grandson one last time.

┿

Luke had vowed never to return to that hospital—a foolish oath for a doctor and a son to swear. For sons and doctors, there will always be one more hospital. He had left his grandfather's room educated in the telltale signs of death. Now he was returning to read the signposts for his father.

This time when they stepped out of the elevator, his mother was the wide-eyed one. As they wandered down the corridor looking for Martin's room, his mother broke the silence.

" 'Never in my worst nightmare did I ever believe my life could end this way.' That's what Father told me."

Luke stopped short. "Those are Dad's words, not yours?"

"Father said he doesn't want to die in a hospital. He'd rather be home in his favorite chair. Who would want to die in a place like this?"

Luke remembered Nancy Anderson's request to find Martin's living will. "Did Dad ever write those words down?"

"Father doesn't need to write things down. He tells me what to do, and I do it. We've always done it that way."

They found Martin's room by following a bellowing noise.

"He's stable now," a nurse said as Martin took a swat at her.

There was nothing wrong with his lungs. "Johanna!"

The nurse tied a wrist restraint to his bedrail. "He keeps asking for someone named Johanna."

"Hi, Dad. It's Luke."

"Where's Johanna?"

"I spoke to her a few minutes ago. She sends her love."

Martin struggled against the restraints. "I want Johanna!"

"Did Sister say when she'd be coming?" Edith asked.

Luke shook his head and hoped the conversation would move on. Johanna, Martin's favorite, had told her brother she couldn't leave California for the time being. She had an editorial to write for a philosophy journal. Luke kept that excuse to himself as he sat down at the bedside and took his father's fettered hand.

"Johanna?" Martin asked.

Luke let go of his father's hand and sank back in the chair. He had labored at Yale for seven years, holding his own among the nation's leading egomaniacs. Compared with coming home, Yale's competition was easy. Luke could tolerate rivalry from colleagues more easily than his father favoring his sister.

A doctor entered the room, presumably Martin's attending physician. Ignoring Edith, he spoke directly to Luke. "When I looked through your father's chart, I didn't see DNR orders. Does he have a living will?" Nancy's question, repeated sooner than Luke had hoped.

"I tried talking to Dad about that yesterday, but he didn't give me a direct answer."

Edith tugged at the doctor's sleeve. "Father wants to die at home in his easy chair."

"I understand you're a physician yourself," the doctor said, still ignoring Edith. "You know how important this is."

"I'll look through his desk tonight."

Edith poked at the doctor's arm. "At home in his easy chair."

"The sooner the better," said the white-coated demigod with the power to return Martin to his favorite chair.

Edith set the Thanksgiving table at home for two. Islands of linen separated the dishes on the table. She had even put in the table extensions as if a legion were coming to a banquet. The turkey looked as lonely on its platter as Luke felt sitting at the opposite end of the table from his mother. She had given him his father's place, and like his father, he found it necessary to shout for his mother to hear him. Luke longed for a room full of chatter so he couldn't hear his thoughts. Holidays meant full tables and table talk, didn't they?

After Luke and Johanna had left home, Edith became accustomed to eating in silence. In their childhood, the children had filled in the conversational gaps, not noticing their parents' failure to communicate. Luke put down his fork after a bite of meat and a mouthful of squash. His appetite had disappeared.

His mother looked up and smiled. "Father prefers oyster dressing."

Luke passed on the pumpkin pie and excused himself. "I'm going to see if I can find Dad's living will."

Instead of finding words in the desk that defined Martin Tayspill's preferences for his final days, Luke uncovered a manuscript that might spell out his own death. He was sitting on the floor with *The Deaths of Lucas Tayspill* in his lap when his mother screamed from the doorway.

"Father! What are you doing here?"

Luke dropped the composition book on the floor.

"Oh, it's you, Luke. Why are you sitting here in the dark?"

The light of the winter afternoon had almost vanished from the study. "I lost track of the time," he said, retrieving the manuscript.

"Did you find what you were looking for?"

He shook his head. "There's no living will in his desk. I've searched every possible place it could be."

His mother sat down on the Chippendale chair.

"Do you know anything about Grandpa Giles writing a book?" he asked.

"A book? I didn't know, but that doesn't surprise me. Grandfather often tried his hand at something new."

"While I was looking in the desk for Dad's papers, I found a book Grandpa wrote based on the Tayspill family. From the look of things, he wrote it in the fifties but never finished it. Did he ever talk much about his folks?"

"His grandfather was a Quaker who came from England to Philadelphia. His father, Lucas Jr.—they called him 'Junior'—was a little boy when Lucas Sr. died. Sometime before Grandfather was born, the family moved here to Ohio."

"Were there any Quakers in recent history?"

"Junior was a Friend, I think, but his wife left the faith after she remarried. Her new husband didn't believe in God. Mr. Morton was an Antioch professor, just like Father."

Edith went back to the dishes and Luke returned to the manuscript. Standing alone on the first page, an epigraph begged for his attention— "If you have no cause worth dying for, do you really have a reason to live?" Luke shuddered as he turned on a lamp to read about three men with the same name—his name—whose deaths Giles had woven together. First, the author provided the background history.

Until he committed a capital crime, my great-great-great-great-grandfather was a noted cloth maker in Flanders. The Grand Inquisitor of Ypres called Giles Tayspill an iconoclast. Mijnheer Tayspill interpreted his activities differently from his ecclesiastical critics. He smashed idols in the temple of God. Giles escaped death by seeking exile in England.

An old English rhyme goes like this: Reformation, bay, and beer / All came to England in the very same year. So did Giles Tayspill. You know what the Protestant Reformation and beer are. Let me tell you about the bay.

When Giles escaped across the English Channel, he brought the bay—cloth making—and a restless brand of religion with him. For him, reformation was a process, not a moment fixed in human history.

The citizenry of Colchester hailed Giles—for whom I was named—as a champion of a bold new faith. Even more warmly than his religious zeal, they welcomed his weaving skills. Alas, their warm welcome deteriorated into bigotry. To the English burghers, the hero on the run for "Gottes Worde" became the Dutch stranger who made more money than they did.

As he thumbed through the manuscript, Luke read about characters and adventures that were foreign to everything he had known about the Tayspill family. He had been sitting on the floor so long that his eyes burned and his back hurt. He stood and paced the book-lined room.

Nowhere in Martin's collection of philosophy, history, and literature could Luke find any book about religion. Not even the Bible had earned shelf space. The only gods represented in Martin's books were Greek deities who popped down to earth to solve mortal problems when a playwright couldn't come up with a better last line. Luke wondered what solution his grandfather would propose for Lucas I, II, and III. Giles's manuscript stirred up as many questions as it answered, if not more.

In his BlackBerry, Luke entered notes about the first Lucas Tayspill. For a Philadelphia sailmaker who lived during the Civil War era, he seemed to know important people. "Check Eliza Gurney Fry," Luke wrote, "English woman who visited Lucas I. Knew Abraham Lincoln."

Luke tried to remember his American history. In the nineteenth century, blacks in the South were illiterate as a matter of law, but Northern Quakers were already educating freed and runaway slaves. Luke entered another name in the BlackBerry. "Af-Am teacher, Charlotte Forten." He made medical notations as well. "Malaria in coastal south. Slaves survived;

owners didn't. Partial immunity? Genetic protection?" He wondered what kind of malaria it had been, but he didn't imagine that country docs in South Carolina at the time had microscopes in their doctor's bags to make that fine a distinction. He intended to research these questions when he got back to Yale.

Giles peopled his book with enough Tayspills to make Luke dizzy. Sometimes more than one character entered on a page. By the end of the first Lucas story, Luke had made a list of all the Tayspills to keep them straight. The second part of the book found the family on the move.

The story tracked the second Lucas from South Carolina to Ohio. Junior settled in Hobart Corners, a few miles down the road from Yellow Springs. *Now*, Luke thought, *we're getting closer to home*. But the Hobart Corners described in the manuscript sounded nothing like the Ohio he knew. It sounded more like a story from the Reconstruction South.

Junior, a cabinetmaker, tried to stop the Ku Klux Klan from burning a cross at the home of a neighbor. But the Klansmen lynched him instead, along with the black man he tried to protect. "Lucas II—my great-grandfather," Luke entered in his notes. "Why have I never heard this story before?"

Unlike the first two sagas, the third Lucas Tayspill's story was incomplete. Set in the twenty-first century, the story spoke of future events as if they had already taken place. In one short paragraph on an otherwise clean page, Giles had sent this Dr. Lucas Tayspill on a mission to a plague-ridden, war-torn African country. This third story—and the manuscript —ended with the hero's arrival in an unnamed and treacherous land.

In the same envelope containing the manuscript, Luke found scraps of notes and a genealogy of the Tayspills dating back to 1395. The name *Lucas* appeared twice in the family tree, corresponding with the first two stories. The names and dates of birth of Giles and Martin were listed, but the author hadn't noted Martin's marriage to Edith Yancey or the births of their two children, Johanna and Luke.

Springing out of his chair, Luke went over to Giles's easel and picked up an old paintbrush.

Over Luke's desk in his Connecticut home hangs a painting of an old dock jutting out into a peaceful bay. In the lower right-hand corner stand some chaotic blades of grass that don't fit with the rest of the marsh grass. A few months before Giles's death, Luke had watched his grandfather work on that painting.

✛

"Can I paint too, Grandpa?" the child asked.

Giles took Luke's hand. "Sure you can. I'll help you."

He placed the brush between Luke's fingers and covered his hand with his own. The child tried to paint some blades of grass. After a few strokes, he was disappointed with what he saw. "Can you fix my grass?"

Giles put the brush back in its holder and put his arms around his grandson. "Oh, I think we should leave it just that way. I love having your grass next to my grass."

"But my grass isn't perfect like your grass."

"That's okay, child. Life isn't about perfect grass. We can have a perfect day like today together. Isn't that perfect enough?"

Luke looked at his haphazard strokes on the canvas and scowled. "My hands aren't as good as your hands."

His grandfather took Luke's hands to his lips and kissed them. "These are wonderful hands."

Luke spread his fingers and frowned at them. They weren't strong enough to do most things grownups do. "What can I do with my hands?"

"You can take care of sick people."

"Me, Grandpa?"

"Yes, Lucas. That's your calling."

"Who's Lucas?"

A cloud passed over the old man's eyes, a thin film of tears. "Someone I knew a long time ago."

"Are you going to cry, Grandpa?"

"Someone you knew a long time ago?" Luke asked, shaking the manuscript at the portrait of Giles, with its unfinished whiskers. Luke's eyes blazed. "All those times I sat with you in this room, all those times we sat together at your desk, you were planning my death?"

He flopped onto the stool where his grandfather used to sit to paint. His anger dissipated as he stroked the face in the portrait. "Were you a prophet, Grandpa? Or a perverted writer plotting my demise?"

He wanted to talk to Theo, but he didn't know where or how to find her. He took out his BlackBerry and started to compose an e-mail. "Dearest Theo," he began to write, but then he didn't know what to say about *The Deaths of Lucas Tayspill.*

Six

Marta was stirring up a cloud of flour in the kitchen when her houseguest returned from Dr. Garvey's office. Waving a wooden spatula at Theo, she said, "I hope you're hungry." Without answering, Theo took off her coat and sat at the breakfast bar. Her hostess pointed to a roasting pan where potatoes and vegetables surrounded a lonely looking chicken.

Marta prodded her guest. "Come on, ducky. I can't eat this all alone."

Theo shrugged. "Maybe I'll have an appetite later."

Marta plugged in the teakettle and then fussed some more with the chicken. "So tell me what happened after you sat down at Shane's table."

Theo's face darkened as her thoughts returned to Sarajevo. Like a reporter scribbling in a notebook, she picked up her story in choppy sentences. Marta settled in for the staccato recitation.

"Young woman came into the café. Scarf covering her head. Bunch of roses in one arm. Baby in her other arm. Moved from table to table peddling flowers. Only a teenager. Felt sad for her. Must be very poor to beg."

Marta frowned. Theo's stories never led back to her true self. She gave up on hoping for a major Sarajevo disclosure and changed the subject. As she returned to the chicken, she asked, "How did the flat search go?"

Theo lit up a cigarette and took a drag. After high tar and nicotine *Drinas,* British cigarettes were far too mild. "Disappointing. The estate agent suggested I try Hampstead. She said it's not a bad commute, but I had hoped to be closer to the British Museum and all."

Marta thought for a moment before speaking. "A two-bedroom flat has come available in this building, one floor down. The super asked me if I'd like it. You and Luke could share it with me for the sabbatical, and after you go home, I'll find myself a flatmate. Porchester Gardens is just a short tube hop from everywhere you want to be."

Theo looked down at the table. "I don't think so."

"It's not easy to find a short-term lease in this city."

"We like our privacy."

Marta put down the chicken and turned to Theo. "You mean *you* like your privacy."

Theo's face darkened. "It's hard for me to trust you."

"Luke is my cousin. I have never thought of him as anything else."

"Ninth cousin six or seven times removed. That's as good as unrelated. It wouldn't exactly be incest."

"Luke is my family."

"In his parents' house, you couldn't keep your hands off him. You traipsed around the house in baby-doll pajamas."

"I'm his cousin. I was his parents' guest. Uncle Martin and Aunt Edith told me to make myself at home."

"You certainly did."

Marta turned her back on Theo. "I take you into my home, and this is the thanks I get?"

Theo spotted an open canister on the kitchen counter and grabbed a handful of flour. When she threw it at her hostess, Marta decided she had had enough. She reached for the faucet, her hands already covered with flour. When she had added enough water to make a gooey paste, she grabbed Theo's long hair, smeared and yanked. Soon they were wrestling on the floor, both women scratching and pulling at each other's hair.

In the struggle the canister, poultry shears, and chicken flew off the counter. The two women skidded on the chicken-greased floor, clawing at each other until clotted flour and chicken fat stained their clothing. Suddenly Marta drew her nails down Theo's face, drawing blood. Theo responded by grabbing the poultry shears.

Marta struggled to get away from her, but Theo held her fast by a fistful of hair.

"No! Don't!"

With the strength of a mad woman, Theo jerked Marta around by her hair and brought her to her knees. Then she raised the shears and brought them down toward Marta.

"*Kurva!*" Theo screamed. "Whore!"

With four blunt chops, Marta's long blond hair fell to the floor.

Theo dropped the shears and collapsed sobbing onto the floor. Grabbing the shears, Marta withdrew to a corner of the kitchen. With a trembling hand she slid the weapon under a cupboard. Finally Theo stopped sobbing and sat up. When she saw the damage she had done to Marta's hair, she started crying again.

Out of breath, Marta helped Theo to her feet. "Maybe sharing a flat isn't such a grand idea after all."

Theo pulled away from Marta and stumbled into the sitting room. She fell onto the couch and stared like a frightened child as Marta stood over her. "Are you going to call the police?"

"I should, but I won't."

Theo curled up with her shoulders hunched over her knees. She could see Marta's feet anxiously tapping. She tried to smooth her own hair, but it was too junky to straighten.

Shaking off her anger and fear, Marta resumed the posture of a conflict mediator and reached out a hand. "Come on, Theo. Shower time."

The two women stripped and bent over the bathtub. As warm water flowed through the showerhead, Marta shampooed Theo's hair then turned the stream on her own butchered locks. Clean again, they went to the kitchen for a pot of tea. Marta retrieved the chicken from the floor and rinsed it off.

"Instant rubber capon," she said as she popped it into the microwave.

They ate in silence, both women afraid to talk. Eventually Marta spoke. "Why did you call me this morning?"

Theo kept her eyes on her plate. "I had a panic attack in Café Sarajevo. I felt one coming on at the hotel." She took another small bite of chicken. "I feel very tired."

Marta helped Theo to the bedroom and stretched her out on the bed. She watched her fall asleep then returned to the kitchen to make another cup of tea. "British Prozac," she mumbled to herself as she poured water into the kettle. "Good for whatever ails me." She took her cup to Theo's bedside to consider her options.

When Marta heard the scream, she bolted from her chair. At first she couldn't remember the events that had sapped her strength. Then she saw Theo and shook her awake.

"It's just a bad dream," Marta said. "You're in London. You're not in Sarajevo." She wrapped Theo in a thick robe and led her to the kitchen. "Do you want your cigarettes?"

Theo shook her head. "Time to quit. Awful habit."

Running her hand through her short hair, Marta thought about calling someone for professional help. Ordinarily she felt strong enough to handle any emergency the world threw at her. *When everyone else falls apart, Marta gets organized.* But that was before she saw poultry shears coming toward her. Not even on humanitarian missions in African war zones had she felt so close to death.

Given the events since Theo had arrived, Marta was less willing to take responsibility where Luke's wife was concerned. For the moment, all she knew to do was offer Theo a cup of tea, so she refilled the kettle and waited for her troubled guest to speak.

"I remember thinking how innocent she looked," Theo said, staring into her tea.

"Who?"

"The Muslim mother in the café. She was wearing a dusty rose dress with a blue scarf over her hair, like a classical Madonna. Her face was oval, not round like most Bosnian women. Her eyes drew my attention; they were hazel, not the usual sad pools of dark brown. My first reaction was that she was a woman just like me. I had been pursuing a cold terrorist trail. Finally, I thought, I've found a genuine human-interest story."

Theo paused to sip her tea and then looked up at Marta. "I felt so bad for her, you know, that she had to beg like a gypsy. I remembered the women I met during the war. Serb rapists had ruined their lives. Faithful wives and tender virgins, all deliberately impregnated and hidden from sight until they were too far along to abort. I got to leave Sarajevo after the war, but they had to stay there living in shame they hadn't brought upon themselves."

Theo returned to her tea. Finally her storytelling had led where Marta had hoped it would, but Theo fell into silence.

Marta risked probing further. "During the war you wrote about those women so the world would understand their pain. I read those articles. Your words breathed life into women the world had left for dead. You named the true villains and vindicated the women's shame."

Theo started sobbing. "I've wondered so often what had become of them and their half-Serb babies. When I saw this young mother in the café, ten years melted away. I was back in the hospital with Jasmina and…" A door closed in Theo's mind. She fell silent again.

Unwilling to leave the door shut, Marta asked, "What did you do when the mother came over to your table?"

"I had a few Bosnian marks left. I held up the coins and pointed to her roses. She smiled at me and bowed politely." Theo smiled as if she were there in the story, but her face soon became contorted. She stood up and started pacing the kitchen. "That's when reality ended and the panic took over." Theo dropped back into her chair.

That last sentence, Marta thought, was a description of Theo's life. For more than a decade, Theo had lived between the real and imaginary, between life and death. Marta got up to fill their cups.

Theo didn't seem to notice and went back to her story.

"She put her baby down on the table next to me while she took out her purse. All of a sudden I started screaming. I thought she was a suicide bomber with explosives in her baby's nappy. Shane tried to restrain me. I was furious, especially when he grabbed my arm and dragged me out of the café. It was quite a scene. I cursed at him to let me go."

Marta didn't touch her fresh cup of tea. She was far too concerned about Theo, who was beating her fist on the breakfast bar as she spoke.

Theo stopped pounding and massaged her painful hand. She picked up her tea and sipped again before she returned to her story. "There were no explosives. I felt humiliated. Shane took me back to the hotel and then put me on a plane."

Marta hoped Theo would finish the story before she did any further damage. Ironically Marta had what she had been waiting for—a path into Theo's true story. Finally she had a chance to hear what had been eating at Luke's wife for a decade. "You were screaming when you woke up. You said, 'She killed her baby.' But that didn't happen, did it?"

Theo answered without emotion in her voice. "I wasn't dreaming about her. That dream was about me."

Marta waited a moment before speaking. "Somebody once said that we're the characters in our own dreams."

But this was an old dream, Marta realized, an old story. Last week probably wasn't Theo's first panic attack.

"Do you take any medications?"

Theo looked up as if Marta had jogged her memory. "I have a prescription in my purse that a doctor gave me to relax."

Marta found Theo's purse and pulled out a pill bottle. From the date, it had just been filled today. Lorazepam—a powerful sedative. She read the directions on the bottle and tapped out the prescribed number of pills. Marta made a mental note of the prescribing doctor's name.

Obediently Theo swallowed the pills. Marta risked another question. "There was something else you said when you woke up. 'Forever locked in.'"

Theo melted into tears.

Marta reached a hand toward her. "You're not locked in, Theo. That Bosnian mother and her baby are alive. Listen to me. They're alive, and so are you. You're not locked in anything or anywhere."

Theo jerked her head and snapped back to something she had forgotten. "Do you mind if I check my e-mail?"

Marta frowned. "Would you rather use the phone?" Until Theo's outburst in the kitchen, Marta hadn't heard her mention Luke's name. If Theo's cell phone wasn't working—as she had claimed—why hadn't she asked if she could call him from the flat on an important family holiday?

Theo shook her head, so Marta showed her where she could plug her laptop into a phone jack behind the desk.

Marta settled into a chair at a discreet distance from the computer screen as Theo scanned her messages.

Theo's eyes narrowed as she scanned the titles of some e-mails, then she clicked them out of sight and mind. Her focus sharpened as she came to one message that seemed to hold her interest. She drew in her breath and moistened her lips. Her lips moved as she read the e-mail. Then she started to shake.

Marta was on her feet. "What's wrong?"

"My steady anchor just pulled loose from its moorings," Theo said.

Marta walked toward the desk. "What are you talking about?"

Theo snapped down her laptop cover before Marta could see what was on the screen.

"Bad news?"

Theo started to breathe heavily, rhythmically at first. Then her breathing intensified, as if she was trying to suck all the oxygen out of the room. "I've got to get some air." She stood up and staggered toward the front door. Sweat was pouring down her face.

"Come over to the window. I'll open it for you so you can get some air."

Theo froze and then moved away from the window as far as she could. "No!" she yelled and then tried to control her voice. "Just let me sit for a few minutes."

"I'm taking you to the casualty ward."

Theo clutched her chest and tried to breathe. "No emergency room! I'm just having a panic attack."

"*Just* a panic attack? You make it sound so simple."

"I felt it coming on a few days ago. That's why I didn't want to be alone."

"How do you feel now, Theo?"

"I've never felt so alone in all my life."

As Marta ran her hand through her ruined hair, she caught the look of despair on Theo's face. When Theo had escaped from Sarajevo and arrived in London ten years earlier, her waist-length black hair had been as short and bluntly cut as Marta's.

SEVEN

Ohio

M y baby, my baby!" Martin bawled his eyes out and reached for Johanna when she walked into the room. At the sound of his daughter's voice, he came back from the grave and wandered his way out of brain fog. Luke, who had put Yale on hold for a few more days, might as well not have been there.

"I'll be staying for a while," Johanna told her brother.

"Fine," Luke said, not looking at her.

Edith heard familiar edges in her children's voices. "Why can't we all get along like friends?"

Luke and Johanna looked at each other, but their expressions didn't change.

When brother and sister had endured as much of each other as they could stand, the family left the hospital and went home. Waiting for them in the garden was Johanna's only child.

"Down!" Luke yelled at the Rottweiler that was ten times Moose's size.

The beast salivated and pawed at the Yorkie who quivered in the safety of Luke's arms.

"You call that monster off," Luke told Johanna, unsure how long he could protect Moose. "Chain him up, or I'll find a gun and shoot him."

"Muffin is a she, not a he."

"I don't care about its chromosomes. Call it off before I break its neck."

Edith came out into the garden with a tray of drinks. "Hot mulled cider, anyone?"

Muffin snarled. Edith dropped the tray and fled into the house.

"Muffin, come!" Johanna called.

Reluctantly the dog retreated to her owner's side.

"That's my sweetheart."

Muffin accepted the lavish praise.

There was no mistaking it. Martin's favorite child had come home.

Johanna looked around as if something was missing. "Where's 'La Bella Simonetta'?" she wondered aloud.

In a corner of the yard, Johanna set up a portable dog run. Muffin settled down with a giant bone, ignoring and ignored by the humans and the pipsqueak dog. Edith brought out more cider.

Luke and Johanna had nothing to say to each other, so they sat wordlessly on the patio, trying to stay warm.

Edith pulled a heavy sweater around her shoulders. "Father loves to sit out here every day of the year."

Muffin barked at an imagined intruder.

"You tell 'im," Johanna urged.

Edith surveyed the garden as if it could demand peace of its visitors. Decades before, Martin had dug out a section of the backyard and surrounded it with railroad ties to create a small Japanese garden. He was proud of his patch of paradise with its topiaries and goldfish pond. Even in winter he preferred to bundle up and sit out there rather than remain in the house. Edith fretted that his garden had fallen into disarray.

"The yardboy didn't show up again this week. Father's garden has grown thick with weeds."

Eager to make peace with Johanna for his mother's sake, Luke suggested they weed together.

Johanna agreed but pointed to Moose. "You keep that little eunuch inside the house."

"You come in the house with Granny, Moosie."

The Yorkie gladly complied.

Luke set his sights on a large topiary, the centerpiece of the garden. "I'll have to trim the shoots back to the last pruning to figure out its shape."

Rap! Bang! Snap! Edith pounded on the French doors of the family room to summon her children's attention. She motioned for them to come closer so she could shout through the glass. "Father says it's a rooster." Martin had always communicated through his women. He did so even in absentia.

"That looks more like porcupine than poultry," Luke said. "I hope Charley Chicken doesn't have feet as part of his grand design."

Johanna hacked away at the branches. "Well, Charley won't get feet today." The bird didn't even have a neck as of yet.

Rap! Bang! "Father said to tell you to clean up the cuttings."

Two green lawn bags were already full. "Ahead of the folks this time," Luke and Johanna said in unison.

Finally Edith returned to the patio. Moose followed and jumped on her lap. Soon both old folks nodded off.

Johanna pointed to a bed of pachysandras circling the weeping cherry tree. "While I finish Charley, you could pull the briars out by hand. Careful though. They're prickly."

"What else would they be?" Luke said.

The weeds came up easily, but they took wads of sod along for the ride. *The better to float off,* Luke thought, *so they can re-implant themselves in a more congenial spot.*

Edith woke up. "Father said to knock the dirt off the roots before you put them in the leaf bag."

"It's Daddy's garden," Luke and Johanna said in chorus.

Edith dozed off again as brother and sister worked together. Moose slipped off his granny's lap, taking a pull toy with him. Unnoticed, he wandered over to Muffin's lair.

While Charley Chicken got a neck and the weed seeds were returned to the soil, the eunuch and the monster sniffed each other. Then each took an end of Moose's toy and pulled each other around the garden. When they had enough of their game, they fell asleep, with Moose's head on Muffin's rump.

"Weeds and wildflowers grow together in Daddy's garden," Johanna said, taking hold of her brother's arm. "Which do we pull up, and when do we let a wildflower have its chance?"

Luke scowled. "Weed is still a four-letter word."

At sunset Edith woke up and shivered. "Is anyone interested in leftovers?"

The dogs responded first and raced each other into the house.

Edith fell asleep in Martin's favorite chair while Moose chased Muffin up and down the stairs. Johanna tied an apron behind her brother's back as they tackled the dirty dishes. "Daddy's tough on you," she said.

Luke rolled up his sleeves and plunged his hands into the dishwater. "I might as well not be here, for all he cares."

"He's proud of you. We all are."

"His pride is about him. Just once I'd like him to be thankful. That might be about me."

"Thankful? That's an odd choice of words. Almost nobody says thank you these days."

"I have patients who say thank you."

"Why would people with AIDS be thankful?"

Luke turned off the faucet and leaned against the counter.

Seeing peace pass over her brother's face, Johanna put down her dishtowel and listened.

"There's this old black guy I take care of named Woodrow Emmons. I've never seen a family member visit him, yet he always has a smile on his face."

Brother and sister walked to the living room and sat on the sofa together. Luke continued his story.

"One day I went up to the ward to make rounds. Mr. Emmons's eyes were shut when I walked into the room, but somehow he knew I was there. Without opening his eyes, he said, 'Docta Luke, seddown, sed-down. Take a load off you feet.'"

Johanna smiled. "You're different when you talk about your patients."

Luke was distracted from his story. "How so?"

"Dr. Luke Tayspill isn't the scrappy brother of my childhood; he's a man at home in his own skin."

Touched by her comment, Luke continued. "This Mr. Emmons is an elder in a storefront church in New Haven. Before he found Jesus, he found heroin and HIV. He's been in and out of our ward all year."

"I don't think he found gratitude in drugs."

Luke shook his head. "I told Mr. Emmons I had just stopped by for a minute to see how he was doing. I asked him if he was feeling any better. He told me, 'I be glad fa ebry day de good Lawd gimme.'"

Luke continued, mimicking Mr. Emmons's dialect: "'I jes be prayin, Docta. I be thankin God fa you.'"

Johanna watched as Luke threw his body into his narration, raising his hands high like an Old Testament prophet.

"'I thank you, Jesus, fa sendin Docta Luke,' I tole de Lawd, 'Ma Docta Luke, he have a healer's heart.'"

Luke stood up and paced the living room, then he returned to his sister. "The contrast kills me. Picture two hospital-room scenes: Dad's and Mr. Emmons's. I go into Dad's room, and he closes his eyes to ignore me. I go into Mr. Emmons's room, and he opens his eyes and smiles. Dad couldn't care less when I'm there, but Mr. Emmons couldn't care more."

Johanna reached out a hand to draw her brother back to the sofa, but he resisted.

Luke continued to pace. "Dad worked overtime to keep Jesus out of our lives, and he doesn't seem to care if I fly out here almost every month to see him. But some poor black man thanks Jesus every time I walk into the room. What's wrong with this family picture? Or perhaps a better question might be, 'What's right?'"

"You're getting to sound like Grandpa Giles," Johanna said.

Her comment caught Luke by surprise. "What about Grandpa?"

"He used to do the same thing you did when telling a story. He'd slip into the dialect of the people he was talking about, the way you just did talking about your Mr. Emmons."

Luke sat on the couch next to his sister. "Tell me about that. I need to know."

"Need to know? That sounds serious."

"I am serious, Jo. Tell me."

"One time I went for a walk in Glen Helen with Grandpa. He told me a story about his father and how he had come up from the South. When he talked about his daddy, he talked just like you did now when you were telling me about Mr. Emmons."

Luke's mind was spinning, turning pages in Grandpa Giles's manuscript to the story of Lucas Tayspill II. "Keep going."

"You know the spout that comes out of the rocks in the glen, where the iron in the water has stained the rocks orange?"

Luke nodded. He knew the place well.

"Grandpa knelt down. I thought he was going to take a drink. Instead, he cupped his hands and spilled water on his head three times. It was the oddest thing."

"Did he say anything?"

"Nothing that made any sense. He went into that dialect again and said, 'Ma papa be pleased.'" Johanna stood up and faced Luke. "Back to your question, What's wrong with this family picture? Remember when you called me about Pop?"

"Of course I remember. You, his favorite, didn't come straight home."

"There's something I didn't want him to find out. I was afraid if he woke up, I'd have to tell him. Then I was afraid he wouldn't wake up, and I'd never get to say good-bye. That's why I came."

"Tell him what?"

It was his sister's turn to pace. "I didn't get tenure at Stanford."

Luke looked at her. "When? For next year?"

"No. I've been out of a job since June. I couldn't tell Dad about it. Or about Mark and me."

Luke was afraid of what was coming next. "What about you and Mark?"

"We split up a year ago."

"And you've never told anyone?"

Johanna shook her head. "I didn't need to tell Mom and Pop yet. Mark and I have been sharing the house, but not a bed. As soon as our divorce is final, we'll cash out our shares in the house. Neither one of us will be able to afford to stay in Palo Alto. So you see, brother dear, I'm homeless and unemployed."

Luke reached out to hug his sister. "I'm so sorry."

She dabbed her tears and changed the subject. "Where's Theo?"

"I wish I knew," he said.

EIGHT

H i, Luke."

The phone line was so clear, he thought Marta was next door. "Are you here in the States?"

"I'm home in London. I'm calling about Theo."

Luke stood up and paced with the phone. "Is she with you?" he asked. "You were the only one in London I didn't think to call."

"She was here, but she's not here now. I was hoping you'd know where she is."

"Theo has me worried sick. She hasn't called or answered an e-mail I sent Thanksgiving Day."

"She was reading an e-mail Friday morning. We had a long night— long story—and she hadn't gotten much sleep. After she read one message, she slammed down the laptop lid and went bonkers."

"It's my fault. I couldn't find her at her hotel or the *Times,* so I sent her an e-mail. I was rather emotional at the time."

How had he phrased it in his e-mail? "My emotions are playing Ping-Pong with my brain." This was no time to tell Marta about *The Deaths of Lucas Tayspill.*

"Your e-mail might have tipped her over, but she was very fragile before that."

As the longcase clock struck midnight, Luke calculated the time in London. "We have a five-hour time difference. What time did Theo disappear?"

"I skipped work yesterday and took her to the doctor around ten. Zipper-lipped chap named Garvey. He wouldn't tell me a thing."

"I'm so glad you were able to get her help. How did you get his name?"

"I didn't. Theo knew him. She had a prescription from him in her purse. She had seen him the day before she wigged out. His name is Sir Nigel Garvey. A posh Harley Street neurologist."

"Neurologist?" *Probably a neuropsychiatrist,* Luke thought. The only doctor Theo knew in London was the psychiatrist she saw when she first came back from Sarajevo. But Luke didn't think his name was Garvey.

"Do you remember what the prescription was for?"

"I wrote it down. Lorazepam."

"She's had that before for panic attacks."

"She told me about that. She knew a panic attack was coming on. That's why she showed up at my apartment. She didn't want to be alone."

"What happened at the doctor's office?"

"When Theo came out, she seemed very calm. Garvey had given her a shot for her nerves, I guess, but he seemed very concerned. He wouldn't tell me anything, but he did ask me if I could fly back with her on Sunday. That's the first time I knew her travel plans. I said yes and asked her what flight she was booked on."

Luke turned on his BlackBerry and scrolled to the right place. "United Flight 907. It gets into Newark at half past noon."

"That's right. *If* Theo is on the plane."

"If she doesn't come back to your flat, could you go to the airport prepared to fly? I'll pay for your ticket."

"I can come over with her, but I have to fly right back."

"Sure you can't stay for a few days?"

"Wish I could, but I have to get back by Monday afternoon for a very important meeting. The war is coming to an end in Sierra Leone, and I'm getting involved with the peace plans."

"Okay, okay. I'll leave here in the morning and meet you at the airport."

"You're assuming Theo's going to do something logical. From what I've seen the past few days, don't count on it."

"What happened after you left the doctor's office?"

"We came back to the flat. She was very calm by then. I made some tea, but she didn't want to talk. Around three she said she was tired and wanted to take a nap. I had an appointment at the hairdresser—that's another long story I need to tell you—and left her asleep. When I came back, she was gone."

"Did she take her things with her?"

"She left her suitcase in my bedroom. Only her purse is missing. Oh, she took her laptop."

"She never goes anywhere without that. Listen, Marta, did she mention anyone else she's been in touch with in London?"

"Other than an estate agent, not really. I called the *Times,* but they hadn't seen her since early in the week. I checked with United Airlines and confirmed she's booked on that flight."

"Call me if you hear from her. Anytime, day or night. I'll see you Sunday at Newark."

Estimating how long it would take to drive from Newark to New Haven, he calculated the time he should leave Yellow Springs and entered it in his BlackBerry. As he hung up the phone, he imagined the ride from the airport to the emergency room, alone in the car with Theo. Then he made one further entry: "Page Bishop Paul from ER."

PART II

Dey holla say, "Jedus! Masta! Habe mussy on we!"
—LUKE 17:13, *De Good Nyews Bout Jedus*
Christ Wa Luke Write (Gullah)

NINE

Pennsylvania hastened by in autumn shades of gold and green and gray. Luke's eyes blinked like a camera framing the highway landscape. Suddenly he hit the brakes. A hunter darted into the median with rifle held high, risking his life to poach a deer. The does were safe from his antler lust, but not from the semis that splayed them out by the side of the road. Not even on the highway could Luke escape thinking about death.

With the threat of his father's death lifted for the moment and his sister settled in Yellow Springs, it was time for him to concentrate on Theo. When her return trip to Sarajevo first became a possibility, he had thought it would serve as an exorcism for her. Now he dreaded what lingering demons might accompany her home.

On the car radio, Billy Crockett crooned the final ditty of the Thanksgiving season.

Let us be thankful boys and girls, for eyes and ears and toes, and puppies with wet noses…

Luke reached over to pat the wet nose on the seat beside him and told Moose, "You're the only one who loves me who doesn't make my life harder." The dog sighed and licked his master's hand.

A snow squall poured over Quakers Knob, dusting some plain folks' bones. Luke was too weary to continue driving, but the gentle voice on the radio gave him hope, and hope was all he had: Hope that his marriage wouldn't suffer another setback. Hope that a psychiatrist could glue Theo back together again. And hope that he could survive *The Deaths of Lucas Tayspill*.

"Why didn't you write about life instead of death?" he asked, as if Giles, not Moose, were sitting beside him. *The Lives of Lucas Tayspill* would have suited Lucas III much better than his grandfather's title. "Help me," he pleaded in his heart.

Halfway through painting a cloudy sky, Giles put down his palette knife and wiped his hands on an oily rag. "Come here, Lukie. Give me your hands."

"What are those bumps on your hands, Grandpa?"

"Oh, just getting-old stuff."

Giles's gnarled fingers moved over the upper side of Luke's hands as he studied the unlined flesh. With the eye of an artist, he conducted his examination. Tears came as he stroked the child's palms.

"Why are you crying, Grandpa?"

"A little epiphany."

"What's a pifany?"

Giles laughed. "An epiphany is a discovery, like looking at something you see every day and noticing something new you never noticed before."

"Like a circus fortune-teller reading the lines in your palm? Can you see the future?"

Giles laughed. "No, child, I can only see your heart."

A husky voice had muscled out the gentle Billy Crockett.

Sometimes you're the windshield. Sometimes you're the bug...

To drive away Mary Chapin Carpenter's pessimistic view of love, Luke pushed the CD button. White voices whispered open John Rutter's *Requiem*.

Requiem aeternum dona eis, Domine...

An invisible choir sang of eternal rest, but Luke knew no one at rest right now. Martin slept fitfully in Good Sam Hospital. Theo might get a nap on her transatlantic flight.

A patient had given him the CD several years ago. Greg, who contracted HIV through a hemophilia clotting factor, lived long enough to resist all the anti-retroviral drugs modern medicine had invented. Eventually his viral load skyrocketed out of control.

On hospital rounds one day, Luke heard the music when he walked into Greg's room. He sensed the connection to the haunting melodies and provocative texts that the young man felt. Other patients were waiting for the doctor, but Luke sat down at the foot of Greg's bed. Wordlessly the atheist doctor and dying youth listened together. When Greg died, he bequeathed the CD to his favorite doc.

O let thine ears consider well the voice of my complaint...

"Do you want to hear a complaint?" Luke said to the object of Rutter's lament. "I have a good one. I'm a doctor, and I live with death. But no one has ever taught me what to say to a dying man."

By all rights Luke should have been an expert on the process of dying. For more than a decade, he had cared for victims of a viral death sentence. Despite twenty years of research, HIV/AIDS still meant automatic death, even if postponed. Who, Luke wondered, had prepared him for this role with his fellow mortals? Oh, he had had sporadic advice from his med-school professors, but they were of no real help. "We wage war against disease," Professor Goff had told him. "We don't negotiate peace with the enemy. Never compromise with death."

In the laboratory, Luke had engaged in negotiations of a sort. He wanted to engineer a tamer strain of HIV. He would take the innocuous mutant and design a vaccine against the potent real thing. *No, Dr. Goff, sometimes you have to hold a conversation. If you stand at too great a distance, death may win. The trick is to come close enough to see and disarm death.*

What about his father's beloved philosophers? The Greeks didn't seem to have any better advice about death than Luke's medical warriors did. Socrates had cooperated with his executioners. The French existentialists might have been wiser about the absurdity of human existence, but Luke rejected that idea. Giles would never have considered life absurd, no matter how tortured it became.

Thus said the man kneeling in the garden—locked in Giles's desk—looking up to heaven.

✠

When Giles died, Martin didn't want Luke to attend the funeral service. But the child cried so much that his father relented. The proceedings were over in ten minutes. One of Martin's colleagues read a poem. Something was missing. Someone.

✠

A dozing bluebird on a billboard beckoned Luke to Sleepers' Inn for the night. As he prepared for bed, he couldn't hear his father bellow out in the quiet night of Good Samaritan Hospital, but other patients could.

"Mussy, Lawd!" lamented the private-duty nurse Edith had hired. She put down her knitting and measured a sedative into a syringe. "Sleep now, honey," she crooned as she squirted liquid silence into the old man's mouth.

Kyrie eleison. Christie eleison. Kyrie eleison.

Lord, have mercy.

✠

As Luke tossed in the motel bed, Justin Bland, senior flight attendant on United 907, studied two passengers in the business-class section. Marta noticed his scrutiny and his inability to keep his eyes off Theo. Justin frowned as he looked over the passenger list and tapped his pencil on a name. Marta listened as he approached a man seated two rows in front of her. She could only catch the end of the conversation and the interchange that followed.

"Please feel free to call on me," the man horse-whispered to the attendant.

As Justin moved off to survey his other charges, the woman seated next to the subject of interest complained to her husband. "Why can't you mind your own business? You have to show everybody what a bigshot doctor you are."

Marta tuned her ear to hear the conversation.

"Better me than some incompetent," the man answered.

"You're a pathologist, Arnie. You haven't taken care of a living patient since medical school."

Marta scratched the doctor in row six from her emergency plan and finished tucking a blanket around Theo.

"Have we taken off yet?" Theo asked without opening her eyes.

"Not yet, but soon."

Theo nodded and seemed to doze. Then she sat up and asked, "Do you believe in heaven?"

"Hush," Marta said as Justin arrived with a tray of orange juice and water.

Theo kept her eyes closed as she answered, "I'm serious."

Marta waited for Justin to make his way down the aisle before saying, "I'd like to believe, but I've never heard any convincing evidence."

"Why do you want to believe?" Theo said, punching her pillow to make it mold to her head.

"I'd like to believe in a final justice for those who have suffered."

Theo smiled and sank back into her nest. "I'd like to believe in mercy."

Marta closed her eyes and hoped Theo would fall back asleep.

"I believe in hell," Theo said, resuming her stream of half-consciousness. "I have more than enough evidence of that."

"Maybe that's the proof there has to be a heaven. There has to be something better than the hell you've been living through." Marta hoped the flight would go quickly and uneventfully.

"Is Luke meeting us at the airport?"

"Yes, ducky. He's on his way there now."

Marta tried to imagine the customs process in Newark. Airport procedures had changed considerably since 9/11. Holding an EU passport rather than a U.S. one, Marta would be channeled through a different line than Theo. As Justin Bland came by again, she caught his attention. "May I chat with you in the galley for a moment?"

As she got out of her seat to follow him, Theo asked again, "Do you believe in heaven?"

On the ground in Newark, the flight attendant escorted Marta and Theo to the transit lounge for international passengers. Once he had them settled, he went off to carry out his plan.

Justin paged Luke and asked him to meet him at customs. "This man is a doctor," he told the agent. "I have a sick passenger in the transit lounge who needs his attention."

The agent waved them through. As Luke helped Theo toward the gate, Marta gave him a quick update before saying good-bye. Then Luke and Theo followed Justin down a VIP lane to customs.

In the car Theo curled up with an airline pillow stuffed against the door. Moose hopped on top of her and started to lick her face. She didn't respond, but Moose continued to comfort her anyway. When Luke tried to touch her, she responded by pulling away.

From the airport to Yale–New Haven Hospital, they drove in silence. Light snow was starting to fall as they reached the George Washington Bridge and traffic became congested. Luke chose to concentrate on driving. He couldn't think of anything to say to Theo that didn't sound too clinical, too intrusive, or just plain dumb. "How do you feel?" "What happened to make you flip out?" "May I get you something?" He wished

Marta hadn't gone straight back to London. Awkward silence likes company.

Finally Theo broke the silence. "Do you believe in heaven?"

Her question frightened Luke. To the doctor it sounded like suicidal ideation. He answered her question with a question. "Why do you ask that, sweetheart?"

"I want to be with you forever," she said, as Moose rolled over on her chest to make himself comfortable.

Luke reached out his hand toward Theo, and she grasped it tightly. "Let's make our time on earth as long as possible," he said.

Theo opened her eyes and placed her other hand over their clasped hands. Luke steered with one hand until he pulled into the emergency-room parking lot. Theo sat upright. Moose dropped to the floor. As Luke turned off the ignition, Theo recaptured his hand. "Were you and Marta ever lovers?"

"I've never loved anyone but you."

Theo let go of his hand and reached for the car door. "That's not what I asked."

TEN

As a nurse took some information from Theo, Luke picked up the phone on the triage desk to page Bishop Paul. When the phone rang, he grabbed it at the first ring. "Dr. Tayspill," he answered.

"Oh, hi, Luke. This is Rita on Sixteen West. I'm answering for Bishop Paul. He's here on the ward. Mr. Emmons is dying."

Luke frowned, torn between the needs of his wife and his patient. Without looking up at him, Theo asked, "Your mistress?"

Embarrassed, Luke saw the nurse trying not to overhear. "A little family joke," he explained. "My wife thinks medicine is my mistress."

"And he thinks my muse is my paramour," Theo said, as if she were repeating the lines of a famous poem. "We're a ménage à quatre."

Luke couldn't remember the last time he had heard Theo use those phrases. Rather than let her bait him into their destructive old repartee, he let the metaphor die, the way he should have ten years earlier.

Their marital squabbles began while Luke was in residency. Life at a New York City hospital was tough enough for a young doctor without additional stress at home. If Theo had had a normal nine-to-five job, she might not have felt as lonely as she did in their small hospital-subsidized apartment. She spent most of her time at home alone working on her first novel.

Frustrated by the reality of the publishing world, Theo hacked out chapters of *Murder in the Marketplace,* a novel in which the police suspected an author of murdering her marketing manager. Luke made the mistake of telling Theo no one would ever publish it. What publishing house would expose its own industry for placing the bottom line above art? Later an agent told her the same thing.

Luke put in long hours at the hospital, even when he wasn't on call. This contributed to Theo's resentment and added a character to her novel's plot—the author's workaholic husband. She also added a nurse-mistress.

Even if Luke's long hours stemmed from his sense of duty—as he argued—medicine was just as real a mistress to Theo as another woman could be. Either way, she thought she was losing Luke to forces she couldn't control.

The loss worked both ways. Luke sensed there was someone else in Theo's life. Their intimacy seemed to stir her urge to write. He hated the nights she slipped from bed and took up her journal to trace their private devotion in the mouths of some fictional characters. Too often Luke saw a faraway look on Theo's face, as if she were looking into another man's eyes.

"Who are you looking at?" he asked one night.

"My muse, darling."

Her joke became his ammunition.

Where was the adoring girl who loved to hear him talk about his future career in medicine? Where was the awkward boy who treasured reading every word she wrote? Back in Yellow Springs they had always found enough to say to each other, and many ways to say "I love you." Then they married and moved to Manhattan, where they agreed on only one thing: There wasn't room enough for all of them in one bed—husband and wife, mistress and muse.

In the sixth year of their marriage, Theo was tired of hearing about his patients, and Luke didn't want to hear about her writer's block. Theo was the one to make the break.

She found a walk-up in Queens. They let the Fifty-ninth Street Bridge delimit the bounds of mistress and muse. She gave up on her novel and took a job at the *New York Times*. At least journalism paid her for passion.

Theirs had been a separation in name and geography, but not in heart. North of the city, they trysted in the Sleepy Hollow Motel.

Together they created an illusion that old Rip would wake up and tell them their nightmare was over. They wanted each other again, but without the failure and the pain. Van Winkle slept on, and so did their marriage.

After a year of separation with no reconciliation in sight, Luke accepted an infectious-disease fellowship in England. He hoped Theo would miss him, but she didn't miss him enough. The same year, the *Times* promoted her to cover international news.

When Luke came back to New York, he claimed to have problems finding an apartment. Theo took him in but didn't resume the marriage. Luke and Moose shared the living-room sofa bed while Theo slept alone behind a locked bedroom door. Then she accepted an assignment to cover the Bosnian War. She left Luke the apartment and Moose. In many ways, Theo's first trip to Sarajevo represented another desertion to her husband.

When Theo came home from the war, she stayed in a psychiatric hospital for a month. The doctors discharged her with pills and the diagnosis of post-traumatic stress disorder. The Tayspills resumed their marriage, although nothing was the same as it had been before. Luke thought things were going fairly well until Sarajevo burst back into their world. Now he wondered why he had ever encouraged her to go back.

The night of Jasmina's call, Luke came home to find Theo shaking on the front porch. Moose was licking her face, trying to comfort her. When the dog saw Luke, he whimpered as if to say, "You're a human. Do something."

"What happened?" Luke asked.

She fell into his arms. "I'm really scared."

He listened to the story of Jasmina's call and the invitation of Theo's editor. He began to feel angry. "We're just getting our lives back together again."

"I know. That's just the way I feel."

But she pulled away from him and started to walk. Moose started after her first, and Luke quickly followed.

"Talk to me, Theo."

"I can't."

"You won't, you mean. Isn't it time you tell me what really happened, so we can put it behind us and you can get on with your life?"

She started to run. "You don't understand."

"Run away! That's just like you. You're too much of a coward to talk to me."

"You don't know what you're talking about," she screamed and kept running.

Later that night she came back, long after Luke had gone to bed. In the dark she climbed in on her side and stayed as far away from him as possible. Luke, too, lay on the edge of his side of their bed. Moose paced on the blanket, not understanding the human positioning in his family bed.

Luke was the first to speak, although he addressed his words to the wall. "The way I see it, you have two choices. You can stay here and tell me what besides the war happened ten years ago, or you can go back to Sarajevo and face it there again. Personally I'd prefer that you stay and talk to me. Either way, you need to get rid of those ghosts."

"I'm booked on a flight tomorrow," she told him.

He sat up in bed. "Then you won't be with me for Thanksgiving at my parents'?"

"Not this year."

"Are you flying through London?"

"Yes. I can get a job at the London bureau nailed down while I'm there."

"Would you be good enough to find us a flat for sabbatical?"

"Sure."

"Good night."

"Good night."

✛

"What did you tell Rita?" Theo asked, bringing Luke back to the present.

"I told her I'd try to stop by later, but I have important business in the ER right now."

She took his hand. "Thanks, sweetheart. I'm really scared."

Luke stared at the locked door that led to the psychiatric holding area of the ER. "It's all my fault."

"No, Luke. None of this is your fault, but it's time for me to get well."

"That's what I had hoped ten years ago."

"It's not too late," she said, squeezing his hand.

The door opened and a voice called, "Could you come this way?" As Luke rolled Theo's wheelchair through the door, he wondered whether they were taking a step forward, or another one back. His head spun as he relived their first separation. *Is that where this is leading?* he wondered.

Once Theo was in the examining room, a resident psychiatrist motioned Luke to follow him. The doctor took careful notes as Luke told Marta's brief version of the episode with the poultry shears. Marta said she had yelled, *"Kurva!"* How many times had Luke heard Theo call out that word in her sleep and pull at her hair? She never would explain the word or why she had come back from Sarajevo with her hair cut short.

✛

Their reconciliation had its price. Where the Bosnian War was concerned, Theo had created a don't-ask-won't-tell policy. Sarajevo was always with them, just not available for discussion.

"What was your wife like before she left on this trip?" the psychiatrist asked.

Luke wanted to say "Fine," as if he knew of no reason she might be in danger. But that wouldn't be an honest answer.

"When my wife came back from the Bosnian War, she was treated for panic disorder and PTSD. At the time I thought PTSD was a crock. I saw it as a matter of the will—she had a secret she didn't want to tell. She quit foreign correspondence, and she seemed happy until—until this. An old friend of hers called from Sarajevo."

"How did she react to the phone call?"

Luke's throat went dry. "She was shaking just like she did when she came back from Sarajevo the first time."

"But she decided to go anyway?"

Luke was uncomfortable with the question. "I suppose it's my fault, but I was tired of living with ghosts."

The doctor rose. "I'm going to talk to her now. Let's see what's going on."

Luke wanted to escape to Sixteen West and plunge himself into work. Didn't Woodrow Emmons need him—and wouldn't he say thank you for coming? But Luke knew that if he left now, his marriage would finally be over.

An hour later the psychiatrist came out of the examining room with Theo. She was walking on her own steam and smiling at the man.

Luke put his arm around her. "Hi, sweetheart."

Theo kissed him on the cheek. "This doctor called Dr. Weiss at home to make an appointment for me for tomorrow."

Luke looked at the psychiatrist. "You're not going to admit her?"

"No need for that. The panic attack is over. The doctor in London gave her the right meds. But your wife does need help. It's best that she see the same man who saw her ten years ago."

Luke's cell phone rang. He recognized the number as Sixteen West. "It's Bishop Paul."

As soon as he heard Paul's voice on the phone, Luke relaxed a bit.

"Hi, Docta Luke. I heard you were in the ER looking for me."

"I was hoping you could come down here and help with my wife, but I hear you have your hands full upstairs."

"Brother Emmons is going home tonight. Lot of folks from church are here with us. The nurses were kind enough to move his bed down to the end room so our singing wouldn't bother anybody. We're in Room 331."

Theo saw the worried look on Luke's face. "I can wait in the conference room on the ward."

Luke looked at the psychiatrist for guidance.

"You feel okay now, Mrs. Tayspill?" the psychiatrist asked.

"Thanks to you, yes." She turned to Luke and kissed him on the cheek. "I want to meet your mistress."

"What happened in there?" Luke asked as they walked to the elevator.

"That doctor asked me one question."

"May I ask what that was?"

"He asked me if I want to live."

ELEVEN

Music surged under the door of Room 331, changing Sixteen West from a hospital AIDS ward to an African American church. Luke noticed the smile on Rita's face—an odd reaction for a nurse to have about the imminent death of her favorite patient. Coming from the room Luke heard a familiar voice singing. *In de River of Jordan...*

Muffled voices responded. *I believe...*

Luke opened the door to a conference room near Room 331 and pulled out a chair for Theo. "Let me see what's going on first. I'll only be a few minutes."

"I've heard that one before." Theo was calm and smiling.

Luke tried to close the door, but she held it open. *What did they give her?* he wondered. This wasn't the woman who had just come home on the plane in a fetal position.

A bass voice boomed again, reminding Luke why he had come to the ward. *In de River of Jordan...*

Luke found it hard to believe that the bishop had not always been a member of his team. Ward Sixteen West had the dying man to thank for the introduction.

✠

"Docta Luke," Woodrow Emmons asked him one day, "you be de bigman here on de ward?"

Luke laughed. "My wife and dog think I am, but I'm not always sure of that when I get to work."

"Well, I be sure."

The patient didn't look like a man in a bargaining position. An IV with three piggybacked bottles feeding it looped under the top of a hospital-issue johnny coat and pierced through the skin of his chest. Beneath the hemline of the coat, a Foley catheter poked out and into a drainage bag. But if Luke could have chosen one word to describe Woodrow Emmons, he would have said *dignified.*

Luke grinned as he answered. "Why do I think this conversation will cost me something?"

"Won't cost you nothin, Docta Luke. Be I right dat you want de best fa you patients? Nothin but de best?"

"You've got me there. You and all our patients deserve the best."

Mr. Emmons seemed satisfied. He relaxed, and his blind left eye drifted. "Tell me dis. If you go way, would you leave a student doctor in charge of we?"

"Of course not. You know how closely I supervise student doctors."

"Den why we see only student pastors on de ward?"

Luke knew he was cornered. "The chaplains aren't my department."

"You de bigman?"

In the years that Luke had been chief of the AIDS Care Service, Sixteen West had waded through a series of seminary students assigned to clinical pastoral education. For students it was an obligatory course on their path to ordination. More often it was their trial by fire. Often the doctors ignored them. What the seminarians hadn't anticipated was that patients like Woodrow Emmons might ignore them too.

Mr. Emmons took a cloth from his bedside table and wiped his forehead. He was trying to ignore the chills and fevers he got from the amphotericin. "I aksed dis young preacher pup, 'Son, you know Jedus? I don't know dis "Groun of All Bein" jazz you be talkin bout.'"

Luke gave in. "I don't know much about Jesus or anything about a Ground of All Being, but I'll see what I can do."

Woodrow Emmons took a business card from his bedside stand. "Dis be ma pastor. He go to dat Yale preacher school too, but he unnerstan people."

Luke winced, thinking of how many Yalies needed help in that department. "Okay, sir. I'll see what I can do."

"You de man, Docta Luke. You de bigman."

Luke took the business card for Bishop Paul Pinckney—Shepherd of Sweet Holy Spirit House of Praise—to the nurse manager. "Mr. Emmons thinks we need help with our chaplains. This is way out of my league."

Rita smiled when she read the card. "I know who he is. When he visits his church members, I don't have as many calls for pain meds. It's worth a call to the director of religious ministries."

By Woodrow Emmons's next admission, Bishop Paul was in charge of the student chaplains. Within a week he had replaced Luke as the bigman of Sixteen West.

✠

I believe…

Before Luke walked through the door of Mr. Emmons's room, he could imagine the faces that went with the voices. When Mr. Emmons was in the hospital, he had a dozen or so visitors.

Woshup Day have no end…

The solo voice had changed from bass to soprano—Mariama Pinckney, Bishop Paul's much younger wife.

As Luke opened the door, he saw a circle of people stomping around the dying man's bed. Mariama stood by the pillow. Next to her an old man with a cane tapped out the rhythm on the floor.

Bishop Paul was at the bedside holding Mr. Emmons's hand. "Docta Luke, our broda be goin home."

Luke looked around the room. "This looks more like a celebration to me."

Mariama came over and hugged Luke. "Paul told me about your wife. How's she doing?"

"Much better, thanks. She's in the conference room."

Mariama motioned to Paul to lead the singing. "I'll go visit with Theo for a while."

I gone down to de River of Jordan; Water take hold my throat;
Jedus Christ was de Capt'n; An de Holy Ghost was in my boat.
I gone down to de River of Jordan when John baptize three;
Look in de Book of Redemption, Where you find
Jedus Christ de docta
Turn water into wine.

Something in that song stirred Bishop Paul, and he let out a whoop. "Hooey!"

Woodrow Emmons pulled off his oxygen mask and started to laugh. Luke watched Paul strut around the room clapping, as the others stomped and circled.

Ain't dat a docta? Bishop Paul sang and waved his arm to invite the response.

I believe.

Ain't dat a docta?

I believe.

Sabbath have no end.

Mr. Emmons motioned for Bishop Paul to come closer. His voice was very weak.

"Read me de Word you done read at ma bactizum."

Bishop Paul picked up a Bible from the bedside stand and looked for the right passage. "And then shall they see the Son of man coming in a cloud with power and great glory. And when these things begin to come to pass, then look up, and lift up your heads; for your redemption draweth nigh."

"Thank you, Jesus!" one woman cried. Others peppered the reading with "Amen" or "Hallelujah."

Bishop Paul slowed his pace of reading to let their voices blend with his. "And he spake to them a parable: Behold the fig tree, and all the trees;

When they now shoot forth, ye see and know of your own selves that summer is now nigh at hand. So likewise ye, when ye see these things come to pass, know ye that the kingdom of God is nigh at hand."

Luke moved over to his patient's bedside and placed the oxygen mask closer to his face. Mr. Emmons squeezed his hand.

Paul smiled. "Every time I pray with Brother Emmons, he thanks Jesus for his Docta Luke."

From the doorway Luke heard Mariama's voice again. *Time a drawin nigh. Judgment a comin.*

Aye...

The singers responded as they resumed the dance pattern and stamped their feet.

Mariama had returned to the room with Theo, whom she led into the undulating circle. Theo was laughing as Mariama showed her how to clap on the offbeat.

Bishop Paul came over to Luke and put an arm around his shoulder. "These are Gullah songs I learned growing up in South Carolina. The dialect is close to the Krio my wife spoke in Sierra Leone."

"Are all the folks in your congregation 'Gullah'?" Luke asked.

The bishop shook his head. "No, but they sure like learning my traditions because they take us all back to Mother Africa."

Luke watched as his wounded woman caught the beat and started to dance. Bishop Paul doubled the beat by clapping his hands and slapping his thighs. "Brother Emmons told us at his baptism, 'You sing dat song when I be dyin.' He knew he had the virus at the time."

Mariama sang as she danced over to Mr. Emmons's bedside. *How you know it?*

Luke heard Theo singing with the rest.

Aye...

By de buddin of de fig tree.

Time a drawin nigh.

Mr. Emmons gasped and let out a death rattle. Luke watched his breathing change to Cheyne-Stokes respirations—the brain telling the lungs good-bye. Emmons's hand went limp, and one of the women began to wail. Others began to cry. Theo came over and put her arm around Luke.

Mariama clapped her hands to start another song.

Theo whispered, "Come on. Let's go home."

Luke held his wife for a long time before taking her to their car.

On the back deck of their house, Theo leaned over the railing and called into the darkness of the water garden below, "Where's my Swimming Flower?" A two-foot blur of metallic yellow and delicate fins sprang up from the water. "A treat for the pond puppy," Theo said, tossing a koi cookie. "Where are your friends?"

A splashing chorus of happy beggar fish quickly joined the Flower.

"If you feed them cookies, they won't clean up the leaves at the bottom of the pond," Luke said, as he threw cookies to the new arrivals.

"Aw, be nice. They'll be hibernating under ice pretty soon."

Theo was right. This was no time for him to play the heavy with her beloved fish. They lured her back to a sane country life set in Guilford's woods. Moments like this gave Luke hope about her answer to the psychiatrist's question.

The night was nippy enough for a sweater, but not bitter cold. Luke grabbed some piñon wood to make a fire in the bulb-shaped chiminea on the deck. Theo settled into a lounge chair, and Moose hopped on top of her.

"Mommy Dog is home," she said, offering him a Beggin' Strips treat.

"Moose never lets you forget when you feed the fish first," Luke said.

To the sounds of fire and water, Theo repeated the comforting word. "Home."

"Do you want to talk about it?" Theo asked.

"About Sarajevo?"

"No. About Mr. Emmons."

Luke lay back on his lounge chair and closed his eyes. "Funny thing, I don't feel sad. His death was beautiful, full of hope."

"That's nice," she said. "I felt like I was part of a family I never knew about but rediscovered after many lost years."

Luke sprang up. "You put your finger on it. *Family.* But not my family—at least not Mom, Dad, and Johanna. When I was a little boy, Grandpa Giles told me I was going to be a doctor when I grew up. I don't think he was talking about science or Yale or any of those things. I think he was talking about moments like that."

"Healer," Theo said, then fell silent.

In the gentle womb of darkness, a murder of crows moved boisterously through the skies in search of late-night lodging. As Theo listened, she ticked off a list of other flocks that had accepted their hospitality in the Westwoods. "A scold of jays, a cast of hawks, a charm of finches, a host of sparrows, a parliament of owls, a rafter of wild turkeys. Did I miss anybody?"

Luke offered a hint. "Pik…pik."

"A descent of woodpeckers. How could I forget them? I'm sorry," she called up to the trees.

In the darkness a downy woodpecker scolded his wife. Turning toward the tree that held a suet treat, Theo teased Luke. "It's nice to know that humans aren't the only ones who fight but still stay married."

It feels good to be teased, he thought. *At least I know she wants to stay.* But he worried how she had so quickly been transformed from the depressed woman in the car to the confident one who was able to walk out of the psychiatrist's office because he asked one simple question.

Pik…pik. Mr. Woody announced his intention to dine. With a beak full of peanut butter, he belched his satisfaction and then marched up the tree as his wife tiptoed down backward. They had seen other species working the suet cakes at the same time.

"His separate dining from his missis can't be from sheer gluttony," Theo said. "Do you think there's a pecking order in their marriage?"

"Maybe they divide up the baby-sitting chores," Luke said, hoping to segue to their king-size bed and the opportunity to work on a flock of little Tayspills.

Theo's face grew dark. Through seven seasons of Westwoods woodpeckers and seven prior years of Gotham pigeons, she had suffered from childlessness. *Suffered.* There was no better word. Glancing down at her body, she saw no promising swelling, only an old Yorkie pretending to be a human child. There was no life within her. Thirty-four years had already expired from her lifetime allotment. *Ticktock, ticktock goes the little bioclock.* She changed the subject. "Tell me about Mariama."

In Mr. Emmons's room, Luke had noticed the bond that had formed between the two women.

"Interesting gal. She's a nurse-midwife, born in Sierra Leone and educated in London and at Yale. She must be at least fifteen years younger than Bishop Paul—I don't know what that story is. She works with HIV-positive pregnant women. Things have been different in the women's clinic since she joined the team. We already had these great drug combos, but not many women came in for testing. Since Mariama came on board, the women really believe that we care."

"I can understand that," Theo said. In their short conversation in the conference room, Theo felt like one of those mothers. She had been willing to bare her soul to this stranger.

From the direction of the driveway, Luke heard a heavy footfall. Moose, aroused and ready for action, hopped off Theo's lap and took up his position at the deck gate.

Luke got out of his lounge chair. "Maybe it's Tommy. I haven't paid him yet for raking the leaves."

Theo peered through the woods, but she didn't see a flashlight beam from the direction of Tommy's house. "I don't think so, hon. With all the stones and branches hiding under the leaves, no one would walk through the woods without a flashlight on a moonless night."

Moose's nose twitched toward a spot next to the waterfall. Adjusting his eyes to the darkness, Luke stared at where the dog was looking.

Theo placed her hand on Luke's elbow and whispered, "Do you see her?"

Suddenly Luke caught sight of another pair of eyes staring back at him. As a fawn bent to sip the cool running water, its doe monitored the strange creatures on the deck.

"New life," Theo said and closed her eyes to let the beauty of life shut out Sarajevo. And, for the moment, Luke turned his back on death.

Twelve

Still groggy from sleep, Luke slipped out of bed and started down the stairs to make coffee. A trail of Theo's clothing brought a smile to his face. As he placed the coffee beans in the grinder, he felt something move behind him. He turned to face Theo, half-awake and happy. She put her arms on his waist.

"What time do you have to be in this morning?" she asked.

"I'm sorry to say I have a conference at 8:30."

Theo moved away but kissed his nose. "Your loss."

"I could call in and say I'll be late."

"Actually, my appointment with Weiss is at nine. Can I ride in with you this morning?"

"Sure, but what will you do all day if you don't have your own car?"

She smiled. "Oh, I have some plans."

After her fifty-minute hour, Theo left Dr. Weiss's office and walked over to the hospital atrium. She bought a latte in the coffee shop and took it over to the fountain. She turned when a musical voice called to her.

"How de body?" Mariama hugged Theo and sat down on the edge of the fountain. "That's how we say good morning in Sierra Leone."

"De body fine, and the rest of me isn't doing bad either. It's nice sitting here with the sun streaming into the hospital and the music of running water."

"Creation sights and sounds. I'm so glad you called me. One of my belly ladies is in labor, so I've got a bit of time."

"I couldn't forget what you said last night when we were sitting in the conference room. For the first time I believed I could get better."

"I spoke the truth."

"Last night in the ER, the on-call psychiatrist asked me if I wanted to live. I didn't answer his question in words, but I answered in my heart."

"Life isn't about us; it's about God. Life is another sign of Creation."

"Creation sounds like starting all over again. How I wish I could do that."

"You can. And you will."

Theo laughed. "You and your God are certain about a lot of things. This morning, Dr. Weiss wasn't sure what to make of me."

"What did you tell him?"

"I told him the truth. 'My husband took me to see a man dying of AIDS. People were singing and dancing in his room. An African woman prayed for me, and then I started to sing and dance too.'" She giggled. "Weiss looked at me as if he should walk me to the loony bin."

"Why didn't he?"

"He could see a change he couldn't account for. He wanted to hear more."

Theo stood up and put her coffee cup down. "I got off his couch and stood in front of his desk. Then I started clapping, but I couldn't get the beat right. 'White woman's disease,' I told him. 'No sense of rhythm.'"

Mariama stood and faced Theo. "Sistah, when I look at you, I never think about your skin. And you do have rhythm. You just haven't found it yet."

Mariama started clapping and motioned Theo to follow her beat. Hospital staff and visitors were streaming through the crowded atrium on their deliberate ways.

"Who cares what anybody thinks," Theo said and started to clap.

Mariama nodded. "We don't have a stick man today." She stamped her foot to reinforce the beat and sang in a whisper until Theo's whole body got into the motion. Behind them, they heard other hands clapping and turned to see that they had attracted a crowd.

Mariama sang louder, *I so glad I here.*

A few black people around them answered, *Yes, Lawd.*

When Mariama called, they responded. Other voices joined in. Theo felt more confident in the beat.

Mariama sang, *Hallelujah now, I so glad I here.*

The crowd answered, *Lawd knows.*

Doctors and nurses, in a hurry just a moment ago, stopped to join the circle around the two women. Soon they started clapping too.

I gwine sing while I here.

The crowd was swaying to the music. A security guard ambled over to check out the disturbance. "Sing it, sistah!" he shouted and clapped his hands.

Joy brought me here.

At the end of the song, the crowd erupted into applause. Theo and Mariama collapsed in each other's arms, laughing.

When Mariama's beeper went off, she looked at the phone number. "That would be my belly lady." She kissed Theo. "God bless you. I'm off to bring new life into this world."

Theo stayed at the fountain for a moment and listened to the water. The staff and visitors streamed off in different directions, their day brighter than it had been just a few moments ago. *Moments like this may be short,* Theo thought, *but their effect lingers on.* She remembered the fawn last night, drinking from her water garden. She sighed and threw away her coffee cup, then she headed toward Luke's office.

Her step was steady but more reluctant than while she'd been dancing with Mariama. Deliberately she sang the song to herself, carrying Mariama with her. Above the sound of her singing, she could hear Dr. Weiss's voice from earlier this morning—"Today would be a good day to start. Practice telling your husband the truth."

At his desk Luke was performing a sort of last rites for Woodrow Emmons. He started to write a note in the hospital chart, but his pen hadn't yet moved. *How do I sum up his story?* he wondered. He had never stopped to think about that for any of the many charts he had laid to rest over the years.

Instead of scratching out a brief death note, he made an outline. "Patient expired from complications of staph sepsis." That would be accurate, succinct, and typical of his death notes, but just-the-facts-ma'am medspeak seemed inadequate and unjust for the events of the night before.

He took up his pen again. "Mr. Emmons died peacefully, with members of medical staff and church family in attendance." More personal perhaps, but did that note fit in a clinical chart? Before he had met Bishop Paul, he wouldn't have wondered about it at all. The answer would have been no.

✠

"Docta Luke, don't you think spiritual diagnosis is just as important as all the medical detective work you do?"

The question came from Bishop Paul the first time he had joined the team as its permanent chaplain. Somehow Luke knew that there was only one answer allowed to this question. The bishop was a persuader.

"God bless you for all your wonderful work for these dear folks." Paul was casting his net for a big doctor fish.

Team rounds finished, Bishop Paul had walked with Luke to his office, his arm around the doctor's shoulder like a father's arm around his young son. In the office the bishop went over to Luke's coffee maker and helped himself to a cup. He knew how to make himself at home. "Sugar and cream?" he asked Luke. He also knew how to serve.

Paul took a seat on the sofa, not in the chair across from Luke's desk. Diverted from his power seat behind the desk, Luke sat down across from the chaplain.

"All I know about is science and medicine. I've never heard of spiritual diagnosis."

Bishop Paul laughed. "I'd be happy to fill you in."

Do I really have a choice? Luke wondered.

Paul took a yellow pad from Luke's coffee table and started to make a list. "Let me show you the system I use—two pairs, four spiritual concepts." On the first line he wrote "A Sense of the Holy" and underlined it. "You know that patient we just visited, Brother Emmons? What would you say? Does he have a sense of the holy?"

"That stuff is your department, not mine. I'm not a Christian. I'm not a believer in any religion. To tell you the truth, I try not to notice what other people say or don't say on the subject."

"I'm sure you notice lots of things. If Mr. Emmons said to you, 'Docta, ma heart be racin,' would you say, 'Sorry, but I'm not a cardiologist'? Would you try not to notice heartbeats?"

Luke laughed. None of Bishop Paul's questions had two possible answers.

"You've got me there. It would be my job to notice, even if I had to call in someone else to follow through."

"There you go."

"When you say 'the holy,' do you mean like the 'higher power' that Twelve Step people talk about?"

"The Gullahs call it the sweet Holy Spirit. The Quakers call it the inward witness. What it boils down to is this: When God created us, he made sure we had enough of him in us to make us pine for more."

"Nobody in my family has that kind of pining."

"They might have if they'd hush up and listen."

Luke thought for a moment. "Okay, I'm hushed up. Does 'the holy' have to have a name?"

Paul grinned. "Inevitably, yes. Otherwise you might think it's you."

"I'm not likely to make that mistake, not the way my life is going."

Pinckney howled a bishop-sized laugh. "Let's go back to Brother Emmons. From what you've seen, do you think Jesus has been good for his health?"

Luke looked out his office window. "I have to agree that Mr. Emmons does better because of his faith. I hate to think what his hospital admissions would be like without those church people visiting."

Paul kept his triumph to a modest minimum. "So you *have* noticed."

"Well, that would be hard to miss. I trip over your congregation every time I make evening rounds."

"Good start for a beginner."

Paul started a second line on the page. "Now, someone who has noticed the holy surely has to pay attention. Can you imagine someone seeing the big ol' handprint of God and not having anything to say about it?" On the paper he wrote "A Response of Gratitude."

Luke saw what the bishop had written and replied, "Gratitude doesn't just belong to religion."

"Ah, but where do you think it came from?" asked Paul.

Luke grinned. "Why do I think I'll have to read the Bible to find the answer to all your questions?"

"Not a bad idea. Now tell me about Brother Emmons. Is he a grateful man?"

Luke would have to concede this point to Bishop Paul as well. "How could I miss it? Every time I enter his room he tells me, 'Docta Luke, I thank God dat you be ma docta. Ebry day I thank him.' "

Paul laughed. "Pretty soon you'll be fluent in Gullah. That's what they speak down where Brother Emmons and I come from. At home they call it 'flat talk.' When I was a boy, I was ashamed to speak it. You could say I wasn't very grateful for my heritage."

"Most people would say they are proud of their heritage, not grateful."

"God gave me my heritage as a gift. Now, that isn't a human accomplishment. We don't choose our parents. Which brings us to the second set in spiritual diagnosis, something that almost never originates with people—a Sense of Forgiveness and a Response of Reconciliation."

"To err is human, to forgive divine? I guess I'll have to get to know Mr. Emmons better before I can work on that pair."

To Luke's relief, the telephone rang. He jumped up to answer the call and mimed to his visitor that it would take awhile. Bishop Paul nodded but made no move to leave. Although Luke had little interest in speaking to the medical-records department, he listened as a clerk upbraided him for his unsigned charts. Paul poured himself another cup of coffee and returned to the sofa. When Luke couldn't drag out the call any longer, he hung up but stayed standing. "I'm so sorry. Perhaps we can chat about this another time."

"We surely shall," the chaplain said as he tore the page from the pad. Taking a tack, he pinned the paper on the corkboard facing Luke's desk. "This is a good place so you don't lose it. Every time you sit down, you'll think about our conversation."

Paul put down his coffee mug. "You make a great cup of coffee. I can't wait until our next chat. Then we'll talk about forgiveness and reconciliation."

✠

The page was still on Luke's pin board, the list complete. Over the months Bishop Paul had stolen time from Luke's busy days to complete his lecture.

"Think of spiritual care as support for your patients," Paul had told him, "just the way your antibiotics help folks with AIDS."

Doodling on a page from the same pad, Luke wrote down the numbers one through four. When his notes were complete, he picked up Mr. Emmons's chart. At the top of a page, he wrote "Discharge/Death Note." He couldn't bring himself to use the word *spiritual* in a medical document, but he entered the following paragraph: "On the Sunday night following Thanksgiving, Woodrow Emmons died peacefully on the in-patient unit from complications of AIDS. In the company of his church family and members of the medical staff, he was joyful to the end. His last words expressed his sense of reconciliation with God and his fellowman."

Luke closed the chart and put it on a corner of his desk, not willing to dispatch it yet to the dead files ruled over by Medical Records. *The Death of Woodrow Emmons,* he thought and picked up Giles's manuscript from another corner of his desk.

His grandfather's stories contained medical facts—death from malaria, death by hanging—but the cause of death wasn't the main plot. They were just footnotes, passing comments to satisfy a reader who might need to suspend disbelief for a moment to join the Tayspills on their journey.

Taking the composition book in his hands, Luke looked at something that had bothered him all weekend. This book about death was full of the holy, gratitude, forgiveness, and reconciliation.

"I think I just had a 'pifany' experience," he whispered as he stroked the book.

"Knock-knock," a voice said.

He turned and saw Theo at the office door.

"Have you got a few minutes?"

"How was your visit with Dr. Weiss?"

She moved into his arms. "It went quite well, but I had an even better appointment after that. Mariama and I had coffee in the atrium. We caused almost as much of a ruckus there as we did last night in Mr. Emmons's room."

Luke noticed she was giggling—a hopeful sign. "What were you two up to down there?"

"She was trying to teach me rhythm. We got a little loud." She reached up and took Luke's face in her hands. "I've got a great idea. Let's have the team Christmas party at our house this year instead of a restaurant. It would be fun."

"Are you sure it wouldn't be too much stress? You just got back from a traumatic trip. The Christmas party is only a few weeks away."

"Mariama said she would help me."

If the bishop's wife was as persuasive as her husband, Luke was facing a plan already in motion. Bodies still linked, Luke walked Theo over to the door, snapped it shut, and turned the lock. He moved her to the sofa and, with one arm, swept his stacks of journals off the sofa and onto the floor.

Once again Luke forgot to tell her about Giles's manuscript, and Theo lost her resolve to tell him about Sarajevo.

Thirteen

Theo's elaborate preparations contradicted her intention to keep their Christmas brunch simple. From Luke's point of view, that was a good sign. Plain and simple would not have been Theo.

Rather than encourage her guests to wear holiday finery, she invited them to dress for a walk in the woods. Nothing could work off a meal better than a hike on the snow-covered Westwoods Trails.

After her guests finished eating, Theo organized the hikers for action. She called Moose to join them. But instead of leaping up for a walk, he yawned from the comfort of Bishop Paul's arms and tucked his muzzle under one of the bishop's chins.

Luke stayed in his rocking chair by the fireplace. "We'll stay and do the dishes," he said.

Theo eyed the men. "Which one of you?"

"All three of us." Luke spoke for Paul as well as himself and Moose.

As soon as the hikers were on their way, Luke poured himself a mug of hot cider and settled back into the rocking chair. Then Paul slumped down in his chair, smiling in his sleep as Moose nestled on his chest. The dishes could wait. With eyes closed, the three dishwasher designates relished the peace of the moment.

Although the cooking pot was empty, the aroma of Mariama's West African stew still overpowered the fragrance of the Christmas tree. As Luke nodded off, content with the events of the day, Paul let out a snort that startled all three nappers. Moose reached up to plant a kiss on his lips and discovered the bishop's mustache. As the dog explored the bush under his nose, Paul exploded in an enormous sneeze.

"I suppose we should start on the dishes," Luke said without much conviction or motion.

Paul started to rise from his chair, but his host motioned for him to stay put. Luke got up and threw the used paper plates in the garbage.

Then he set the dirty serving dishes on the floor. "Moose does the pre-wash," he explained as the dog moved in to offer his services.

Without moving from his chair, Paul said, "And I thought you were an infectious-disease specialist."

"Just don't tell Theo," Luke answered, returning to his rocking chair.

Paul reached down to one of the shopping bags parked by the side of his chair. He pulled out a Christmas-wrapped package and handed it to Luke. "This is for you from Brother Emmons."

Luke tore off the paper and found a small paperback book with an African-looking title. He tried to sound out the words. "*De Good Nyews Bout Jedus Christ Wa Luke Write.* This reads the way Mr. Emmons talked."

"It's Luke's gospel from the Bible in the Gullah dialect. Brother Emmons loved his Docta Luke."

Luke stroked the book and smiled. "Sometimes being a doctor is a bit like being a parent. You're not supposed to have favorites, but the fact is you do."

"I know what you mean. A pastor shouldn't have favorites either, but not every sheep makes you feel glad to be a shepherd."

"You two don't have any children?"

Paul shook his head. "That doesn't seem to be part of God's plan for the Pinckneys."

"I wish it were part of his plan for us."

Paul sat up. "Aha! So you do believe in God!"

"You didn't let me finish. *If* there were a God."

"Everyone's life has a plan."

Luke's excitement over receiving the gift evaporated into sadness. Then it exploded into anger. "What was God's plan for Mr. Emmons—sickness, suffering, and death?"

"God saved him, Docta Luke. That's 'de good nyews.'"

"No offense, chaplain, but you're playing with words. I don't know anything about saved souls. I only know about lost bodies, Emmons's included."

"You're splitting hairs, Docta Luke. The Bible doesn't make those distinctions. Health means salvation. Curing means healing."

Luke laughed. "I can just see the look on a patient's face if I walked into a room and said, 'I have this medicine that can heal you.'"

Paul smiled. "I'd rather think about the look they'd get on their faces if you brought Jesus into the room in your heart." His face changed, signaling a more serious thought. "Can you imagine how hard it was for a simple man like Mr. Emmons to take on his Yale doctor? That's why he gave you this gift."

Luke looked down at the book in his hands and ran his fingers over the words of the title.

"You know what Brother Emmons said? 'If I give him de reg'lar Bible, he put it on a shelf an tell de peoples dis nice old darky wid de virus gave it to him. Maybe he read de Bible in Gullah an unnerstan."

Luke's face softened as he remembered Mr. Emmons. What Bishop Paul had quoted sounded just like something Emmons would have said.

"I guess this is my year for learning. Before I met you, I had never heard of Gullah. Where do people speak it?"

"Off the Georgia an South Carolina coast. I grew up on an island called St. Helena. Ma papa was a farmer an a preacher. He never made it pas de sixth grade. Brother Emmons was our neighbor. He worked ma papa's farm."

Luke noticed a subtle shift in Paul's storytelling style when he started to talk about growing up. The sad, nostalgic tone was not the flowery preaching style he had crafted to win a hearing. Paul's Yale-perfect grammar started to fade when he talked about home.

"In 1953 ma papa an me both got polio. Papa, he died. Docta York Bailey, our island's first black docta, took care of us. When folks needed de doc, dey knew where to find him. After Papa died, Doc Bailey stayed by ma bed. Doc an Momma—God bless her soul. I stopped breathin three times, an three times de doc breathed life back in me. I shoulda been in de hospital in an iron lung, but dey be no special polio beds fa colored folks. Ma momma—Miss Maggie, ebrybody called her—she say she had two patients den, de doc an me."

Paul got up from his chair and spread his hands in front of the fireplace. "I don't remember much on ma own from what done happen back den, but momma tole de story so many times, I reckon like I remember. One night, when I was close to death, Doc Bailey an Momma couldn't sleep—neither one of dem. Miss Maggie, she had her a vision. Doc Bailey said he didn't see or hear nothin, but de doc knew somethin was happenin from lookin on her face. Now, some island folk mix voodoo stuff with dey Christian beliefs, but dis was no blue-root hallucination."

Paul moved away from the fireplace and stood in front of Luke. He used his hands to set the stage for his story. "Miss Maggie came outta dat spell certain I would survive. She tole de doc she saw me sittin on de dock by de salt marshes, lookin out over de water. Another shore appeared, like someone held a mirror to our coast. Dis other piece of land kept comin close, so you could see de people on de other side.

"Dey was a boy ma age wid cuttin marks on his face, like an African from de bush. She hear him callin over de waters to me, 'Come over an help us.' "

As he told the story, tears filled Paul's eyes, and his voice shifted to a whiny contralto. The memory was no longer Miss Maggie's but his own.

" 'I's a cripple,' I tole him, 'I cain't come.' He look so sad, like I tole him I didn't wanna play wid him. He say it agin. 'Come over an help us.' "

Paul reached for the fireplace mantle to support his bulk and shake out his weak leg. Luke had noticed how, after a long day at the hospital, Paul's slight limp became more pronounced. "I tried to stan, but ma legs didn't wanna work. I fell back down on de dock agin. De water tween us, it be growin an de shoreline moved futher and futher way. I could hardly see de boy on de other shore. His voice be a faint echo. 'Come over an help us.' "

The storyteller's voice changed back to Bishop Paul's bass. "Doc

Bailey said Momma began to hoot an shout an dance. She went out on de porch an called to all de church folks who were holdin watch outside in our yard. She was convinced I would live an walk agin. An she was convinced God was callin me to dat other shore, where our people come from."

Paul's face fell as he finished the story. "Miss Maggie thought I missed my calling. She died thinkin I got happy in the fleshpots of academia."

"Have you ever been to Africa?" Luke asked.

Still solemn, Paul nodded. "That's where I met Mariama."

Suddenly Moose ran to the front door barking. Luke scrambled to his feet and stuffed the dishes into the dishwasher. The party guests bounded through the front door, energized from their walk in the woods. They chattered as they took off their hiking shoes.

Mariama and Theo were the last of the hikers to arrive. The first thing Luke noticed was that both women had tear-stained faces.

Mariama was the first to wipe away her tears. "Listen up, folks. Time to gather round the fire and tell Christmas stories."

Both the hikers and those who had stayed home ambled toward the hearth. "Who will be first?" Luke asked, watching Theo emerge from the bathroom with less makeup on than before she went for the walk.

"I'll be first," Rita said. "My parents came from the Ukraine. Their big day for gift giving was Saint Nicholas Day in early December. We had a European version of 'You'd better watch out.' If children were bad, Saint Nick would leave a piece of coal in their stockings."

"What did you do?" Theo asked. She was smiling as she dabbed at her smeared face.

"I hid all my stockings!" Rita answered, and the whole group exploded in laughter.

"Any other naughty children?" Luke asked.

Bishop Paul giggled. "Not when you had Miss Maggie on your tailpipe. We didn't have money for gifts for each other. But we had to do chores to earn money and give it to Miss Maggie. Late on Christmas Eve, she went around St. Helena Island leaving money under doormats for families less fortunate than ours."

Theo smiled and joined in the storytelling. "Greeks don't celebrate Christmas Day proper. Three Kings Day, a week later, is our big day for gift giving. By that time everybody else in Yellow Springs had finished with holidays and forgotten Christmas. But Momma baked extra baklava and *spanikopita*. My father served it to everyone who came in the diner that day." Luke watched her eyes fill up again with tears.

"What about you, Mariama?" Rita asked. "How did you celebrate Christmas in Sierra Leone?"

Like Theo, Mariama wandered back into childhood memories of Christmas. "We went to church to celebrate Christ's birth, but we didn't have money for gifts until Bishop Paul came to my village. I was only eight years old then. Somehow that year every family in our village found something on their doorstep Christmas morning. I wondered at the time who had left it there, but now I am sure." She went over, settled in Paul's lap, and planted a big kiss on his brow.

Luke roared. "If a black man could blush, this is what it would look like."

"What about you, Luke?" Mariama asked. "How did your family celebrate?"

Luke stopped smiling. "We didn't. My father said Christmas was a pagan holiday with Christian trappings. He made certain no one gave anyone else a gift."

"Scrooge!" Rita declared. "But certainly you must have a happy Christmas memory."

Luke shrugged. "I let my colleagues with children have the day with their families."

Silence fell over the group, but Paul refused to let the magic of the moment die. "Come on, gang. Let's sing Christmas carols."

"Oh, let's!" Rita said. " 'Joy to the world, the Lord is come.' Everybody know that?"

Luke shrugged. "I guess I can learn."

After the guests left, Theo looked around the kitchen. Luke took her half smile as a three-quarter invitation. "Want to take a bubble bath together?"

Theo swiveled in his arms. "Why don't you start the water running?"

He bounded upstairs to their master bathroom. Despite the chill of the evening, he opened the window that overlooked the water garden. Plugging in the towel warmer, he chose two oatmeal-colored bath towels from the shelves against the wall. Moose joined him to check out what was happening. Luke rejected "Sweet Dreams Bubble Bath" and poured a healthy slug of "Theodora" into the sunken black-marble tub. As the fragrant steam rose, Moose sniffed it and sneezed.

"Sorry, fella," Luke said, but he wasn't sorry. It was time for the humans to have some privacy.

From aroma, Luke moved on to choice of music. Rather than selecting one of his classical CDs, he picked a Greek chanteuse Theo favored. Haris Alexiou had set the right mood on other nights, so he slipped *Di Efchon* in the CD player on a shelf behind the tub. Finally he lit jasmine candles that circled the sunken tub and turned off the overhead lights. "Oh yeah," he said as he felt Theo hug him from behind.

Theo looked out the window at the water garden below. "It's snowing again. We'll have to take the underwater lights out of the pond before it freezes over."

"Tomorrow," he whispered and pulled her into the sudsy water.

✠

"I'm sorry," she said as they lay on their separate edges of the bed. "I didn't mean to spoil everything by crying."

"It's my fault. When you and Mariama came home, I saw that you had been crying. I should have waited until we had a chance to talk."

Theo leaned over and kissed Luke on the forehead. He took a deep breath, thinking that the moment had finally arrived when she would open up her heart.

"I've never felt as much at ease with anyone in my life as I do with Mariama," she said.

At first Luke tried to disguise how wounded he felt, but then he said what he was thinking. "I'd like to believe that you could be at that much ease with me."

"Sometimes it's healing to listen to someone else's pain."

That word again, Luke thought. *Healing.* The right word, he had to admit. *Salvation.* That, too. In the context of Theo's story, she needed both, not the type of cure he tried to give his patients. He wished he knew how to be that type of healer. And he wished he knew what it was she needed to be saved from.

Theo reached over, still willing to talk. "For so many years I've felt as if no one in the history of the world has ever suffered as much as I have."

But Luke didn't want to hear Mariama's story, however tragic it was. He wanted to know what had turned his young wife into an aging time bomb. "But you *have* suffered. Your pain is very real."

Theo preferred to talk about Mariama. "Sierra Leone is a dangerous place. Mariama watched rebels murder her parents, rip her pregnant sister's baby from her body, and kidnap her little brother. She doesn't even know if her brother is still alive. The last she knew, he was one of those wretched child-soldiers enslaved by the rebels."

"What else did you two talk about?"

Theo gave him a chaste kiss on the cheek, then rolled away. "I'll tell you sometime."

Moose migrated up between them on the blanket. Better than Luke, he knew when the loving was past. On her side of the bed, Theo lay thinking about Mariama.

✠

As Theo and Mariama walked along in the snow, Mariama asked, "Do you have any children?"

"I was pregnant once," Theo told her, "but the baby didn't live."

"What is your baby's name?" *Is,* not *was.*

"It didn't live long enough to have a name."

"Didn't you and Luke talk about names?"

"Luke didn't even know I was pregnant. We were separated at the time. I was in Europe."

"Your baby still lives in your heart. Your heart holds his name."

Theo had always thought it was a boy, but she had no evidence for that. The fetus was too small for anyone to tell. "Luke. I would have named him after his father."

"Someday you'll have another child." Mariama had certainty in her voice.

"I don't think so. At least the doctors don't think so."

Mariama laughed. "Doctors don't know everything."

Theo thought about Sir Nigel. And her husband. And her psychiatrist. Doctors who didn't know how to heal her filled her life. "Isn't that the truth!"

"Have you ever read the Bible?" Mariama seemed to change the subject.

"Not really. Well, maybe once in college. I took this course—Ancient Women in Literature. Some of those readings were about women in the Bible."

"Which stories do you remember?"

"I can't remember their names now, but I remember women with fertility problems."

"Sarah, Hannah, and Elizabeth."

"Very good. I'm sure those were the names."

"What do you remember most about them?"

Theo's face grew grim. "I remember that they won. They got the babies they wanted. They were all happy."

"Why do you think they got their babies?"

"The women said it had to do with God, at least that's what it said in the stories. But why did God make them jump through hoops in the first place?"

Mariama smiled softly. "That's the type of question you have to ask God."

╬

Luke remained silent as he reached over and drew Theo's head to his chest. She came to him but didn't do more than sleep. *How does a guy get into a woman's mind?* he wondered. With Theo, it surely wasn't through lovemaking. Sex was a lock for her, not a key. The last sound Luke heard before falling asleep was Moose sneezing.

Theo couldn't sleep. When she closed her eyes, she saw hoops high above her head and out of reach. How could she tell Luke she had lost a child he never knew about? Could she ever jump that high?

In a holiday shop the next day, Theo purchased a manger scene and placed it on their fireplace mantle. She found three kings, too, to keep the holy family company. Throughout the rest of the season, in private moments, she fingered the small figure of Mary, dressed in blue like Botticelli's Madonna. Each time, she caressed the halo the artist had placed around the virgin's head and whispered, "So you had a hoop over your head too."

On Christmas morning she came down to the living room before Luke and moved the holy family under the Christmas tree in front of their packages. This time she touched the small figure in the manger and stroked the golden ring around his head. "Why did you come into this world, little one? Did you come to turn hoops into halos?"

Fourteen

A scold of blue jays woke Luke on New Year's Day. The noisy bird visitors came the same time each morning and didn't want to hear about humans sleeping in on a holiday. Through a half-open eye, Luke could see them lined up on the railing of the bedroom balcony, outdoing one another with their complaints. He pulled his pillow around his ears, dislodging Moose.

Except for the dog, Luke was alone in bed. In one corner of the balcony, Theo was pouring shelled peanuts into a dish. One jay landed in the dish while it was still in her hand and weighed three different peanuts in its beak. When it found the largest peanut, it fled to the trees, while its buddies zoomed in toward the feeder like top guns heading home to their aircraft carrier.

Luke stumbled out of bed. "You've spoiled them," he told Theo as more jays cackled from nearby trees.

Theo smiled but had no intention of rationing the peanuts. She held some out to Luke and asked, "What's on your schedule for today?"

"New Year's resolutions," he answered, but he didn't offer specific details. He was determined to explore Giles's manuscript, specifically the settings of the three Lucas Tayspill stories. He had also promised himself that he would put Sarajevo on the table every time he had the chance.

He took a handful of peanuts and spread them out for the birds. He didn't look directly at Theo when he asked, "Do you have any resolutions?"

"I'd like our sabbatical to be a honeymoon," she answered, brushing past him and squeezing his hand.

Why did he think she'd say, "I've resolved to tell you the whole truth and nothing but"? He settled for what she offered and grabbed the hem of her bathrobe.

"I'm going to make breakfast now," she said, continuing to walk away.

Ah, well, he thought, *my sabbatical hasn't started yet.*

After breakfast Luke settled on the sofa with a large yellow legal pad. Moose hopped up and burrowed under a blanket. The bundled dog slid closer to Luke and rested his head against Luke's thigh.

Theo brought Luke a cup of coffee, took off his slippers, and started to massage his toes.

He wanted to surrender to the mood of the moment. Instead, he asked, "Do you remember the e-mail I sent you in London?"

Theo let go of his foot and shook her head. Then she resumed stroking. "I've probably blocked it out of my mind. I was so consumed with my own problems that I didn't have room for anything else."

The doctor in him wanted to drop his own agenda and ask her about those problems. Instead, he picked up the composition book and handed it to her.

"The day I found this manuscript was the worst day of my life since you were trapped in Sarajevo."

Theo dropped the book as if it had burned her hand. "Now I remember. I panicked when I read your e-mail. I count on you to hold the world in place for me."

"I'm not Superman—or Atlas. I feel about as powerful as Moose." At the invocation of his name, a wet nose appeared from under the blanket fringe.

Theo reached over to pet Moose. "You know what I mean. You're my safe anchor. I need your stability."

Luke lifted the dog and moved him and his blanket to the other end of the sofa. This was no time for a buffer zone between him and Theo.

"People change. Marriages grow. I'd like to think you could sometimes be a safe anchor for me."

"I wish I could. Maybe I should make that one of my New Year's resolutions."

"How about a promise rather than a resolution? There's something more sacred about a promise. 'Resolution' implies that you know you'll fail."

Theo thought for a moment. "Could you settle for a resolution for right now?"

Luke lifted her face in his hands. "We need to talk. What would you say if I told you that my life is in danger?"

She stiffened and pulled away from him. "How? From working with AIDS?"

"No," he said, drawing her back. "From forces outside my control that I don't understand."

She drew away again and frowned. "I'd say that sounds melodramatic, and you're scaring me."

He pulled her down onto the sofa and kissed her hair. "I'm scaring me too."

"So stop scaring both of us. I'm serious." She started to nibble on his ear.

Breaking away Luke sat up and placed Giles's manuscript in her hands. "I found this while I was in Yellow Springs." He covered her hands with his own to keep her from dropping it.

Withdrawing to a corner of the couch, Theo frowned as she mouthed the words in the title. "What is this—a whodunit? And whose handwriting is this?"

"It's three parts of the Tayspill family history. Grandpa Giles wrote it."

As Theo flipped through the pages, the tension in her face increased. "Wasn't your grandfather—different? At least that's what Johanna told me."

Luke sprang back, offended. "No one else has ever loved me as much as Grandpa."

"Present company included?"

Luke reached a hand toward her, and she accepted the touch. But she didn't move toward him.

"Have you read the whole thing?" she asked, looking at the manuscript. "What's all this death stuff about?"

Luke took the book from her and slipped it back into its envelope. He drew Theo into his arms and stretched back on the sofa. "It means that our sabbatical is going to be a little different than we had planned."

"No London?"

"Yes, London."

The telephone rang, breaking the tension. Theo popped up to take the call. "How de body, girlfriend?" she asked.

It had to be Mariama. Luke smiled and tried to listen in on Theo's side of the conversation.

"We don't usually do anything special. Just stay home by the fire." She placed her hand over the phone and summarized for Luke. "Mariama and Paul are inviting us over for some Gullah cooking left over from their New Year's Eve at church. How do hoppin john, red rice, and sweet-potato pie sound to you?"

"With Paul and Mariama? Sounds like fun."

Theo turned back to the phone. "What time? And what can we bring?"

She was smiling when she hung up the phone. "That's one of my New Year's resolutions—to spend more time with Mariama."

The Tayspills rang the doorbell of a modest house on upper Chapel Street. You would expect to hear squealing children in a house like this.

But when Mariama opened the door, all they heard was music. Paul limped to the door to greet them. Post-polio syndrome, Luke diagnosed, a painful late reminder of Paul's long-ago suffering.

The bishop caught the doctor's examining look. "I got carried away at the ring shout last night."

"Looks like you could use some physical therapy," Luke said.

Paul ducked the doctorly advice. "PT stands for 'physical torture.' You don't know what it was like in the old days for polio patients."

Mariama ushered them to the kitchen. "Most of these dishes are a handful of Africa with a fistful of Gullah."

Paul ladled a generous portion of a black-eyed-pea mixture on their plates. "Folks down home say hoppin john brings good luck the whole year if you eat it on New Year's Day."

Mariama smiled. "Where Paul comes from, they put pork in everything. In Sierra Leone we add pieces of whatever protein we have on hand—chicken, fish, beef. Sometimes we put all three in the same meal. Either way, we're both getting fat." She laughed as she patted both Pinckney waistlines.

After dinner, both Luke and Theo peeked down at their own bulging waistlines. Mariama, however, wasn't finished with them yet. "Let's move into the living room. I'll bring out dessert and coffee."

"You guys go ahead," Theo said. "I'll give Mariama a hand washing up."

Luke noticed pain pass through Paul's face as he thought about standing. He stood by the bishop's chair to give him a hand. As Paul accepted Luke's arm for support, he said, "The spasms come and go. Good to have someone to lean on."

Paul settled into his favorite chair in the living room. Luke sat down next to him and drew him back to his unfinished story about his childhood illness. "At the Christmas party, you told me about your mother's vision and how you almost died. What happened after that? Did you get much rehabilitation?"

Paul nodded and resumed the story. "Once Doc Bailey was certain I was gonna live, he went up to Warm Springs to learn some rehab at the place where President Roosevelt went. Doc came back and taught Miss Maggie what to do. I can still remember the agony."

Paul stood up to shift his position and shake out his lame leg. He walked around the room until the spasm passed.

"Miss Maggie took to the treatments with a holy vengeance. Of course, she sprinkled her torture with Bible verses and spirituals. I'd start crying as soon as I saw her boiling the kettle on the fire.

"First she'd lay me on my stomach with rags rolled up under my chest to support my shoulders—they were still very weak. Then she'd dip strips of wool into the water. She'd fish them out with a fork and let the extra water run off. I'd lie there, unable to run away, watching the steam rising up from the cloth. Then she'd wrap the red-hot rags around my arms and legs. I thought I was gonna go up in flames. She'd boil and wrap until I couldn't stand it no more. Then she'd roll me over me like a side of meat and start pounding on my muscles. I was too weak to fight her off. To this day, when I hear the word *massage,* I start running the opposite direction."

The women appeared with sweet-potato pie and coffee. Mariama settled on the arm of Paul's chair. "Paul won't let me do any PT for him," Mariama said.

Still standing, Paul took a bite of pie and a sip of coffee. Revived by dessert, the spasm passed, and he relaxed. He slipped back in his chair and picked up his story.

"Once Miss Maggie was done pounding on me, she'd stretch my arms and legs. But they didn't want to go nowhere. Didn't matter to Momma. She stretched and I howled. Lawdy, how I hated her! All those cuss words I had learned but never dared say came to my lips. Oh the names I called her that no Christian man, black or white, should ever have coming out of his mouth."

"She must have been a strong woman," Luke said. "In the old days they didn't let mothers visit children during polio therapy. The woman who developed the treatment you're describing—Sister Kenney—was known as a blessed brute."

Paul pointed to his head. "I know that all here. I even knew it when I was a boy, but oh how I hated my momma. One day she just couldn't do it no more. I was in bed when Doc Bailey came to call. Momma went outside with him on the porch. I could hear her crying. 'I cain't do it no mo. Jes cain't do it.' No matter, she did do it, and I got better. But in my heart, I hated my momma."

Luke felt there was a gap in the story. "What happened to take that hate away?"

"Once I was better, Miss Maggie hammered away about her vision. She said God saved me for a purpose. He healed me to be a preacher and do something special for my people. 'You gwine go over an help,' she'd say. 'That's your vision, old woman, not mine,' I'd tell her.

"Doc Bailey, he made sure I got an education. He wanted me to get out of the South for college. He had connections with Quakers and got me a scholarship to prep school and one of their best universities."

Luke watched the transformation in Paul's face as he moved to the next part of his story.

"It was the sixties, and the civil rights movement was just under way. Dr. King even came to our island to plan the March on Washington." Paul's face turned dark again. "I was in college when he was killed. I couldn't believe it when I heard some of those white boys cheer. 'Christians,' they called themselves, and some of them Quakers. The professors didn't laugh, though. I think those Quaker teachers mourned as much as I did. But there was a gap between the Quaker ideals of the college and daily life on campus, something I couldn't figure out. During the Civil War, Quakers came to teach my people how to read, even before Lincoln signed the Emancipation Proclamation. How could they have forgotten my people? We have never forgotten them.

"All the rage I had building up inside me started spilling out. My limp even got worse for a while. I grew me an Afro and wore dashiki shirts. I even joined the Black Panther Party. When I went home to St. Helena Island, Miss Maggie would rag on me. She didn't like the way I looked, the way I talked. Lord knows how I made it through college with honors, but I had no plans for the future. I wasn't sure if America could be my home, with all the hatred on the streets. So I saved up some money and went to Africa.

"In 1970 I arrived in Sierra Leone. That's when I met this sweet lady for the first time." Paul put his arm around Mariama's waist. "She was only eight years old at the time."

Paul stopped speaking. A bittersweet look passed between him and his wife, pleasure blended with pain.

Luke waited, assuming the storytelling would resume, but Theo tugged at his sleeve as if responding to a silent signal. "It's getting late, and you've got an early morning tomorrow."

Mariama rose. "I'll get your coats." She didn't beg them to stay.

Luke wondered how Theo knew the polite time had come to leave. He shook hands with Paul. "I want to hear the rest of that story sometime."

Then he noticed the look that passed between Mariama and Theo.

FIFTEEN

Bishop Paul continued to limp around the hospital until one morning in mid-January. That day he showed up for rounds in a warm-up suit. It was the first time Luke had seen him wear something other than his signature jeans and clerical collar. He slapped Luke on the shoulder. "Either my pain tolerance has improved since I was a kid, or physical therapists have learned how to heal you without making you wish you were dead."

"I can see a difference in your walk. What gave you the incentive to go back to therapy?"

Paul handed him a piece of paper. "Do you remember the talk you helped me get together for the International AIDS Conference? They've accepted my paper for the main session."

"No way! Have you ever been to London before?"

Paul shook his head. "I'm excited enough to make sure I enjoy London. From what Mariama's told me, London is a walking town. By the way, her abstract has been accepted too. She'll be presenting in the maternal-fetal workshop. She's all excited about seeing her nursing-school chums. That's about as close as she ever wants to come to Sierra Leone again."

"Stop by my office after rounds so we can make plans."

Instead of smiling, Paul's smile faded. "That's the good news."

"With news that good, what could be so bad?"

Paul handed him another piece of paper. "Came in the hospital mail today."

Luke's smiled faded even faster than Paul's had. "How can they eliminate your position? It feels like you've just barely begun."

Paul tore up the letter. "I'm beginning to feel like Job. The Lord giveth, the Lord taketh away, but blessed be the name of the Lord anyway. As long as Mariama has her job, we'll have a roof over our heads, food on the table, and health insurance. And as a community pastor, I can always drop in to visit the patients."

Luke shook his head. "It's not right. It's rotten economics. Your salary is a small investment in the bigger picture. Thanks to you, patients feel they have something to live for. They're leaving the hospital earlier than they used to."

"That's the irony. I called the hospital administrator to ask why they cut my job. He said they're looking at the whole AIDS program. Fewer inpatients, shorter hospital stays, so fewer staff needed."

On his desk Luke saw Mr. Emmons's Christmas gift. He had made a resolution to read a little bit of the book each day. It was already January 15, though, and he hadn't gotten started yet. Above his desk was the page with Bishop Paul's four-point list, soon to be presented to the worldwide AIDS community.

Paul poured himself a cup of coffee and raised it as if to toast. "Elixir of life."

If Paul could be jovial after what had happened, Luke thought, he, too, could shake off the dark cloud that had settled over their conversation. He lifted his own coffee mug to salute Paul. "If they ever prove this stuff causes cancer, I'm in trouble."

"How about helping a friend? My physical therapist says I need to lose weight."

Without staring, Luke agreed with the opinion.

"She says I need to do some power walking to get my legs moving again."

Luke scrutinized Paul. "I presume she didn't mean your sweet Holy Spirit does all the walking."

Paul grinned. "The therapist says I need to find me a walking partner."

"I'm game. We could walk to the Green and back over lunchtime. I'll meet you at the Hunter entrance at noon."

✢

Luke was running in place when Paul showed up. The bishop sighed and fell into pace with his new taskmaster.

"Have you noticed that our wives have become bosom buddies?" Luke asked.

Panting, Paul answered, "Uh-huh."

"Have you noticed that our wives seem to cry together?"

Panting even harder, Paul said, "Uh-huh. Better than crying alone."

Luke stopped in his tracks. "Does Mariama tell you why she cries?"

Still panting, Paul stopped to catch his breath. "As the years go by, she smiles more often than she cries."

"I'd give my life to see Theo smile without time out for tears."

"Maybe you're holding on to Theo too tight. Sometimes you have to give something away to gain it, whether it's your wife or your life."

Luke stood still, frozen in place.

"Let's move it, Doc," Paul said, setting the pace down the street. "We've got a lot more work to do."

Part III

An dat day been de Preparation Day, de day wen dey git ready fa de Jew Woshup Day.

—LUKE 23:54, *De Good Nyews Bout Jedus Christ Wa Luke Write* (Gullah)

Sixteen

Theo settled on the sofa, half ignoring her husband. "You at it with list making again?" she asked.

Luke handed her the pad on which he had drawn two columns. "Here's my to-do list for our sabbatical in the order of priority. I'd like to settle the top three things this week."

She put the pad on the coffee table without reading the list. "You should have been an accountant," she said.

Luke refused to respond to her deflection. "We've got a lot to do before we leave for London, including finding a place to live. Is someone at the *Times* still looking for a flat?"

"Yes, but they haven't had much luck."

"There's always Marta," he said. His cousin had promised to remove all potential weapons from the flat.

Theo's expression didn't change. "Let's save that as a last-ditch option."

"Okay, that's number one. Next, are we going to rent our house for the six months we're away?"

When Theo's face didn't register a response, he went on to the third item on his list. "What are we going to do with Moose? His cataracts are getting worse." He saw a spark of concern and zeroed in while he had a chance. "He could spend the time in Yellow Springs. At least he'd be with family in a house he knows."

Theo was skeptical. "What about Muffin, the most misnamed big dog in America?"

Luke laughed. "Some people say the same about Moose. Anyway, by the time we left Yellow Springs, Moose and Muff were playing together like long-lost pals. They got along just fine." For a brief moment, Luke sounded like his mother.

"We'll see," Theo said without enthusiasm.

She started playing with his hair, but Luke pulled away. "Is there anything on the list you think we could take care of today?"

"I don't want strangers in our house. I'd rather suck up the financial loss."

"So we leave the house empty?"

"Not necessarily."

For the first time in years, she was working with him rather than against him. As she moved to the kitchen, she stacked the breakfast dishes and talked. "Mariama called me this afternoon. She said their landlord has sold their house. They have to be out of there by the end of the month."

Luke frowned. "No! That's awful. First Paul loses his job. Then they lose their home. No wonder he was comparing himself to Job." Suddenly Luke perked up. "We could rent the house to the Pinckneys for the six months we're in London."

Theo nodded. "Let them stay here as long as they need to at whatever rent they can afford to pay. I think the going rental rate for a house like this is out of their reach."

Luke's wallet was hurting, but his heart was feeling good. In the second column, he wrote the word *DONE* in large letters. "Why do I have the feeling you and Mariama have already settled this?"

As Theo batted her eyes at him, Luke moved from one problem solved to take on another. His pen stopped and tapped at problem number three. He tried to remember either Paul or Mariama mentioning a passion for canine companionship. "Do you think they'd mind a furry head on their pillow until Johanna can come to fetch the Moose man?"

"Mariama and I have solved one of your problems. You and Paul can solve that one."

Theo moved out of his reach and into the kitchen. Luke followed her. "We've solved two out of three. Stick around and we'll finish our list."

"*Your* list. Any solution without Marta is fine with me."

Standing behind her in the kitchen, Luke noticed something mirrored in the kitchen window. He smoothed Theo's hair behind her neck and turned her toward him to get a better look at her face. His finger traced the line between her nose and the corner of her mouth. "For a moment I thought the crease on the right side of your nose is flatter than the left."

She kissed his finger and moved away. "You don't have enough patients at the hospital to play with?"

He looked again and shook his head. "I guess it was just my imagination."

"Guess so," Theo lied and tossed her hair to let it fall loose around her face again.

Luke woke up in the middle of the night not because of a noise but because of the silence. He rolled over toward Theo's side of the bed, careful not to squash Moose. But Moose wasn't there. He missed the sound of Moose snoring. *That was what woke me,* he thought. Sitting upright in bed, he saw that Theo was gone as well.

Assuming Theo and Moose had gone on a joint call of nature, Luke appropriated more space in the bed than he was usually allotted and fell back to sleep. At 4:00 a.m. silence woke him again. Finding himself still alone in the bed, he grabbed his robe and slippers and gave up on sleep. He found his missing bedmates together, asleep in the living room.

Theo slept on her side, eyes closed, face turned toward the television. Moose was nestled on her uphill hip, his snores competing with the off-the-air signal coming from the tube. Theo might have slept longer had Moose not bolted off her body when he saw Luke.

"Did I wake you?" Luke asked.

Half asleep, Theo groped for the TV remote. As she clicked on

CNN World News, Luke moved in for a kiss. She accepted his affection but didn't respond. "I've been waking up in the middle of the night. I came down here so I wouldn't disturb you."

How many nights had Luke gone without sleep during the first year she came back from Sarajevo but stayed in their bed? "Disturb me," he said.

Theo sat up and paid more attention to the news than his invitation to early morning love.

Rebuffed, Luke tried a different approach. "Does the TV help you sleep?"

She turned up the volume. "Sort of."

The next day, on the way home from work, Luke bought a small television. He installed it on Theo's side of the bed. At 3:00 a.m. he woke up alone. As he had the night before, he got up and went downstairs. Theo was asleep on the sofa again, her back to the television. This time Moose sat on her uphill hip watching *Lassie* reruns.

Finished with sleep for the night, Luke took up refuge in his study. He sat at his desk and stared up at Giles's painting with the imperfect blades of grass he had drawn. His gaze moved up to three figures on the horizon. Marsh hawks, his grandfather had called them, come to scavenge what fishermen left behind on the boating launch after they cleaned their catch.

"You should have hung around longer," he whispered to his grandfather. He picked up *The Deaths of Lucas Tayspill* and started to read.

How many times had he read it through without finding even the smallest clue to Lucas III's unfinished story? He picked up the Gullah *Good Nyews* and held the two volumes in his hands. Giles's book and this part of the Bible—were they part of the same story? *Let's see what Luke wrote,* he told himself.

He came to the story of a sick woman Jesus healed and sent on her way. *I wish it could be that simple for Theo,* he thought. *Believe in Jesus and you're healed. But healed of what?*

The night Mr. Emmons died, Paul's church folks had sung a song that Luke now remembered.

Jesus Christ de docta turn water to wine...

Ain't dat a docta?

I believe

Sabbath have no end

The Gullahs believed that with Jesus you can have peace in your heart. Luke remembered Giles's words the day Luke painted his blades of grass.

"These are wonderful hands," his grandfather had said.

And he remembered his own reply—a question. "What can I do with my hands?"

His grandfather had answered, "You can take care of sick people."

When Luke responded, "Me, Grandpa?" Giles had said, "Yes, Lucas. That's your calling."

Lucas. Not *Luke.* And called where?

Luke set down the books and put his head in his hands. "My sabbatical may be my end."

He looked at his to-do list and the last memo he'd made to himself that afternoon: "Call Dr. Nigel Garvey." It was the middle of the night in America, but noontime in London. He picked up the phone.

"Dr. Garvey, please. Professor Luke Tayspill calling." He hoped his salutation sounded suitably impressive to Sir Nigel's receptionist.

"One moment, please," she said and then transferred the call. Garvey was cagey but cordial. "I hope Mrs. Tayspill is feeling better. Please give her my warmest regards."

"I appreciate your care for my wife. I was wondering if you're a psychiatrist as well as a neurologist."

"I was glad to be of service."

Garvey hadn't answered his question, so Luke chose another approach. "You must treat a lot of doctors' family members."

The Harley Street consultant paused for a moment. "That's only an advantage when the patient brings the family into the consultation. Otherwise, it's a special kind of purgatory."

Sir Nigel was revealing only as much as he felt he could, even if he was dealing with Luke on a collegial footing. He might be keeping Theo's revelations in confidence, but at least he had confirmed the fact that she harbored a medical secret.

Luke struggled to phrase his next question. "This morning I thought I saw a flattening of her nasolabial fold. Did you make any similar observation?"

"I understand you'll be in London for a sabbatical soon. Please tell Mrs. Tayspill I look forward to seeing you both at her next visit."

Luke read between the lines of Garvey's words. That's what doctors do for a living.

SEVENTEEN

"A re you sure this is the right building?" Luke asked. On the stoop of Porchester Gardens, laden down with luggage, he wasn't at all certain.

"It won't look much better on the inside," Theo said.

Luke looked for the super's bell. "Marta said she'd leave a key for us in case she wasn't home." He tried to force a smile. "It's only for a few months."

"Sure," Theo answered without enthusiasm.

They heard the clopping of Birkenstock sandals echoing in a high-vaulted hallway. Suddenly the door sprang open.

"I heard a taxi outside," Marta said. "Sorry I couldn't meet you at the airport." After kissing Luke, she grabbed two pieces of Theo's luggage. "Come on, you two," she said as she clopped up the stairs.

Luke saw no reaction on Theo's face, positive or negative. She started up the steps and called after Marta in measured tones.

"Thanks so much for taking us in. The only short-term lease we could find was in a hotel."

At the door of her new flat, Marta ushered them in. "Wait till you see how much roomier this is than my last place."

"I see," Theo answered without looking around.

Luke followed Marta to a bedroom and dropped his luggage onto the floor.

Marta called to Theo, who remained by the door. "Come see how big your room is." When Theo didn't move, Marta shrugged her shoulders and went to the kitchen. "I'll make us some tea."

Ignoring Marta, Theo spoke to Luke. "I have an important meeting this morning, so I have no time for a bath or a nap. I'll be back in time for high tea."

After she left, Luke stared at the door. This was the first time he had heard of this meeting.

Marta drew close to Luke and slipped an arm through his. "Sir Nigel Garvey's office called yesterday. They were confirming an appointment for Theo for today."

Luke sat down on a sofa in the lounge and rested his head in his hands. Marta followed him and massaged his neck. Gradually the tension in his muscles eased.

"I don't know what to do. My marriage is built on lies and half truths."

"Poor cuz."

"What time is her appointment with Garvey?"

"Half past two," Marta answered as the teakettle whistled.

"I think I'll take a nap. No sense meeting Sir Nigel if I'm suffering from jet lag."

"I'll run you a calming tea bath. Twenty minutes and you'll be in dreamland."

Luke awoke in the darkened bedroom and tried to figure out where he was. He stumbled into the sitting room where Marta was folding laundry. "What time is it?" he asked.

"A quarter to six."

"Why didn't you wake me up?"

"I didn't have the heart. You were so tired. To tell you the truth, I wasn't certain what good a confrontation at the doctor's office would accomplish."

Luke still felt disoriented and confused. "I suppose you're right. Have you heard from Theo?"

"She rang a few minutes ago. Said she was finishing up at the office and would be here around six."

Luke ran his hand over his chin. "I'm going to get ready."

☩

Theo appeared on schedule. "I'm hungry," she said. "That was a long day of meetings on my first day here. Nathan's leaving on holiday next Monday and wants to turn everything over to me."

Luke caught the look on Marta's face but kept his attention on a cucumber sandwich.

"Dr. Garvey's office called," Marta said. "They said you missed your appointment."

Luke looked up and stared at Marta. She hadn't mentioned that before.

If Theo was upset, he couldn't tell from her face. She nodded, her eyes focused on her sandwich. "I couldn't get away from the office. I have to reschedule."

Luke wondered whether there had been such a call or if Marta was bluffing. From the shrug of his cousin's shoulders, he gathered the latter was true.

"Who's Dr. Garvey?" Luke asked.

Theo smiled at Luke. "A doctor who helped me the last time I was here. I know he'd like to meet you."

With what seemed to be a concession, Luke didn't want to push Theo any further. "That sounds great. My schedule is very flexible."

"What are you going to work on in the lab?" Marta asked.

"I'm trying to modify HIV to make it less virulent."

Marta scowled. "Is that genetic manipulation stuff safe?"

"Sure, if you know what you're doing."

"And the good guys are the ones doing the manipulation," Theo added.

After a few tense weeks in Marta's flat, Luke and Theo moved to a hotel for the week of the AIDS conference. Sharing a suite with the Pinckneys lifted Theo's spirits.

Mariama was excited to be back in London. "I came here for the first time almost fresh from the bush. To me, Freetown was a big city, but big isn't the same as sophisticated."

"Have you gotten in touch with your nursing-school friends?" Theo asked.

"Oh yes! They live in North London. I was the only one who went back to Sierra Leone. Several are registered for the conference."

✠

The audience had applauded Paul's paper on spiritual diagnosis. At first Luke was nervous that they might look down on a religious topic, but he shouldn't have underestimated a master preacher.

During the week of the conference, Luke and Paul skipped lunches in favor of their power walks.

"You should have seen Moose when your sister came to pick him up," Paul told him. "He was so excited to see that big Rottweiler."

Luke grinned, thinking about the reunion. "A response of reconciliation."

"There ya go. Even dogs need spiritual diagnosis."

As he walked with Paul at a peppy pace, Luke asked, "Is a lie ever justified?"

Paul stopped walking. "Now you're talking about serious stuff, brother. Any lie is a land mine, no matter how innocent we think it is at the time we set it out there. Some land mines are worse than others, like when you set a trap to catch someone you love in a lie."

"Ouch!"

"You seem to know that trap. Most married men and women do."

"When you said that, I felt like something pierced my heart."

"Dat's de Holy Sperit peckin at you chest. Dat ole dove love to tell you heart when you doin wrong."

"Was that Holy Spirit of yours ever married?"

Paul roared and picked up the pace again. "I never planned to get married myself."

"Then you tell that bird of yours to stay off my breastbone."

"Don't have the power to do that, Docta Luke. You gotta take that one up direct with the Holy Dove."

Paul took a drag of water from his sports bottle. "Okay, so your little woman told you a whopper. And you never lie to her?"

"Not about anything important."

"Who's to say what's important and what isn't? You ever meet anyone that you're certain told you the truth all the time?"

Luke nodded as he drank from his own water bottle. "Grandpa Giles."

"Why are you so sure?"

"He was a bearer of the holy."

"Your brain has been working overtime. Or maybe it was your soul. Have you been reading that Gullah gospel?"

"Yes. Fascinating reading."

"How so?"

"Gullah is the most expressive dialect of English I've ever run across. I can't sit still while I'm reading it. My mouth starts moving me into the words, and then my body starts moving me into the story."

"Sometime I'm gonna take you to St. Helena Island."

"I'd love to go. Shall we take our wives?"

Paul stopped laughing. "No, son. Those two beautiful oomans will just add confusion for two little boys." He brightened. "You like to go fishing?"

"I haven't caught any fish since..." Luke's voice trailed off.

"Since Grandpa Giles went to heaven?"

Luke nodded. Paul took a pull on his sports bottle and tipped it toward Luke's in a toast. "Two young uns goin fishing. I'm gonna teach you how to catch you some crabs."

"I'll drink to that," Luke said, taking a long slug of water.

"Here's another toast: to the taming of the AIDS virus. May the plague soon come to an end."

"Amen," Luke said and emptied his bottle.

As her husband puffed around Knightsbridge with Bishop Paul, Theo plunged into her work at the *Times*. All eyes were on her when she walked into the conference room of the London bureau for her first full staff meeting. She was the only woman in the room. Most of her new colleagues had greeted her during her visit in November, but there was one man at the table she wasn't expecting to see.

Shane Callahan rose to pull out the chair next to him. Grinning, he reached for Theo's hand and held it to his lips longer than a courtly gesture required. "I'm covering Africa for the *Times* now."

Theo had forgotten how grating his manners could be. She looked around the room for another chair far away from Shane, but there was none. As she settled into her seat and turned her full attention to the bureau chief, she felt Shane move his chair closer to hers.

"Any news from the Africa desk? Is this bloody war in Sierra Leone really over?" The bureau chief spoke without enthusiasm. Theo could see why Nathan was ready for holiday. When you ask a question for which you expect no answer, it's time to do something else.

"All's quiet on my front," Shane said. "The refugees are coming back from Guinea and Liberia. They've got democratic elections planned for May."

Lionel Atwater, the Middle East correspondent, frowned. "I've heard some vague rumors about Islamic terrorists nosing around Sierra Leone's diamond mines." Except for his commitment to Dewar's White Label, most of Lionel's efforts were ineffectual.

Shane rejected the notion. "That's old news. Every country with a substantial Muslim population gets tarred with that brush these days."

Remembering her recent wild-goose chase to Sarajevo, Theo had to agree. "That's the truth."

When Shane started undressing her with his eyes the way he had ten years ago, she reminded herself not to agree with him too often.

╬

Three weeks after Theo had arrived in Sarajevo for the first time, Shane Callahan had watched her enter the Café Sarajevo. She had already taken a lover, but that didn't stop her from responding to Shane's attention. He took her left hand in his and massaged her ring finger. Tan skin surrounded a wide, pale circle.

"You're married." A declaration. Not a question.

Theo nodded. She had been using her failing marriage as a cover for her relationship with a Bosnian doctor. No one in Sarajevo knew that she and Luke were heading for divorce. She was also attracted to Shane, compelled by the sense of power he emanated. But she wasn't willing to let him come dangerously close. At least not yet.

"Where's your ring?" Shane didn't surrender her eyes.

She broke away from his gaze but left her hand in his for the moment.

"My rings are at home. I didn't want them stolen."

"You're an expert," Shane said, retaking her eyes.

"An expert at what?"

"Obfuscation," he said, massaging her ring finger.

When he pulled her hand toward his mouth, she broke away from his hold. "I didn't lie."

"You intend to deceive." Shane surmised she was either separated from her husband or was cheating on him. He also knew that her husband wasn't his greatest obstacle to this woman with a perfect face. He had seen Samir Oric drop her off at the Holiday Inn and followed him back to the hospital where he worked.

"Do you specialize in doctors?" he asked.

"My husband is a doctor." Theo wondered what else he might know.

Shane lit a cigarette and offered it across the table. She wanted to reject the *Drina,* to keep her hands in her lap. Nicotine seemed too cheap a price for selling your soul. She shook her head, and Callahan tipped back his chair. He moved away from Theo but continued to search her eyes.

"Filthy habit," he said, enjoying a long drag on the cigarette.

The burning ashes mesmerized her. She moistened her lips and reached out to take the cigarette and lose her secrets to this man.

"Ciggie?" Shane asked, pulling Theo back to the present. He lit up a *Drina* and passed it to her.

"Do you mind?" Lionel said, waving his hand to dispel the smoke.

Shane ignored Lionel and looked into Theo's eyes. She shook her head with as little conviction as she had in Sarajevo, but she didn't move to take the cigarette. He shrugged his shoulders and smiled. After one more puff, he put it in the ashtray between himself and Theo without crushing the butt. Each time she looked down at the *Drina,* instead of paying attention to the conversation, she willed herself—unsuccess-fully—not to look anymore.

Nathan tried to bring his fragmented team back to business. "Shall we get back to Sierra Leone?" Terrorism was front-page material. Nathan's team hadn't been off the back page of the second section for a long time. "How can we find out if this al-Qaeda rumor is true?"

Shane shook his head. "Sorry, mate. My best Sierra Leone source just got deported. Now that the war is over, the Brits are hastening these chaps home."

"Who do we know in the Antwerp diamond market?" Nathan asked the Western European desk.

Theo tapped her pencil on the table as if the action helped move her thoughts from her brain to her mouth. "I'd like to cover the International AIDS Conference," she said, looking around the conference table.

Callahan sneered. "My, my. We still have our interest in doctors?"

Theo ignored him.

"Shouldn't the medical-news blokes cover that?" someone else asked.

"Or the Africa desk," Lionel said. "Didn't 'they' start the whole epidemic?"

"And queers spread it?" Callahan said. "What other prejudices would you like us to chase today?"

Funny, Theo thought, how fast the professional jealousies set in. If it's not your idea, make sure no one else gets the assignment either.

She looked at the bureau chief and kept her back to Shane, "The only way to get a fresh story out of the conference is to let someone who can get inside the medical community cover it."

Weary from sitting in London rather than working out in the field, Nathan agreed. "Okay, then. Let's get to work." He turned to Theo and asked, "Promise you'll bring back more than the usual boring science sagas?"

"I know exactly what to do," Theo said, still keeping her back to Callahan. She picked up her materials and stood up to leave.

"Care to share," Callahan asked, "or do you intend to register your idea as a state secret?"

She looked around the table and tried not to look smug. "You boys have your locker rooms, and I have mine."

Callahan whispered, "How many doctors are you doing these days?"

Theo wanted to get out of there fast. She knew she had privileged access: Mariama had connections to many Sierra Leonean expats and had entrée to tea salons and back rooms the press couldn't penetrate. She closed the conference-room door behind her but stood listening a moment. She heard Shane's voice through the door. "Sure she can handle this? I hear she went wacko after her lover was killed in Sarajevo."

"Shut your mouth, you fool!" Nathan said. "There isn't anyone in this room with Theo's instincts for a story. And I'd put your sorry excuse for a brain at the bottom of that list."

"Whatever you say, mate. You know I'm a team player."

As she rushed from the building, Theo's brain raced faster than her feet. Whatever else happened in London, she had to make sure that Luke never met up with Shane Callahan.

Eighteen

As an African man in a Muslim cap left the tearoom, Theo watched to see which direction he turned. She was waiting for someone who could lead her to Finsbury Park's radical mosque. For a moment, she regretted her bravado. The only white person in the tearoom, she felt conspicuous and couldn't concentrate on Mariama and her friends. She turned back to the women and asked a question. "Will you ever go back to Sierra Leone?"

Tiki answered first. "I send money to relatives, but I'll never go back. My parents are dead. Murdered. There's nothing for me there."

Mariama nodded in agreement. Theo had expected her friend to show some expression of homesickness, especially since the war was over. "What about you?" she asked Adama. "Doesn't your country need your skills?"

"I'll never go back. Let the devil take Sierra Leone. He's worked hard enough to earn his prize."

The interview was not going the way Theo had hoped. She had yet to pose her harder questions, but she took a deep breath and moved in that direction. "Did you see many cases of AIDS in Sierra Leone?"

Again, Tiki spoke first. "Some of our people don't even believe in the disease. They think white men made it all up to keep Africans from making babies. There's a saying that AIDS stands for Americans Intent on Destroying Sex."

Theo wrote down the quip but doubted it would be enough to make Nathan happy with her reporting. She was getting nothing new or particularly interesting.

The meal was clearly over. Skewered balls of fried bean paste remained on the common plate. Theo, who liked to experiment with cuisine, was sickened by the sight of them. Mariama was examining tea leaves in the bottom of her cup. Adama and Tiki murmured their good-byes to Mariama in a language Theo didn't understand.

Alone with Mariama at the table, Theo said, "I guess I blew that."

"We come from a world that's hard for westerners to understand."

"I hope I didn't offend your friends."

"Oh no. You didn't say anything they haven't heard before."

They parted ways, Mariama heading back to the conference, Theo ducking into an alley next to the restaurant. After her stomach heaved back the African food, she wiped her mouth and headed for the office of Dr. Nigel Garvey.

Theo was almost asleep when Luke returned to the suite. He slipped into bed and nested against her back.

"Promise you'll never leave me," she said, turning into his arms.

Her question alarmed him, as if she saw the final blow coming to their marriage. Before he responded to her touch, he reacted to her question. "Promise me you'll always tell me the truth."

"The truth is that I adore you," she said and tried to roll away.

Luke held her tight until she gave him an answer. "Promise me."

"I promise I will never tell you another lie."

Luke released his hold, but she could sense from his silence that his mind was racing. Never telling a lie was not the same as always telling the truth.

As soon as she was sure Luke was asleep, Theo slipped out of bed and took her laptop to the sitting room. She stared at the e-mail template on her laptop screen, not knowing where to begin. Rather than starting with her husband, she began a letter to her boss.

From: Theodora Tayspill <ttayspill@nytimes.net>
To: Nathan Green <nwinters@nytimes.net>

Subject: Hate to spring this on you, but...
Date: Thurs, 31 Jan 2002 23:39:26 UTC
Hate to spring this on you, boss, but by the time you read this,
I'll be on my way home to the States. Doctor's orders. Health
problem. Fire me if you must, but I hope you understand.
Theo

That was easier to write than she thought it would be, but what could she say to Luke? She could have said it when she promised to tell him the truth. But a lie masquerading as truth had started in Sir Nigel Garvey's office that afternoon.

✠

"Promise me you won't tell my husband," she asked the neurologist. This was her week for extracting promises without giving much in return.

"I had hoped to meet Professor Tayspill this visit," Sir Nigel answered.

"I have to tell my husband in my way and in my time."

Good old Sir Nigel liked to get to the point. "Time isn't something you have on your side. Are you certain he doesn't suspect? Your symptoms aren't as subtle as the last time we met."

"Luke thought I had drunk too much wine."

"Wine wears off in the morning, Mrs. Tayspill. ALS doesn't."

She nodded and frowned. "Is there any doubt about the diagnosis? I mean, I thought Lou Gehrig's disease only affects men."

"A common misconception. There are some tests you need. I can schedule them for later this week."

"I can get those done at home."

"The end of the sabbatical would be too long."

"I'm going home to the States."

"I thought you were here for a six-month stay."

"That was Plan A. The plan when I had a future."

"Speaking of planning, it would be wise to avoid pregnancy, given your condition."

Theo looked up at the doctor like a hurt child. "Do you know what it's like to be barren, Sir Nigel? No, you wouldn't. You're a man. Skip it. I'm sorry. That was rude. What can I do?"

"Plenty of sleep. Healthy diet. Effective contraception. I'm writing you a script for a medication to take. It will help somewhat, but the drug is another reason not to get pregnant. This treatment for ALS is harmful to a fetus."

Theo looked up at the clock. "Thank you for your time. I've got a plane to catch."

As Theo packed her suitcase, she thought about leaving a note, but she didn't know what to say. "Dear Luke, I'm running away. See you, Theo." That might be truthful, but it wouldn't be helpful. She felt like a child again, overwhelmed by the world, in need of her mother's arms. She could hear her mother's voice from a time when she'd cut her lip. "Ah, Theodora! Don't cry. Here, let momma kiss that and make it better."

A few hours later on the plane, she started typing a second letter that her mother would never read.

Oh, Momma, you left the world too soon. I'm making a mess of my marriage. I adore Luke but don't know how to let him come close. I'm afraid that if I tell him the truth, I'll have to believe it myself. I'm on the run again, Momma, running to you.

Finally she started the e-mail she had been dreading to write.

From: Theodora Tayspill <ttayspill@nytimes.net>

To: Luke Tayspill < luke.tayspill@yalemed.edu>

Subject: Don't hate me

Date: Fri, 1 Feb 2002 11:56:026 UTC

Dearest Luke,

Last night I promised I would never lie to you again—and I won't. I made you promise never to leave me—and I just left you. Forgive me if I don't explain the reasons right now. Believe me that I've only left you so I can find myself.

All my love,

Theodora

Theo snapped her laptop shut and stowed it under her seat. A wave of nausea hit, and she unbuckled her seat belt and ran for the rest room. An attendant knocked on the door. "Are you all right?" she asked.

"I'm pregnant!" Theo blurted out.

Nineteen

"How long does mourning last?" Theo asked. She knelt on the ground in front of her mother's grave, filled the *kantili* with fresh olive oil and lit the flame.

"As long as it needs to," Edith answered. "For some people it takes a lot longer than others, but I'm not the one to say."

Between the two Kannoudakis graves, Moose kept watch and softly whined. Edith reached down and ran her hand down the little Yorkie's back. "Whenever Moose comes to stay with us, he wants to come here to the cemetery and sit by their graves. The two of us old folks come here to visit, don't we fella?" Moose licked Edith's hand but stayed at his post. She patted her lap, inviting him. "Want to come snuggle with Granny?" But the dog stayed where he was, keeping watch.

Edith trimmed some flowers and placed them in holders on the graves. Theo pulled weeds from around her mother's grave. She kissed her fingertips and touched them to the photograph in the center of the marble cross. Eleni Kannoudakis was a young woman in the picture, almost as beautiful as her daughter.

"I'll always be grateful to you and Martin. You were such good friends to my parents."

"We missed them when they went back to Crete. Father was so happy when they came back. He and Dimitrios used to talk about being grandfathers together. I only wish your parents could have lived long enough to…" Edith stopped talking and placed her hand on Theo's belly.

Tears formed in Theo's eyes.

After Theo's marriage to Luke, her parents took their profits from the Antioch Diner and moved back to their native island of Crete. Secure with their savings and content with their daughter's marriage to Luke, they bought a restaurant in the harbor town of Chania.

Before Theo went to Sarajevo for the first time, she brought Moose to stay with them. With her parents, the dog looked out over the sea toward the self-destructing Yugoslavia. When Theo escaped from Bosnia near the end of the war, her first stop was Chania. She looked out over the same sea and wondered how she could find her way back to the husband she had abandoned. Dimitrios was the one who had decided that they would return to Yellow Springs, taking Theo and Moose home to Luke.

Later that evening Theo stood in the shadows near the door to Martin's study. She checked out the room before she entered. Giles's self-portrait was no longer in its corner. Martin's reclining chair had replaced it— a kitschy contrast to the period pieces that had once tied this room together. From her place in the shadows, Theo could see that Martin was asleep.

Since he had liberated himself from hospitals and nursing homes, Martin didn't like to wander far from his chair. He tilted back with his eyes closed and a book on his chest. He would read a sentence or two and then doze off.

"Baba," she whispered. After Dimitrios's death, she had taken to calling Martin by the Greek term for papa.

He opened his eyes and struggled to straighten up his chair. "La Bella Simonetta!"

Theo sat on the floor next to him and held his hands. She looked around the room. "What did you do with Grandpa Giles?"

"I put him in the closet where he belongs," Martin said. Like a child caught in a naughty act, he added, "Don't tell Luke I said that."

Moose ran into the room, chased by Muffin. The two dogs raced around Martin's recliner until they wore each other out. Then they sat at

Martin's feet to beg. He reached into a compartment in the arm of his chair and pulled out two dog cookies. Moose and Muffin found a spot on the oriental carpet to settle with their treats.

"I won't tell Luke if you put Grandpa back where he belongs."

Martin scowled. "He belongs in the closet."

Theo withdrew her hand. "I guess I'll have to tell Luke."

Martin retrieved her hand and patted it. "Take the old troublemaker, if you want him in your house."

Theo rewarded Martin with a kiss on the cheek. "Not just yet, Baba. Grandpa still belongs here." She resumed stroking his hand. "Do you know anything about a manuscript Grandpa wrote?"

Martin shook his head. "Mother told me Luke found it in my desk. That's what he gets for snooping. Some things are best left buried—like my father."

"I couldn't make any sense out of it."

Martin pulled himself up in his chair but landed at an awkward angle. "You read it?"

Theo nodded. "The first two parts, but the third was never finished."

"What did it say about me?"

"Nothing at all."

Martin relaxed back in his chair. Relieved, he changed the subject. "Will you be going back to London?"

"I don't think so. I left a mess over there."

"Have you left Luke for good this time?"

"No. It's harder to go back every time I panic and run."

"Does he know about the baby?"

"Not yet."

Martin reached for her face and stroked her cheek. "That's how you'll get him back. This time you have the world's most perfect excuse. Pregnancy makes women do funny things."

"Was Mom weird when she was pregnant with Luke?"

Martin's brow furrowed while he thought for a moment. "She had to have chicken-fried steak at midnight when she was carrying Johanna."

Theo stood up but didn't let go of Martin's hand. "We'll bail each other out. In exchange for your suggestion to plead pregnancy as my excuse, I'll take Grandpa's portrait off your hands."

Martin nodded in submission. "Take the easel and paints too, if you want them. He'd probably like it better that way."

"Luke or Giles?"

"Both, I guess."

She moved the easel out of the closet and set it up in its old place. "I'll pack them tomorrow."

"Are you going home?"

"Yes, Baba. It's time."

Theo went to the bedroom that had been Luke's as a child. Next to the bed was a vase of yellow roses. She smiled, assuming Edith had placed them there. A trail of petals led from the bed to the guest bathroom. Moose was following the trail, sniffing as he went, and Theo followed. Even with the door closed, she could smell the fragrance of roses in the bathroom. That's where she found her husband, in a tub filled with floating yellow rose petals.

"I hope you removed the thorns," Theo said, grinning.

Luke reached out a hand to her. "Come in and find out."

Theo looked around as if Luke's parents might come through the door.

Luke grinned and hugged her with wet arms. Theo giggled as she looked at the inviting cloud of yellow petals. "You think of everything."

Luke tried to pull her fully clothed into the bath, but she resisted.

"Dad told me you have some great news."

Theo felt trapped by her husband and her father-in-law. She remembered Dr. Weiss's words. *Practice telling your husband the truth.*

"I'm pregnant," she blurted out.

Luke let go of her and stared. "How many weeks?"

"Twelve, I think, I'm not really sure. I haven't been to an OB yet."

Luke climbed out of the tub and grabbed his robe. "But I *have* been to see Nigel Garvey." He pulled the plug on the tub and let the rose petals sink to the bottom.

"Don't run away from me," Theo said.

"Who's the one running? You couldn't even tell me yourself. Why can't you tell me everything?"

"I've been living with secrets for so many years. I don't know how to begin."

Luke put his arms around her. "Theo, you can't keep this baby. You know what it means to your health."

"I can't give up this baby. I *won't* give it up."

"Do you know how terrified I am right now? After Garvey told me, everything I've noticed started to make sense. I may hate that you have ALS, but I accept it. I want you as long as I can have you. I was without you for too long. Now that I have you back, I don't want one minute less than I can have with you."

"What makes you think you'll still want me after you hear everything that's happened?" She ran out of the bathroom and into Martin's study. Luke's father had gone to bed, but Grandpa Giles was still there on the easel.

Luke followed her into the study and kissed her on the cheek. She leaned away from him toward Giles's self-portrait, as if he could help her. She pointed to Martin's chair. "Please, go sit over there. I want to tell you a story."

Luke withdrew from her and sat down. Theo blinked away tears as she returned to Sarajevo.

There was a long silence before Theo asked, "Do you forgive me?"

"For what?" Luke said. "You haven't told me anything yet."

Theo shook her head. "Before I begin, I want to know if you'll forgive me, no matter what I tell you."

Luke leaned down to pet Moose, who had followed them into the room. "You're just like Moose," he said. "I come home and find him rolled over on his back in a submissive pose. I know there's some mischief he's done, and I want him to tell me where it is so I can clean it up. But, no, he wants me to rub his belly and forgive him before I even know what it is."

Theo smiled. "If I have to roll over and ask you to rub my belly, I'll do it."

Luke glared at her. "Your belly is an unfortunate analogy."

"Will you forgive me?"

"Why don't you tell the whole story first?"

Theo shook her head. "This is hard enough for me as is, sweetheart." *What was it Bishop Paul had said? "Forgive and you will be forgiven."* Theo persisted. "Do you forgive me?"

"Yes, I forgive you," he said and then added, "I have a feeling this is going to be a very long night."

Slowly Theo relived the weeks she spent in Sarajevo ten years earlier.

"The first day in Sarajevo, I went to a hospital full of Muslim women who had been raped and impregnated by the Serbs. Abortion was legal in Bosnia at the time, but the Serbs didn't release the women until it was too late for them to terminate even if they wanted to. The Serbs made the women's husbands and fathers watch their bellies grow large before they murdered the men. Samir was one of the doctors who cared for the women."

Luke sat up straight. The enemy now had a name. *Samir.*

"The rest of the press corps covered the mass graves. I wanted to write about the survivors. Samir allowed me to follow him around the hospital." She stopped her story and looked down at the floor. Then she looked at Luke. "I wasn't planning to fall in love with him, but I thought you and I were through."

There was no change in the expression on Luke's face. Theo remained silent, waiting for him to react.

"What am I supposed to say? 'I forgive you'? Sure, I forgive you. I guessed there was another man. We were separated. Okay, I was even thinking about divorce." *Forgive and you will be forgiven.* Luke's face softened. "Do you forgive me for letting you go?"

"I'm the one who needs forgiveness," she said.

"I drove you to it, but it still hurts to hear a name to fill in the story."

Theo nodded. "Do you forgive me?"

"Yes, I forgive you if you'll forgive me."

Theo nodded again and took a deep breath. "A few weeks after Samir became my lover, I suspected I was pregnant."

The color drained from Luke's face. This other doctor, a Bosnian and a Muslim, had accomplished what he had failed to do.

"It wasn't Samir's baby. It was yours." She hastened to continue the story rather than give Luke a chance to respond. "One night we were on the way to the hospital. The snipers were very active, so Samir was taking a big chance by coming to the Holiday Inn to fetch me." Tears interrupted the flow of her story.

"Why were you going to the hospital at night?" Luke's voice was cold.

"Samir was going to perform an abortion."

"On my baby?" Luke's voice trembled.

Theo nodded. "We never got as far as the hospital. Samir drove down a back street he thought was safe, but a band of Serbs was waiting there. It was as if they knew who we were. They caught us and dragged us out of the car." Theo began sobbing.

Luke got up and went over to Theo but didn't reach out to touch her. Her eyes stayed downcast. He reached out a hand, but she withdrew from him. "Let me finish the story. I've gotten this far. Let me finish to the end."

Luke nodded but didn't move. Theo paced around the room as she took up her story again.

"Ski masks covered their faces. One man—very tall—was especially brutal. He gunned down Samir. I thought the others were going to rape me, and they meant to, I'm sure. I was fighting them off while the tall man pumped Samir's body full of bullets. When he was finished with Samir, he called the others off me. I lay in the street, covered with bruises and bleeding. I thought the tall man was going to rape and then murder me, but he took out a knife and cut off my hair. '*Kurva,*' he called me. Whore. And then he threw me on top of Samir's body."

Luke could bear no more and took her in his arms. "You don't have to finish."

Theo pulled away from him. "Yes, I do." She began to pace again.

"I was cramping and bleeding. I lost the baby."

Luke took her into his arms. "I'm so sorry."

She placed his hands on her belly. "I don't want to lose this baby, Luke."

"But I don't want to lose you!"

"I won't have an abortion."

Luke let go of her and paced the room, pulling at his hair. "Oh, God! I don't know what to do."

Luke endured a restless night, watching Theo toss in her sleep. Disturbed by Theo's movements, Moose hopped over Luke and commandeered his pillow.

Whatever happened to my simple life as a doctor? Luke wondered. His thoughts switched to the portrait of Grandpa Giles. What about Lucas

III and his path that Giles left blank in his book? *"If you have no cause worth dying for, do you really have a reason to live?"* Luke wasn't at all certain he wanted a cause.

In her sleep Theo turned toward him and nestled her head on his shoulder. "We'll go home tomorrow," he said, kissing her hair.

She groaned softly and murmured, "I can't. Not just yet."

Luke sat up in bed. "What do you mean 'not just yet'? You are home. You're with me."

Theo started to cry. "I need to be near my mother, just for a little while. And you need to plan what you're going to do with the rest of your sabbatical."

He didn't know how to argue with a pregnant woman. "Promise me you'll come home soon?"

She nodded and rolled away from him.

Part IV

De Lawd Sperit da libe een me an gee me powa.
Cause e done pick me fa tell de good nyews ta de
po people.

—Luke 4:18, *De Good Nyews Bout Jedus
Christ Wa Luke Write* (Gullah)

TWENTY

"Interesting reading?" Paul asked, leaning on Luke's office door. The doctor was sitting at his desk, poring over *The Deaths of Lucas Tayspill.* He picked up his coffee cup and rose to fill it. "The way my life is going lately, I'm almost afraid to read it."

Paul helped himself to coffee and sank onto the sofa. "I assume you're not going back to London. Have you made any new plans for the rest of your sabbatical?"

Luke shook his head and sat across from a man who had once been a stranger. He placed Giles's manuscript on the table, next to the Gullah gospel. "I guess I'm looking in these books for an answer."

Paul picked the two books up and held them side by side. "Maybe you should be looking for questions instead of answers."

"That's an interesting way to look at it. My grandfather would have called it an epiphany experience." Luke's smile changed to a frown. "How would you like your life to be on hold while a force you can't identify takes a whack at you whenever it wants its jollies?"

"I get what you're saying. That's how I felt when my momma did my physical therapy. I think I'd rather tackle the ways of God than the ways of women. Let's get back to this wacko 'force' of yours. Does it have a name?"

"These days I'm calling that force 'Author'—and a malevolent one at that. Author cares more about his plot than his characters."

"Is that how you feel about God?"

"You're assuming I believe in God. *If* I believed in God—and that's a mighty big if…"

"Big ifs are the only kind worth having."

"That sounds like a corny sermon title. Sometimes I feel as if your God has just finished writing a rough draft of my life. Right now he is deeply engrossed in the editing process. Then along I come with one of my problems—like my powder-keg wife who flirts with danger or my elderly parents running amok while I'm half a continent away. Maybe I just might like Author's advice. So I stand in front of him, politely waiting for him to look up from the manuscript and notice me."

As he spoke, Luke moved around the room, gesturing the drama of his words. Paul grinned and sat back as he listened.

"I wait and I wait. Surely, in his godly know-it-all-ness, Author might notice this poor, little slob character standing in front of him. I'm anxious for help, so I clear my throat—ever so slightly. *Ahem.* But Author doesn't pay any attention to me. He breaks out into an almighty laugh. Not, mind you, because he's laughing at *me.* Oh no. Author just came to a particularly twisted part of his plot. Except he won't tell the character what's coming next."

Paul scratched his chin and wet his lips. "What if Author gave the character the power to choose what comes next? What would you tell him then—*if* Author existed?"

Luke scowled at Author's black bishop. "Trust me. You don't want to hear what I'd say."

"Trust me, Luke. God wants to hear."

"The first thing I'd do is knock the manuscript out of his hand."

"Bravo," Paul said, then swept the Gullah gospel off Luke's coffee table. He started to applaud. "Good move."

"Hey, what are you doing?" Luke bent over to retrieve the book and brushed the cover to remove lint it had picked up from the carpet. "A friend gave me that. Treat it with respect."

With the ham of his hand, Paul made another swat at the table, this time sweeping Giles's manuscript to the floor.

Luke's face was red as he went back on his knees to retrieve the composition book. "Have you gone mad?"

Paul reached over and put his foot on the book so Luke couldn't pull it away without tearing the cover. "If you had been in Giles's study while he was writing this manuscript, would you have interrupted him?"

Luke looked blank for a moment and then sat back on his heels. He shook his head.

Paul strengthened his foothold on the manuscript. "Would you have tried to change a word on any page?"

Again Luke shook his head. When he finally spoke, his voice was thin. "Once, a long time ago, I interrupted him while he was painting. I begged to use his paintbrush and add to what he had on the canvas."

"What did your grandpa do?"

"He let me paint. I was only five years old at the time. I picked up his brush and tried to make some blades of grass."

Paul moved his foot to allow Luke to retrieve the manuscript. "And if you, esteemed Yale professor and doctor, were sitting in Grandpa's study today, watching him write, what would you do?"

Luke stared at the mostly blank page that constituted the third part of Giles's saga. Lucas Tayspill III's whole story was two lines. "Sometimes I wish he had finished the story and filled in the blanks."

"It sounds like he left the manuscript blank for you to fill in yourself, the same way he let you have your hand at painting."

Luke looked at Paul. "That's what terrifies me. What if my life turns out as childish and purposeless as those blades of grass I added to his beautiful landscape?"

"That's a mighty big if, son."

"That's why I'm sitting here, unable to plan for the future. I can't even make a list."

Paul laughed. "If Dr. Luke can't do his to-do list, the world may just as well come to an end." Then he stopped smiling, took two letters out of his pocket, and put them on the coffee table. "Good news and bad news."

Luke looked up, startled. "Again? What more bad news could there be?"

Paul pushed one letter toward him. It was addressed to Mariama by the chairman of ob-gyn. " 'Approved but not funded,' " Luke read. " 'Your position will terminate with the current grant year.' "

"I can't believe this! What are you going to do now?"

Paul's expression changed. "I'm going to fix on the good news." He handed Luke the other letter to read. "If you can't control the future, how about making plans for the present? This letter might give you a clue."

As Luke read the letter, his own mood lifted. "This is great, Paul. Obviously your paper in London made a strong impression. You're moving up from plenary to keynote speaker. I bet you'll be getting more invitations like this. Where is this Beaufort Memorial Hospital?"

"In the low country, son. Only a few miles from St. Helena Island."

"You must be excited. Maybe they'll even offer you a job."

"I haven't decided yet whether I'll take them up on their invitation."

"Of course you will. Why on earth not?"

"I'll only accept the invitation if they also invite you to speak at the conference. They probably didn't know they could get a big expert like you. St. Helena Island is a great place for two guys to go crabbing." He headed out the door. "If you want to go, page me before you leave work this afternoon. I'm planning to call them at the end of the workday."

Luke poured himself another cup of coffee and began to reread the first Lucas Tayspill story.

Many chapters in the American fight against slavery began or ended with a Quaker twist. So does our story. Blacks and whites, slaves and free—all who cared about justice and human dignity knew a small Englishwoman adorned in black dress and bonnet. So did the busiest man in America. Just as they did, Abraham Lincoln called her Aunt Eliza.

In the darkest hours of the Civil War, the president invited the woman in black, Elizabeth Gurney Fry, to visit the White House.

The American leader may not have shared Aunt Eliza's penchant for pacifism, but he admired her commitment and passion.

When she crossed the ocean to visit Mr. Lincoln, she made time for a side trip to visit her Philadelphia nephew. Lucas Tayspill's sail loft on the wharf of Philadelphia was no longer prosperous. When he bought the business from the Forten family, he worked hard to keep it as strong as they had made it. Alas, with the advent of steam engines, few shipbuilders sought his handsewn sails. Lucas's needle fell idle, but not the man. As he waited for sail orders, he stood before three black boys seated on his workbench. When his Aunt Eliza arrived, he was giving them a reading lesson.

She smiled when she saw the eager children seated on the bench. "Thee should have chosen school teaching for an occupation like thy father," she said.

Lucas glanced over at his young pupils. "These fresh sails need to be stitched tight against the winds of change in America."

Eliza nodded. "I thank the heavenly Father for the winds of promise. We must negotiate rough seas till that wind blow us all safely into that fair haven of equality."

Abandoning the bench, the lads chased each other around the loft—little boys at play, unaware of the dangers outside the loft and the companionship of Quakers.

"I went to see the commissioner today," Lucas told his aunt.

"Is thy news good?"

"Better for Friends here in Pennsylvania than in the northern commonwealths, I fear. At least the Philadelphia militia will accept our scruples against bearing arms."

"That is indeed wonderful news," Eliza said.

"Unfortunately there is a stipulation. Someone must take the conscientious objector's place in the war. That costs money—three hundred dollars, to be precise. Not all Friends at Meeting agree that one can support war making with such a payment—if one had the money."

"What says thy inner light, Friend Lucas?"

"Wait and listen, it says." Lucas took his aunt's hands. "No sorer trial have I ever passed through in my life."

Looking toward the three waifs, Eliza Fry told her nephew, "Practice them well in their letters and numbers. An inner urge advises me to say that to thee."

As the woman with the gift to soften the hearts of the powerful left the sail loft, she heard her nephew call to his pupils.

"Come, young Friends. Our time for rest is past." Lucas reached for his well-worn Bible and gave it to one of the boys. He pointed to a page. "Here, Friend Daniel. Commence thy reading here."

Daniel stared at the page and frowned. He took a deep breath as he stumbled over the words. The Spirit of the Lord is upon me, because he hath anointed me... The boy stopped reading and shook his head. "Scuz me, Mistah Lucas, but dem people in de book sho do talk funny."

Lucas roared and cuffed Daniel's ear affectionately. "Do thee think that thy humble teacher sounds funny too?"

Reverently, Daniel held up Lucas's Bible. "Dis be de way God talk?"

The sailmaker shook his head and answered the question with a question. "Before thee came north by the Underground Railroad, where did thee dwell?"

Daniel grew sad. "On a beautiful island wid palm trees an big oak trees. Pa wanna grow corn to feed we, but Masta done say grow cotton."

"On that island, who taught thee to read and write?"

Daniel shook his head. "No one. Masta say slave mus no
read."

"Not even the Bible?"

Daniel shrugged. "Masta say all we needa know from de Book
be, 'Slaves, obey you masta.'"

"Friend Daniel, would thee read the Bible in thy own
tongue?"

The child shrugged. "Can God talk de way de home people
talk?"

Lucas smiled, "Nothing would please him more, dear Friend.
Perhaps thee can help God teach me de way de home people talk."

Forgetting his own situation, Lucas Tayspill started to translate the passage. "All right, young Friends, we shall start here. As
I read the words in King James English, tell me how thee would
say it on thy island. The Spirit of the Lord is upon me, because he
hath anointed me to preach the gospel to the poor..."

Daniel scratched his head. "Say dat agin."

They went back and forth, word by word at first, then by
whole sentences, then again word by word, until Daniel smiled
and took a deep breath. "De Lawd Sperit de libe een me an gee me
powa."

"Gee me powa," Lucas repeated. "Well done. Now let us see if
I can write that down."

Luke put down the manuscript and picked up *De Good Nyews Bout
Jedus Christ Wa Luke Write*. He flipped through its pages until he came
to the fourth chapter and the eighteenth verse. Then he grabbed the
phone and punched in the number of Bishop Paul's beeper.

TWENTY-ONE

Luke pushed open the door of the airline terminal in Charleston and started to sweat. He put down his suitcase and stripped off his overcoat. "It may be winter in New England, but it sure isn't here."

Paul found their rental car and opened the passenger door for Luke. "I be gone so long, ma bones done turned Yankee."

Luke laughed and mopped his forehead. "My bones were never anything else."

Paul grinned at the sweat stain growing on Luke's back. "We could stop at Wal-Mart and get you a seersucker suit."

"And a pair of two-tone wingtip shoes?"

"Wouldn't that be a sight?" Paul popped open the trunk. "Docta Luke, you be leavin de world you know behind."

Luke relaxed as Paul drove to St. Helena Island. Entering new worlds was getting to be a regular event in Luke's life. So was the sound of Paul singing.

Before he met the Pinckneys, Luke had already appreciated the throbbing beat of spirituals and their power to relieve suffering. In the hospital on summer Fridays, a musical group would play for the employees eating their lunch outdoors. When a black gospel-music group played, he watched black faces in the audience. The same low-paid employees, who rarely smiled during the week, broke into ecstasy. Luke had never listened to the words of the songs or thought of them in terms of his own life. He could tell from the transformed faces that the working poor of New Haven knew all about Pharaoh.

The night Mr. Emmons died, Luke started to hear the words. Sometimes the message conflicted with his way of viewing the world. Like the song Paul belted out as they rode along.

Jesus make de blind to see; Jesus make de deaf to hear;
Jesus make de cripple walk. Walk in, dear Jesus.

"If your Jesus has the power to heal, why didn't he heal Mr. Emmons? If he healed the blind, the deaf, and the crippled, why not heal one poor man with AIDS who loved him?"

Paul stopped singing. "That's a question I've asked him myself. I guess that's one big if we'll have to leave till heaven."

"If there is a heaven."

"Oh, I believe there's a heaven, and I do believe Jesus heals."

Luke sank into his seat. "I wish I could believe that. Sometimes I think Jesus is your fantasy friend, like the kind little children conjure up to make them feel better in the dark. But Jesus doesn't make me feel better when I hear that song. If he can heal and he doesn't, Jesus is a sadist."

"If I were God, I would run the world a lot different. But then, I'm not God."

"If I were a Christian—and I'm not—I'd be afraid to pray for healing. What if the answer was no?"

"Many big ifs this morning, Docta Luke," Paul said.

"Quote. The only kind of ifs worth having. Unquote."

"Let me ask you this. Remember the drug with the funny name that you gave Brother Emmons for his fungal infection? 'Amphoterrible' brought him back from the grave as I remember."

"As I remember too. Amphotericin is powerful stuff."

"I was there when you talked with him about the drug. You told him amphowhatever didn't work all the time."

"Yes, I did. Not every drug works for every patient. I couldn't guarantee amphotericin would work for him."

"But you've seen it work, and it did pull Brother Emmons through. So even though you've seen cases where your ampho didn't heal the fungus, you prescribe it just the same?"

"Sure. Sometimes it works miracles."

Paul nodded. "That's the way I feel about praying for healing. I believe it *can* work miracles, and I've seen some of those miracles for myself. I've also seen cases I can't explain, when God didn't choose to heal a good person of an awful disease. But I can tell you this—I would be committing spiritual malpractice if I didn't pray just because of those cases where it didn't seem to work."

Luke didn't want to concede the whole point, but he had to agree that the analogy had its merit. If he had been so pessimistic about Mr. Emmons that he hadn't even told him about amphotericin, he would have committed medical malpractice.

For the next thirty minutes, silence filled the car. Paul refrained from singing, and Luke was lost in his thoughts. Paul saw his companion blink to control tears.

"The whole congregation of Sweet Holy Spirit House of Praise is praying for your wife and baby."

As they drove down the palmetto-lined road, Luke broke out in a grin. "Sweet Holy Spirit House of Praise. Now that's the name for a church and a half."

"Wonder what our women are up to tonight," Paul said.

Luke shook his head and smiled. "I'm glad Theo invited Mariama out to Yellow Springs. That wife of mine hasn't even seen an OB yet."

"Let's just pray she doesn't need a midwife yet," Paul said.

"Amen," Luke answered. "I'm getting used to thinking of myself as a daddy."

They both fell silent for the next few miles. Then Luke reached into his briefcase and pulled out Giles's manuscript.

Paul tried to see where he was reading. "Have you gotten to the part where Giles tells how Lucas got from Philadelphia to my neck of the woods?"

"I'm just getting to that part of the story. Want me to read it to you?" Paul nodded.

Consider the plight of a gentle Quaker schooled in the ways of peace. War has broken out around him, North against South, abolitionists against slave owners. Glory hallelujah. Lucas Tayspill thought truth was on his side. However, the only way Lucas knew how to fight for truth was with love.

If I had been a pacifist in 1862, I would rather have lived in Pennsylvania than any other state in the fractious Union. Founded by the Quaker conscience, the Pennsylvania militia understood that Friends weren't cowards because they chose not to fight. As I've reported, Lucas had a possible way out. If in obedience to a higher power than the State, he refused to bear arms, he could pay another to take his place. The struggling sailmaker didn't have the cash, but he did have friends.

When he heard a knock on his door, Lucas opened to find a visitor. "Friend Margaretta, how are thee this glorious day the Lord has made?"

"I am always touched when you greet me as a Friend, dear Lucas."

The sailmaker laughed and cleared a place for Margaretta Forten to sit. Then he placed a kettle on the fire to make tea for one of the city's most prominent freedwomen.

"Friend Margaretta, my father spoke so often of thy father's kindness."

"God was good to take my father home before the steamer replaced schooners." Miss Forten took something out of her basket wrapped in a checkered cloth. "These were his favorite at teatime. I made them myself."

"I am twice blessed, then, Friend Margaretta—thy dear presence and thy dear corn bread. How blessed can a man be?"

He opened the fragrant bundle and saw something besides the corn bread. "What is this?" he asked, picking up a thick wad of bills.

"A gift to a Quaker to render to Caesar," she answered.

He counted the money. "The price of my freedom."

"If your conscience allows friends to help a Friend."

"Some of us say that a Friend cannot assist Caesar by providing another warrior."

"And what says your inward light?" she asked.

"My inward light says that I must thank thee with all my heart but say no."

Margaretta left the money on the table. "Did our president grant your cousin Eliza an audience?"

Lucas nodded. "He saw her on behalf of all Friends, here and in England. She said he listened with his heart as well as his head. Abraham Lincoln was not certain what he would decide should there be a national conscription, but he is sympathetic to our plight."

"The Confederates have already passed a conscription bill. With the exception of schoolteachers and a few other professions, all able men will be mustered into their ranks."

Lucas looked grim. "Friends from Massachusetts bring us dark news from their commonwealth. Men of conscience are treated as traitors and no better than the slaves the militias would fight to free."

"These are treacherous times, my friend, but stirring ones as well."

Lucas nodded. "So they are, Friend Margaretta. So they are."

"To be continued," Luke said as he slipped the composition book back into his briefcase. As they pulled onto the causeway leading to St. Helena Island, he felt the pulse of palmettos, loblolly pines, and live oaks laced with Spanish moss lining the road. Trailers dotted the landscape as often as houses and churches with names like Oaks True Holiness. Luke wondered who were the holy but untrue. Next to each old church was a cemetery plot.

"Could we visit the cemeteries?" Luke asked. "I'd like to look at the headstones."

✠

They pulled off the road several times, and Luke wandered from grave to grave to see the inscriptions on the stones. But he found more mosquitoes than information.

"There's one more place you could try," Paul said, pointing toward a section of time-worn stones. "And while you're checking out dead people, I'll check out the crabs in Capers Creek."

Amid tangled brush and marble slabs, Luke found another visitor.

"You find what you lookin fa?" a young voice asked.

Luke spun around and faced a boy in a dark suit, white shirt, and tie.

"Not yet," he answered. "I'm not even sure what to look for."

"You not from roun here," the boy said.

Luke laughed. "No, I'm just a Yankee visitor."

"You come from President Lincoln's state?"

"No, I was born in Ohio and live in Connecticut."

"Uh-huh. Where dey be?"

"A long way from here. Almost another world."

"Any grave special you lookin fa?"

"Do you know if there's a grave here for a Lucas Tayspill?"

The boy scowled and sized Luke up again. "Why you be lookin fa him?"

A booming female voice interrupted their conversation. "Cedric! You comin?"

Luke turned to see an imposing figure standing by a car with her hands on her hips.

Cedric ignored her and led Luke deeper into the brush. "You know Mistah Lucas?"

"He was my great-great-grandfather. I hoped to find his grave."

Cedric stopped and examined Luke again. Then he bent and cleared some vines away from a marker.

Luke knelt down and brushed away the dirt. He could read the words engraved on the stone: *If you have no cause worth dying for, do you really have a reason to live?* "Do you know anything about this man?" he asked.

The boy nodded. "He be ma great-great-great-granpapa."

"Cedric!" The voice was more insistent than before. The boy looked in his mother's direction.

"Morrow's ma bactizum," he told Luke. "Momma and me gotta meet wid de preacherman make sho ma heart be right. I come here firs to talk wid Mistah Lucas."

"Cedric!" His mother's volume had doubled for having to call him a third time. "You gwine git yousef bactized or what?"

The boy walked backward toward her, unwilling to turn away from Luke just yet. His mother took one of his arms to drag him to the car, but Cedric said something to her that made her look in Luke's direction. The way she scrutinized him, Luke felt conspicuously white. This woman, who gave the distinct impression that she was rarely speechless, stood silent, looking him up and down. Then she marched in his direction.

Paul appeared in time to rescue Luke. As he put his hand on Luke's shoulder, Cedric's mother bowed slightly.

"Welcome home, Rev. I hear you preachin at de bactizum."

Paul extended his hand. "Good to see you, Eula May. Have you met my friend, Docta Tayspill?"

"I was jes bout to invite him fa some fried chicken dis evenin. I'd be much obliged if you come too."

"That's very neighborly of you."

"More dan neighbly," she said as she led Cedric to the car. She nodded toward Luke but spoke to Paul. "Him and me, we be fambly."

"What does she mean?" Luke asked, frozen in his place.

Paul squeezed his shoulder. "Maybe it means you'd better read Giles's book again. But right now, you and me got some serious fishin to do."

Reluctantly Luke followed Paul to the parking lot. In the car he returned to the manuscript.

"Lucas Tayspill?"

"Aye, Friend. What can I do for thee?"

"You can pay three hundred dollars to be released from service, sir, or you can come with me right now."

The three boys sat on the sailmaker's bench, wide-eyed with fright.

"My conscience will not let me pay thee to send another in my place, and I cannot fight. If it is the welfare of the Africans you seek, why not allow me to remain here and prepare these lads for the future?"

"I wish I could, sir, but I am a man under orders."

Lucas nodded. "Would thee give me a moment with my pupils?"

The militiaman nodded and walked to the door to wait.

"Now, lads, help me pack for the journey. I travel light."

One boy took Lucas's black coat and hat from the hook where they hung and held them for his teacher. Lucas slipped his arms into his coat. Another lifted up his Bible. "Aye, I'll be needing that."

Lucas carefully placed it in his saddlebag and gathered the boys to him. "The Lord be with thee and me while we are absent one from another."

"Amen," said Daniel, sniffling.

As Lucas walked to the door, his students clung to his coattails.

"Have thee knowledge where thee shall take me?" he asked the soldier.

"You could have done worse. You've been assigned to a Union regiment under Colonel Thomas Wentworth Higginson. You're on your way to South Carolina."

Daniel handed Lucas a sheaf of papers. "Maybe you meet up wid colored folk dey can hep you wid we Bible."

Lucas wiped tears from Daniel's eyes. "Now go to Miss Forten and tell her what has transpired. And tell her to find a new teacher."

As the boys nodded and started to run, Lucas wondered what problems his conscience would offer the army in swamps where only colored folks and mosquitoes survive.

"Malaria," Luke whispered. "I'll bet that's what killed him."

"Hope you've got bug spray in your suitcase," Paul said. "You're about to meet skeeters the size of rhinos."

TWENTY-TWO

Paul pulled off onto a rough dirt road and stopped the car in front of a bungalow on cinder-block stilts. "Let's get us some gear."

"Is that your family's house?"

Paul nodded. "I've never gotten around to cleaning things out."

"You never got around to coming home."

"That, too," Paul said. He went into a shack to the side of the bungalow and emerged with two nets.

"Don't you use a pole?" Luke asked.

Paul laughed. "Not for shellfish, boy." He threw a net to Luke. "First we gotta make our repairs."

He gathered some sticks from the brush and took out a pocketknife. Luke watched him carve out an eye in the center of a twig and thread through it a shredded piece of net.

"When I got to Sierra Leone, I found out they fished just like I did at home and even sewed their nets the same way."

He pointed to a flat-bottomed boat and motioned Luke to give him a hand. They carried the bateau a half mile farther down the road until they came to an inlet with a boat launch and a weathered dock. Paul took off his shoes and rolled up his pants. Luke followed his example.

"You go fishing much?" Paul asked.

"Not since I was a boy."

"Did you have a place like this, all your own?"

Luke shook his head. "I used to go fishing with my grandfather. After he died, I never went again."

"Well, come on. Jump in the boat. Not many gators on this part of the islands."

After an hour of bending into the water over the side of the boat, they had nets full of crabs and oysters, and even a few little trout. Luke straightened up and massaged the small of his back. They rowed to shore and sat on the dock swatting mosquitoes.

"They've got skeeters bigger than these in Sierra Leone," Paul said.

"And pretty women, too. Tell me more about how you met Mariama."

Paul's face changed as he shifted continents. He led Luke out on a rickety old dock. "This here was the spot in Miss Maggie's vision. Right where we're sitting the ocean became small and the other boy called me to come over and help.

"After college I was ready to live out Miss Maggie's vision, but I had to do it my way. Watch out, Africa. Here comes your long-lost son!"

Luke grinned, imagining Paul in an Afro during the black-is-beautiful sixties. He remembered sitting on Giles's lap watching television and seeing a country change, not of its own choosing.

"I signed up for the Peace Corps and went to Sierra Leone. I laugh at myself today when I think how cocky I was. I had no idea what to expect. Half of me thought the natives would be living a better life than their oppressed sons and daughters in South Carolina. The campus know-it-all was ready to spread wisdom with his every word. I knew the story of the schooner *Amistad* and the Sierra Leonean slaves who went all the way to the Supreme Court for their freedom. I fantasized about becoming a fierce warrior.

"I made my way to Makeni—that's the main city in the Northern Province—and from there to a tiny village. I taught English at a primary school, but the children laughed at my American accent. I was humiliated. In prep school I had worked hard to rid the last vestige of Gullah from my speech. But in this village, the kids giggled as if I had the worst flat speech on all of St. Helena Island.

"One little girl, only eight years old at the time, took it on herself to explain why they were laughing. For them, she explained, English was a second or third language. Most of them spoke the local dialect with one another and Krio with strangers who came from other parts of Sierra Leone. I asked her to give me an example of this Krio. At first I thought she was speaking Gullah. The next day her mother came to the school to apologize for her daughter's rude manners. She invited me to come for a meal. That little girl was Mariama.

"I ate often with the Conteh family. I asked them how they could be Christians after all the white man had done to Africa. The colonialists stole Sierra Leone's resources and kidnapped her children. Pa Conteh picked up the Bible that was never far from his side. 'This isn't the white man's book,' he said. 'This is God's book. This book doesn't rob us. It fills us with life and hope and dignity.'

"It didn't take long for me to 'go native.' Little Mariama was teaching me Krio. But there were ominous things happening around me. I was increasingly aware of secret societies. Little boys hinted at the powers they would obtain when they went into the bush for their initiation. The *bundo* society for girls was just as secret, but I imagined women sitting around a campfire passing down recipes to bush Girl Scouts. I soon learned the reason for the secrecy.

"One day when I arrived at the Conteh house, the parents were frantic. Mariama's sister Erna had disappeared. Although the family refused to send their daughters to the bush, they feared pressure from Erna's girlfriends had driven her into the bush to become a *bundo* girl.

"A week later the child came home, pale and sweaty, with blood soaking the lower half of her dress. I wanted to take her to a doctor, but the village women pressured her mother to let them care for her. A week later when I returned to the home, I noticed a foul smell coming from Erna and begged the family again to let me take her to a doctor. The village Mammy Queen gave her mother an evil look, but this time Ma Conteh gave in and let me take her to the mission hospital.

"The doctor frowned when she saw the stains on Erna's dress. She said Erna would be lucky if she didn't get tetanus. I didn't understand why. Female circumcision with unsterile instruments and no anesthesia, she explained. 'The Christian pastors preach against it, the fathers don't want to pay the *sowei* the money for the procedure, but it still keeps happening.'

"I was horrified and asked what would happen to Erna. The doctor shook her head. 'The good news is that now she can find a husband. Many of the village boys won't marry a girl who hasn't gone through the initiation. The bad news, from what I see here, is that she'll probably develop a fistula. She'll have pain during intercourse and trouble in childbirth. Just this week I watched a woman bleed to death in labor. It was an awful sight.'

"The doctor cleaned up Erna's wounds and gave her a powerful antibiotic. When I took her back to her family, Mariama was hiding where she could watch everything. While I was talking to their parents, she came over and told her big sister, 'Mariama next *bundo* girl.'

"I was more horrified thinking of that than anything I had seen or heard that day. I begged the Contehs not to let Mariama go to the bush. I pointed to Erna, moaning on her mat. 'You didn't want that for your daughters, but it still happened.' What surprised me was that her mother walked away.

"For several weeks I didn't go to visit the family. I taught at my school, and every day I saw sweet little Mariama and all the other bright, beautiful girls. When the older girls came back to school from the bush, these little ones gathered around them in admiration. They had nice new dresses and golden jewelry. For poor little girls, they looked so rich. That's when I made my plan to save Mariama.

"I went to Pa Conteh and made him an offer. If he and his wife would do their best to spare Mariama this awful mutilation, I would pay for her education. She could go to England or the States, wherever she wanted. If no man in their village would marry her, she could come to America where she would have plenty of suitors—if marriage were her choice. I wanted her to have choices in her life.

"At first her father rejected my offer, so I started to work on her mother. 'I know you don't want this for your daughter,' I pleaded. After months of hospitality, she began to treat me like an outsider.

"I went back to her father and pleaded with him, Christian man to

Christian man. I told him that Saint Paul told men to love their wives as Christ loves the church. Could he imagine Jesus mutilating the church he died to save?"

Paul was getting weary. Telling the story had sapped all his energy, but he carried on.

"In the end, Pa Conteh agreed to do his best, and I trusted that he meant to save Mariama. My teaching assignment ended, and I came back home. My African romanticism was over, but not the commitment I made to that family.

"I got a good-paying job in Atlanta and put away money for Mariama's education. But the words of Miss Maggie's vision kept haunting me: 'Come over an help us.' Had I helped or meddled? I wasn't at all sure.

"I went home to St. Helena Island and told Miss Maggie the story. Momma wept like a baby when I told her about Erna. 'You did help them,' she assured me. 'And I'll help too. I don't need much money to live on.'

"Together we kept a bank account for Mariama, saving to keep her free from an old hag's blade. And the Contehs kept their promise. They lost their status in their village, but the local pastor stood by them.

"Mariama wrote to me regularly—chatty little letters. She told me when her baby brother was born and what a good little mother she was to Lazaro. I lived for those letters.

"Meanwhile, I needed to make a plan for my life. I knew a sales job in Atlanta wasn't meant for me. Somehow St. Helena would always be a part of me, even if I didn't live on the island. Somehow Africa was in my bones, even if I never went back. I still had some of the money Doc Bailey had given Momma for my education, so I applied to Yale Divinity School. They had a program in black preaching, which brought me to New Haven. To be continued, as they say."

✠

Watching the sun start its descent, Luke remembered their date for Eula May's fried chicken. "At least we can be proper guests," he said. "Look at all the shellfish we can take along." He rose and stretched his legs as three large hawks circled in the sky.

"Marsh hawks," Paul said. "They clean up after the fishermen."

Luke stared at the hawks, then turned to the side of the dock where tall grasses were poking through the bog. Disoriented, he looked in another direction. "I know this place. This is the scene in Giles's painting. He was here! I didn't recognize the dock until the hawks flew over. You see that patch of marsh grass over there? Those are just like the blades I tried to paint when I was a little boy."

"Well, you'll be back here tomorrow at sunrise when the tide comes in. This is the creek where the baptism will take place."

As they raised the bateau to carry it back to Miss Maggie's house, Luke turned one last time to view the scene he'd studied so often while sitting at his desk at home.

As they walked down the dirt driveway, they could see Cedric standing in the front yard. As fast as he could, he ran to the backyard yelling, "It be Lucas!"

"You tink he be somebody special?" Eula May asked. From the time Cedric was a little boy, he had been known as a wise one. Grownups four times his age came to him for advice.

The boy nodded and Eula May sized up the white man in rolled-up Dockers. "Welcome to our home. Ma son could hardly concentrate on meetin wid de preacherman, tinkin bout you comin tonight."

Luke held out a pan full of shellfish. "I hope you have room for two more boys at your table, Miss Eula May."

Cedric ran into the house and brought back a book to show Luke. "This be his journal."

Luke dried his hands on his shirttail before taking the leather-bound book. When he opened the cover, he saw the owner's name written inside—*Lucas Tayspill.*

"That's what your momma meant when she said, 'We be fambly'?"

Cedric nodded. "Welcome to de fambly."

Luke stuck out his white arm and lined it up with Cedric's ebony one. "I'll bet there's an interesting story about how all this happened."

"I know de whole story. I jes didn't know bout you."

Cedric took back the journal for a moment and carefully flipped through the pages until he came to a special place. "Tells here how Lucas met Amoretta Capers. She be ma momma's great-great-granmama. Her masta be her daddy. She coulda passed, but she stayed here on St. Helena Island wid de fambly. Then she married her a white boy."

"So we're cousins?"

"If you know Jedus, we be better dan cousins. We be brodas. You do know Jedus, don't you?"

Luke shook his head. "I'm not a Christian if that's what you mean."

"Why not?" Cedric asked as if he couldn't think of a rational reason why anyone who had a chance to know Jesus didn't.

"My father was an atheist," Luke answered as if that was a good answer.

"Ma daddy be a drunk, but dat no mean I be one."

"I hope not!"

"Mebe I can innerduce you to Jedus."

Luke laughed and squeezed the boy tightly around the shoulders. "An you ain't even be bactized yet!" The doctor was learning Gullah fast.

Luke looked over to the picnic table where a contingency of aunts and uncles surrounded Bishop Paul. From their gestures and glances in his direction, Luke could tell that their conversation was about him.

Eula May came out the back door with a bowl heaped with fried chicken. "Hope you done bring you appetite, Docta Lucas."

Certain that Eula May was the sort of hostess who wouldn't permit her guests to determine how much they should eat, Luke threw his cholesterol to the wind and dug in.

Eula May bobbed her head toward the journal Cedric had put to the side, safe from chicken grease. "Ma son know dat story by heart. When ma daddy be live, he usta read it to Cedric. It be Poppa's book. He usta wonder what come of de boy, de other twin. Auntie Caroline, she stay here on St. Helena—she be ma great-granmama. Junior, he took his wife and lef fa de North. No black boy could marry wid no white girl proper dose days. Not by de State anyways. But de Quakers would marry dem, jes like dey marry Lucas an Amoretta. De las entry in his diary be bout malaria. Lots of white folks be taken dat year. Lucas be taken too, I reckon. We didn't know bout de rest of de fambly. Tayspill a mighty peculiar name."

Luke went back to the car, fetched Giles's manuscript, and showed it to Cedric. "This tells the rest of the story."

Cedric looked at it studiously. " *The Deaths of Lucas Tayspill.* All dead Lucas men? How many he be talkin bout?"

"There are three stories in the book, but the third one has yet to be written."

"Dat you story?" Cedric asked with a worried look on his face.

Luke showed him the first page with its single paragraph.

"Dat be what written on Lucas Tayspill's tombstone," Cedric said, pointing to the page with the epigram. "How come all de Lucases have to die?"

Luke shook his head. "I don't know, son."

Cedric turned to the incomplete page. "How you gwine finish dis page, Docta Lucas?"

"Carefully, I guess."

"Now me, I wouldna finish dat page les I knew Jedus."

Luke grinned. "Quite a little evangelist, aren't you?"

Cedric read the short third story. " 'Plague-ridden, war-torn country.' Soun like South Carolina back when Lucas firs come here."

"May I borrow the journal overnight? Promise I'll take good care of it."

"You be comin to ma bactizum tomorrow?"

"Wouldn't miss it for the world."

"You hafta get up fore sunrise. Day clean be when we go wadin in de river."

TWENTY-THREE

L ong before daybreak Luke sat on the veranda of the Beaufort Inn leafing through Lucas Tayspill's journal.

Unlike our Pennsylvania militiamen, this company has no favorable report of Friends. I have become like an African—the soldiers' slave, subject to their cruelty. They strung up one Friend by his thumbs for refusal to serve. I praise the Almighty Father for his protection thus far. Our company is small, so they seek African recruits to serve with the Union when we reach South Carolina.

He drew closer to the porch light and flipped to another entry.

In his mercy, the Almighty has brought me through to a new day. In faithfulness to the Commandments, I rebuked a soldier who took the Lord's name in vain. My back still smarts from his whip, but his language has been purified. I will be assigned to a hospital when we reach the front. My conscience is torn on this matter. Can I be a peacemaker if I restore men to health so they can take up the sword once more?

To Luke the story seemed both real and surreal. He imagined the tent in which Lucas sat writing by lantern light.

This morning I read passages from Luke's gospel in Gullah. It stirred me to seek the inward light, God's precious Holy Spirit. The poor, the imprisoned, the blind are here in this place. Let me be God's hands, I pray, his voice, his messenger.

We reached South Carolina, but not all our men survived. Some soldiers were taken by fevers. Others fell to Confederate swords. Our commander joined up with us and spoke to the regiment. Thomas Wentworth Higginson of Massachusetts is a man of the cloth and steeplehouse. He has no crisis of conscience to use the sword as an instrument of righteousness. He purposes to build a regiment of freedmen who volunteer to fight. We shall see how "voluntary" their service will be.

The journal read like a continuation of Giles's manuscript.

God of all mercy has reached down and saved his servant. Today Colonel Higginson had a visit from an old friend he knew in the abolitionist movement. Charlotte Forten besought him to assign me to a position consistent with the conscience legislation. Margaretta's niece comes here to teach the emancipated slaves. On their behalf and in full compliance with the law, she seeks to have my services as a fellow teacher. My heart is full of praise for our Lord.

Today I moved from the army camp to the school. My new pupils' speech is harder to understand than young Daniel's, but we have charted out a course together. Each day's lesson begins with a verse from Luke's gospel in the Authorized Version. As with Daniel, I asked my young pupils to repeat it for me in "ole time talk."

Luke grinned as he read the next entry.

A glorious Sabbath Day today, God has made more glorious with the sight of a maiden. Her skin is as fair as mine, but they say Amoretta is a woman of color. I cannot even call her dark, but she is as lovely as Solomon's beloved. The sun darkens her skin less than my own. I seek the inward light, but my heart is stirred with excitation.

Luke read of a struggle between conscience and physical attraction, followed by the record of a Quaker marriage blessing. He read of the long-time bachelor's description of his attempt to tame a free-spirited girl, the arrival of Junior and Caroline, and Amoretta's death in her second childbirth. Finally he came to an entry made shortly before the end of the Civil War.

He couldn't wait to knock on Paul's door. "Let me read you something."

Colonel Higginson called on me today. With him, he brought clothing for the children purchased by his men and foodstuffs to help us through the winter. I remember with gratitude his kindness to me from the beginning and his warm heart toward all Friends. Thus, when he came with a request, I could not easily decline.

A fierce epidemic spreads throughout his company. Many of his Africans suffer from this blackwater fever. Colonel Higginson asks me to help in the camp, not to revive fighters, but to save those black men who so recently won their freedom.

I sought the inward light for hours sitting in silence. When God's Word came to me, it came in the language of these people.
De time done come wen de Lawd gwine save e people.

Luke paced as Paul continued to pack. "He died of malignant malaria, but he could have said no to Higginson."

"He had a reason to live and a cause worth dying for," Paul answered.

Luke sank into a chair. "The first time I read the manuscript, my instinct was to leave the genie in the bottle. I didn't want to unleash whatever power was packed into it."

"And now?" Paul said, scanning the room for any more belongings.

"I've unleashed a tornado, but I wouldn't want to go back to where I was before."

"You can't go back. But where is forward going to lead?"

"Someday I'll have to give a name to that plague-ridden, war-torn country."

"And for now?"

"I just don't know. I'm reluctant to close this chapter of my life. St. Helena Island is a very special place."

"Because of your family?" Paul asked.

"Not just that. I can't really explain it. I had the feeling first when we were fishing, then later on the dock. When I recognized the place from Grandpa's painting, I thought that was it—finding Grandpa Giles again. But I still felt that way when we were at Eula May's picnic."

"Come on, Doc. Surely a Yale man can find a word to describe it."

"It sounds too silly to even say, but I did hear a word in my heart."

"Must be all those Quaker roots. What exactly was the 'inward word' you heard?"

"And it was good."

"Words of a Creator pleased with what he had accomplished."

"Something good was created on this island despite the evil that man intended. President Lincoln created freedom. The teachers shared knowledge. Lucas and Amoretta created their own brand of racial reconciliation."

"And God said, 'Uh-huh, dat be gooood.'"

Luke turned to the preacher. "But it's still going on here, Paul—that sense of the holy. I may not be ready to give the holy the name 'God,' but I can feel the holy happening. Think about the conference we attended. Ignorance once helped AIDS flourish in this country, but you saw the faces in the audience when you gave your lecture. They were hungry for help to fight against AIDS."

Paul smiled. "God saw a new evil that was not part of his original design. He also saw a way out for the people."

"Your analysis, not necessarily mine," Luke countered.

"But would you say, 'And it was good'?"

Luke nodded. "It was good. I sat in on one of the workshops of the community health workers. They were bubbling with new ideas for working through the churches to reach out to the people."

Paul grinned. "That was good." He looked at his watch. "Speaking of good things, I'm wondering what those wives of ours are up to right now."

"Getting ready to meet us at the airport, I hope. After the baptism we need to hustle our bones. Our flight leaves Charleston at 2:45." Luke picked up the journal. "I wish I could pack Cedric and the journal in my suitcase."

"Invite him to visit you in Connecticut. And you can always come back. Remember, you have fambly here."

"I'm wondering how much of this story my father knows."

Paul checked the room one more time for belongings. "You'll find out soon enough, I expect."

As the first rays of sunrise broke over the waters, Luke strained to see the procession moving from the church to the boat landing across the road.

Who those children dressed in red?

God gwine trouble de water.

Mus be de children dat Moses led.

God gwine trouble de water.

"That sounds like a funeral dirge," Luke whispered to Paul.

Paul nodded. "In baptism, a Christian is buried with Christ. Remember what Brother Emmons wanted to sing about the night he died?"

Luke nodded, remembering the songs and the Scripture passage Paul read at Mr. Emmons's bedside. "What do they mean about God troubling the waters?"

"It was a coded song. To Masta, the slaves were singing a Bible story about Moses parting the Red Sea or Joshua leading the children of Israel across the river Jordan. To the slaves, it was something else—a clue to avoid leaving a scent for Masta's bloodhounds. Wade in the water, and the dogs won't smell you."

"Why baptize at sunrise?"

"Outgoin tide gwine wash their sins way."

Who dat yonder all dressed in black?

God gwine trouble de water.

He be de hypocrite who turn back.

God gwine trouble de water.

A deacon came next in line after the pastor. He was dressed in a white robe and carrying a long, crooked stick. Dark-suited men and pastel-dressed women with large hats moved in from the sides to flesh out the congregation on the shore. For a moment there was a buzz among the matrons. Luke felt all eyes on him.

"Dat be Lucas Tayspill," one woman said, using her fan to point to Luke. "He come back fa Cedric's bactizum day."

"Mus be Junior's kin," another said. "Junior done went up north. Dat Lucas be white as a buckra. Tink it be his ghost?"

A fan came crashing down on the ghost-buster's arm. "He jes a man. A white man."

"He sure be white."

Who dat yonder all dressed in white?

God gwine trouble de water.

Mus be de children of de Israelite.

God gwine trouble de water.

As the pastor and elders reached the water's edge, a procession of white-robed young people followed, wearing white cloths wrapped around their heads. As the last baptismal candidate reached the water's edge, Paul nudged Luke to move in closer. Luke spotted Cedric and slipped his camera out of his pocket. Paul grinned. "Jes like a proud papa."

Luke kept snapping photos. As Cedric came out of the waters for the last time, the waters started to churn.

"God done trouble de water!" one of the women shouted, pointing to the sky.

The whirring sound got louder, as if it was coming from the other side of the creek.

"Dem be a locus plague comin outta Egypt!" yelled another sister.

A murmur went up through the crowd, a wail of distress. The pastor and Cedric, still in the water, shielded their eyes to look in the direction of the buzzing noise. Suddenly, from around the bend, a helicopter appeared and plunged toward the crowd.

Some of the women gathered their skirts and ran. Others fell to their knees and prayed. As the chopper landed on a nearby farm field, a state trooper jumped out and ran toward the water's edge.

"I don't think he's the hypocrite who turned back," Luke said to Paul as the man approached him.

"Are you Dr. Tayspill? Could you please come with me, sir? And if this is Bishop Pinckney, he's coming too."

"I've got a sermon to preach," Paul said.

The trooper motioned to them to come quickly. "We're taking you to your wives. They're safe."

"Safe from what?" Luke asked, resisting the arm that hastened him along.

"I'll tell you the story on the way," the trooper answered.

As the trooper spirited Luke toward the waiting helicopter, Paul grabbed their luggage from the rental car parked a few yards away at Miss Maggie's house.

The crowd moved toward the helicopter, and Cedric pushed his way through the mass of hips and chiffon. "Lucas! Where you be goin, man? Bishop Paul! Who gwine preach today?"

As the chopper blades whirled into action, Paul yelled over the din. "Guess you have to do it, son. The text is from Luke's gospel, chapter four, verses eighteen and nineteen."

"De Lawd Sperit de libe een me an gee me powa?" Cedric yelled back.

"That's it," Paul said as they pushed him onto the helicopter.

"I'll be back," Luke yelled to the boy. To Paul he said, "I don't think Cedric heard me."

"He knows you'll be back. You didn't have a chance to give him back his journal."

Eula May came rushing to her son's side and called, "Docta Lucas, you come back fa Easter and bring de rest of you fambly."

Luke smiled and waved to let her know he'd gotten the message.

As St. Helena Island grew smaller, Luke turned to the trooper. "Tell me what happened to my wife."

Part V

Whosoneba want fa be me ciple mus lobe me mo
den e lobe e papa an e mama.

—Luke 14:26, *De Good Nyews Bout Jedus
Christ Wa Luke Write* (Gullah)

TWENTY-FOUR

Luke stared at the weeping cherry tree in his parents' backyard, dusted with snow. He turned to the tableau of mourners, reconfigured since Beauregard's death and shivering in their winter clothes. Giles was gone, but there were two welcome additions—Paul and Mariama. On that day so long ago when they buried Beau, Martin had called God a crutch that no Tayspill should ever need. Now his father was walking around in the snow like a zombie on Risperdal and Ativan—badly in need of a crutch.

On the road to St. Helena Island, Luke had sounded like his father when he challenged Paul about the bishop's dependency on Jesus. What was it Luke called Jesus? A "fantasy friend." Paul had laughed and clapped Luke on the shoulder. "One day you'll find out just how real Jesus is," his friend answered. That day had not yet arrived—if it ever did—but Luke would have felt lost without Jesus's black bishop at his side.

While the rest of the family huddled together, Martin hobbled around the yard, finding weeds to yank and brushing snow off the topiary chicken. Charley was in fine shape, with trimmed neck, comb, and even feet. Martin kept himself busy and away from the rest of his family.

Luke wasn't at all certain that the mutilation of the painting had been an act of dementia as the police and Martin's doctors were eager to believe. He picked up a garbage bag and followed his father.

"I jes don git it," Martin muttered. With his speech slurred from the medicine, he sounded as Gullah as Bishop Paul.

But Luke had to agree. Nothing he had heard in the past few hours had made much sense.

✠

As the helicopter took Luke and Paul from St. Helena Island to the Charleston airport, Luke asked, "What happened?"

"Your families are safe," the trooper told Luke, "but shaken up. Your father is an old man, right? He's had a couple of strokes? As best as the Ohio State Police can figure, he was sleepwalking and went into his study carrying a gun. Something he saw there made him wig out. He pumped bullets into a painting on an easel."

"Grandpa Giles," Luke whispered.

The trooper shrugged. "The dog must have heard the noise and gone into the study. Somehow the gun went off and the poor thing took some hits in the belly and leg."

"Moose?" Luke whispered, his mind working wildly as he tried to follow this bizarre narration.

"Your wife heard the dog and was the next to arrive."

"Is Theo okay? Dad didn't shoot her, did he?"

"She's fine," the trooper said. "That dog, Moose, saved her life. By that time, your father was swinging his arms wildly. Even with his injuries, Moose was able to grab your father's arm and deflect the gun. Your father must have been sleepwalking. Senile people do that, don't they? That's the only thing that makes any sense."

"Will Moose be okay?"

The officer shrugged his shoulders and diverted his eyes. "They didn't tell me."

"It's not fair," Luke said.

The officer wanted to say, "I'm sorry for your loss," but as far as he knew, no one was dead yet. "Your wife grabbed the gun and called 911."

Luke tried to imagine his grandfather's study riddled with bullets and splattered with blood. He tried to blot out the image of poor Moose, a real weenie about pain. Somehow he couldn't buy the sleepwalking story. "Is my father in jail?"

The trooper shook his head. "They said he stayed in the hospital overnight on sedation, and they let him go home this morning. He didn't remember anything that happened. The Ohio police said there will be no charges."

"Is it over?" Luke asked.

The officer didn't answer directly. "Your family is pretty shook up."

Beneath the cherry tree, Bishop Paul rocked Moose, who was swaddled in a baby blanket Edith had knit for her first grandchild. The wounded animal moaned. The vet had been noncommittal about his chances of survival, but Mighty Moose was still with them. A plastic Elizabethan collar transformed him into a droll clown and kept him from licking his sutures. As the dog slept on his back, Paul rubbed his chest. As drowsy as Moose was, he seemed to remember the comfortable nesting place he had discovered at Christmastime.

Moose tried to migrate up to Paul's chest, but his collar got in the way. The bishop unclasped the device and whispered in the dog's ear. "If I take off your conehead, promise me you won't bother your stitches." With his eyes closed, Moose found Paul's mustache. It didn't take much tickling to ignite a sneeze from Paul. Then the dog settled with his head under Paul's chin and whimpered in his sleep. "Ask the animals, and they will teach you," Paul said. "In God's hand is the life of every living thing."

Theo reached over toward Paul and took his hand. "That's beautiful."

"May I pray for his healing?" Paul asked. He addressed his question to Martin, who had run out of bushes to trim and weeds to pull. Martin answered with a movement halfway between a shrug and a nod.

Paul stood up, holding the dog close to his chest. "We lift up your little servant who has served this family well. More so, I raise this family to you. Protect them from the Evil One." He paused in his prayer long enough to place his right hand on Theo's head. "Protect this woman and her child. Heal her of all her afflictions. We love her and we know that you love her too."

From Theo, he moved on to place his hand on Luke's shoulder. "Guide this man into all knowledge and wisdom. Lead him in the path where he should go." He finished his prayer by reaching behind him to take Martin's hand. "I commit this family into your loving arms. Protect and guide them in all their ways. I pray all these things in the strong, strong name of Jesus. Amen."

As they walked back to the house together, Martin leaned on Paul's arm. "Thank you, sir."

Paul smiled. "It's a good time to be with friends."

Luke looked over at Paul and thought, *Too many changes in our lives. And too many losses.* Everyone else seemed to buy the sleepwalking theory. But not Luke. Sure, shooting Moose was an accident. The dog wasn't Martin's target.

That night as Luke and Theo lay entwined in bed, Moose slept in a basket on the floor. The dog's absence from bed unsettled Luke more than Theo. Luke needed the ordinary and familiar. As he drew Theo close and kissed her hair, he said, "I'm so scared."

"There's no reason for you to be."

He broke the embrace and sat up. "No reason? My wife doesn't tell me about a life-threatening illness. She risks her life to carry a baby that could destroy the strength she has. My father nearly shoots her. And now she tells me there's no reason to be afraid?"

Theo put her hand over Luke's mouth. "Hush. You'll wake up the rest of the house."

"I want to wake up my wife. Tell me the truth. I don't think I can stand half truths much longer."

"When were you planning to tell me about the South Carolina Tayspills?" she asked.

"You know?"

"Mariama told me."

"I was waiting for things to calm down before I told you."

"Like I was waiting for Sarajevo to calm down?"

He kissed her. "Let's not fight."

"Are you worried what people will think if the baby looks black?" she asked.

"Let's just say I'm glad you didn't ask me that a month ago. Our baby's color might challenge even liberal minds."

Theo sat up in bed. "Would you have asked me to abort the baby because of its color?"

"No, I don't think so. But it would have made me think awfully hard."

"What was there to think about?"

"A boy and girl meet and fall in love. Bing-bang-boom. All they think about is how they feel."

"And how they dream about the future."

"That, too, but it all seems so simple when you're first in love."

"Then along comes life."

Luke turned on the light. "The new Tayspills were a wonderful surprise. I can't wait till you meet Cedric. They've invited us for Easter."

"From what Paul told Mariama, Cedric is your opposite in more than complexion."

"Cedric is as proud of his Tayspill roots as I am. But I like to think in complex terms, and Cedric likes to break things down to the bottom line. When I met him, I thought that if I had a son, I would hope he'd be as wise as Cedric."

"What if you have a daughter?" Theo asked.

"You're kidding. Do you think we've got a little Theo instead of a little Luke?"

"A little Chloe if it's a girl."

All of a sudden Theo felt a movement within. "The quickening!"

"Did the baby kick you?" Luke asked as Theo guided his hand to the place where she felt the movement.

"It felt more like the fluttering of a butterfly."

"Does that mean it's a girl?"

"No, silly. It just means our baby is alive. Tell your baby you love him—or her."

Luke covered her belly with kisses. "Hang in there, little one. Your daddy loves you." Then he leaned down to the dog bed on the floor. "You hang in there too, Moose."

In the guest room, Mariama snuggled in Paul's arms. "I'm so frightened."

Paul kissed her forehead and held her tighter. "You'll be okay in a couple of days, and then we'll go home."

"Home? Don't you remember we have no home? And now our jobs are gone."

Paul kissed her forehead. "We can stay with Luke and Theo as long as we need to. And God will make another way for us to serve him. He's just taken these material things away so we can find that way. Luke's parents said we're welcome to stay as long as we'd like."

Mariama's eyes filled with tears. "We don't have a home."

TWENTY-FIVE

Moose watching filled the rest of February. They waited for signs of recovery or clues that he might not make it. Then Theo saw a hopeful sign. Moose limped into the living room favoring his right front leg. She covered him with kisses. "It's your left paw, you little fake."

Luke laughed. "If he's healthy enough to malinger, I guess he's going to make it."

Freed from another deathwatch, Luke plunged into work, helping Paul put together his second paper on spiritual diagnosis in AIDS. The hospital might have made the bishop redundant, but Luke had paid for their trip to London. The paper took less than three days to finish. Then the board games appeared.

Luke studied the tiles in front of him. All consonants. Usually that meant high points in Scrabble, but what could you do with *B, R, T, S,* and *D?*

"I'm going to use a stopwatch on you," Johanna told her brother. "You're taking too much time."

"Why don't you help Brother?" Edith asked her.

"No, Ma. I want to win."

"I can find my own words," Luke told his mother.

"I could give you some of my letters," Edith told Luke.

"He doesn't need your tiles, Ma. He just needs to move. Now!"

Luke picked up four tiles and stood over the board to place them in line with someone else's *O.* "B-O-R-E-D." Then he threw the rest of his tiles on the table.

Johanna sprang into action and arrayed her tiles around Luke's *E.* "S-E-X-Y. Fourteen more points for me. I win." As Luke stalked out of the room, Johanna called after him. "Spoiled brat!"

Edith burst into tears and ran into the kitchen.

Paul started to hum. Mariama patted Theo's hand.

"Shall we play Trivial Pursuit?" Johanna asked.

Theo shook her head. "Luke needs something besides games to stay busy. In a good year I can't get him to take more than one week of vacation at a time."

"Same thing with Paul," Mariama said. "He's not going to be able to sit around like this for much longer."

Luke wandered out into the garden where his father was weeding again. He picked up the pruning shears and chopped at Charley Chicken.

"Go gentle with him, Son. You're plucking all his feathers."

Luke had planned to pluck his father's feathers about the shooting, but changed his mind. He noticed that Martin's speech no longer was slurred. He put down the shears. He wanted to hear him speak.

"How do you like retirement, Dad?"

Martin shrugged. "The first few months were awful. I drove Mother crazy."

"And now?"

"Now I'm glad to be alive. Close encounters give you a different point of view."

Luke was certain his dad had learned nursing-home tricks, like parking your pills behind your wisdom teeth, but he didn't know how to catch him *in flagrante delicto* without treating him like an infant. Luke flopped into a lawn chair and fell silent.

Martin took the chair next to him. "Do you think Theo will be okay?"

"She thinks so. She's upbeat these days."

Martin snorted. "Because that colored preacher prayed for her?"

Until that moment, Luke had planned to tell him about St. Helena's black treasures. Given that rude description of Bishop Paul, he decided it wasn't a good time to ask his father whether he knew Junior had left South Carolina with more than a good tan. "Whatever," he answered.

Martin joined the Scrabble game, and Luke used his preoccupation as an excuse to run over to the nursing home. He wanted to fetch a syringe of Ativan in case his father had a violent flareup.

Back at the house again, he avoided the game group in the family room and settled in the living room with his briefcase. He missed having a home office where he could hide, so he took up a corner near the fireplace as his work area. He pulled out Giles's manuscript and the journal Cedric had loaned him. Perhaps this was a good time to work on the Lucas mystery. He hadn't expected his genealogical research to move so quickly from South Carolina to Ohio, but then Junior Tayspill probably hadn't planned his move so quickly either.

In Lucas Tayspill's diary, he found reference to Junior's birth, but not to his departure for the North. Luke put the journal aside and picked up Giles's manuscript. He paged through it until he came to the story of the second Lucas Tayspill.

My mother said I came out of her crying and kept crying for the first year of my life. I wonder now whether I felt close to my father in the safety of her widow's womb. Even when I was in the cradle, she read to me.

Mother's favorite book was the Song of Solomon, although she never told me why. Look not upon me, because I am black, because the sun hath looked upon me. *We were already living in Mr. Morton's house when she read it to me for the first time. By that time I had Morton brothers and sisters.*

My mother, Mary Elizabeth, fell away from the Quaker meeting after my father's death and her second marriage. Mr. Morton wasn't a believer, she said, but he was a good man and wanted to give me his name. I carried my real daddy's name like an honor badge. I wouldn't give up being a Tayspill no matter how kind Mr. Morton was to me. I must admit he was kind to us both.

I wanted to know about my father. Mother said she and Junior were Solomon reversed. I am black, but comely, O ye daughters of Jerusalem, as the tents of Kedar, as the curtains of Solomon. *In the life she had known before she met my father, had my* mother been a queen? Sometimes she talked about their old home in the South on an island that could have been paradise if it weren't for the hatred of men who claimed to be Christians.

When I was older, I read the Song of Solomon and King Solomon's story in the first book of Kings. The Bible told stories of forbidden love. God told the children of Israel not to intermarry with people from other nations. Yet a sun-drenched foreigner offered King Solomon the best love he had ever known. What my mother wouldn't tell me, I made up in my head—my mother, a grand lady in a plantation palace surrounded by wealth and mystery. His left hand is under my head, and his right hand doth embrace me. I wondered if the Quakers ever read the Song of Solomon in their meetings. Solomon's song made me sweat.

I had no picture of my father and asked my mother what he looked like. Curly red hair, she said, and skin with a fine warm glow. My beloved is unto me as a cluster of camphire in the vine-yards of Engedi. I asked Mr. Morton—that's what I chose to call my mother's husband—if I could go with him to the college library one day. Camphire, I learned there, is a plant that pro-duces henna dye. Did my father's skin glow from camphire?

"Why did they string up my daddy?" I asked.

"They were cruel and ignorant men," my mother answered, wiping her eyes.

Forbidden love, I decided, but I knew she wouldn't tell me the real reason. By night on my bed I sought him whom my soul loveth: I sought him, but I found him not.

I asked Mr. Morton, but he wouldn't tell. "I'm your daddy now," he said, but I still wouldn't take his name. Tayspill was all I had left of my father.

When I was thirteen, I borrowed Mr. Morton's horse and rode the nine miles from Yellow Springs to Hobart Corners. That's where they say it happened, but I couldn't find my daddy's grave. I returned to Hobart Corners a few months later, but this time I had to walk. Mr. Morton was sorely vexed that I borrowed his horse without permission.

I went on a Sunday morning to find the Quaker meeting. Perhaps someone there would know and remember the man who gave me life and a name. At the meeting, people didn't need to talk to feel good. The Quakers were waiting, but waiting for what? The voice of my beloved! Behold, he cometh leaping upon the mountains, skipping upon the hills.

For an hour men and women in plain dress sat in silence, and I sat with them waiting for the voice. I never heard anything that morning, but on the way out the door, I saw an old man with a long white beard who looked wise and kind. "Please, sir," I asked him. "Did you know my daddy, Lucas Tayspill? People called him Junior."

"What is thy name, my child?"

"Giles, sir. Giles Tayspill."

"Are thee as brave as thy father, Friend Giles?"

"I don't know, sir. Why did my daddy need to be brave?"

Other Quakers stood listening at a distance. The old gentleman took my hand. "Come, Friend Giles. I'll show thee where it came to pass."

We walked about a mile until we came to a cluster of large oak trees. The Quaker man pointed up to one of the trees. "There, Friend Giles, they hung thy father and another man."

A dilapidated house stood some twenty yards away.

"They burned a cross in front of that house and prepared to string up the Negro. Thy father came and tried to save him. There were two hangings that day instead of one."

"But why? Why did my daddy have to die?"

Greater love hath no man than this, that a man lay down his life for his friends.

"Forbidden love?" I asked.

"The love that is from God can no man forbid," he answered.

"Did they catch the men who did it?"

The old Quaker shook his head. "In those days the Klan had friends in this town."

I returned to Yellow Springs and Mr. Morton's house very late that evening. Mother was crying, and she cried even more when I told her where I had been. She sent me to bed without supper, but I hid in the shadows by the stairwell and listened to her and Mr. Morton talk in the kitchen below.

"I am so frightened," my mother told Mr. Morton.

"He'll never find out, and neither will the hatemongers find out about Lucas's son."

"We should have stayed on St. Helena Island."

"It was against the law, Mary Elizabeth. Lucas knew that. He took you away to protect you."

"Where was God when he needed protection?" she asked.

That day my mother lost more than her thees and thous. She stopped believing in God.

I listened to them later in their bedroom. I imagined that all the noises I heard went along with Solomon's song. My beloved is mine, and I am his: he feedeth among the lilies.

Mr. Morton loved my mother and rescued the two of us— from what, I could not tell you. He couldn't rescue her from what followed their night among the lilies. Nine months after I listened to the beloveds in the night, my mother died in childbirth. I cannot adequately describe the depths of Mr. Morton's grief, but I began to call him father.

Luke had never before thought of "father" as a name to earn. *Father. Daddy. Dad. Pop. Baba. Pa.* What would little Luke or Chloe call him? And what could he do to make sure his child would speak his name with joy?

TWENTY-SIX

On Sunday the Pinckneys found a promising church in Yellow Springs. The pastor was so delighted to meet Paul that he drafted him and Mariama to lead revival meetings planned for the following week to help his flock forget the long winter.

Martin hobbled into the living room and poked his cane at Luke to wake him up from a nap. "You're not going to any of these revival meetings, are you?"

"I'd love to hear Bishop Paul preach," Luke told his father. "I was cheated out of hearing him on St. Helena Island."

Martin's eyes filled with tears. "I don't want you going with them. With all the crazy stuff going on around here, I'm afraid you'll lose your head."

"I'm your son, Dad. My head is locked on good." Luke paused for a minute, summoning the nerve to ask his father a question. "Why don't you believe in God?"

Martin's face turned red. "Because I'm an educated, rational person. That's why."

"Relax, Dad. I didn't mean to make your blood pressure go up. It was a simple question."

"There's nothing wrong with my blood pressure," Martin stammered, a small artery in his temple throbbing at an unaccustomed beat.

"I have a reason for asking," Luke said, hoping he could continue the conversation without his father getting any angrier.

Martin's eyes narrowed. "Does this have anything to do with your grandfather? Theo tells me you found a book he wrote. He probably made up a bunch of fairy tales as phony as the Bible."

"I don't think they're fairy tales. I checked out some of the historical characters. All the facts he cites can be verified."

"I can't see what good can come of rummaging around in ancient family history."

Luke took a deep breath. "Did Grandpa teach you that there wasn't a God?"

Martin started fidgeting. "I didn't need anybody to tell me that. All you have to do is look around you to come to that conclusion. Everywhere you turn, you see the innocent suffering."

Luke didn't want to let go of the subject. "That's what I mean. When you talk about God, you get angry. Why so much emotion for a simple pragmatic matter based on evidence?"

"I'm not being emotional!" Martin raged, the artery pulsating wildly again.

Mariama came into the living room wearing a bright African dress and headpiece.

Edith smiled. "You look beautiful, my dear."

Mariama took Edith's arm. "I have a favor to ask. I'm singing this evening at the revival meeting. If I gave you the music, could you accompany me so I can get in some practice time?"

Edith looked down at her hands. "I haven't played for some time. You can see what arthritis has done to my fingers."

"I could pray for your hands," Mariama said.

Martin stalked out of the room. "That's it. I'm going to my study."

Theo called after him. "Have a nice nap in your chair, Baba."

"I will if they don't make a racket," he said and slammed the study door.

Theo encouraged her mother-in-law. "Since Paul and Mariama's church in New Haven prayed for me, I've been feeling a lot better."

More than Theo's sense of well-being had improved. Her speech had lost its tendency to slur when she was tired, and the tiny tremors around her nose had disappeared. Luke had watched her while she was sleeping. It was true—the tremors were gone.

"I'd like to play the piano again," Edith said.

The women moved to the family room and gathered around the Baldwin as Mariama opened her bag and pulled out a tambourine and a pair of wooden blocks. She handed the instruments to Theo and Johanna. "You can be part of the band for now."

Luke tried to concentrate on the manuscript, but the music was too alluring. He followed the sound of music to the family room and started clapping.

Martin poked his head out of his study door. "A man can't take a nap in his own house anymore." He hobbled into the family room.

"Father, look at my hands," Edith said, holding them out relaxed and straight.

Tears filled Martin's eyes. "Mother used to play for the Columbus Symphony Orchestra," he said. "I wish she could play that well again."

"She will, Pa Martin," Mariama said with certainty. "While you great men were off doing your important things, we humble women gathered around the piano and prayed for Ya Edith's hands. None of God's angels could play more gloriously than Ya Edith."

Martin looked to Theo, pleading for sanity.

"It's a miracle, Baba."

Martin looked to Luke for male consolation. "I've finally figured out women. When they want to bend you to their little schemes, they call you 'father' in their mother tongue."

At 6:45 p.m. Martin and Edith came into the living room dressed in formal attire. "You're going to the revival meetings?" Luke asked his father.

"I always go to Mother's opening nights." He turned to Bishop Paul. "Is this the hand-clapping, foot-stomping kind of music?"

✠

After breakfast the next morning, Martin kept his eye on the mail slot and raced to the door when the newspaper dropped through. "I saw the photographer take a picture of Mother. Here it is. Doesn't she look beautiful?"

The telephone rang and Edith picked it up. "It's Marta. She's calling from New York. She's there for a conference."

"I'd better talk to her," Theo said, taking a deep breath.

Luke mouthed the words, *Everything will be fine.*

Theo hung up the phone after two minutes. "She'll be here in a couple of days."

Twenty-Seven

M arta wound a wool scarf around her neck as she and Theo set out the front door. "Fifteen years as a conflict mediator, and I'm ready to call it quits. This conference at the Quaker UN is my last try."

Theo took Marta's gloved hand and steered her onto Corry Street in the direction of the Women's Garden. Although last night's snow was still on the ground, a bright sun warmed them. Despite her heavy winter clothes, Theo bounced along, still carrying the energy and optimism of the revival services in her step. "No one ever said conflict mediation was easy."

Marta spun around to face her companion. "No, but they never said it would be this hard. They said the conciliator stayed outside the passions that caused the conflict."

Theo laughed. "I've never seen you pass up a good passion."

Marta sighed and watched her breath turn to mist. "You're right. Not me. Besides which, without passion, life and work wouldn't be any fun."

They came to the garden that promised a better world for women. With the toe of her boot, Marta cleared snow from some of the stones in the walk, each revealing the name of a woman. Theo joined in, polishing stones with her toe until a woman's name caught the sparkle of the sun. "Do you remember coming here when we were students? We thought women could make a difference in the world."

Marta sighed, her foot falling away from the stones. "I used to think I could make a difference."

"And you'll feel that way again. When I was in London, you were all excited about the end of the war in Sierra Leone. Their war was coming to an end, and you saw a place for yourself in the peace process."

Marta looked up at the sky. New snow clouds were moving in, covering the sun. She shivered, and they started walking again. "This conference in New York is about child-soldiers in Sierra Leone. This is my last chance to make a difference."

For a few minutes the two women said nothing more. Theo thought about how dangerous it might be for Marta if she went to that terrible country where they hack off arms and legs. But Theo had something else on her mind as well. "Have you and Luke ever been lovers?"

Marta caught her breath and measured her words. "You're the only woman Luke has ever loved."

"That's not what I asked you."

Marta fidgeted. "We've never been lovers."

"How can I believe you?"

"Because it's the truth."

In search of an admission, Theo rephrased her question. "Are you in love with Luke?"

Marta started walking again, forcing Theo to catch up with her. Theo ran ahead of her and blocked her way. She wanted to see Marta's eyes as she spoke.

"I admit I had a crush on him when we were younger, but your husband never gave me the slightest encouragement."

"I wish I could believe that," Theo said, but she smiled to herself that Marta said "your husband" rather than "my cousin."

At the risk of agitating Theo, Marta decided to tell the truth. "The year that you and Luke were separated…"

Theo interrupted her. "The year he was in England?"

Marta nodded. "Yes, that's the year. I had a little too much to drink one night and made a pass at him." Marta stopped to watch Theo's reaction.

"And?"

"And he pushed me away—politely, of course, or at least as politely as a gentleman pushes away a lady who's had too much to drink. He told me then that he had never made love to anyone other than you. Even when you were separated—which you were at the time—he couldn't imagine being with another woman."

Theo nodded as if she believed the story. "It helps me to hear that. You could have told me that nothing ever happened and left out those details. But thanks for telling me."

Marta nodded, relieved that the story was out and nothing violent had happened.

Theo stretched back with her belly pushed forward and looked down at her bulging coat buttons.

"Pregnancy does funny things to a woman," Marta said.

Theo had to agree. "After a lifetime of keeping my abs flat and pouring myself into the smallest dress size I could manage, I'm buying maternity dresses before I need to. I want the whole world to know I'm pregnant." A movement of the baby interrupted her thoughts.

"Have you checked with Sir Nigel about your pregnancy?" Marta asked.

"I'm fine, Marta. Honest. It's nothing short of a miracle."

Suddenly the baby kicked again.

"May I feel?" Marta asked.

Theo took her hand and placed it where she had felt the kick.

"I'm jealous," Marta admitted.

A shadow fell over Theo's face as she looked across the Antioch campus lawn. Each time the two women tried to mend fences, another conflict erupted. The last time it cost Marta her long hair.

Finally Theo spoke. "A few months ago Luke and I met the black couple you saw at the house. They helped us keep our marriage together. Paul and Mariama didn't stay outside our conflict. They embraced our passions. If they had been only a neutral sounding board, I don't think Luke and I would still be married today. I don't even think I'd be alive."

"Blessed are the peacemakers," Marta answered.

"Maybe they—you—are more blessed than you know. Look at what war has done to my marriage. The conflict that started in Sarajevo isn't over yet."

They turned around and started walking back toward the house.

"Maybe the diagnosis was wrong," Marta said. "Maybe the symptoms were stress-related instead of ALS. Somewhere there's got to be a logical explanation."

Theo shrugged. "I don't need to explain it. I just need to be glad that it happened."

"Don't you *want* to understand it?"

"Mariama told me a story a lot like mine. Jesus healed a man everyone knew had been blind from birth. All the skeptics crowded around the man and demanded an explanation. I love what he said: 'All I know is once I was blind, but now I see.'" She grasped Marta's shoulder. "That's me, cuz."

"I remember that story. The disciples asked Jesus who sinned, the man or his parents, that he was born blind."

Theo nodded. "And Jesus said, 'Neither one.' The man's illness wasn't punishment for sin. His healing was to glorify God."

Marta shook her head. "Who would have believed any of this?"

Theo reached over and stroked Marta's short hair. "I'm so sorry."

"Me, too, ducky, but at least now I look like Princess Di. She looked plain till someone bobbed her hair."

Twenty-Eight

While the women were walking, Luke settled down in the family room with Giles's manuscript. He picked up Junior's story where he had left off.

I buried Solomon's song with my mother, but the story came to life again when I met my sweet Kate. O my dove, that art in the clefts of the rock, in the secret places of the stairs, let me see thy countenance, let me hear thy voice; for sweet is thy voice, and thy countenance is comely. *I would have stayed in those secret places forever had WWI, the "war to end all wars," not intervened.*

I signed up with the U.S. Marines and said farewell for boot camp on Parris Island. I was on leave one day with some of my buddies when I saw the road sign for St. Helena Island. I made my way to the island where my parents were born.

In a church graveyard, I saw the name Lucas Tayspill and words on the tombstone that marked his life. I found no one at the church that day and met no one on the road who knew anything about the man who rested under palmettos and live oak.

I went up the road to Penn School where a woman told me what she knew. She said that near the end of the Civil War, some white folk came from the North to teach the slaves set free. Some Yankee soldiers came to keep the Rebels away. Somehow, Lucas Tayspill, a man of peace, came with those soldiers. When Lucas died, he left a wife and children, she said. But she didn't know what became of them. Perhaps they went north.

They all hold swords, being expert in war: Every man hath his sword upon his thigh because of fear in the night. *The war carried me to foreign shores. I passed through the same poppy fields of Ypres that the Tayspills had abandoned centuries before.*

I've traveled the world in search of my father's story. I wanted to fill in the blanks. I charge you, O daughters of Jerusalem, if ye find my beloved, that ye tell him, that I am sick of love.

After the Great War, I went back to Hobart Corners and the tree the old Quaker had shown me so many years ago. Into its wood I carved the words I found on my grandfather's grave.

Edith pulled on a pair of gloves as she walked into the living room. "It's time to leave for the cemetery."

Martin turned to Luke. "Are you coming with us?"

"Sure. First, let me get a few things."

Luke set up a camp chair for his father in Glen Forest Cemetery so he could sit as he attended to his tasks. Martin asked Edith for some olive oil to fill the *kantili* on the Kannoudakis's graves.

"It's good to be remembered," Luke said as he swept snow off the markers.

"I can't get down on my knees anymore," Martin said as he bent over to light the flame. "Dimitrios wasn't very religious, but I know he'd really like this."

Martin crossed himself right to left. "What are you staring at?" he asked Luke. "It's part of the ritual. That's all it is."

Next to the ornate Greek tombstones, Grandpa Giles and Grandma Kate rested beneath simple markers. Martin reached into a canvas bag and pulled out roses they had bought at a florist on the way. As he trimmed the stems, he handed half the roses to Theo and Johanna, who placed the flowers in the holders on Eleni's and Dimitrios's graves.

"Father wouldn't want a *kantili*, would he?" Martin asked Luke.

"No, you're right. I don't think Grandpa Giles needs one." Then he asked, "Can I talk to you about Grandpa's book?"

Martin tried to stand up. "Mother!" he yelled.

When Luke tried to help him, Martin slapped his hand away and fell into the snow. When Edith reached down to help him, he swatted her away too.

Edith looked alarmed. "Father, what's happening to you? Are you having another stroke?"

Helpless as a baby, Martin floundered and wept. Theo knelt and put her arms around him. "Come, Baba. I'm making pastitio for supper."

He stroked her face. "La Bella Simonetta."

"And a nice Greek salad. Today I found a market with the best feta cheese in Ohio. If we get home early enough, I could braise a lamb shank."

Martin let Luke hoist him to a standing position but then broke away from his son and leaned on Theo.

"Would you like some rice pudding for dessert? Tomorrow I can make baklava." Martin was upright but shaky, so Theo continued. "Let's go home, Baba. A little chicken soup with egg drop and lemon."

As helpless as Luke felt, he agreed with Theo's prescription. He had nothing better to offer than Greek comfort foods. And no way to bridge the chasm between him and his father.

Twenty-Nine

A fter dinner Edith closed the kitchen door and whispered to Luke, "I need to talk to you about something very important."

Luke frowned. It wasn't like his mother to be conspiratorial. "Do you have a headache?"

"Yes, dear, but not for much longer. I'm leaving your father." Her eyes were dry.

Luke came to full attention. "What are you talking about? People your age don't do things like that!"

"They do all the time in the real world."

"What real world are you talking about? Daytime soap operas?"

"You don't know the real world of Antioch. It's not all faculty teas and poetry readings."

No, Luke thought. *Sometimes esteemed faculty members pump their father's portraits full of bullets.* "I admit Dad's not an easy person to live with, but why leave him now? Don't we have crises enough in this family?"

"I can't sleep in the same bed with Father any longer. He's built our marriage on deceit and lies."

Luke wanted to say, "Welcome to the club," but he didn't. He thought of all the mistresses and headaches his mother had suffered through when his father was younger. His mother wasn't a newcomer to deceit.

He put his arms around her shoulders and guided her to a kitchen chair. "This is your home. You can't just leave."

"All right. Then I'll kill myself."

He was glad he had removed all the guns from the house. "You won't kill yourself. That's not an answer. Tell me what created such a crisis right now."

"Mothers don't talk with their sons about things like this." She was sniffling.

"Sure you can tell me."

Her headache broke. She shook her head and straightened her shoulders. "I promised Father I wouldn't tell you."

Now Luke was thoroughly confused. "Let me get this straight. You want to leave Dad, but you can't tell me why because you won't break a promise to the man you want to leave."

"I swore I would never tell."

"A long time ago?"

She shook her head. "Tonight."

"So unswear."

"I can't." She sniffed again.

"If you don't tell me, I'm going to ask him."

"He won't tell you."

Luke was frustrated. "Does he know you want to leave him?"

His mother shook her head. "I couldn't tell that to a man in his medical condition."

"So you think walking out without telling him is good for his medical condition?"

Edith sniffed again. "I wish you had never found that manuscript."

"Is that what this is all about?"

Edith's demeanor changed completely. Her face brightened. "You're right, dear. It was silly of me."

"So you're not leaving?"

"Of course not."

"And you're not going to kill yourself?"

"No."

"Come on, Mom. Everybody else is already in bed."

As Luke and his mother walked into the living room, they heard Martin stomp down the hallway toward his study and sit down in his favorite chair. Edith straightened her skirt and rubbed her eyes dry. Then she followed her husband into his study and shut the door.

Theo came out of the bedroom, and Luke kissed her lightly on the cheek.

"I just found out the most remarkable thing," he told her. "We have the healthiest marriage in this family."

"Oh dear."

There was a fire in the fireplace and no one in the living room to attend it. "I think Dad is losing it," Luke said and went to put out the fire.

On the floor he saw his open briefcase with papers spilled out in disarray. In the center of the flames, he saw the corner of a black-and-white composition book and the frayed leather binding of the journal Cedric treasured.

Luke screamed and plunged his hand in to try to rescue Giles's manuscript. "How could he?" He withdrew a handful of ashes and collapsed on his knees.

Theo rushed to the kitchen for ice to soothe Luke's burned hand.

"This time he's gone too far," Luke said as he let her care for his hand.

"Talk to him. There's got to be an explanation."

"Right now all I want to do is wring his neck."

"He's your father, Luke. Someday you're going to have to find a way to forgive him."

"Not in this lifetime! First the painting; now this."

"Do you know how I would have felt if you had said that about me? Do you know how it is to feel unforgivable?"

"That's not the same. You love me."

"Baba loves you. He just doesn't know how to say it."

Luke struggled to his feet and headed for the front door. "I've got to get out of here. I can't stay here a minute longer."

Theo followed him, pulling him back into the house. "What are you saying?"

"I'm going back to New Haven with Marta and the Pinckneys tomorrow. Are you coming with us?"

"To do what? Watch you seethe with anger? You can save yourself this agony by talking it through with your father."

Luke pulled his hand away and turned to find Martin standing by the door.

"We need to talk," his father said and grabbed Luke's injured hand.

Luke tried to pull away but recoiled from the pain in his hand. "How dare you talk to me after what you've done!"

Martin flinched and turned to go back to his study, but Edith stood blocking his retreat. She pushed him into the living room so roughly that he almost lost his footing. "No more headaches," she told him. "I can't bear the pain. Tell him!"

The women left them. Father and son sat on opposite sides of the room, Martin rubbing his weak leg, and Luke nursing his burned hand.

"Your mother says she'll divorce me if I don't tell you the truth."

Luke scowled and looked at his hand. "When did you lie to me?"

"I never lied outright. I just failed to provide you with information."

"Why did you shoot at Grandpa's painting? Why did you burn his manuscript and Lucas's journal?"

Martin shifted in his chair. "I'm going to tell you a story, and I want you to wait till I finish it before you say anything."

"What makes you think I'll hang around to listen?"

"You will," Martin said, looking at his son for the first time. "You need to hear this. Especially now."

Moose needed someone to rub his itchy scar and hobbled over to Martin. At first Luke moved to pull the dog away from his shooter. But Moose rolled on his back, and the old man reached down and rubbed his belly. Muffin wandered off, leaving three male companions to contemplate their wounds.

"Your grandfather searched all his life for the truth about his father's murder. Then one day a lawyer named Harrison from down in Hobart

Corners called our house and asked for a Giles Tayspill. He was searching for your grandfather on behalf of his own ninety-four-year-old father.
I was a grown man at the time. Johanna was just a little tyke. But Father
treated me like a child.

"'You're coming with me to Hobart Corners,' he said. 'Whatever I
learn, you need to know too.'"

Luke closed his eyes and tried to resurrect Giles's voice as he listened
to his father narrate. He wished he could hear Giles tell him the story.

"When we got to the house, young Harrison was so glad to see us.
He ushered us into the sickroom to see his father. Old man Harrison
didn't pay any attention to me. He looked Father up and down. There
was an oxygen tank in the room, but the old man lit up a cigarette just
the same. I thought he brought us there to kill us. Then he said to Father,
'You don't look like a Nigra.' I thought he really meant to use the ruder
term.

"Father told him our family was Flemish.

"'Do your children pass too?' the old man said.

"Father told him there was a black man strung up with his daddy.
He must mean the other family.

"'Your name Giles Tayspill?' Harrison asked.

"Father said yes.

"Then the man looked him over again. 'Your hair is kinky, but
otherwise you couldn't tell.'

"I wanted to leave. I didn't know what this old man was talking
about, but Father kept his hand on my arm. He asked Harrison why he
went to so much trouble to find him.

"'Three boys hung your daddy and the other darky,' Harrison said.
'I was one of them. I'm dying now, and I want you to forgive me.'

"Father looked at him in disbelief.

"The old man started coughing and put out his cigarette. Then he
reached for his oxygen mask. Between puffs he said, 'In case you didn't
notice, I'm dying. I want to make things right with God.'

"I stood there in shock. Father said to him, 'You're saying my daddy was a black man?'

"Harrison laughed. 'Everybody knew that,' he said.

"Well, I didn't know that, and from the look on Father's face, he didn't know either."

Luke opened his mouth. "Don't interrupt me," Martin said. "Let me finish the story before you say anything.

"The man kept jabbering, 'I want you to forgive me.'

"Father said it wouldn't be easy, but he was willing to start trying. Then your grandfather started with God-talk. 'You need God's forgiveness far more than mine.'

"I had never heard him talk this way before. Harrison said he had already asked God, but he needed Father's forgiveness too. Father asked him about the family of the other victim. Harrison said he tried to find them but couldn't. Then Father wanted to know how Harrison found the Tayspills.

"He told us about an old Quaker who came to call on him almost sixty years before. The Quaker told him about a boy who came down from Yellow Springs asking about his daddy. Father remembered a day when an old Quaker took him to the hanging tree. He asked Harrison if the Quaker man had known all along who was responsible. The whole town knew, Harrison said, but there were no witnesses. No one could prove who was under the white hoods. Father wanted to know about the other murderers.

" 'Long since gone to meet their Maker—or the other one,' Harrison told him. 'Which leaves you. Are you gonna forgive me or what?'

"Father motioned to me that we were leaving but told Harrison that we'd be back. Young Harrison pleaded that his father wouldn't last very long. Then Father asked him if he knew the name of the other man they lynched. The name was Capers."

Luke couldn't keep silence any longer. He wanted to stop his father and tell him what he knew. There had been no reason for Martin to upset

Edith and burn the manuscript. Luke wanted to tell him about Cedric and Eula May. "Dad, I know."

Martin waved his hand, dismissing his son's interruption. "You don't know anything," he said. "Now let me continue."

Luke fell back in his chair, wishing his father were as interested in listening as he was in talking.

"The son gave us directions to a neighborhood on the other side of Hobart Corners. He asked us to hurry. Father told him to tell the old buzzard to hold on.

"We drove through streets where no white person was visible and pulled up to a convenience store. There were a couple of kids browsing through girlie magazines. 'My name's Tayspill,' Father told the proprietor. 'I'm looking for the Capers family.'

"The man told him, 'You look awful white for a Tayspill.' Father said Tayspills seem to come in many different shades. Then Father pulled his Social Security card out of his wallet and showed it to the man. Everyone in the store was staring at us. 'Watchu want wid Capers?' the man asked.

"Father said, 'My daddy and their daddy were lynched together.'

"The proprietor reached over the counter and shook Father's hand. 'I'm Magnus Capers. You daddy tried to save ma granpapa.'

"Father explained the reason for his visit and asked him to collect his children. We returned to Harrison's home with the Capers family, but Magnus was perturbed when he saw whose house it was. 'We're going to a hanging,' Father told him. 'We'll see what kind of thief Mr. Harrison wants to be.'

"Father told Capers that just like the two thieves who hung on either side of Jesus, old man Harrison had a choice to make. One crucified thief mocked. The other begged for mercy. Capers didn't want to go into the house. He told Father that Jesus and all his angels could deal with this devil. Capers asked him if he walked away, would old whitey go to hell. But he went in with us anyway.

"When Harrison's son saw the Capers family, he wasn't too happy. Father had this droll look on his face. 'Your father's prayers have been answered,' he said. 'I found the other family.'

"The son's jaw was agape, but he let us pass through the door. Father picked up the Capers's's baby girl and carried her into the dying man's bedroom.

"The dying man eyed them suspiciously. 'Here's your chance to make things right with God,' Father told him.

"Harrison said, 'Cute little monkey.'

"Father slammed his hand against the bedside table and sent the oxygen mask flying. 'Listen to me, you scum! If you think you can get into heaven by choosing which man's forgiveness to ask, you're the dumbest white man I ever met.'

"I stood against the wall watching this exchange. I had never seen Father so forceful with anyone. Suddenly Harrison started to gasp for air. His son tried to come to his rescue, but Father restrained him. 'Take her into your arms,' he told Harrison. 'Ask her forgiveness.'

"The dying man pulled away. 'Why she's a little pickaninny.'

"Then Father said, 'Inasmuch as you have done this to the least of these, my brethren, you have done it unto me.'

"The dying man pushed the baby away and said, 'I'd rather go to hell.'

"Father gave him back his oxygen mask. 'Enjoy breath as long as God gives it to you,' he told him. Then he gave the baby back to Magnus Capers. He nodded to me and said, 'We're finished here.'

"Mr. Harrison's son called after us. 'Wait!'

" 'Wait for what?' Father asked. As we walked away from the house, Harrison's son was weeping."

Martin paused in his storytelling to wipe his eyes. Luke said nothing and waited for him to pick up the thread and finish.

"When we got home to Yellow Springs, our little Johanna came crawling to the door to meet us. I remember thinking that my baby could have been born colored. I picked her up and examined every inch of her. This time we were lucky, I reckoned, but I was frightened what might come in the future."

Martin struggled to his feet, waving Luke away. He wanted no help. He hobbled over to the fireplace and resumed his story with his back to his son.

"I made a decision that day. I sent Mother and Johanna to visit relatives in Tennessee. While they were gone, I went to a doctor in Dayton and made sure I would never again father a child. Mother was anxious to have another baby and coaxed me to keep trying. Of course, she didn't know. When another child didn't come along, she assumed she had a fertility problem. I've never told her what I had done. She wanted another baby so bad she became melancholic. I felt so guilty that I couldn't touch your mother. I started to stay out all night. All the while, your grandfather kept giving me these looks as if he knew what I had done—I never told him either.

"One day I came home and heard laughter in the house for the first time in a few years. Mother was so happy. Your grandfather was there with her. In her arms was a little baby boy.

"'Whose baby is that?' I asked her.

"'He's our baby,' she said. 'Giles brought him to us.'

Martin turned to face Luke. "That, my son, is how you came into our family. Now you know what Mother and I were fighting about when she threatened to leave."

Luke stared at his father but didn't really see him. This time it was his own temple artery pounding. "You're telling me I'm not your son?"

"You are my son, even if not biologically. That day I learned about my own heritage, but Father refused to tell me anything about yours. 'Love him, not his ancestry,' he told me."

Martin made a move toward his son, but Luke stiffened.

"Luke, I can't tell you if you're African or Flemish or anything else. That was the way your grandfather wanted it. I am and always was your father. I love you with all my heart."

"You're a thief," Luke said. "You even took away my grandfather. You don't deserve to be his son."

Tears were pouring down Martin's face. "Can you ever forgive me?"

Luke stormed out of the room, heading for the front door. "You and Harrison are two of a kind."

"Luke!" his father called after him.

"It's too late, old man. I'm not your son anymore."

In the shadows of the hallway by his study, Martin Tayspill gazed into the faded looking glass and saw his father staring back. His eyes narrowed as he said, "Mind your own business, old man."

THIRTY

A s Luke drove back to the East Coast, he told Paul about his father's confession. "Maybe that's why Giles didn't finish my story."

The bishop shook his head. "It doesn't matter, Luke. Christ died so that there would be neither slave nor free, Jew nor Greek, African slave nor Flemish Huguenot. That's what your granddaddy tried to teach your father and that old Klansman. And your father seems to have learned that lesson." Paul paused for a moment. "What are you going to tell Cedric?"

Luke looked startled. "I hadn't even thought of him. I can't tell him the truth. He'd be so disappointed."

Paul smiled. "Do you remember what that boy said to you at the picnic? If you know Jesus, you are better than cousins. You are brothers."

"But I'm not Lucas Tayspill."

Paul shook his head again. "You are. Your granddaddy kept your past a mystery to free you from other people's biases. He left your future a mystery to free you from your own."

"I feel totally empty."

"You're not empty. You're a father-in-waiting. You have a baby on the way and a wife healed from everything that was destroying her from within."

"I'm dying within, Paul. Lucas Tayspill III is dying. And I don't need a plague-ridden, war-torn land to finish me off."

Marta leaned over the backseat, interrupting their conversation. "I've made up my mind," she said. "I'm going to Sierra Leone."

Luke almost hit the brakes. "And just when did you make that decision?"

"Just now. I've been thinking about the end of the war. Sierra Leone has planned a truth-and-reconciliation process. They'll need someone with experience to help with the child-soldiers."

Mariama was skeptical. "The Loma Accord sounds more like a

South African cookie cutter to me than a solution tailored to Sierra Leone. South Africa had Nelson Mandela and Desmond Tutu to stand behind what amounted to a spiritual resolution for what they thought was a secular problem. Who are Sierra Leone's larger-than-life heroes?"

Paul took up the train of thought. "All warfare is spiritual."

Luke was confused. "But I thought Sierra Leone's war wasn't about religion."

Paul shook his head. "A war doesn't have to be between two different religions to be spiritual. Christians, Muslims, and traditional peoples— they all believe in the powers of darkness."

Marta was having a hard time sitting still. "Michael Wilson is the man I met with in London. He would agree with Mariama. Like other Quakers, he believes in an inward light that overcomes the darkness."

"*Does* Sierra Leone have any larger-than-life heroes?" Luke asked.

Marta smiled. "If she doesn't, then we'll just have to be the heroes she needs."

"We?" the others asked in unison.

"Well, it would be nice to go with friends," Marta said. "As I said, Michael Wilson believes in an inward light that overcomes darkness."

Luke laughed. "What's he gonna do? Light a lamp and run home to England when the rebels say 'boo'?"

No one laughed with Luke, but he returned to his skeptical thoughts. "A long time ago some white men called Africa the Dark Continent. To my knowledge, no one since has argued with that label, although they might have split hairs over how dark it was."

"Sierra Leone plans elections in May," Marta said. "That's only a few months away. Everyone will participate, even the former rebels. The truth-and-reconciliation process guarantees even the rebels a right to field candidates for president and parliament."

Luke shook his head. "If you believe that one, cuz, you probably think Hezbollah is a charity that cares for the poor."

Marta interrupted him. "Wasn't there a democratic election in Sierra

Leone a few years back? I remember a wonderful motto: 'The future is in your hands.'" She turned to Mariama. "Don't you vote with your thumbprint in Sierra Leone?"

Tears welled up in Mariama's eyes. "During that election, the rebels swept through the country, hacking off arms and legs."

Paul leaned over the front seat and reached for his wife. "That's when Mariama's family was killed and her little brother disappeared."

Mariama wiped a tear away. "The rebels hacked off my father's arm and threw it at him. 'Give that to President Kabbah,' he said. 'Tell him that's your vote.' At the time, the president was in exile in Guinea. Most of the people of the Northern Province followed, and the rebels ruled our land."

"Oh, I'm so sorry!" Marta whispered as if she had said too much. However, she couldn't forget what she had heard. "Who will help those poor people?"

Mariama murmured, "'Whom shall I call, and who will go for me'?"

Paul saw determination replace the fear he always saw in his wife's eyes whenever she talked about Sierra Leone. "Here am I," he said.

This time Luke hit the brakes and pulled over to the side of the highway. "Send you where?" he asked Paul. "To Sierra Leone?"

"Home to Sierra Leone," Mariama said, and then she turned to Marta. "We're going with you."

Luke turned around to face Mariama. "You can't do that!"

Bishop Paul touched Luke's arm. "Docta Luke, surely there are people with AIDS dying there. Yale doesn't think it needs this pastor to pray with the dying or a nurse-midwife to shepherd those ladies. I bet in Sierra Leone they wouldn't turn us away."

Luke pleaded. "They'll die just the same, whether you go there or stay in America. I'll call the vice president of the hospital tomorrow. I'll tell him how desperately we need both you and Mariama on our staff. You just wait. I'll fix everything."

Paul got out of the car and started singing.

We have heard the Macedonian call today...

Mariama joined him and started to dance in the snow.

Send the light! Send the light!

Luke shook his head, wishing he could bring back the simple days when all he had to worry about was a crazy wife.

That night, home in bed, Luke was restless. He dialed Theo's cell phone.

"I miss you," she said when she heard his voice.

"I have to tell you what happened today."

Theo held her tongue as he told the strange tale of his ride back to New Haven. "You're not going with them, are you?"

Until that moment Luke hadn't admitted it to himself. "I have to, baby."

"No, Luke, you don't have to. Don't blame anyone else. This is your choice."

He closed his eyes as if that would turn off the conversation.

Theo responded to the silence. "Don't shut me out."

"I'll come back to Yellow Springs and fetch you," he said. "You and Moose will be happier in Connecticut."

"Oh, you know what will make me happy, do you?"

"That's not what I mean. I can't imagine what else Dad might try when the medicine wears off."

"I'm safe here," she complained. "I'm not the target of his frustration."

"But you saw what happened when Moose got in his way. You saw what happened with the painting..."

"You seem to need your grandfather more than you need me."

"The whole house in Yellow Springs reminds me of my grandfather!" he cried.

After a long silence, he heard Theo's voice. "So, you're going to Sierra Leone..." In the background Luke heard Moose moan softly in his sleep.

Part VI

Ef oona waak on snake an scorpion, dey ain't gwine hut oona.

—Luke 10:19, *De Good Nyews Bout Jedus Christ Wa Luke Write* (Gullah)

Thirty-One

Like a paratrooper preparing for his first jump, Luke began to sweat. Cramped in a Russian helicopter left over from the Afghanistan War, he scanned the distance from his seat to the door. Terror mixed with hope, but terror seemed to have the upper hand. Acid surged from his stomach to his mouth as he imagined young Russians jumping into thin air. Were they still party-line atheists when they reached for the rip cord, or did they cross themselves before they took their leap of faith? No one had offered Luke a parachute.

As the machine shuddered toward liftoff, Luke stared across the unsecured load of luggage that separated him from the passengers seated on the opposite bench. He wished his friends were there to take his mind off the helicopter trip. Bishop Paul could launch into one of his hypnotic sermons, or Mariama might line out a reassuring song. Even Marta's nervous energy would be a welcome distraction from current reality. Why, he wondered, had he allowed himself to be separated from his friends? That had been a serious blunder.

The engine whined and sputtered without promising success. Luke reached for his handkerchief, already soaked with sweat. He swiped at his brow, mixing red African dust with the brine that poured from his face. Would this be the defining moment that would spell the death of Lucas Tayspill III? The manuscript had never said how the third hero would arrive in his unnamed plague-ridden, war-torn land.

Luke had never imagined his arrival in Sierra Leone as a twenty-first-century event. When he pictured Lucas III, he conjured up a strapping younger version of himself, tanned and fit, leaning against the mast of an eighteenth-century schooner anchored in Freetown Harbor. A cool breeze would play with his sun-bleached hair and billow out the tall sails. Why did he think the breeze would be cool just because air was moving?

His wristwatch chimed the hour—midnight, three hours late for arrival. If his welcoming party was still waiting at the heliport, that would be the first thing on this trip that went right.

✠

Two days earlier, Luke and the Pinckneys had arrived at London's Gatwick Airport to find Marta sitting on her luggage. She wasn't smiling. She was on the verge of hysteria.

"Krio Airlines canceled our flight," she told them. "The plane is still sitting on the tarmac in Sierra Leone."

Luke had left all their traveling arrangements up to his usually efficient cousin. "Were you able to find us another flight?"

"Yes, but that airline doesn't fly out till tomorrow."

Deflated and exhausted, the quartet of would-be humanitarians went back to Marta's flat to rest, but no one slept. The next morning, burdened with the maximum load of allowable luggage, they were wearier than the night before.

At the Crescent Airways counter, they asked for seats together, but the ticket agent informed them the flight was overbooked. He handed Luke a boarding pass but asked the others to wait. They would have to take their luck as standbys.

Marta protested. "We all booked at the same time."

The agent fiddled with the keyboard of his computer but didn't look up at her. "You booked yesterday along with everyone else from Krio Air."

Luke handed back his ticket. "When is the next flight you can confirm all of us on together?"

The agent continued to look at the screen. "I can confirm three seats three days from now, but I can't confirm four seats for two weeks or more. Krio Air's problems are spilling over onto us. We were already fully booked. You'd be best off taking what I give you. Hopefully your friends will get on a flight by going standby."

"Maybe I should be the one to go on ahead," Marta said to her companions. "That way I can prepare for your arrival. I know the contact person who's meeting us, and I've been to Sierra Leone before."

The agent raised his head from his computer but looked past her at the long line of passengers. "If Mr. Tayspill gives up that seat, none of you will get on board. There are twenty-five people ahead of you on the wait list."

"That doesn't make sense," Marta muttered and took out her wallet.

Still without looking at her, the agent said, "Forget it."

Marta turned red and returned the intended bribe to her purse. She beckoned to the others to move away from the counter. "I'll think of something," she said.

At the entrance to the screening area, they waited for a miracle. When Crescent Airways called the flight, neither cancellations nor no-shows worked in their favor. Marta hadn't thought of another way to get on the flight. She squeezed Luke's hand and tried to be cheerful.

"Don't worry. Michael Wilson will be waiting for you at the helicopter terminal."

Luke's eyes widened. "Helicopter terminal?" That was the first he had heard about a chopper flight.

"That's how you get from Lungi Airport to Freetown proper. There's no land route. Just grab your baggage from the carousel and go through customs. Turn left when you walk through the door."

At the point of no return, Luke placed his carry-on bag on the conveyor belt and lifted his arms for an electronic pat-down. Then he nodded to his friends and resigned himself to traveling alone.

Not fortunate enough to get an aisle or window seat, Luke took his place between a brightly dressed African woman and an Arab-looking gentleman in western garb. He scolded himself for wondering if Crescent Airways did security checks on Arab passengers and tried not to look to his right. All the same, the man struck up a conversation.

"What takes you to Sierra Leone?"

Unwilling to encourage conversation, Luke stared at the magazine sitting in his lap as he answered. "Medical work."

The man smiled. "Are you a doctor? Our poor country needs all the help we can get."

Luke nodded and turned a magazine page. He wondered why an Arab called Sierra Leone his country. "Are you going to Freetown on business yourself?" he asked.

The man pulled out a business card. "Sierra Leone is my home and where I do business. My grandfather started a grocery chain in Sierra Leone many years ago." He handed the gilt-edged card to Luke. Three words were printed on it: *Farid Nassour, Merchant.* There was no address or telephone number.

Was Nassour a Lebanese name? Luke wondered. Hadn't he read somewhere that a Lebanese from Sierra Leone had founded Hezbollah? The idea did not cheer him. What kind of merchandise did Farid Nassour peddle?

"What are your plans in our country?" Again, Nassour used the possessive when talking about Sierra Leone.

"I'm an AIDS specialist," Luke answered as he put away his magazine. Nassour would give him no peace. "I'll be working with a Quaker relief organization in Freetown."

Nassour pulled out his wallet, extracting a thick wad of American bills. "A donation for your work, Doctor. Such a worthy cause."

Luke started to refuse but remembered the limited supplies he had been able to bring with him on the plane. "Thank you, Mr..."—he looked at the card—"Nassour. I can use this to buy medicines in Freetown." Luke turned the business card over to look for an address. The reverse side of the card was blank. "Do you have a mailing address?" he asked. "I want to make sure the organization acknowledges your gift."

Nassour shook his head. "Our postal service has not been in good working order since the war. A letter probably wouldn't get through. But I need no thanks other than knowing that you care about my people." Nassour took back the business card and wrote something on the reverse side. "This is my mobile number. If I can be of any help to you while you're in Freetown, please let me know."

Luke reached under the seat in front of him for his briefcase and brought it to his lap. As he fished for an envelope for the money and a piece of paper on which to write a receipt, Nassour pulled out a silver money clip. He clipped the money and business card together and dropped them into Luke's briefcase. "Please take this small token of my admiration for your mission to my tragic nation."

As the plane banked toward Lungi Airport, the two men shook hands. Luke stood for a moment on the steps leading off the plane, and a hot breeze slapped his face. After thirty seconds in Africa, he already felt washed out and dehydrated. Considering the events of the past few days, he wondered whether a sabbatical month in Sierra Leone was such a smart idea after all, especially traveling alone.

The horde of passengers bustled toward the carousel and then toward Mammy Yoko Airlines for the helicopter. Luke couldn't imagine all these passengers and their luggage on board one small helicopter. Since the flight from London had arrived so late, he wondered whether the helicopter was still waiting.

At baggage claim a porter loaded Luke's things on a cart and pushed it through customs toward the waiting helicopter. Luke followed the crowd in the same direction as his luggage. On the tarmac the hot breeze assaulted him again.

He had forgotten to save bottled water from the flight, but Marta had assured him that Michael Wilson would have water waiting for him.

Now he regretted that he didn't have even one small bottle to quench his thirst. Luke remembered the advice he had received at Yale's Travel Clinic: *Keep drinking! You have more to risk from dehydration than infection. If you wait for thirst or convenience, you'll end up with kidney stones.*

As he reached the tarmac, Luke saw the machine that would carry him to Michael and potable water. An MI-8 helicopter stood in front of him. A thin layer of black paint barely covered its former camouflage colors. Luke felt like an actor cast in an old war movie—on the losing side. What was it they called the planes that carried dead young Russians home from Afghanistan? *Black Tulips.* Too bad they hadn't painted this tulip white.

Farid Nassour, merchant and philanthropist, appeared at his side. "We're fortunate," he said in a calm voice. "We'll be on the first flight over."

"Are you sure that thing is safe?"

"The alternative is a ferry."

Luke remembered stories about ferries sinking into third-world waters. All of a sudden, the helicopter looked more appealing.

Nassour held out a large water bottle to him. "This water comes from a local spring. Very safe, I assure you."

Luke opened the 1.5-liter bottle and drained half its contents. "Thanks so much. I'm not sure I would have lasted till Freetown."

On board the chopper, Nassour smiled across the luggage and lifted his own water to toast Luke. The weary doctor tried to smile, but he had barely enough energy to nod. With his feet he used all his remaining strength to stabilize a large wobbly carton that threatened to fall into his lap.

When they landed, Luke tried to rush toward the exit, but his legs were shaking as badly as the helicopter. He ordered his feet to get moving and hurried toward his baggage. He wanted to find Michael Wilson as soon as possible. Ignoring a herd of porters, he pushed his luggage load out of the terminal into total darkness.

"They don't waste generators on outdoor lights." Nassour was at Luke's side again, reading Luke's mind. "The rebels destroyed the electrical grid for Freetown. Electricity wasn't very effective before the war anyway. Do you see your friend?"

In the darkness Luke strained to see a white British-looking face. "I can't see him or anyone else."

"Does he have a mobile phone?" Nassour asked as he pulled one out of his pocket. He offered it to Luke.

Luke checked the number Marta had given him and punched it in, but he got no answer. "I'm getting voice mail. That's very strange."

Nassour's driver appeared and carried his employer's luggage to a waiting Mercedes. "Do you know where you're staying in Freetown?" Nassour asked.

"Yes. I'll just catch a cab."

"You don't want to travel with any of these men waiting for naive westerners. My driver can drop you wherever you'd like."

If Luke had any reluctance, the second bottle of water Nassour's chauffeur held toward him overcame it. "I'm staying at Lumley Guest House."

"Excellent. That's on my way. Why don't you leave a message for your host and let him know I'm taking you to your guest house."

Luke didn't feel he had a choice, so he slid into the backseat of the air-conditioned Mercedes.

Nassour's driver passed potholes in the road the size of craters. Luke was glad he wasn't driving.

"Were the roads damaged during the war?"

"Many of these potholes were already there," Nassour told him. "I never drive here myself."

Without warning, a motorbike cut them off. Nassour's driver lurched and narrowly missed going off the road. "Dangerous pests!" Nassour complained.

Luke chuckled. "At home we call them 'donorcycles.' Sorry. That's medical humor. I know it sounds ghoulish, but most of the transplanted organs at my hospital come from motorcyclists."

"An apt phrase, I would say. Too bad we don't do organ transplants in our hospitals. We could contribute a significant number of kidneys and hearts."

As they drove along the beachfront, Luke peered out through tinted glass at strings of lights illuminating a hotel.

"The UN peacekeepers go to the bar at that hotel when they're off duty," Nassour said. "Since war came to Freetown, that's about all the business the hotel gets."

"Looks nice," Luke said, hoping Lumley Guest House would be equally well lit.

"American tourists stayed at that hotel until the rebels came. They used to love our beaches. Somehow a marine rescue has changed their idea of a vacation destination. Do you see this next hotel?" They were passing another appealing string of lights. "A special-ops force landed a helicopter on that roof and rescued a thousand stranded Western expats. An American warship was waiting out at sea to carry the lucky ones home."

Remembering the helicopter ride from Lungi, Luke turned away from the bright lights on the beachfront. Maybe in Sierra Leone it doesn't pay to keep your lights on at night.

Lumley Guest House had no lighting at all. Nassour's driver honked at a corrugated tin gate, rousting a security guard from slumber. As the Mercedes passed into the courtyard, its headlights fell on a Land Rover with two logos on its side. One was for UNICEF, and the other noted the vehicle's loan to "Friends for Freetown."

As the driver unloaded Luke's luggage, Nassour spoke to the guard in a rapid-fire brand of English Luke now recognized as Krio.

"This fellow says Mr. Wilson went out on his motorbike in the middle of the afternoon. He heard him tell his driver he'd be back by 7:00 p.m., but he never returned. His driver thought he might have made other plans to pick you up, so he didn't go to the heliport."

"May I speak to the driver?"

After another exchange in Krio, Nassour explained that the driver was in bed. Luke could speak with him at breakfast if he wished.

The security guard and Nassour's driver carried Luke's baggage to a room with two beds that he appeared to be sharing with the missing Michael Wilson. Luke looked from his roommate's net-covered bed to the one he would be taking. Pointing to a motionless fan positioned over his bed, he asked, "Does that thing work?" He had already sweat out as much water as he had drunk since they left the airport.

Nassour flipped a switch on the wall, and the fan limped into lazy action. "They'll probably turn off the generator in the middle of the night," he warned. "You had best get to bed as soon as you can."

"I can pay them extra to leave the generator on."

"I wish things were that simple," Nassour answered, motioning his driver to climb up on Luke's bed. "Hand him your mosquito net so he can fasten it for you."

Before he undressed, Luke separated Nassour's business card from the money clip of hundred dollar bills. Who knew when he might need him?

Within the confines of the mosquito netting, he waited for the generator propelling the small fan to go off and for Michael Wilson to return. Sometime during the early morning, he fell asleep. In his dream he jumped into his parents' fireplace after Giles's manuscript.

It was not yet light when he awoke abruptly and sat up in bed. The bed next to him remained empty. Reaching out of his mosquito net, he pulled over the satellite phone Theo had given him as a going-away gift. Before he went to bed, he had plugged it in for recharging. He calculated the time difference—5:00 a.m. Freetown time was 10:00 p.m. in Yellow Springs.

No light came on when he flipped open the lid. With the generator off, the phone had not recharged. Luke lay back in bed and stared up at the mosquito net until dawn.

THIRTY-TWO

A table in the breakfast room was set for four people, but no serving staff was in view when Luke walked in. Paper napkins covered open dishes of sugar and butter and a breakfast roll on each plate. Luke lifted a roll and smeared it with marmalade but left it on his plate uneaten. He had no appetite. Ants moved in on his rejected portion of bread as he poured hot water from a carafe to make himself a cup of tea. Through the open door, he watched a man place something inside the UNICEF vehicle. The man was slim and sinewy, like one of those African runners who always win the Boston Marathon. Assuming the man was Michael Wilson's driver, Luke rose to greet him as he came into the restaurant.

"How de body?" Luke said, extending his hand.

The man flashed a wide white smile and offered his hand in return. "De body fine, I tank God. Are you the American doctor Michael's expecting? I'm surprised you speak Krio."

Luke shook his head. "You just heard all the Krio I know. Are you Michael Wilson's driver?"

The man shook his head. "My name is Brima. I'm a nurse working out of Michael's office while I'm in Freetown."

Another African arrived and greeted the nurse. The driver perhaps? The two Africans spoke in Krio, but Luke didn't need a translation. They spoke in hushed tones and shook their heads. More than once Luke heard the name of the missing Michael Wilson.

"It's not like Michael to disappear," Brima said in English. "For safety's sake, he set up a buddy system. We don't go anywhere without informing our partner."

"Who is Michael's buddy?" Luke asked.

"I am," Brima answered. "He never said a thing to me about going into town yesterday afternoon. I knew he was planning to pick you up at the heliport, but I never heard about a change in plans."

A waiter came over with a carton of bottled water. Brima placed two large bottles in front of Luke. "Drink at least three liters a day. Use this rather than tap water to brush your teeth."

"Shall we go to the office? Maybe Michael's there," Luke asked, rising from the table. "I'm anxious to get started."

Brima nodded. "What medical supplies did you bring with you?"

"I brought anti-retroviral drugs," Luke said, then he remembered the silver money clip in his briefcase. "I've got cash for generic drugs we can purchase here."

As Brima helped Luke load cartons of medications into the Jeep, he read the labels. "How are you going to decide which AIDS patients to treat?"

Luke frowned. "We don't have enough drugs for all those who are infected, but if we focus on pregnant women, we have hope of saving the next generation."

Brima grunted. "I've read about that. What do you propose to do after the baby is born?"

"The mothers can't breast-feed, of course. Breast milk transmits the virus."

"What alternative do you recommend for nutrition?" Brima lifted a bottle of water and took a swig.

Luke shrugged. "The pediatricians will have to solve that problem. I only treat adults."

"In Sierra Leone a doctor is a doctor. Sometimes a nurse is a doctor. We have to deal with what we find on our plate."

Luke's shoulders sank. "I hope that problem will be on someone else's plate. Other members of my team are coming on a later flight. Mariama, our midwife, was born in Sierra Leone. She can counsel the mothers."

Brima continued loading the cartons. "Do you know what happens in the bush when a mother doesn't nurse her *pikin?*"

Luke had seen the same pictures of starving babies as everyone else— the West's five minutes of Africa before they change the channel. "Maybe we can get someone to donate powdered formula for those infants."

"And a supply of bottled water?" Brima asked as he watched Luke take another long drink. "Most of the villages upcountry don't have a safe water supply. The rebels have destroyed our country."

"I hadn't thought of that, but formula also comes reconstituted."

"And needs refrigeration once opened."

This time Luke said nothing, but Brima wasn't finished with him yet. "Even if you provide formula, safe water, or refrigeration, by doing so you mark these women in their villages as infected with the virus. Their neighbors would wonder how they got access to these scarce supplies."

Luke looked defeated. Did the third Lucas come to Africa to die of humiliation?

Brima continued. "AIDS is more than a viral infection, and Africa is more than a challenge." Before they left for the office, he led the way back to Luke and Michael's room. "I'm looking for anything that might tell us where Michael might be."

"Maybe he has a girlfriend. Maybe he doesn't want to be found."

The nurse shot Luke a look but held his tongue. "Let's see if he's at the office."

Before leaving, Luke took the money clip out of his briefcase and slipped it into his pants pocket. Meanwhile, Brima returned to the restaurant, picked up the bread Luke had discarded, and covered it with a paper napkin.

Wilson was not at the office. Brima took a cell phone out of his pocket and punched a speed-dial number. Instead of Michael, the voice mail picked up. As Brima sent the driver off with instructions, Luke saw the worried looks on their faces.

"Do you have a photocopy of your passport?" Brima asked. "We should keep one in the office on file, just in case."

"In case of what?"

He shrugged. "You never know."

As Brima put the passport copy in a desk drawer, he pulled out a similar-looking paper. "I need to run some errands in town, but I don't want to leave you here alone. Until we find Michael, I'm your buddy."

"Fine with me." However, Luke knew things were not fine. He wished Brima would smile again, the way he had at their first meeting.

"You can ride on the back of my motorbike." Brima said.

"Do you have an extra helmet?"

Brima laughed. "I can't even afford one for myself, Doctor. Besides which, you need to be able to hear to drive safely in these streets. Hop on."

Luke thought about the Russian paratroopers jumping to their date with destiny.

Brima shouted over the traffic. "When we get off the bike, stick close to me."

They wove through rows of cars that couldn't move in the thick Freetown traffic. As they passed bombed-out buildings and faded colonial facades, Luke watched children duck through the vehicular chaos, hawking their goods. A teenage girl passed by with a tray of pared grapefruit on her head. The white globes, devoid of the outer skin, looked tempting, but Luke would have to be very hungry before he ate anything he hadn't washed and peeled himself. A small boy peddled terry-cloth towels for sweaty foreheads. Luke wanted to stop to buy one, but he didn't want to distract Brima from steering through an intersection without traffic lights or police officers.

As they came toward the center of town, Brima pointed to a large tree. "That's our famous landmark, the Cotton Tree. In the old days, lepers came here to beg." As they passed the tree, hundreds of bats fluttered up into the air. Beneath the tree, hundreds of men with missing limbs stood or lay down in the shade.

"Can you reach into my sack?" Brima asked. "Take out the bread."

Luke pulled out his discarded breakfast roll. "Now what?"

The nurse slowed down and came close to a group of amputees. "Toss it to one of them."

Luke chose a man sitting in a wheelchair with two bandaged legs and missing feet. He heard Brima shout something in Krio and saw the men smile. As they pulled away, the nurse said, "The amputees are our new lepers."

Luke didn't know much about what had happened since the end of the war. "Did they jail the rebels?"

From the rear of the bike, he couldn't see if the nurse had frowned, but holding on to Brima's waist, he felt his muscles tense. "The war ended with an amnesty. Only a few top leaders were thrown in jail. The rest were sent home."

"That doesn't make sense."

"The UN feared another ten years of war."

Luke wanted to ask personal questions, such as "What happened to you during the war?" and "What about your family?" Instead, he fell silent.

Brima pulled up at a police station and parked the Honda. "Stick close to me. Pickpockets move in fast on a white man."

At the front desk Brima pulled out a copy of Michael's passport and pointed to the picture of a serious-looking, young white man. The desk sergeant shook his head. For a moment Brima stood there, contemplating his next move. Then he took Luke's elbow and guided him out of the station.

Zigzagging on foot through the marketplace, past corrugated roofs with laundry laid out to dry, Luke stuck as close to the nurse as he could. When they came to a courtyard of tin-roofed stalls, Brima took a sharp turn into the dimly lit enclosure. He spoke in rapid-fire Krio to a man peddling carved figurines. Just as quickly he darted back out into the bright midday sun.

"Do you mind telling me what our plan is?" Luke asked.

"Our plan is to find Michael," Brima answered, failing to add specifics.

Luke was concentrating so hard to hear the answer that he didn't see a man coming straight toward him.

"Watch out!" Brima yelled at Luke and said something less friendly in Krio to the man. "Do you have your money and passport in a safe place?" he asked as Luke recovered his footing. Luke patted the body wallet secured to his waist under his shirt and smiled.

Luke and Brima returned to the office of Friends for Freetown, where two women had prepared a midday meal for the staff. Brima loaded his plate with a tall mound of rice and spooned over it a sauce of greens with specks of white and orange. Luke tentatively placed a small portion of rice on his plate and a few tablespoons of sauce.

"Better eat up, Doctor. This rice chop is our main meal of the day."

Luke looked at Brima's plate. "It looks like you haven't eaten in a week."

Brima's face grew solemn. "There were times like that during the war."

Luke fell silent again. Not knowing what to say had become a common phenomenon for him. He played with his food and picked out what looked like a malnourished baby carrot. As Luke popped it into his mouth, Brima's eyes opened wide.

As the innocent-looking vegetable hit Luke's tongue, Brima asked, "Do you like your peppers hot?"

Luke's mouth was on fire. As he grabbed his water bottle, his eyes filled with tears, and his nose started to run.

"They're good for you," Brima added. "Keeps down the intestinal-parasite load."

Luke shook his head and blew his nose. "I think I'd rather take a dose of Vermox."

Brima shrugged his shoulders and reached over to Luke's plate to fish for more of these little beauties. He popped one into his mouth to savor the experience and left it on his tongue for a while.

"Your palate must be as hardened as your feet," Luke said, wiping his nose and eyes.

Brima grinned. "We've had different life experiences, my friend. Mine have prepared me for survival."

Luke looked at the man across from him, whose shining ebony skin required no protective sunscreen. His hair was close cropped rather than fashioned into dreadlocks or the Afro that had been so popular with African Americans during the seventies. No louse could gain a foothold on Brima's scalp. Luke tried to laugh. "How many white men have you buried?"

Brima's face grew dark. "In the colonial era Sierra Leone was called the White Man's Grave, but they forgot to count all the black bodies. Half of our children die before the age of six months. We have the highest maternal mortality rate in the world. And that was before the war and before HIV/AIDS."

Luke fell silent. He resisted the temptation to turn his thoughts toward home and all the worried-well who crowd the clinics of Yale Faculty Practice. He looked across the courtyard and saw a huddled group of women. He saw nothing poor in their spirits. They dressed in colorful West African *lappas,* with babies nestled in the small of their backs or fixed to a breast.

Brima followed Luke's gaze. "Friends for Freetown's microcredit ladies," he said. "The organization loans them small amounts of money to start a business, and they pay back Friends for Freetown out of their earnings."

Luke smiled. "Neat. Cottage industry." He looked around the court-yard. "Where are the men?"

Brima returned his attention to his plate. "Men aren't as conscien-tious about paying back money. Friends for Freetown only loans to women. The better the organization's payback, the more people we can help."

Luke looked back at Brima. "I've got a lot to learn about Africa."

The nurse flashed the wide smile Luke was learning to treasure. "As I would in America."

"Have you ever been to the States?" Luke asked.

Brima shook his head. "I've only been out of the country once, and that was to Guinea."

Luke drew a mental map, locating Guinea to the north of Sierra Leone. "Is Guinea a vacation destination for Sierra Leoneans?"

Brima laughed but didn't smile. "Hardly."

The driver from Friends for Freetown pulled up in the courtyard and searched until he found Brima. From the look on his face, Luke knew he had news about Michael.

Brima listened and then sprang up from his chair. "Come on!" he yelled to Luke as he ran to the Jeep.

THIRTY-THREE

It never gets easier, Luke thought as he followed Brima through a hospital maze. He had spent his adult life walking such corridors, but none as cluttered as those of Lumley General. When they reached the door of the intensive-care unit, he took a deep breath.

No doctor or nurse hovered at Michael's Wilson's bed. They were attending other patients who had a chance of survival. Brima crouched by Michael's bed—even chairs were in short supply. Luke watched the nurse pray, with eyes closed and silently moving lips. *How do they handle futile cases in Africa?* Luke wondered. *Does it take a village to pull a plug?*

Another nurse came and detached the ventilator from a tube in Michael Wilson's mouth. Before rolling the machine to another patient, she and Brima conversed in Krio. Luke waited for an agonal gasp, but Wilson was silent as the rest of his body caught up with his dead brain. Brima eased away the adhesive tape and removed the tube from his friend's mouth. After a moment he pulled the sheet over the dead man's face and began to walk away. Luke hurried to catch up with the nurse.

"Why did you come to Africa, Doctor?" Brima asked without turning toward him.

"Please call me Luke," he said, avoiding the question.

"Why did you come to Africa, Dr. Luke?" Brima asked, splitting the difference but maintaining the formality. The nurse stopped walking. He wasn't smiling.

"It's a long story. I want to help."

"How do you think you can help us?" The answer wasn't apparent to Brima.

"AIDS patients live longer every day at Yale. I want to share what I know with your people."

Brima started walking again. "How do you plan to accomplish that?"

As if the events of the day were not depressing enough, now Luke felt that his motivation was in question. Nevertheless, Brima had put his finger on a problem. Luke didn't have a plan. Somehow he thought if he came to Sierra Leone with bushels of medicine, the plan would make itself. He hurried to catch up with the nurse. "I honestly don't know."

Brima nodded as if he had heard the answer he sought. In a softer tone, he asked, "Why didn't you come before?"

Before what? Luke wondered. *Before AIDS swept over Africa? Before Giles's manuscript changed his life?* "What do you mean?" he asked, running to catch up with Brima. "Why should I have come before?"

He watched the tension around Brima's face dissolve to sadness and melt into a gentle smile. "I had hoped you came to Sierra Leone not because of what you had to offer but because you love us."

Brima walked out into the dark night as Luke stood with his mouth agape.

They rode back to the guest house in silence. As he turned off the ignition, Brima turned to Luke. "Michael's family has made arrangements with the embassy for his body to be shipped back to England. Would you like to go with me to the airport tomorrow night?"

Luke nodded.

"Actually, you have to go. I'm not leaving you alone."

The next morning there was more news waiting for them at the Friends for Freetown office. Krio Airlines was flying again. The rest of Luke's team would arrive that night on the plane that would turn around and carry Michael Wilson home.

A British embassy van doubling as a hearse sat at the pier waiting for the ferry to Lungi. Luke climbed out of the Land Rover to get some fresh air. Soon he was swatting at mosquitoes and cursing himself for forgetting his DEET cream.

"I'm going upcountry later this week," Brima told him. "For the last month I've been making plans for mobile clinics in villages that haven't seen a doctor since the start of the war. Would you like to join me?"

Luke brightened. "It may not be what I had in mind, but I'm willing, if my friends can come with us."

Brima nodded. "What do you know about malaria, leprosy, onchocerciasis, typhoid fever, elephantiasis, whipworm, schistosomiasis, and amebic dysentery?"

"I know what they look like in the textbooks, but I can't say I've ever treated a case."

Brima was smiling again. "I'll give you a chance to correct that deficiency."

This trip, thought Luke, was either going to be an infectious-disease specialist's fondest dream—or his worst nightmare. At least he had a plan worth taking a ferry ride with a corpse.

When his friends got off the plane, they looked as tired as Luke when he had arrived. Before they had a chance to adapt to the heat, he told them about Michael Wilson. Wordlessly they rode to Lumley Guest House in the darkness. Brima, seated next to Bishop Paul, broke the silence. "Why did you come to Africa, Pastor?"

For the first time since Luke met him, Bishop Paul Pinckney was outranked. The title of "pastor" seemed to be a demotion from "bishop," but Paul answered in his usual confident manner. "God called me here a long time ago."

"What did God call you to do?" Brima asked in a neutral tone.

"Come over and help," Paul said as if his Macedonian call was self-explanatory.

Brima had recently heard the answer to the same question couched in medical rather than theological terms. "How are you going to help?"

Brima's tenor was casual and conversational, but Luke knew he wanted to hear a plan.

"I'm going to pray with Docta Luke's patients," Paul answered, this time with a tinge of defensiveness in his voice.

"I see. You pray for his AIDS patients in America?"

Sensing a trap, Luke leaped to Paul's rescue. "Every doctor needs someone like Bishop Paul. Our AIDS ward became a different place when he joined our team."

"You've seen many patients with AIDS miraculously healed at Yale?" Brima asked them both.

Paul shook his head. Luke wished he hadn't jumped into the conversation. Brima didn't drop the subject.

"Tell me about one AIDS patient healed by your prayers."

Paul shook his head again but added, "That won't stop me from praying."

Brima smiled at Paul. "I'm glad you're here. We have many pastors here who serve the same Jesus you do, but they don't know as much about medicine as a hospital chaplain. I hereby appoint you our team pharmacist."

Paul's eyes widened as if he didn't know what had just hit him.

Brima looked in the rearview mirror to catch Marta's eyes. "You're going to be our triage officer." Before Marta had a chance to react, he moved on to Mariama. "You're in charge of belly ladies and *pikins.*"

At least, Luke thought, Mariama's assignment made sense. "Dare I ask my assignment?"

Brima smiled. "You and I will be treating around five hundred patients a day."

It could be worse, Luke thought. *Brima could leave me in the bush to see all those patients alone.*

"What kind of lab facilities will we have?"

"None. We don't have electricity to power a microscope. We'll bring a small generator with us, but we have to save it for important things."

Luke wondered what could be more important than a correct diagnosis. "If we can't diagnose or we don't have the drugs to treat what we diagnose, what then?"

"You can remove the word *if* from your vocabulary," Brima answered, "and the words *can't* and *don't*. Those words won't get you very far in Sierra Leone. You'll learn how to diagnose and treat anemia without knowing how low the hemoglobin is or what shape the red cells have taken. You'll diagnose worms from looking in large slop buckets rather than sending small samples to the lab."

"You run clinics like this all the time. Why do you need me?"

Brima grinned. "You're my continuing-education program. I may know *what,* but you know *why.*"

"I may know *why,* but you know *how.* I don't want you out of my sight."

"I said you're my buddy."

Paul stared straight ahead into Africa's darkness, thinking about the responsibility foisted upon him. For many years he had heard doctors talk about their solemn oath: *Above all, do no harm.* That sounded like great advice for a bush pharmacist, too. As he mopped his brow, Paul heard another voice in his heart—*Come over and help us.* Help us, the voice said, not harm us.

"Don't worry, Bishop Paul," Brima said, guessing his thoughts. "As soon as we get upcountry, I'll show you the system. You're going to be a big help." Luke noted the friendly tone that accompanied the ecclesiastical promotion.

"Where exactly upcountry are we going?" Marta asked.

"Near my home," Mariama whispered. "Near the diamond mines and my family's graves."

"We'll start in a village called Lonko," Brima told them.

Marta brightened. "That's where the Whitlocks said they'd be working. I met them in New York at the Quaker UN. There should be former child-soldiers in that region. It sounds like a great place to make our base."

"The children of war aren't the type of little boys you cuddle on your lap and read a bedtime story," Brima said. "These *pikins* saw their parents slain. The rebels doped them up and trained them to murder. Then they sent the boys back to their own villages to mutilate and rape."

Mariama's face darkened. "Those devils knew the West doesn't care about Africa."

"We're here because we care," Luke said. Then he remembered Brima's words: *Why didn't you come before?*

"These boys are in great need," Marta said. She tried to sound positive, but she ended up sounding melodramatic.

As they pulled up to Lumley Guest House, Brima honked the horn for the night guard to open the gate. "Tomorrow morning we'll pack the Land Rover and buy additional supplies."

Suddenly Luke remembered the gift of money from Farid Nassour. He reached in his pocket to pull out the money clip. Then he remembered the face of the man who jostled him in the marketplace.

At Lumley General Hospital the morgue attendant who had released Michael Wilson's body placed another corpse on the slab. Frothy blood covered the tattered shirt. The attendant reached for a mask, knowing what tuberculosis looked like at the end. He copied the number from the toe tag onto the plastic sack that held the dead man's effects. Opening the bag he found a silver money clip holding a wad of American bills. When the dead man's relatives came to claim his body, would they know what had been in his pockets? The man was an amputee, a beggar from upcountry. His relatives were probably dead. Now a plague of the earlier centuries had caught up with him. The attendant looked around to make certain he was alone, and then he pocketed the silver clip and cash.

Thirty-Four

The Quaker Whitlocks had traveled from North Dakota to dig wells in Sierra Leone. Philip and Constance also planned to model peace, which proved to be the easier of the goals they had set for themselves. Philip's first well in the village of Lonko wasn't finished yet, so Constance walked two miles to a river every day and carried water back on her head. During her first month in Lonko, she dropped as much water as she safely brought home. Three little Whitlocks had come with them to the bush, two boys and a girl. Moses, Aaron, and Miriam loved to climb mango trees with the village children. Black and white *pikins* were scooting down a tree together as Luke and the team arrived.

"Snake! Snake! Snake!" the children shrieked in unison.

Constance put down her water jug and stepped into a hut. She returned with a shotgun as calmly as if the children had asked her for milk and cookies. *Cutchoom! Cutchoom!* Two green mambas fell to the ground. Luke stepped out of the Jeep into a heap of green coils.

"You've got to get both of them," Constance explained. "If you get just one, its mate will be very mad. You don't want to meet a mad mamba."

As Luke watched the disposal of the reptilian corpses, the oldest Whitlock boy came over to greet him.

"You got any kids?" Moses asked as if snake slaying was a lackluster daily event.

Luke shook his head. "Not yet," he said with his eyes fixed on the motionless mambas. "But my wife and I have a baby on the way."

Six-year-old Miriam tugged at Luke's hand. "Too bad your baby's not born yet. It's so much fun living in Sierra Leone."

Luke stooped down to the child's level. "You're not afraid of snakes?"

Her mother answered for her. "We didn't come to Africa to live in fear."

"I didn't know Quakers toted guns," Luke said, returning to adult height to shake Constance's hand.

"I'm a mother," she answered, keeping a grip on Luke's hand longer than the protocol of courtesy required.

He shook his head. "I think I can understand a Quaker with a sawed-off shotgun. What I can't understand is a mother allowing her children to climb in trees with deadly serpents."

"We came to Africa to bear witness to the love of Christ."

Luke's eyes narrowed. "I'm sorry, but I don't understand that kind of love."

As he turned away from Constance, Luke saw Brima listening to them with the same sad smile he had on his face at the hospital. What was it Brima had said to him? "I had hoped you came to Sierra Leone not because of what you had to offer but because you love us."

As the little Whitlocks raced off with their African pals, Constance smiled after them. "These children love each other in the same unconditional way Papa God cares for us."

"I couldn't imagine putting my child in harm's way."

"Papa God put his only *pikin* in harm's way for the sake of the world."

Luke wasn't prepared for Jesus-talk. "What kind of papa is that?"

"A loving Papa," she answered as Paul poured his frame out of the Land Rover and saved Luke from further theological debate.

The bishop smiled. "Hooey, this place reminds me of home."

"Except for the snakes," Luke answered, mopping his brow.

"No, son, *because* of the snakes. South Carolina has more varieties of poisonous snakes than anywhere else in America." Paul pulled on a green vine tangled in the mango tree. "See this here liana? We have this in the low country. Didn't you see it in the old church graveyard on St. Helena?"

Luke had seen the vine growing over Lucas Tayspill's gravestone and on the trees down by the old dock.

"If you see liana, you watch out for belly crawlers," Paul said as he picked up his luggage.

Luke grabbed his own suitcases. "I'm glad you didn't tell me that when we were on the island. That was one of the happiest weeks of my life."

"I was watching out for you, son. If you had focused on snakes, you might not have noticed the people."

Luke bent over to fit through the entrance of a hut with a thatched roof. Brima came up behind him and directed him into to an unfurnished common room with a dirt floor and an open window frame.

"Don't they use screens on their windows?" Luke asked.

Brima shook his head. "Even if they could afford it—which they can't—the metal mesh would cut down on the breeze." He reached up and tapped on a bamboo crossbeam near the roof. "As good a place as any to hang your mosquito net." Brima tossed a rattan mat to Luke. "Your bed."

On the other side of the common room, Mariama was hanging a curtain to separate their sleeping quarters. Suddenly Luke felt very much alone. He envied Paul for having his wife with him. With a wife, the rustic sleeping arrangements might even be romantic. Longing to hear Theo's voice, he went outside and set up the generator to juice up his satellite phone. Longing for an intimate moment, he hadn't counted on attracting a crowd. Curious children surrounded him.

Brima poked his head out the window and grinned. "They don't understand English."

"But you do," Luke said, moving the sat phone farther away from the hut.

"We made it to the bush," he told Theo. "How's my baby?"

"Which one of us?" she asked.

"Both of you."

"The baby-baby is kicking hello to Daddy right now. I just got a powerful belly whupping."

Luke laughed. "Know what they call a pregnant woman here?"

"A belly lady. I've heard Mariama use the term at Yale. Meet any snakes yet?"

He decided not to tell her about his first reptilian escapade.

"Love you," he said as his old life faded to silence.

Luke wanted to sleep, but he thought he'd better study for a while. He took his mat out of the hut and sat against the building to read. He set a kerosene lamp beside him and focused on a chapter about snakebite in his tropical medicine handbook. Paging through, he committed the pictures to memory. If he ever met one of these uglies again, he wanted to know its name, rank, and serial number. Armed with facts, he could construct a treatment plan. Suddenly he jumped up and grabbed his mat and textbook. Seated on the ground, he might meet one sooner than he had planned. He returned to the stifling hut and sat against the wall of his room.

In his journal Luke made columns to chart Sierra Leone's poisonous snakes. *Bad news,* he wrote. *Day number one as bush doctor, I saw a green mamba. Good news: No mamba bite. More bad news: No antivenom with us. Worst news of all: No antivenom available anywhere in the world for one kind of local viper.*

Luke tried to fall asleep. After ten years of sleeping with a war survivor, he had reservations about sharing digs with Brima. He wondered if an African man would have nightmares and suffer from post-traumatic stress disorder. He put his mixed feelings on hold and asked, "May I help you put up your mosquito net?"

Brima shook his head and stretched out his own pallet. "Nets are for women and *pikins*—and white visitors. Not all of us have the same risk of malaria."

Or have to sweat under a net, Luke thought as he lay awake.

In the night he listened to villagers passing by on the path outside the hut. They were striking walking sticks hard on the ground.

"Why are they doing that?" he whispered to Brima. It sounded the way Gullahs stomp in a ring shout, but the local natives weren't moving in circles.

"They're warning the snake that a mortalman be passing by."

"You don't look like you're afraid of snakes."

"I treat them with respect. They were here first."

Luke lay quietly before speaking again. "Did you learn how to control your fear in the bush?" He had read about the mind-over-matter techniques some of these indigenous societies employ.

"Peace isn't the absence of fear, Dr. Luke. Peace is a gift from Jesus Christ."

Luke frowned in the dark. "To me, peace of mind comes from controlling what threatens you."

"You've been successful with that method? You have peace of mind?"

Given the events of the past few months, Luke had to concede that his method hadn't worked at all. "The more I try to control my world, the more threatening it seems to become."

"The peace of Christ isn't the power to control the world with your mind. His peace is a gift he gives to the heart even if our circumstances don't change. Through his Spirit he gives us the power to love people more than we fear snakes."

"After everything Sierra Leone has been through, you still can believe that?"

"Do you remember the sign at the crossroads in Makeni when we were passing through? 'God is here. Peace is here in Sierra Leone.' God's peace is the peace Sierra Leone needs most. The devil may have kicked up his heels for a time, but that's not how the story will end."

"I wish it were that easy for me to believe."

"It is easy, Dr. Luke. You just make it hard."

Luke heard other sounds in the night—the blowing of the wind, mangos dropping onto the thatched roof. He fell asleep wondering what else fell out of the trees.

THIRTY-FIVE

Luke was up the next morning long before the others—he thought. He found Marta already at work building a fire in the cooking shelter.

"Think you could boil me some water for oatmeal?" he asked.

She looked up from stirring. "How about some fluffy rice?"

"Brown rice?" he asked.

Marta held up a ladle full of the white stuff. "You'll have to get your fiber another way. Processed white rice is cheaper and not as subject to pests."

Luke groaned. "I didn't think to bring fiber tabs with me. I was worried about…"

Marta raised her spoon like a sword. "Spare me the clinical details of your digestive tract."

Luke shrugged and sat down with his calculator. "The way I figure it, we've got to start seeing patients by 8:30 if we're going to make a dent in the patient load."

He looked down the path at the procession of women and children. Each carried a heavy jerry can, the same kind he had seen used for gasoline, but they were coming from the waterside.

"Where are the men?" Luke asked.

"Dreaming about the hard day they have ahead, sweeping the front entrances to their huts," Marta answered.

Luke shook his finger at her. "You think you can run the world without men?"

"You just watch," Marta said as Constance Whitlock and her children deposited their burdens.

"Good morning," Luke called to them.

Constance waved, and the little Whitlocks rushed to Luke. "I bet you're going to be glad when that well is finished," he told them.

Moses shook his head. "I'll be sad."

"You like walking two miles with a heavy jug on your head?" Luke asked.

Moses shrugged. "When Daddy finishes this well, we'll move to a different village. I'll miss my friends."

"Hey, Moses!" called one of the village children, whose chores were also complete.

"See you later, Mr. Luke," Moses called as he scampered off with his friend.

Around 8:30 but surely not sooner, Brima and Bishop Paul appeared. Breakfast wasn't finished until 9:00, and Luke was getting more agitated by the moment as he calculated how many more patients they'd have to process per hour, if Brima's estimates were correct. He tried smiling and asked Brima, "Where will we be setting up shop?" He hadn't noticed any building suitable for a clinic.

Brima pointed toward a clump of trees. "We should get decent shade there for the morning. Best air-conditioned examining room in the bush. After lunch we'll move somewhere else."

Luke meditated on the prospect of an outdoor clinic. "Not much privacy," he noted.

Brima shoveled in a mouthful of rice and shrugged. "These folks haven't seen a doctor for ten years. Privacy is not something they're going to worry about."

Luke sighed and stretched. "Fine, I'm raring to get going." By his watch, it was already 9:15.

Brima grunted. "So am I, after we take care of a little matter."

"What little matter is that?" Luke asked, his mental calculator adjusting for lost time.

"We can't get started until we pay a call on the paramount chief in this region. We are here as his guests."

It made sense to Luke that the chief might want to say thank you, so he looked around for a hut that came closest to a bush palace. "Which is his house?"

Brima waved his spoon seemingly over the horizon. "We have to drive to get there."

At 9:30 the team poured into the Land Rover and drove for miles until they came to another village. Brima followed a dirt road to what appeared to be an oasis in a desert—a freshly painted brick house and the sound of a large generator.

A woman came out on the veranda and greeted Brima. Luke watched her shake her head and shrug her shoulders. Then he saw Brima pass a wad of money into her hand. Brima jumped back into the car and turned it in the opposite direction.

"Wasn't the chief home?" Luke asked.

"His big wife said he's in his bath and can't be disturbed right now."

"Will he come see us later?"

"Maybe. Maybe not."

Luke glanced at his watch. It was 10:15.

When they got back to Lonko, Brima took Luke by the arm. "Do you have twenty dollars?" he asked.

So much for the chief wanting to say hello. Luke wished Brima had just asked for the money an hour ago so they could have gotten the clinic started.

Marta came up behind Luke and whispered. "Blessed are the flexible, for they shall not break."

"Did they teach you that in conflict-management school?" he growled. Then he looked over at the grove of trees where half of Africa seemed to be standing. He put on a smile and sauntered over. "Well, it looks like we're open for business."

Luke was relieved when the first hint of sundown came. Many of their patients had walked great distances from other villages and still had to walk miles through the bush to get home. He stood up and stretched. Brima rose as well, but not with a mind to finish up business.

Brima walked to the triage desk and looked through Marta's cards for the patients they had not yet seen—fifty all told. He called out ten names and motioned for them to follow him to the desk.

"I thought they needed to leave by dusk to make it home," Luke said.

"If they're dead, it won't matter," Brima answered and called over to Paul. "Get out the bottles of chloroquine and penicillin, broda. We got some sick ones coming your way."

A mosquito landed on Luke's wrist, and Brima swatted it dead. "Time to lotion up again," the nurse told Luke. "We can't afford for you to get sick."

As Luke covered himself with the day's second dose of DEET, he wondered how much pesticide the human skin could endure.

Thirty-Six

Before breakfast the next morning, Luke and Paul struggled down a path with loads of firewood balanced precariously on their heads. Ahead of them, Mariama and Marta carried jerry cans of water. Luke stopped walking and whispered to Paul, "The women's loads look heavier than ours."

"It's hard to be a woman in Africa," Paul answered.

Luke agreed. "But it doesn't have to be this hard. I tried to help Marta, but she called me a cultural imperialist."

Paul stopped and mopped his brow. "Let's sit down. Right about now I'm dreaming of a nice North American winter."

Luke laid down his burden and joined Paul on the ground. "Last year we had twenty-four inches of snow."

"Right about now snow sounds pretty good to me. Didn't think so when I had to shovel it."

"Minus seven degrees in March. A record for the last two centuries."

"Give me snow."

"Give me a deep chill."

"Amen." Paul almost got up again, but he flopped back down. "No sense rushing to breakfast when it's always the same as lunch and supper. If I never see rice when we get home, that would be fine-o with me."

Luke agreed. "I'd give my next year's pay for a bowl of oatmeal right now."

"When I get home, I want chitlins three meals a day."

"I'm losing weight."

Paul rubbed his belly and scowled. "I'm constipated."

"You need oatmeal."

"Chitlins. They'd put some meat on your ribs."

"Please don't tell me what part of pig chitlins come from."

"The best part, son."

"That's disgusting."

"Maybe the Tayspills are all white after all."

"That's intolerant."

"I bet you don't eat no grits neither."

"Only if you drown them with garlic and cheddar cheese."

"That's disgusting."

"That's intolerant."

They both laughed, but Luke got wistful. "Right about now I'd even eat chitlins and grits if it meant I didn't have to see another plate of rice chop."

"You don't think none of the tough white stuff floatin on top is dead snake, do you?"

Luke stood and picked up his burden. "As long as it isn't that mangy dog that stopped coming round the house."

Paul fetched his bundle of wood. "Wouldn't know. All the dawgs in Africa look like they have the same daddy."

They carried their wood the rest of the way back to the cooking shelter where Mariama and Marta were ready to serve the first daily dose of rice chop. Slivers of mystery meat poked through the palm-oil-soaked greens. Paul held his hands up to offer a blessing. "Nourish us, Papa God, but don't bother us with the details."

Luke was the first to say, "Amen!"

As Brima had predicted, they saw almost five thousand patients in the first two weeks. How long, Luke wondered, would their supply of medications hold up? He checked with their ersatz pharmacist.

Paul shook his head. "Let me put it this way, Docta Luke. Did you ever read the story about Jesus feeding the five thousand?"

"I think I've heard about it. Does the story start with a couple of puny fishes and a little bit of bread?"

"That's the story. We're down to the little bit of bread. Think twice before you prescribe pills for something that might take care of itself."

Luke scowled. "Is that what Jesus did—ask the hungry people how hungry they were before he fed them?"

Paul shook his head. "Okay, okay. You prescribe. I pray."

If the masses of people waiting for them didn't vary, neither did the diseases. Luke saw diseases he had read about only in textbooks: leprosy, elephantiasis, river blindness, tuberculosis, meningitis, and lots of malaria. He learned how to diagnose by using his eyes rather than a laboratory.

"I haven't seen one case yet that looks like AIDS," Luke told Brima.

"It's here, but not to the degree you would see it in Freetown. Once they repair the roads to upcountry, the long-distance truckers will come north again, and HIV will follow in their tracks. There should be enough drugs in your supplies to take care of the women we see."

"I mean… I guess I meant to say… Well, I expected I'd only be seeing AIDS. That's my specialty."

"Africa is more than AIDS, Dr. Luke."

"I'm beginning to see what you mean."

Occasionally excitement interrupted the orderly flow of patients. Marta rushed from triage yelling, "Snakebite!" Some villagers followed with a man on a makeshift stretcher.

Mariama translated from the Limba dialect. "They say it was a cobra bite."

"That's a neurotoxin," Luke said, wishing he wasn't getting so much experience with snakes.

"He stopped breathing!" Marta shouted.

"Do we have an ambu bag and mask?" Luke asked Brima. He might as well have asked the nurse for a ventilator to plug into the electricity that also didn't exist. "He's got a heartbeat. We just need to ventilate him, but we'll have to do it mouth to mouth."

Luke leaned over the man and started to breathe for him. After a few minutes he was breathless and motioned to Mariama to take his place. When he caught his breath, he asked Brima, "Any idea how long cobra neurotoxin lasts?"

"About four hours."

"Then that's how long we need to breathe for him."

Hundreds of patients were waiting for the doctor, but the clinic had come to a halt. Brima looked at the line. "There's nothing we can do for him. The villagers know that."

Paul was horrified. "He can't breathe on his own." To the bishop, this wasn't a case of snakebite, but a reenactment of his childhood polio when he couldn't breathe. He dropped to his knees and took Mariama's place.

Brima took Luke aside. "We are working here in wartime conditions. Sometimes you can't do things in the field that you could do in a hospital." He pointed to the people waiting. "Somewhere on that line is a life you can save. We have to make tough choices."

Luke stared at the curious villagers, who looked on at the team's futile efforts. Paul stood up from the patient, and Marta took his place. The bishop found his second wind and began to sing.

Let everything that hath breath praise the Lord.

As Paul sang, he beckoned to the village men and motioned for them to come take a turn helping the victim breathe. Mariama took up the song and lined out the words in the local dialect, but only the women sang. The men saved their breath to be the next in line.

In the second hour after the cobra bite, the victim's heart gave out, and the women began to wail. "Come on," Brima said, steering Luke back to their table. "We have patients to see."

Luke went with him and started to move the long line of patients along. He watched the victim's family carry the man away. Meanwhile, Paul shifted uncomfortably in his pharmacist's chair. He was no longer his cheerful self.

During the night Luke turned to Brima. "It's so hard for me to make decisions about who lives and who dies. How do you do it?"

"We just do our best and leave the rest to God."

Luke shook his head in the dark. "I saw so many patients today who could easily be treated if they lived in the West, like that young woman with a new case of diabetes."

"The one who said she had ants in her urine?"

Luke laughed. "I've got to admit her observation was as accurate as any lab test I could have used! I can just imagine her squatting in the bush and the ants lining up, licking their chops. I'm learning how to get along without a lab, but I can't say I like it."

Brima wasn't interested in the lab. "That woman has a hard road ahead of her."

"Exactly my point," Luke agreed. "I wrote out a referral to a hospital, but I bet she never gets there. And what if she does get to a hospital? Here in the bush she has no refrigerator to store her insulin, no machine to monitor her blood glucose, and no high-risk obstetrician to help her through her pregnancies. She's going to be dead within a year."

"Probably sooner."

"And what about that baby with meningitis? All I could give was a shot of penicillin and a quarter tablet of an antibiotic we don't give to children in the States. I'll bet that poor little guy never gets to a hospital either."

"Probably not."

"So what am I doing here? Putting a Band-Aid on Africa?"

"You're doing your best, Dr. Luke. What about those people you were able to help? I never knew that sickle-cell patients get leg ulcers because of their blood disease. You knew that, and now I know what to do next time I see it. Or that woman who wasted all her money on *juju* medicine. No one had ever examined her, but you did. You made the right diagnosis, and now she's on the way to a hospital to have her prolapsed uterus fixed. The whole village thought she was crazy. You not only treated her, you vindicated her with her people."

"But what about the ones we can't save?"

"You're not God, Luke. You're a mortalman, just like me."

"That's a hard lesson to learn."

"On the run during the war, I learned about my own mortality."

"Did you make it to Freetown?"

In the dark Luke couldn't see the grim look on Brima's face. "I don't talk about it much. Everyone has a story, and mine isn't the most important."

"But the rebels didn't catch you."

"They almost did. While they were busy stealing my motorbike, I grabbed my pants and scampered out the window."

"Was that all you had with you?"

"My pants, a pot, and a bag of rice. Later I went back and got a bag of dried peppers I had hidden. That's how most of us survived in the bush."

"After a few days in the bush, could you go home?"

Again Brima shook his head in the dark. "We traveled through the bush to the border. I was in a refugee camp in Guinea for over a year."

All of a sudden something made sense to Luke—why a slim man like Brima ate as if there might not be another meal anytime soon.

Thirty-Seven

By the end of the first week, Luke was worried about Paul. After long clinic days, he limped rather than walked. On Saturday afternoon when they took a rest from their busy clinics, Luke followed Paul to the hut. He found him sitting on the ground with his head in his hands.

Paul looked up when Luke entered and waved his Bible at him. "Look at this text I was going to preach on tomorrow. *The Spirit of the Lord is upon me, because he hath anointed me to preach the gospel to the poor.* Growing up on St. Helena, I thought I knew what it meant to be poor. But you've seen the poverty here. How can I tell stories about people at home who only think they're poor?"

Luke didn't know much about the Bible, but he did recognize the text. "Isn't this the message you gave Cedric when we were spirited away by the trooper?"

For the first time in days, Paul smiled. "Hooey, I bet that boy preached quite a sermon. Probably better than what I would have preached."

"Even if Cedric saw the poverty here, I bet he wouldn't be shy about preaching to these villagers."

Paul nodded. "He has what the Gullah call the silver trumpet. That boy is a born preacher."

"And your horn is made out of tin? Guess you need some *powa de Sperit.*"

Paul's shoulders drooped as he shook his head. "I'm not feeling very powerful right now. First, there was that man with the cobra bite. Then yesterday, a boy came on crutches to see you. I looked at him and saw myself."

Luke remembered the case better than hundreds of others he had seen that day. He had seen polio only in textbooks. "They didn't have vaccines here for the ten years of civil war. I saw you praying with him. You were praying up a storm."

Eyes vacant, Paul looked off in the distance. "That boy was still on his crutches when he left the clinic."

Luke sat down on the ground next to his friend and placed his hand on Paul's knee. "I've seen you pray for patients with AIDS at Yale. They didn't walk out of the hospital, but you didn't take that personally. I've heard you tell Brima that you'd never stop praying, even if people aren't healed."

Paul looked at Luke. "For some reason, it matters here more. At home I prayed for miraculous healing, but I always knew miracle medicines and miracle workers were just around the corner. More often than not, I saw God heal through people like you."

Luke wasn't giving up that easily, or taking any glory. "What about back on St. Helena Island when you were growing up and there was only old Doc Bailey to take care of all the poor people? What did you believe then?"

Paul nodded. "Prayer and old Doc Bailey were all we had."

Luke watched a hen scurry across the floor to her nest in the corner of their hut. "Well, all you got here is prayer and old Docta Luke. I think you saw yourself in that boy. Maybe when you prayed for him, you were praying for the poor child within you. When that boy couldn't throw away his crutches, neither could you. That's when you started to limp again."

Paul grimaced with pain. "I felt so ashamed my prayers couldn't heal him. When I saw him in the courtyard later, I looked the other way. I turned my back on that child."

Luke wasn't buying into Paul's feelings of failure. "These people love you, Paul. When you get up to preach tomorrow, start with your own story. Tell it the way you told it to me when we sat around my fireplace back in Connecticut. If there really is a sweet Holy Spirit, don't you think he can take it from there?"

✠

On Sunday morning Paul went to the "town hall" and beat on the goat-hide gathering drum used to call villagers to important meetings. Men, women, and *pikins* poured out of their huts. A few goats and a lot of chickens tagged along to see what was going on.

"Come right on in," Paul said, ushering them to the bamboo benches. Luke chose a seat on the front "pew" and watched Mariama go over to a blind man. She took his stick and tapped it against the bamboo bench as she spoke to him. The man flashed a toothless grin that he understood what she wanted. Mariama had found herself a stick man.

Luke marveled how quickly the villagers caught on to songs they had never heard before. Paul's Gullah spirituals pulsed with rhythms of Sierra Leone. When the bishop got up to preach, his face was no longer con-torted with pain. Dressed in a long yellow kaftan, Paul pranced. He danced. He glowed with more than sweat. When he came to the last verse of his text from Luke's gospel, he put down his Bible and repeated the line by heart. "This day is this scripture fulfilled in your ears." Paul motioned to the congregation to repeat the words and gathered in their responses with his arms. Luke relaxed. This was the Bishop Paul he knew.

Suddenly Paul stopped preaching and looked at the rear row. All the villagers were murmuring. Luke turned to see what was causing a distur-bance and noticed people pointing to a robed figure. Marta drew in her breath and whispered, "I hear there's a witch doctor operating in this area."

Brima rose and walked toward the intruder. Luke watched the nurse shake hands with the man, linking thumbs. He had seen Brima execute that African handshake only with people he really liked. A foot taller than the nurse, the stranger stood majestically in a tie-dyed robe of blue, crimson, and purple. Over the robe he wore a vest embroidered with the same royal colors and studded with clear stones. Luke wondered if they might be diamonds. When the man moved, golden bells tinkled on the hem of his garment. On his head he wore a golden pillbox with what seemed to be Hebrew letters stitched into the fabric.

Behind the man, almost hidden in his shadow, stood a group of Africans dressed in rags. More striking than their garments were their twisted bodies. Each of them was missing an arm or a leg. Some were missing both arms. They looked like the war wounded Luke had seen at the Cotton Tree in Freetown on his first day in Sierra Leone.

Brima ushered the amputees to places of honor and their leader to the seat next to Luke. Brima whispered, "This is Rabbi Hilkiah," as he took his seat on the other side of the stranger. Luke did a double take as he got a better look at the dark-skinned man with a long hooked nose and flowing gray beard. Luke wished that Brima was not sitting on Hilkiah's other side. He wanted to ask him what a Jew was doing in the middle of the African bush.

Hesitantly at first, Paul resumed his preaching and began telling his own story. He started with the saga of American slavery and told how slavers had carried his own ancestors away from a village much like Lonko to a land across the sea. In this New World the Africans worked under a slave owner's yoke, just like the children of Israel had under ancient Pharaohs in Egypt. Paul used words to paint portraits of African men working in American rice fields and African women weaving baskets in the same patterns he had seen the women of Lonko weave. He spoke of the hardships under which they labored and the diseases they endured. Luke stole a look at the regal rabbi to his right and saw tears stream down his face.

Paul told how the enslaved Africans found hope when missionaries told them about Jesus. At first the white plantation owners were afraid of what might happen if the black men heard the Christian good news. The gospel story, after all, has revolutionary effects on people. On the other hand—he explained the owners' reasoning—the slaves might become docile and obedient. Didn't Scripture tell slaves to obey their masters?

With some hesitation, the masters allowed the missionaries to invite the Africans to church. The gospel had sewn the first seeds of freedom.

"Today in America," Paul told them, "some people say that Christianity isn't an African religion. But when the slaves heard the good news, their hearts cried, 'Yes!' That day the scripture was fulfilled in their ears." Paul lifted his hands and invited the congregation to respond. *This day is the scripture fulfilled in your ears.*

From slavery, the bishop moved on to the story of abolitionists and Quaker teachers who came to his village on St. Helena Island. Eventually a bigman named Abraham Lincoln set the captives free. As Mariama translated, Luke watched the villagers listen carefully and nod to one another. Wasn't this their story too?

Paul slipped back into his childhood Gullah as he described St. Helena Island and his own poverty, hunger, and sickness. The Gullah words were so close to Krio that Mariama didn't even need to translate. Paul talked of his near death from polio and spoke of his mother's vision. The bishop wove stories together like a sweet grass basket, mixing colorful strands with the basic message.

Luke watched the villagers weep as Paul told of his prodigal years after college. Throughout the sermon the preacher worked the congregation, call and response, just the way he did at home. *This day scripture is fulfilled in your ears.*

No wonder the first Lucas Tayspill began his Gullah translation of the Bible with this text, Luke thought. His ancestor's life was also part of this story. And he, Lucas Tayspill III, was being drawn in.

So mesmerized was Luke by Paul's sermon that he forgot Hilkiah by his side. As Paul whispered for the final time, *This day scripture is fulfilled in your ears,* Rabbi Hilkiah rose and spoke to Paul in flawless English. "My brother, your sermon moves me. The prophet Isaiah spoke about a day like our own. As you can see, I have brought the brokenhearted with me—at least those who have survived the rebels' cut."

Hilkiah moved to center front, turned to the congregation, and spoke in their dialect. "My children, let me tell you what else the prophet said would happen when the scripture was fulfilled. The Anointed One will comfort those who mourn and give them a garland instead of ashes, oil of joy instead of mourning. The people shall build up the ancient ruins and raise up the former devastations."

Rabbi Hilkiah resumed speaking in English as he turned to Luke. "Doctor, I have no doubt that the Spirit of the Lord God has sent you here to help his Anointed One fulfill his words to these poor people." He put his hands on the shoulder of one man who had both arms hacked off below the elbows. "Dr. Luke, won't you come to our village, too? My people have lived in darkness too long."

Brima stepped up. "We'd be honored to serve your people."

Bishop Paul moved forward to greet Hilkiah and clap him on the back. "Of course you and your friends will stay and share a meal with us."

Mariama's eyes opened wide as she calculated the amount of rice the crowd would consume. Marta slipped out of her seat and headed for the cooking hut.

As the service concluded, Luke walked out in lockstep with Brima. "What's a Jew doing in the middle of the bush?"

Brima grinned. "I'm sure Rabbi Hilkiah would be happy to answer that question himself."

The amputees and their leader gathered in a circle around the large dish of rice. Marta had stretched the small pieces of meat and fish as far as she could with cassava greens. Hungry men dug in with their hands and filled their mouths as quickly as they could. Luke watched Rabbi Hilkiah, the guest of honor, waiting to serve himself. First he took a handful of rice and lifted it to the mouth of a man without arms. Embarrassed by his own hunger, Luke followed his example and fed another man who could not feed himself.

Hilkiah settled down next to Luke. "I've always wanted to visit America. I hear there are more Jews there than in Israel."

"Certainly more than in Sierra Leone. So how did a black Jew wind up in the African bush?"

Hilkiah took a handful of rice and filled his mouth before answering. "My family left Jerusalem when the temple was destroyed. They wandered down through Ethiopia and, two generations ago, came to the nearby village of Kameara. For all these centuries, they assimilated to survive, but someone among them always knew who we were and where we came from."

Hilkiah rose and stretched his long legs, then he sat down next to Bishop Paul. "The only school in my village was Islamic, and I was taught the Koran. Later I learned English. Then I found a copy of the Hebrew scripture written in English. When I read the chronicles of the Jewish people, I knew the book spoke the truth. One of the stories was about a man who almost lost his Jewish identity until he found the holy word and read it to the others who had forgotten their roots. I made a vow to God that day to always sing his praises."

Paul looked at the writing on Rabbi Hilkiah's cap. "I took a Hebrew course in divinity school, but I'm not sure I can make out those words."

"Holiness unto the Lord," Hilkiah translated.

Luke watched a great grin break out on Paul's face. "I know the Gullah translation better than the Hebrew." He motioned with his arms and hips. "Walkin straight."

Hilkiah roared. "I couldn't have said it better."

Paul clapped his hand on Hilkiah's shoulder. "So, Rabbi, tell me what you think of Jesus."

Hilkiah looked off into the distance, measuring his words. Luke thought he had long ago prepared his answer for countless Christian missionaries who had discovered this Jewish treasure in Africa. "I believe he is the spiritual son of God," he answered.

Paul thought for a minute and nodded. "Well, that's not a bad start."

Mariama came to her husband and poked him on the shoulder. "Could you grab another handful of faggots for the cooking fire?"

As Paul tossed them onto the fire, he let out a scream. A foot-long snake had attached its fangs to his hand.

"That's a bush viper!" Luke said. The doctor's alarm added to Paul's apprehension.

"It feels like somebody splattered hot bacon grease on my hand."

The bishop reached his hand into the fire, and the viper withdrew its fangs. None of them could take their eyes off the snake as it fell into the flames.

"You'd better sit down," Luke said. He grabbed Paul's wrist but found his own throbbing pulse obliterating his patient's. His mind raced as he ticked off the symptoms. First would be nausea and dizziness. Then, as the venom started to destroy red blood cells, the victim would feel panic. Nowhere in the textbook did it mention that the doctor might panic first.

"Do we have the antivenom?" Paul asked.

Luke didn't want to have to tell him what he knew. "There isn't any antivenom for bush vipers."

Paul stared at his hand. "Then I guess we ought to pray."

As Paul and Mariama prayed in loud voices, Luke closed his eyes but kept his fingers on the bishop's pulse. As long as Paul's pulse remained steady, Luke kept his eyes closed. When he heard "Amen," he released his fingers and opened his eyes.

Paul grinned. "Thank you, Jesus, I'm still alive!"

Luke saw no swelling at the puncture site. If the venom had entered Paul's system, his hand should be horribly swollen by now.

The amputees, who were far more familiar with snakebites than Luke or Paul, crowded around the doctor and patient. When they saw no swelling at the puncture site, they murmured to one another and pointed at Paul.

The bishop looked down at his normal-appearing hand. He took a deep breath and decided he felt okay. Finally he stood up. "It's okay, folks. Show's over."

Hilkiah took Paul's hand and inspected the wound. His amputee companions murmured in a dialect Luke could not understand. Finally the visitors started heading back to their village, turning every few feet to stare at Bishop Paul.

Luke watched Paul and Mariama walk to the hut, arm in arm. Paul stooped to kiss her on the forehead, and Mariama giggled.

"My dear brother, have you been sipping palm wine?"

"Kiss me with the kisses of thy mouth: for thy love is better than wine," Paul answered.

Luke ducked into the hut ahead of them. "Just let me get the sat phone and then you two can have your privacy."

As Luke strolled down the path away from the hut, he imagined his grandfather as a young teen reading the Song of Solomon. He found a good spot for reception and dialed.

"Hey, babe," he whispered to Theo.

"Hey, you," she whispered back. "You have no idea how much I miss you."

"Me, too, sweetheart. All I ever think about is you."

"You mean you think of me when you have nothing more exciting to do."

"Nothing is more exciting than you."

"Have you found a number-two wife over there?"

"I'm a one-woman man."

"One woman at a time?"

"You're my big wife and only wife."

"How's Marta?"

"She's got more energy than the rest of us. Poor thing, she spotted a louse on her head this afternoon. She shaved her hair down to a buzz cut."

"Gotta go, sweetheart," Theo said, shutting out the picture of Marta's kitchen and the poultry shears in her hands.

THIRTY-EIGHT

On Monday morning of their second week upcountry, the team headed a short distance to the village of Kameara, where Hilkiah and the amputees lived. En route Brima suggested a slight detour.

"Another paramount chief to visit?" Luke asked.

Brima laughed. "No, just the UN peacekeepers. We're getting close to an area where there might be holdout rebels. I just want to let the UN know we'll be in the area."

As they pulled into the command post, Luke watched a tall African in camouflage mufti emerge from a tent. Luke waved. "Hi. I'm Dr. Luke Tayspill from America. We're here to run a clinic in the bush."

The tall Yoruba from Nigeria towered over Luke. He shook Luke's hand and laughed. "And I'm Dr. Joseph." He pointed to the large tent. "That's my hospital. Would you like to see a few patients?"

Luke shrugged. "Sure. Why not?"

The two men walked off together to the medical tent. Half an hour later, they shook hands, and Luke climbed back into the Land Rover. "Teach him a thing or two?" Brima asked.

Luke lifted a water bottle. "I wouldn't mind having him on my team."

As the vehicle pulled into Kameara, dozens of villagers rushed to meet them. They were eager to greet one of the passengers, but it wasn't the doctor.

"*Kusheh,* Pa Paul," they cried to the miraculous survivor of the viper bite.

"*Kusheh* yerselves!" Paul called as he accepted an extended stump to shake. His new role as an African elder seemed to please him.

Luke was surprised to see another familiar face in Kameara. "Now there's a pair of strange bedfellows," he said to Brima, pointing to Rabbi Hilkiah and Farid Nassour, Lebanese merchant and philanthropist.

Luke watched as Nassour's driver unloaded provisions from a dust-coated Mercedes SUV. A crowd of amputees surrounded the vehicle, the most able-bodied carrying sacks of rice and other foodstuffs to the storehouse. Nassour smiled when he saw Luke and came over to greet him.

"We meet again, dear doctor. I see your adventures have taken you out of Freetown."

Luke offered him his hand. "And I see that your generosity extends all over the land."

Nassour smiled. "Hilkiah and I are old comrades, both sons of Abraham. How could I refuse him when he tells me of these people?"

The doctor couldn't make the connection. "How do you know each other?" he asked.

Nassour laughed. "Diamonds."

Luke didn't understand. "I can see why a merchant might be involved with diamonds, but what does the rabbi have to do with them?"

"Before the war he was an expert appraiser," Nassour said.

"And during the war?" Luke remembered that the rebels had taken over the diamond mines and used the world's best alluvial gems to finance their reign of terror.

"Our friend spent most of the war in a Makeni prison, reading his Jewish Bible. He came out singing God's praises. He said he never wanted to see diamonds again."

Nassour excused himself to resume his conversation with the rabbi. Luke noted the unusual distance in Hilkiah's body language. He kept shaking his head, and although Luke couldn't hear Nassour's words, he could tell his voice was getting louder. In their short acquaintance, Luke had seen Hilkiah regal and friendly. None of that was visible across the dusty path.

A band of the ever-present war widows appeared, as if on command, and crowded around Farid Nassour. Behind his back Hilkiah had signaled to the women to surround the visitor. The women wrung their hands, repeating pitiful stories. Hilkiah shrugged his shoulders at the merchant and grinned slightly at Luke. The doctor was sure Farid Nassour was about to part with another wad of bills from his pocket.

"I wish I had a gaggle of widow beggars to whistle for when I had uninvited guests," Luke said as he walked with Brima toward the intended clinic location. He stopped short when he saw the lineup near the table where they would be conducting business. "Let's do the women and children this morning," he suggested. "Those amputees look like they'll need our undivided attention in the afternoon."

Hilkiah appeared and took Mariama by the hand. She beckoned the others to follow. He led her to a tall mound overgrown with scrub grass, next to the bombed-out shell of what looked like a church.

Mariama fell to the ground weeping, and Paul went to her side. "Her family is in this mass grave," Hilkiah explained. "When the rebels came, the villagers all ran into the bush. But the rebels found them anyway. They took away the children and herded the adults into the church. Then they set the church on fire. After the war, when I came to this village with the amputees, we dug a grave to bury all of them."

Luke kept his head bowed for a moment and then wandered a few yards away to what looked like overgrown grave markers. One simple cracked stone read *Willard C. Boardman, Died March 27, 1902, Aged 37 years. Asleep in Jesus.*

"Who was he?" Luke asked.

Hilkiah's face was reverent. "One of the early missionaries who died of malaria. This village is the reason they called Sierra Leone the White Man's Grave."

Luke felt a chill down his spine, hopefully not a malarial chill. He moved a row away to look at another marker.

Irvin F. Johnston, Died January 8, 1894, Aged 5 years, 4 months, and 4 days. Blessed be the name of the Lord.

Luke shook his head. "I can't imagine blessing the name of a God who swallowed up my children." He walked from one grave to another. Each told a similar story. "Child sacrifice," Luke mumbled.

Miriam L. Day, December 29, 1888–December 27, 1917. She hath done what she could.

"What exactly did she think she could do?" Luke asked about the young woman in the grave.

"She could pack her worldly possessions in a pine coffin to come here. She didn't want anyone to have to pay for her to be buried."

"Strange folks," Luke murmured.

"No stranger than your friends," Hilkiah said and slipped away.

Luke would have traded his bowl of rice chop for a nice nap if he had had the choice. The morning had been hot enough. As the shade moved across the courtyard, Brima dragged the tables and chairs to a different cluster of trees for the afternoon. Fifty men and half as many women with missing limbs pursued them.

A man sat down in front of them and rubbed his stump, telling his story. Luke didn't need a translator to understand what he was saying. He was describing a phantom limb.

"This is a very unusual case," Brima told him.

Luke held up his hand. "Now wait a minute, buddy. That's what you say when you don't know what's going on."

Brima laughed, but then he caught himself and grew serious. "You're right, but I'm telling you the truth. This man had his arm hacked off below the elbow, but he still can feel his hand burning with pain. He believes the machete took off his arm and left a devil in its place."

Luke recognized the symptoms but disagreed with the cause. "Phantom limb is very common, even after a clean surgical amputation. The brain used to know a hand was there and still thinks it is."

"How do you treat that in the States?" Brima asked.

Luke had to reach back to his medical-school days before he became an infectious-disease specialist. "Sometimes with drugs, but nothing we have in our packs. Sometimes massage helps. But the best thing is for the patient to stay busy, to take his mind off the feeling."

"Mind over matter?" Brima asked.

Luke nodded. "We do it every day. I've seen you walking barefoot on the path. Your foot feels everything beneath it, but your brain doesn't pass the message along to your conscious mind."

Brima nodded. "I only think about where I'm going and what I want to do."

"Exactly," Luke continued. "Your brain doesn't make you pay attention because it knows your plans are to get from here to there uninterrupted."

"So we have to help these patients find a life plan that's so important their brains don't want to interrupt them with the pain."

"I guess you could say that," Luke answered, thinking of the elaborate pain clinics at home with drawers full of medicines and machines to distract the nerves.

Brima slapped Luke on the back. "I may know *what*, but you know *why*. We're quite a team, but what are we going to do for this man?"

For a moment Luke was baffled, but then he noticed Bishop Paul at his pharmacy post chatting with Rabbi Hilkiah. "I think I have an answer," he said and motioned for Brima to join him.

"Hey, Docta Luke!" Paul yelled as they approached. "How de body?" Clearly Paul was enjoying his new friendship.

Luke looked from the black American Christian to the black African Jew. "You two seem to have formed quite a team."

Paul slapped his fellow clergyman on the shoulder. "You know this fella knows all the Psalms by heart?"

Hilkiah bowed modestly. "I had little else to do while sitting in my jail cell."

Luke laughed. "Well, maybe you two rabbis can do what Brima and I can't." He outlined the problem of phantom pain for them—the demonic and the Western views of the problem.

It was Luke's turn to receive a friendly slap. "Now you jes leave it to us, broda. Ain't nothin bout dat problem we cain't handle. Right, Hilky?"

Luke would never have dared be so familiar with the dignified rabbi. As he and Brima returned to their post, they watched the two men huddle. As their next patient sat down before them, Hilkiah called to a small child hanging around the courtyard. He whispered something to him, and the boy nodded that he understood. Hilkiah turned back to Paul as the boy ran off on whatever errand Hilkiah had sent him. A few minutes later the boy returned with the remarkable robe he had worn the first time they saw him at Paul's church service.

"That's quite a getup," Luke whispered to Brima.

"Have you ever read the Bible?" Brima asked.

"Got me there, but what does the white man's Bible have to do with African tie-dye?"

"The Bible belongs to all of us, not just to the westerner. Sometime you should read the instructions Papa God gave to his priests about how they should dress."

Luke did a double take as Hilkiah held out an identical robe for Bishop Paul and slipped it over his head. "Do you mean that design has a purpose?" he asked.

Brima nodded. "Every part of it."

"Looks to me like Paul is tickled pink—or whatever color a black man gets tickled to."

"Bishop Paul is a man of the Book, Dr. Luke. He knows Jesus didn't come to destroy the Jewish law, but to fill it full of meaning."

"Well, something's filling up the friendship of those two men with meaning." Luke hoped that somehow the two new buddies could translate their clerical collegiality into an effective pain protocol. All the patients' stories sounded the same that afternoon. So was the prescription. Luke and Brima pointed to the pharmacist's bench.

As the two clinicians worked their way helplessly through the line of patients, they heard tandem contrasting voices on the other side of the courtyard.

"I can understand what Rabbi Hilkiah is doing," Luke whispered to Brima. "It sounds like he's reciting something. Even though I can't understand the words, they sound very soothing."

Brima nodded. "That's one of the psalms. 'Hallelujah, praise the Lord. He heals the brokenhearted and binds up their wounds." The nurse turned his gaze from Hilkiah to Bishop Paul. "How come you can't understand Bishop Paul?" he asked Luke. "His voice is ten times louder than the rabbi's, and he's speaking in English."

Luke shook his head. "I understand too well what he's up to. He's talking to demons and telling them to get lost."

"You think the devil only belongs to Africa and ignorance?" Brima asked.

Luke shifted uncomfortably in his chair. "That's not what I said."

Both men turned at the sound of a third man yelling and dancing. The amputee was praising Papa God as Paul and Hilkiah were slapping each other on the back. Bishop Paul called over to them, "How's that for combined modality therapy?"

The doctor shook his head. "As long as it works, I won't say a word."

"How about praising Jesus? He's the one who healed the man."

Hilkiah broke into another psalm, dancing around the pharmacist's table with the amputee. "Come, everyone, and clap for joy! Shout triumphant praises to the Lord!"

"We'd better stop chatting and get back to work," Luke said, remembering the long line of waiting patients. But their table was empty. Dozens of victims of phantom pain had moved over to where the healing was happening.

Brima motioned for Luke to carry his chair over to the holy corner. "There's nothing I can do over there," Luke complained.

"You can help me make occupational therapy plans for the men who have forgotten their pain. They were subsistence farmers before the war."

In the distance Luke saw Farid Nassour. The diamond merchant had extracted himself from the group of widows and was fleeing to his car as fast as the demons had fled the amputees. Luke smiled that the merchant had allowed himself to be trapped for that long. Nassour's day hadn't turned out the way he had planned, but neither had Luke's sabbatical.

Thirty-Nine

Marta dubbed her hut "Bethany House" and started to make plans to take in children. For her, Kameara began to feel like home. She sat out front most mornings, watching the village women carry water to their huts.

One morning Luke was awakened by her shout, "Come quickly!"

Brima was the first to come running toward the sound of the commotion. As quickly as they could, Luke and Mariama followed. They found a little boy dragging the dead weight of a teenager covered in dirt.

"How did he get so dirty?" Brima asked the little fellow.

"Dey kill him wid white powder an bury him in de groun," he answered. "He be ma friend so I sleep by his grave all night. When I wake up dis mornin, he push his way out de groun."

"I know who he is," Mariama said, her lips quivering. "He's my brother Lazaro."

Luke checked the boy's pupils and then listened to his lungs. "If I were back home, I'd swear he had overdosed on heroin."

Brima nodded grimly. "The rebels gave the boy soldiers cocaine during the war and then brought them down from the high with heroin or *jamba.*"

"I don't suppose we have any naloxone in our medical supplies?" Luke asked, hoping for a simple antidote for narcotic overdose.

Brima shook his head. "If he goes into withdrawal, we won't have enough morphine to ease his way."

Since Luke had arrived in Africa, every case he treated turned into an adrenaline moment. *I'm a virologist,* he thought, *not an ER doc.* He felt a small hand tugging at his shirt. The boy who had dragged Lazaro into the compound was standing next to him, shaking uncontrollably.

"Get him a shot of chloroquine," Luke shouted as he carried the boy to a pallet. "He doesn't look good." The boy's complexion was a sick shade of yellow. "What's your name, son?"

"Samura," the child answered.

Brima pulled down the boy's eyelids. "He has more than malaria. He's also in opiate withdrawal."

"This boy can't be more than ten years old," Luke said.

Luke looked over at Lazaro, awake now and trying to talk with Mariama and Paul. His brow was dripping sweat, and he was starting to shake. "Bring him over here," Luke said, pointing to a cot next to Samura. "We're about to manage two kids going through withdrawal cold turkey."

Mariama huddled with her brother as Marta took over the care of Samura. In the midst of the steamy jungle, they covered the boys with blankets. For three days the women mopped their brows and cradled their tortured bodies. Paul never slept, going from boy to boy praying.

As Lazaro and Samura began to recover, neither one wanted to talk about his experience. Only gradually did Lazaro's story come out.

"Dey kill mi parents dead," he told them, "den de rebels take me wid dem and gimme strong juju."

"The war is over," Luke said. "I thought they had liberated all the boy soldiers, and the rebels went back to whatever they were doing before the war."

Lazaro shook his head. "Not all de rebels go home. Not all de boys got to go."

As Lazaro adjusted to normal village life, Mariama became more a mother than a sister to him. Samura, on the other hand, was not so easy to nurture. On a good day the boy mixed charm with guile in equal measure. But his cunning escalated when Marta decided to take him firmly under her wing.

"Someday Bethany House will be a haven for boys just like you," she told him. "After our team goes home, Lazaro could be the head boy, and you could be his assistant."

Marta's model of English public-school life did not appeal to Samura. "Auntie Marta put me in cage."

As Marta and Samura matched wills, the other team members bore the burden of arbitration.

"This is getting to sound like a badly written soap opera," Luke grumbled one day when Marta wasn't around.

"She's your cousin," Mariama answered. "Maybe you could talk to her."

Luke shook his head. "Don't look at me. She may be my cousin, but she's come close to ruining my marriage."

It was Mariama's turn to complain. "When we needed help with travel plans, it was nice to have someone so organized. But now that we're here, I don't need someone telling me how to run my life."

"Have you talked with Marta about your concerns?" Luke asked.

"I did," Mariama said. "She told me I don't help enough around the place."

"Sounds like we need a conflict mediator," Paul said.

"Bad joke," Luke said.

Brima tried to intervene. "We don't want to gang up on her."

Outside the hut they could hear Marta screaming. "Sammy, you come back here right now!"

"Are you sure the boy isn't the problem?" Brima asked.

Luke disagreed. "He's just a child, and I've seen Marta in her control mode before. It's not a pretty sight when she goes into overdrive."

"Any other ideas?" Brima asked.

Paul nodded. "Here's a thought. Why don't we alternate handling the crises? Each day we have a 'chump-du-jour' to arbitrate?"

Luke agreed. "Better than sticking one person with the assignment."

The task of Marta management didn't find a first volunteer. They drew straws to decide who would be first. Bishop Paul lost.

"I'm going to my prayer chamber," he said. An hour later he emerged and led Marta and Samura into the hut.

Luke tried to relax to write in his journal, but loud voices soon emanated from within the hut. Samura stormed out first and ran west toward the bush. Marta followed and shrieked after him. Soon Bishop Paul was in pursuit.

"It doesn't look good," Mariama said.

"Want to flip me for day two?" Luke asked.

Mariama watched the peace coalition stalk off in three different directions. "I don't think we need a second day. We need a whole new plan."

The next day Marta looked at her four teammates, all childless. "I need the advice of an experienced parent."

Brima reached over and took her hand. "As far as we know, Jesus never had children, but he knew what to do with children."

Marta looked up. "What would he say in this type of situation?"

"He said never to do anything that might cause a child to sin. Rather than offend a little one, he said it would be better to have a millstone put around your neck and be tossed into the sea."

Marta moaned and ran to leave the hut.

"Where are you going?" Luke asked.

"To find Sammy before it's too late."

Paul lifted his hands toward heaven and mouthed the words, "Thank you, Jesus!"

✠

Peace returned to Bethany House. Philip and Constance Whitlock finished their work in Lonko and moved to Kameara to drill another well. Marta had plans for them after they finished the well and the pit latrines—building a home for former child-soldiers.

"Are you sure that's a good idea?" Brima asked Marta. "We'll only be in this village for another week."

"The need will be here long after we're gone."

"What's up for you after Sierra Leone?"

For the first time in her life, Marta said, "I really don't know."

That evening, when the last of the patients had left and the sun had followed them back to their villages, Luke had a visit from the Nigerian doctor he had met at the UN compound.

"Dr. Joseph! How nice to see you again."

The tall Yoruba smiled and motioned to Luke that he wanted to talk in private. "I'm here to see you on a personal matter."

Luke signaled for Brima to leave them alone, and he sat down behind his table. "How can I help you, Doctor?"

"I came here six months ago. My men have been here a lot longer."

Luke nodded, accustomed to long medical stories that would vindicate what would follow.

Shoulders slumped, the doctor seemed to be weary of whatever was bothering him. "Not even in medical school did I see such things. I'm a city man from a good family."

So far the two men were even. For Luke dinner would have to wait. The military doctor had come with a heavy heart.

"My men are very young and far from their families."

Luke felt the story moving closer to his field of expertise.

"Some of these young village girls are married to very old men. If a girl doesn't get pregnant, she sneaks off at night to a young man who doesn't want to do it with a condom."

Rumor had it that the so-called peacekeepers were leaving more than babies in the bush. They had a high percentage of HIV infection. But the picture of those reckless young men didn't help Luke understand why Dr. Joseph had called on him. For certain, they had long since exhausted his supply of anti-retroviral drugs and the rapid field tests for the virus. "But how can I help *you*, my friend?" Luke asked.

Dr. Joseph pulled his wallet out of his pocket and showed Luke a picture.

"You have a beautiful family," Luke said, looking at a well-nourished mother with two smiling children.

The Yoruba smiled sadly. "I won't see them again for at least another year."

Luke grew sad as well, imagining what it would be like to be away such a long time from Theo and his soon-to-be-born child. "You have a hard life," he said as he waited to hear the rest of the story. A trite but true answer.

The black doctor sighed deeply and looked over at the triage desk where Marta was sorting cards from the day. "A fine woman," he said. "Not your wife?"

Luke sat up straight, no longer the objective medical inquisitor. "My cousin," he answered, "here under my protection." As if anyone could protect Marta from herself! Luke laughed silently at himself. His last remark sounded like something he had heard in a movie.

"I can pay a good bride price," the doctor said.

Luke saw the desperation on the man's face. "She's not available," he answered as firmly as he could without sounding rude.

The Yoruba doctor sighed. "I can understand—a fine woman like that."

Luke's heart went out to the man. He whispered something in the doctor's ear and pointed to a distant hut.

As his visitor departed, Brima came back and sat by Luke's side. "A difficult case?" he asked.

Luke nodded.

"What did you do for the man?" Brima asked.

Luke stood up and gathered up his instruments. "Rabbi Hilkiah says he can cure AIDS, so I sent Dr. Joseph for a lesson on Jewish safe sex."

Around the cookpot that night, Luke laughed as he told the story. Everyone smiled except Marta.

"Next time someone asks you that, you send him to me!" Then she went off in a huff.

"How much was the man willing to pay?" Brima asked.

Luke laughed. "Why? Are you interested too?"

Brima shook his head, watching the proud woman disappear into the hut. "I doubt there is a mortalman who can afford that woman."

Luke was asleep that night when the sat phone rang. On the line he heard Theo crying.

"It's Baba," she said.

Luke reached for a flashlight. "Another stroke?"

"He's gone."

Luke pulled on his pants. "I'll get an earlier flight home."

"You don't need to do that. Johanna and I can help your mom with the arrangements. Baba didn't want a memorial service anyway. When you get home, we can decide what we want to do."

"Could you put Mom on the phone?"

His mother's voice was strong and clear. "Father was in his favorite chair. I heard him laughing. When I went in his study, he was talking to someone. Nobody was in the room, but he kept saying, 'Daddy. Daddy.'"

"Thank God he didn't suffer," Luke said.

"I've never seen Father so happy."

"I'll be home soon, Mom."

Theo came back on the line. "I'll be home soon," he said.

"I love you. Our baby loves you," she answered.

"Good night." Luke hung up the phone, then whispered, "Daddy, do you forgive me?"

Part VII

A done see Satan fall down, come out ob heaben like lightnin.

—Luke 10:18, *De Good Nyews Bout Jedus Christ Wa Luke Write* (Gullah)

FORTY

Marta turned away from the window. "I've never seen nights as black as an African night without a moon in the sky."

Mariama shone a flashlight on Marta as she handed her a long white dress. "Sunrise is in half an hour."

As she slipped the dress over her head, Marta said, "I've wanted to do this ever since I came to Sierra Leone."

Mariama smoothed the homespun robe over Marta's hips. "Sistah, you're taking a big step."

Marta took a strip of white cloth and wrapped it around her head. "Am I tying this right? It's hard to tell without a mirror."

Mariama put down her flashlight and rewrapped the seeker's headpiece on Marta's head. "I remember when I put this on for the first time. To choose Christian baptism in my village was a bold step at the time."

"Was your life in danger like the early Christians?"

"Not really, but it did set me apart from the other girls my age. They wanted to go through initiation into the *bundo* society. Sometimes they called me names for not going with them into the bush."

Mariama took up the flashlight again and shone it on Marta. She was pleased with what she saw. "You always pay a price to take a stand for what you believe."

Marta heard a touch of sadness in Mariama's voice. "Your parents backed you up, didn't they?"

"My father was adamant that I would not go to the bush with the other girls, but sometimes my mother felt pressure from the Mammy Queen. She passed the pressure onto me. 'Lots of Christian girls are *bundo* girls,' she would tell me. Finally my father sent me to school in England so there would be no more fighting."

Mariama turned off the flashlight and led Marta out the door of

Bethany House to the place where the others were waiting. It was still too dark to discern faces, but she could make out who was who.

Luke stood in the dark next to Rabbi Hilkiah. "Are you going with them?" Hilkiah asked him.

Luke shook his head. "I'm going to the water, but not in it."

"Ancient Jews believed in water too, when they wanted to repent of their sin."

Luke shrugged. "What about Muslims?"

"Ah, our ancient brothers, born on the other side of Abraham's blanket."

Luke thought about his own birth on an unknown blanket. "What would it take," he asked Hilkiah, "for brothers to live in unity?"

Hilkiah looked in Paul's direction. "An authentic prophet to announce the coming of the Anointed One."

At home Luke had known a few Jews who still waited for their Messiah. Unlike Hilkiah, they had grown up with their Torah and taken it for granted. But this tall African Jew had known the Law only in the whispers of his father and grandfather, hidden in a Muslim village. Then, as Luke had done with Giles's manuscript, Hilkiah discovered the Torah and devoured its words.

"I can't claim my journey is the same as yours," Luke said, "but I think I understand in some small way."

The rabbi bowed graciously. "I'm very certain you understand."

"One question," Luke added. "Where is your journey leading?"

Hilkiah gathered his robe around him. "To Messiah, dear doctor. The same place your journey is taking you."

There was just enough daylight for Luke to see the rabbi's face. "Bishop Paul says that someday Jesus will come again."

Hilkiah turned to leave. "And on that day some of us will be more surprised than others."

"What are you saying?" Luke asked, but the rabbi had disappeared into the early morning darkness.

Bishop Paul came over and placed his hand on Luke's shoulder. "It's not too late for you, you know."

Luke smiled and shook his head. "It's just too early."

"What would make it just in time?" Paul asked.

"I don't know the answer to that question yet."

"I bet you'll know before you leave Africa."

Marta joined them, looking like a bride in her white baptismal gown. "Baptism is a form of death," she said. "Maybe that's the kind of death Grandpa Giles had in mind in the manuscript."

Luke shook his head. "I'll just have to wait and see."

He thought about the time Giles splashed himself by the spout in Glen Helen. What did Johanna report that he had said? *"My papa be pleased."* It wasn't long after that incident that Luke's grandfather had died.

Marta tried to read Luke's thoughts. "You don't think you'll get out of Africa alive, do you?"

Luke's face darkened for a moment. "I honestly don't know, but I think I'm ready to go home."

Preparing to lead the procession to the river, Bishop Paul clapped his hands. Brima, serving as his deacon and carrying a long, crooked stick, moved up behind Paul. As the candidates lined up, Mariama began to sing.

Wade in de water, children.

Lazaro and three amputees fell into place.

Wade in de water, children.

Marta took a deep breath and stepped forward as the procession started to move.

Wade in de water, children.

Only one person drew back from the larger group. Samura stood at the edge of the bush.

Luke beckoned to him. "Come on, Sammy. You can go with me."

The boy hesitated and stepped farther back.

"Don't you want to see Auntie Marta baptized?" Luke asked, moving in the boy's direction.

God gwine trouble de water.

Samura's eyes widened as Luke approached, but he stayed fixed in place. "Come on, Sammy."

Finally the boy accepted Luke's outstretched hand, and they followed the baptismal party to the river.

When the group reached the water's edge, Brima stepped into the river and sounded the depth with his stick. When he had located the proper depth, he nodded to Paul, and the bishop waded in to join him. One of the amputees was the first to follow.

"Do you renounce the devil and all his works?" Paul asked.

"I renounce de devil an all his works," he answered.

Luke felt Samura's palm sweat as Paul lowered the man into the river. "There's nothing to be afraid of. This is a safe place to be." He let go of the child's hand and placed both his hands on Samura's shoulders.

Three times Paul brought the man under the water. "In the name of the Father, the Son, and the Holy Ghost. Amen!"

Even Luke added his benediction, but he felt Samura trembling as Marta stepped into the waters.

Paul repeated the formula. "Do you renounce the devil and all his works?"

Sweat broke out on Samura's brow as Marta answered, "I renounce the devil and all his works."

As she emerged from her third time underwater, Marta began to shiver. Luke let go of Samura to take her a towel.

When Lazaro's turn came in the river, Mariama started to weep. Luke smiled at Brima, who had so expertly guided the boys through the time of drug withdrawal, but the nurse wasn't smiling. He was looking toward the bush.

Luke turned toward Samura, but the boy was gone. *Too bad,* he thought. He wouldn't see Lazaro take a further step out of the clutches of the devils that stole his childhood.

"Do you renounce the devil and all his works?"

"I renounce de devil an all his works," Lazaro answered in a strong voice.

His years as a child-soldier, with all his murders, mutilations, and countless rapes, were forgiven in the three-personed Name. The ceremony complete, Bishop Paul waded out of the river. "Hooey! Nothing like a baptism to make me hungry."

As the party made its way back from the river, Mariama started another song.

Sheep know his shepherd's voice...

"Where's Sammy?" Marta asked, looking around for her charge.

Yes, Lawd, I know de way...

"He saw you go into the river," Luke said, "but I lost track of him after that."

Every sheep know his shepherd's voice...

At the front of the procession, Luke saw Brima come to a full stop.

Yes, Lawd, I know de way...

"Quick!" Brima said in a hushed tone with his fingers to his lips. "Into the bush." He pushed Luke and Marta off the dusty trail and motioned for them to be silent.

"I've got to find Sammy," Marta yelled.

"He's gone back to the rebels," the nurse said, motioning her to keep quiet. "Your lives are in danger."

"He wouldn't hurt me," Marta said. "And how do you know our lives are in danger?"

"Samura is an addict in need of a fix," Brima answered as he signaled the others to follow him.

"Where are we going?" Paul asked.

"Deep into the bush behind Bethany House."

"Isn't that the witch doctor's devil bush?" Mariama asked.

"We'll have to take our chances," Brima said. "They'll find us on the road."

FORTY-ONE

Marta stood paralyzed before a column of fire ants. As Brima grabbed her by the waist and hoisted her over the ants, she asked, "Why are we zigzagging like this?"

"We don't want to give them a clear trail to follow," he said.

"Who is it we're running from?" she asked.

Brima scowled. "Whoever it was who kept Lazaro and Samura prisoner."

The fire ants missed, but not the mosquitoes. Marta swatted at her ankles, remembering the can of insect spray in her suitcase. She tried to drive away the alluring mirage of the chemicals she had once thought of as poison. She turned away from Brima and frowned. "We've been on the move all day."

Brima struck the elephant grass with his stick. "You do fine-o."

When she heard his Krio phrasing, she relaxed. When Brima was most concerned about their welfare, he spoke Standard English. Still, she had to be honest with him. "I don't know how much longer I can walk."

Brima spun her around so they were standing face to face. "You work in Sierra Leone not be done-done."

Marta tried to smile, but her face froze when she saw him lift a finger to his lips. Brima let go of her and snapped a branch to capture the attention of the rest of the group who were walking ahead of them. Then he motioned toward the east.

The small band of refugees turned in the new direction. Mariama had to support Lazaro, who was still weak from his narcotic withdrawal. Luke had linked his arm through Paul's to support him as he limped. Three days of walking through thick underbrush had taken its toll on the most vulnerable in the group.

I want to sing praises to the Lord...

Paul crooned softly, trying to lift his own spirits as much as the others'. He was almost as depressed as Marta.

"Talk to me, Paul," Luke said. "Don't sing me jingles. I want to hear what you're really thinking."

Paul stopped dead in his tracks. "I'd rather praise than think. Right now thinking is getting me in trouble." He sat down without even looking to see what might have crawled beneath him. "You remember meeting Sister Jackson when Brother Emmons died?"

Luke squatted down next to him. "Sure, I remember. She was using a cane then. Now, thanks to the virus, she's stuck in a wheelchair. It breaks my heart."

Paul nodded. "Before we left, I told the congregation where I was going and what we were planning to do here. I watched them turn their eyes away while I was preaching. They were afraid I might ask them to give money or come with us."

"You shouldn't feel guilty about that," Luke said. "They're sweet folks, but no one we could use on our team."

"But do you know what happened? Everyone looked away except Sister Jackson. She rolled her wheelchair up to the altar rail and shouted out, 'Here am I! Send me, Lord.'"

Luke turned toward Paul and laughed. "Has she ever flown on a plane?"

Paul shook his head. "I don't think that mattered to her—or should have mattered to me."

"Then why did it matter?" Luke asked.

"It was truth time, Docta Luke. Every Sunday I prayed with her, believing God could heal her of AIDS. But I sure didn't have the faith that he could take care of her in Africa."

Luke looked around at his friends who were struggling to make it through the jungle alive. He shook his head at the thought of a wheelchair-bound, three-hundred-pound woman in tow. *I'm not the one who makes a career out of believing,* he thought. Then he remembered Theo, who no longer had any signs of ALS. His heart filled with gratitude.

I want to sing praises to the Lord.

"What did you say to Sister Jackson?" Luke asked.

"Oh, I told her that God had called her to a ministry of prayer for Sierra Leone. I gave her some pictures Mariama had of her village and commissioned her as our prayer warrior."

"She was satisfied with that?" Luke asked.

Paul shook his head. "Her eyes filled with tears. 'But I want to go with you,' she kept repeating."

"Someday we'll come back and bring Sister Jackson with us," Luke whispered.

Paul flashed a weak smile. "If I could believe that, I guess I could believe we'll get through today."

At a muddy stream Brima paused to fill an empty water bottle. After the sediment settled, he passed the bottle around. "This is the only water we're going to see for a while. Drink from the top as much as you can."

Marta's face fell. "I think I'm going to vomit."

Brima held the bottle of brackish water to her lips. "Dehydration is more of a risk than infection right now. It's dry season, and we won't find much water along the way."

Marta wept. "I don't think I can do it."

"Vomit if you have to, and then drink as much as you can."

Paul's stomach was rumbling. "How many days can we go without food?" he asked.

Brima frowned. "If I go into a village, someone might report us to the rebels. We'll find some mangoes and cassavas on the way."

Luke pulled Brima aside. "Back on the road I never saw or heard a thing. How can you be so sure there were rebels?"

Brima's face grew taut. "I didn't hear the rebels. I heard the silence that comes before them."

"What about the rice and cooking pot? You told me that when you were on the run, you always had them with you."

Brima reached down into a bush and broke some berries off a branch. "Eats, Lazaro," he told the boy who stuffed them into his mouth. "The next food we find is for Marta."

"You don't think one of those scrawny village chickens might get lost and wander our way?" Paul asked.

"The snakes would find it first," Mariama said.

"Don't think about food right now," Brima said.

"Or snakes," Luke added.

Brima warned them. "If you think or talk about food, you'll be hungry."

Luke took Brima aside. "If rebels were in the area, wouldn't we see villagers on the run?"

Brima knew Luke was right. "Tonight while you're sleeping, I'll sneak back into the village for the rice and cooking pot and see what's going on." He touched his lips again to signify silence and motioned them to start walking again.

At sunset, when they reached a clearing, Brima took a flint out of his pocket and burned away a large patch of grass. Then he gave directions to the team.

"Marta and Mariama, collect some palm fronds. Luke and Paul, find us some long sticks to make poles. We're going to make us a canopy for the night." When the sticks were in place, Brima showed them how to lay palm fronds over them for a roof. As soon as the others settled on the ground, the nurse started in the direction of Kameara.

Luke didn't sleep that night. As he listened to Paul snore, he wondered if Brima would ever return. Finally, almost at daybreak, he heard footsteps near their lean-to. "Did you get the rice and pot?" he asked Brima.

Brima motioned Luke to come away from where the others were

sleeping. "I couldn't get near Bethany House. It looked like they had guards posted."

"What about the rest of the villagers?"

"Some of them fled to the bush on the opposite side of Kameara when they saw the men arrive. Pa Sesay told me that Samura was with them. They were going from house to house asking about you."

"What are we going to do?"

"We've got to wake the others and get moving. We don't dare make a camp like this again. They'll be able to track us."

As soon as the others were awake, they started taking down the lean-to and covering up their tracks.

On the next night Brima signaled the others to wait at some distance as he approached a tree.

With his stick he rustled the branches and stepped back briskly. Just as quickly, a green mamba slithered out from the leaves and hastened down the trunk. As the snake headed into the bush, Brima moved to another tree and repeated the maneuver. Luke took a deep breath as he saw more snakes descend from the trees.

Satisfied that he had routed out all the snakes in residence, Brima hoisted Marta into a tree and settled her in the fork of the trunk. Mariama helped her frail brother into a second tree. Brima beckoned to Luke, and together the two men boosted Paul into the third tree. Finally the nurse helped Luke up into Paul's tree before he took his own place next to Marta.

Brima whispered loudly enough for all the trees to hear. "Remember, one sleeps while the other keeps watch. Keep your eyes peeled for trouble and make sure the sleeper doesn't fall out of the tree."

In the silence of the night, Marta wept. "I'm so frightened."

Brima held her and sang softly, *Sheep know his shepherd's voice...*

Marta smiled and fell asleep with the response on her lips, *Yes, Lord, I know the way.*

In his tree Luke took the first watch and let Paul sleep. The doctor had observed that each day Paul's limp was getting worse. The bishop was snoring, so he reached over and gently touched his arm. The sleeper snorted and then resumed regular but unornamented breathing. Luke wished he had his journal with him, but a flashlight would have been out of the question.

The night air in the jungle was cooler than heat of the day, and Luke felt a slight chill. The chill intensified, this time ripping through his body. Sweat dripped from his brow as he touched his burning cheek with his hand. Long overdue for his pills, he settled back to experience his first bout of malaria.

"We can't stay in the bush," he told Brima the next morning.

"We have to stay here if we're going to survive."

"I'm the one they're after."

"We're staying together. If we left you and they caught us, they'd torture us to find out where you are. We're staying together."

Luke watched Brima wander through the brush examining plants. He came back with a handful of leaves and crushed them into the empty water bottle. "I'll be right back," he announced and headed for the river.

When Brima came back to the clearing, he was shaking the bottle. "This isn't the best way to make a tea, but it will have to do." He handed the herbal concoction to Luke.

"Drink this right down. It tastes terrible, so try to take it all at once."

"What is it?" Luke asked, gagging.

"A bush remedy for malaria. It takes the edge off an attack."

He spilled out the rest of the herbal water onto a terry-cloth towel and used it to bathe Luke's forehead. "I'm going to take the others to the river to drink. I'll bring back a full bottle for you."

Luke nodded, although he didn't relish staying in the jungle by himself. He was too weak to argue—or to go along.

Brima told him, "If you hear any noises, climb a tree."

"Leave me your stick."

The nurse shook his head. "If you hear noise, you've only got time enough to climb."

Brima gathered the rest of the group around him and whispered. "First we go to the river, and then we come back and stay here today. Dr. Luke is in no shape to travel."

While they were gone, Luke drifted into a malarial dream. He was thrashing around calling "Grandpa!" as he watched Giles wheel Sister Jackson over the potholes in the laterite roads. When Brima returned with the water, he told Luke, "Drink all of this."

When the next set of chills took hold of Luke, his friends quietly prayed over him. Then the sun began to fall. Brima helped Paul into the tree with Marta. Then he kept watch all night at the side of the fever-racked doctor.

At sunrise Luke woke up to feel his tree shaking. Brima was already down below.

"Come down!" Brima called. "We've got to get out of here as quickly as possible." He helped Luke out of the tree and instructed the others. "Get down on your stomachs! Crawl into the bush."

At first, all Luke heard was an eerie silence. Then he heard the sound of machetes cutting through the underbrush. As he lifted his head slightly, he saw two black figures with Kalashnikov rifles. One of them was Samura.

"We've got to split up for a little while," Brima whispered. "How are you feeling?"

"Much better," Luke answered. "You take the others and head for Kameara. I'll go the opposite direction."

"Sorry, son," Paul told him. "I'm not leaving you on your own."

Brima nodded. "Go with God, my dear doctor." He motioned to his three traveling companions to follow him.

The sick doctor and handicapped preacher tried to crawl on their bellies through the underbrush. Four hours after they separated from the others, Luke heard a voice behind him.

"Over der!" yelled Samura. "I see de white docta."

Propelling himself with his elbows, Luke moved as quickly as he could away from the sound of the approaching men. Suddenly a heavy-booted foot clamped down on his neck, pinning him to the earth. As he struggled to get free, the boot came off his neck and crashed into his side. His attacker kicked Luke over on his back like a turtle. As the boot came down on his chest, Luke stared up at the most evil eyes he had ever seen. The man he assumed to be a witch doctor motioned to Samura to pull a hood over Luke's head.

FORTY-TWO

With his hands bound behind him, Luke was unable to mop up the sweat pouring from his brow. The brine beads pooled on his chin and seeped into his mouth. As his captors propelled him through the underbrush, thorns ripped at his sandaled feet. Unlike the man whose boot had pinned him to the earth, the guard who pushed him forward was short and had small hands. "Sammy?" he asked, his voice muffled by the hood over his head.

"No talk, Docta Luke. Better dat way."

Ignoring the warning, Luke asked, "What happened to Bishop Paul?"

"Dey capture him, too."

"What about Auntie Marta and the others?"

"No want dem. Men look fa you two."

"Why, Sammy?"

"Bigman say we bring you an de preacherman."

Luke remembered hostage stories in the news, dismembered heads displayed on television. In Sierra Leone, they seemed to favor hacking limbs and leaving survivors to suffer for the rest of their lives. *Which would be worse,* he wondered, *losing my life or losing my livelihood?* For the moment he would settle for getting out of Sierra Leone alive.

About an hour into the forced march, Luke heard a thud behind him. An African voice yelled from a few yards away. "Get up!"

Bishop Paul's response was weak. "I can't with my hands tied."

Luke lunged in the direction of Paul's voice, but a rifle butt came down on his head.

"Get up! Both of you!"

Luke shuffled to his knees to boost himself upright. It took strong leg muscles to stand erect without the help of his hands. He thought of Paul's polio-damaged leg. "Let me help him."

A rifle came down on Luke's shoulder, and he stumbled again. "He's an old man with a bad leg. Let me help him walk."

"You hands stay tied."

Luke listened as the man who yelled at Paul dragged the preacher to his feet. Again Luke tried moving in that direction. "Lean against me," he called to Paul and felt his friend sag into his body. "Sammy?" he called.

"No talk, Docta Luke."

"Listen to me, Sammy. Tie us together at the waist. Surely your friends won't mind. It will make it harder for us to escape, and we'll get to the destination faster."

Luke tried to hear what Sammy said to Paul's guard but could only catch a grunt. Then he felt the ropes digging into his middle and the almost dead weight of Bishop Paul fall against him. "Hang in there, buddy," Luke called to Paul as he thrust both their bodies forward through the dense jungle.

An hour later more voices signaled that they were coming to their destination. Samura pushed them through the low opening of a hut, and they fell bound together on the floor. Paul was silent, but Luke could feel his chest heave.

The doctor fought off sleep, intending to stay alert. Finally the exertion of the march through the bush and days without eating took its toll, and he sank into the darkness.

Luke awakened with a start, not certain how many hours had passed. The sound of Paul's snoring reassured him that his friend was still alive. Luke's mouth was parched, and he licked his lower lip to take in his sweat. He wondered if this was how it felt when men were lost at sea and reduced to drinking salt water.

A startled snort from Paul signaled his return to consciousness. "Are you awake?" Luke asked in the dark.

Paul tried to find a comfortable position as Luke moved with him. They managed to pull themselves upright and lean against the wall of the hut. Then the bishop started to sing.

Let everything that hath breath praise the Lord.

Luke smiled underneath his hood. "You keeping singing, and I know we'll make it through this."

Paul fell silent and tried to listen for noises outside the hut. "Do you have any idea where we are?" he asked.

"Somewhere near that witch doctor's territory."

"While we were on the road, I heard children's voices."

"I'm sure that was the diamond mine. I bet they're using those children to pan for blood diamonds."

"This thing is bigger than you and me, son."

"Don't I know it. I keep asking myself what Grandpa Giles would do."

"You keep asking that, son, and God will show you the way."

Luke remembered the night when he'd seen his grandfather's picture full of bullets. Anger had raged in him at first, but he remembered Martin's last words when he died. *Daddy. Daddy.* Luke felt tears adding to the wet mix on his lips, and he started rocking back and forth. "I wish I could be a little boy again, sitting on Grandpa Giles's lap. For the past few months, my life has been full of surprises and none of them has been pleasant. I want Grandpa to open his desk and let me search for a Matchbox car or a baseball trading card. I want some small surprise that will fill my heart with joy."

In the darkness Paul shook his head. "Neither of us is a little boy anymore."

"If I were that little boy, I would wait for Grandpa Giles to write the rest of my story, but he never finished anything. He wouldn't even paint over my messy blades of grass. I don't know how a man is supposed to act in a situation like this."

Paul smiled to himself. "A wise saint once said something like this:

Work as if everything depends on you and pray as if everything depends on God."

"Sense the holy and then respond?"

"Something like that."

Luke dropped his voice to a whisper. "I hear somebody coming."

Judging from the voices, Luke figured that two men had entered their hut. They mumbled something in Krio and untied the cords that bound Luke and Paul together. Luke waited for the men to take off the hoods, but that didn't happen. He heard Paul grunt as the men dragged him to his feet and through the door.

"Where are you taking him?" Luke called after them.

Luke was alone in the darkness. He moved to the door and tried to follow the sounds. He heard muffled shouting and the high-pitched voice of a child. Sammy's voice. Then he heard Bishop Paul singing.

O when my friends forsake me, give me Jesus.

A dull moan interrupted his song.

When de doctor give me over.

Luke heard more voices, angry and impatient, and the sound of a child crying.

O when my friends forsake me, give me Jesus.

"You tell them, broda!" Luke whispered. Then he heard Paul's voice.

"It won't do you no good to ask."

Again he heard voices shouting in Krio, including Sammy's voice. Luke's joy at Paul's resistance turned to horror as he heard cries of pain, then silence. A low moan and shuffling sounds followed, like a man in pain being dragged. Two voices spoke in Krio, but no one was singing.

Luke heard a moan and hid in a corner until the door opened. Something fell to the floor. The door snapped shut, and the lock turned. Luke heard another moan.

"Paul? Are you here?"

O when, O when...

He moved in the direction of the song.

O when, O when...

Luke reached over in the darkness.

O when I come to die, give me Jesus.

"What did they do to you?"

"Beat me up good around the face and then took pictures. They had a video camera."

Give me Jesus...

"Who did it?"

"He didn't want to beat me."

"Sammy?"

"He was crying."

"How you doing?" Luke asked.

"I've got some tightness in my chest that makes it hard to breathe."

Angina, Luke worried. The beating had put an additional strain on Paul's heart.

"They're coming for you next," Paul told him. "They want to make us pretty for the camera." Then he howled in pain and grabbed his back.

Luke reached over toward where he thought his friend was lying. "What's wrong?" he asked.

"Must be a kidney stone setting off for a southern vacation." Then he howled again and grabbed for his flank.

Luke scooted over toward his friend and tried to find his hand. "Do you know what these guys are asking for? Are they asking for a ransom?"

In the darkness Paul nodded, thinking about the consequences and more. "You can't do what they're asking, son. No matter how much they beat you."

"I can't bear seeing what they're doing to you."

"I'd rather die than think we left those children in slavery."

"Oh, God! I don't know what to do!"

"His grace is sufficient for me," Paul said. "His power is made perfect in weakness."

☩

Luke couldn't sleep, imagining what would happen next. Were they waiting for morning and sunlight to bruise him for the camera? He felt so weak. What was the prayer he had heard Theo say sometimes in her sleep? *Lord Jesus Christ, Son of God, have mercy on me, a sinner.* With Paul leaning against his chest, Luke fell asleep until daybreak when he heard footsteps approaching the hut.

As they took him from the hut, Luke lunged at his captors. Then he heard a demonic laugh, a voice he recognized. He pulled his hands free from the ropes and yanked the hood from his head. The witch doctor who had frightened the villagers was standing before him.

He motioned to his men to fetch Bishop Paul. "Bring him out here so he can see what we do to the doctor."

"So your witch-doctor routine is just an act to scare the villagers. What was your moniker during the war?"

The man laughed. "Captain Cut Hands."

Luke had heard the name from villagers talking about former rebel leaders who never went to jail. The melodramatic name had power over the people.

Captain Cut Hands watched Paul stumble out of the hut and called to his men, "Take off his hood. I want him to enjoy this."

He signaled to two men to hold Luke fast. "Are you right-handed or left-handed, Dr. Luke? Your government has refused to pay the modest ransom we requested. Perhaps now they will come through with the ten million dollars."

One of the henchmen took out a large machete. The phony witch doctor grabbed the machete with one hand and looked at Sammy. "It's time to be a man again."

Sammy wept and tried to run away. "Bring the white powder," Cut Hands instructed. "Let him sniff away his fear."

One man held Sammy as another filled his nostril with powder. *Cocaine*, Luke assumed.

"That's good," Cut Hands encouraged. He pushed Sammy forward. "Now, you know what you have to do."

One of the men came with the video camera while another dragged Luke to a tree stump.

Paul strained against his captors as Luke struggled with the man who was trying to hold his arm on the stump.

When his captor heard a commotion to the rear, he let go of Luke. A dozen of his henchmen turned to see Rabbi Hilkiah arrive with a band of ragtag amputees.

Forgetting Luke and Paul for the moment, Captain Cut Hands sneered at the new arrivals. "What have we here? A Jew with an army of half-dead men?"

Cut Hands' henchmen were unprepared for the ferocity with which the amputees fought against them. Paul sang out, *I have seen the downfall of Satan. Glory be to God! Glory be to Jesus!*

"They're devils!" one man yelled and ran into the bush. Those left standing followed.

Hilkiah moved swiftly to Paul's side and released his bonds, but not before Captain Cut Hands pulled out a gun. Luke saw pure wickedness in his face as he raised the weapon and aimed it at him. Then he saw Paul move quickly in front of him.

"Don't!" Luke cried, but it was too late. The bullet intended for him cut down Paul instead.

Captain Cut Hands turned to run to his Land Rover only to see a UN helicopter circle overhead and then land. He tried to run the other way, but three of the peacekeepers jumped out of the helicopter and caught him. After they secured him, they ran into the woods after the rebels.

As Luke knelt over Paul, Dr. Joseph and Farid Nassour ran to his side. The Yoruba doctor shook his head when he saw Paul's wound.

Paul moaned, and Luke held him as close as he could. "I can hear your heart," Paul whispered. "You have a healer's heart."

"You can't die," Luke said. "That isn't supposed to happen."

"If I get out of here alive, then would you believe in Jesus?"

"If that happened," Luke admitted, "I'd be a fool not to believe." The odds were clearly against him.

"Sometimes, son, the best miracle happens when there's no visible sign."

"How can you say that?"

"Blessed are those who believe but have never seen."

Delirious, the bishop called out to Miss Maggie so tenderly that Luke felt as if he were there on St. Helena Island with him.

O when, O when, when I come to die, give me Jesus.

Dr. Joseph closed Paul's eyes, but Luke wouldn't move.

"How did you know where to find us?" Luke asked.

"Mr. Nassour came to ask for help. Rabbi Hilkiah thought he knew where they had taken you. We followed the rabbi and his men through the bush in our helicopter."

"The children," Luke remembered. "We can't leave them behind. Samura told me they have children here, held captive."

Luke found the huts where the children were imprisoned. He pointed through the bush in the direction of Kameara. "Run, run!" he urged them, pushing them out. "Go to Bethany House."

He found Samura hiding in a corner. "Come on, Sammy. It's time to go home."

Samura drew back. "I can't go. Papa God never forgive me for what I done."

Each time Luke approached him, the boy drew away, so Luke sat on the floor where he was. "Sammy, let me tell you a story about a boy who left home and got into big, big trouble. When he came home, he asked his papa to forgive him. You're just like that boy. You tell Papa God you're sorry and that you'll never do those things again. Say, 'Lord Jesus, Son of God, have mercy on me, a sinner.'"

Samura sat staring at the ground.

"What, Sammy?" Luke asked.

"Docta, de preacherman be dead. It be my fault. You forgive me?"

Luke sat there stunned. How easy it was to talk about God's forgiveness to the child, parroting what he had heard Paul say about the Bible's prodigal son. He looked over at the small hand that had wielded the machete over his own. Like Samura, Luke was at a loss for words.

The boy looked up at him with the puppy-guilt face of a ten-year-old in trouble with his daddy. "You forgive me?"

"It's not for me to forgive you. I'm not the one you hurt."

Samura shook his head. "When I hurt de preacherman body, I cut you heart."

As tears ran down Luke's face, he felt the sharp pain of loss. He nodded, not looking at the boy. "When I feel that pain in my heart, I wonder if it can ever heal. But then I hear Bishop Paul saying, 'Don't listen to de devil. That ole liar says you can't forgive.'"

Sammy sniffled. "Mebe dis time de debil tell de truf."

Luke moved closer to the boy and took his hands. "The devil's an ole liar. He never tells the truth." As he pulled the child into his arms, he said, "It's not an easy thing to forgive you, I admit. But if I don't forgive you, Sammy, there's no hope for me."

"I never meant to hurt you heart, Docta Luke."

"That's good, Sammy. Doctors are no good without a heart."

Rabbi Hilkiah came into the hut. "All the other boys are out of here."

Luke helped Samura to his feet. "Run-run to Auntie Marta. It's time for all of you to be free."

FORTY-THREE

When they reached Kameara, Luke saw Marta and Brima standing in front of Bethany House. He cut short his greeting. "Are you all here?"

"Yes. Mariama and Lazaro are safe."

Mariama came out of the house. She saw Nassour and Dr. Joseph climb out of the helicopter. "Where's Paul?" she asked.

As two of the peacekeepers carried Paul's body out and laid it down, Luke took Mariama in his arms. "I'm so sorry, Mariama, but we brought him home with us."

As she had done at her parents' grave, Mariama fell down on her knees and sobbed. Brima knelt beside her by the lifeless body of the bishop. When he rose, he said, "Let's bury him next to your parents."

Mariama nodded, and they walked together to the horrible place of murder that Paul had just planted with sweet potatoes and the hot red peppers Brima loved so much. Now Brima and Lazaro dug a place next to the mass grave for the man who cherished their daughter.

Nassour helped Luke carry the body and slide it gently into the grave. Dressed in his priestly robe, Rabbi Hilkiah kneeled by the open grave. He quoted from one of the psalms he had memorized in prison.

"Behold, how good and how pleasant it is for brethren to dwell together in unity."

He poured oil over Paul's face and body.

"Unity is like the precious oil upon the head coming down upon the beard, coming down upon the collar of his garments."

Luke motioned to the others to gather. Mariama took his hand. He didn't know what to do other than squeeze her hand as if to say, "I know how you feel." But he couldn't know how she felt, so he kept silent.

He watched the villagers gather, but Marta stood at the fringe of the group, looking toward the bush. *I hope Sammy is on his way with the other boys,* Luke thought. Hopefully? Luke had acted on impulse, telling the boy who had beaten Paul to come back to Bethany House with a bunch of trained young killers. Oh how he wished Paul were there. The bishop would know what to do.

But Brima knew. He took Paul's tattered Bible and turned to a well-worn page. "Hear a word from the New Testament written by a Jew named Paul: 'Who shall separate us from the love of Christ? Shall tribulation, or distress, or persecution, or famine, or nakedness, or peril, or sword? As it is written, "For thy sake we are killed all day long; we are accounted as sheep for the slaughter." Nay, in all these things we are more than conquerors through him that loved us. For I am persuaded, that neither death nor life, nor angels nor principalities nor powers, nor things present, nor things to come, nor height, nor depth, nor any other creature, shall be able to separate us from the love of God, which is in Christ Jesus our Lord.'"

Brima closed the Bible and turned toward the doctor who had become his partner for the past few weeks.

"In the end Paul was not alone. In his final letter the apostle wrote, 'Only Luke is with me.' Paul called this faithful friend 'the beloved physician.' If I were the one facing death, I can think of no better companion."

Luke felt his cheeks burning as Mariama reached up to kiss him.

Hilkiah spoke again. "They say that the first Paul helped turn the world upside down. In our times it may be said that our Paul turned Dr. Luke upside down." Hilkiah stepped back into the gathered circle as everyone looked at Luke.

Luke went over to the edge of Paul's grave. "You all know Samura's story. I must confess that a part of me wanted to leave the boy behind with his captors this morning. I wanted him to pay for what he had allowed to happen to Paul. Then I remembered what my grandfather said about the man who killed his daddy. 'Let's see what kind of thief he wants to be.'

"My grandfather said that Jesus died on a cross between two thieves and that each of them had a choice. Back in that awful place, so did I. In that village where they kept those little boys, it was my turn to show mercy.

"Someday my grandfather's manuscript *The Deaths of Lucas Tayspill* will be complete. On that day when I stand before Jesus for judgment, I pray that Bishop Paul will be by my side. I want to hear him say, 'Hooey, son, you done learned your lesson well.'"

Luke turned to Brima and Lazaro. "I know I'm leaving a lot on your shoulders by sending those boys here."

Lazaro stepped forward. "The work of Bethany House must continue."

Suddenly Luke heard Mariama's voice.

Powa, powa, pour your powa.

The mourners began to clap and answer.

O Sperit, fall on me.

In the near-trance of a ring shout, Mariama started to move.

Good nyews, good nyews, preach de gospel.

Marta was the first one to follow her into the counterclockwise circle, joining in the singing.

O Sperit, fall on me.

Luke watched joy replace sorrow as Mariama continued to line out the song. From Paul's songs, he knew the words from the fourth chapter of Luke's gospel by heart.

Freedom, freedom, free de captive.

The ring widened as more people joined in.

O Sperit, fall on me.

Luke watched Rabbi Hilkiah stomp his feet and move into the circle.

Heal de blind man, heal de deaf man.

The night Woodrow Emmons died, Luke had watched Theo join such a circle. An hour earlier she had been depressed and withdrawn. That night her healing began.

The doctor moved into the circle, clapping to the beat.

O Sperit, fall on me.

Nassour's driver pulled up in the air-conditioned SUV, ready to carry Luke and his friends to Lungi. Luke turned to Marta, "Pack Mariama's bags as well as yours."

"I'm not leaving," Mariama said.

Luke pulled away from her. "Of course you are! You know the danger if you stay here. Not all the evildoers have been dealt with."

As they walked toward Bethany House, Mariama took the doctor's hand. "You must go home to tell the story, but Brima, Lazaro, and I will remain. We want to be here with our people to see the downfall of Satan."

"You can't stay. Theo and I need you at home."

"My dear brother, if you truly know Jesus, you have everything you need."

Luke turned to Marta. "You've got to knock some sense into her. She can't stay here!"

"Luke," Marta said quietly, "she's pregnant."

Dumbfounded, he looked at Mariama. "How did that happen?"

Mariama laughed. "The usual way." Then her voice took on a more serious tone. "You know about the brutal mistreatment of my family and how I returned to Sierra Leone after nursing school. You also know how deeply Paul and I loved each other. Now I want you to hear the rest of our story."

Luke, who had been in a hurry to leave Sierra Leone, took a seat to listen to Mariama's story.

FORTY-FOUR

How beautiful she is, Luke thought. Mariama was young and radiant as she sat down to tell him the story.

"I had studied nursing in England and came home just before the war began. After the rebels killed my parents and sister and kidnapped Lazaro, I stayed on to help the women. So many women were malnourished that their babies couldn't pass easily into the world. When the village birth attendants called me, I went to see what I could do. They needed cesarean sections, but that was impossible. I can't tell you how many belly ladies bled to death as I stood there helpless. I had no real medical supplies, certainly no latex gloves. Afterward, with the help of local church leaders, I escaped to the United States. I already had my visa for midwifery training at Yale School of Nursing. Paul's congregation took me in."

Her face grew sad, and her eyes filled with tears. Luke was glad she left the awful details to his imagination. As he listened to her, Luke wanted to take her into his arms, but he knew she wanted to finish her story.

"A few weeks after I arrived in New Haven, I had a high fever and swollen glands. When I had applied for my visa in Sierra Leone, my HIV test had been negative. Now it was positive."

Luke listened silently, but his mind kept replaying scenes from Connecticut. Since he'd known Paul and Mariama, he had always thought they held some things private, but big, famous AIDS doctor that he was, he had missed the telltale signs of Mariama's illness.

How many times had her wristwatch alarm gone off during the day? Each time she disappeared for a moment. Shouldn't he have noticed that those chimes corresponded with anti-retroviral dosing? But he hadn't noticed. He had chalked up the Pinckneys' secrets to cultural differences that were beyond his comprehension as a white man.

In horror he suddenly remembered that she was pregnant. It was vital that she return to the States for treatment! But he held his tongue until she finished her story.

"My diagnosis created a new dilemma. The student health insurance didn't cover a chronic illness like AIDS. And thanks to the terms of my student visa, I wasn't eligible for any American medical-assistance programs. If I returned to Sierra Leone, I would die at the hands of rebels before the virus got me. That's when a lifelong old bachelor made a decision.

"Bishop Paul had intended not to marry. Yes, he was attracted to women. Sometimes too much, the way he told the story. But the life of ministry he had chosen left little time for the cares of a wife and children. He fasted and prayed until he had a plan. He offered to marry me, but with an important limitation. We could have no sexual intercourse. We would love and cherish each other in nonsexual ways."

Mariama stood and paced, but Luke stayed in his chair.

"If Paul had not already chosen bachelor life, I would have refused his offer. But I knew that if he did not marry me, he would never marry anyone else. I wondered if the schoolgirl crush of my childhood could flower into mature love in this unusual arrangement. Surely I didn't want to infect any man, much less someone I had loved since I was a little girl."

Mariama sat down again.

"What alternatives did I have? A sexless marriage to a good man so many years my senior that guaranteed I could stay in the U.S. with health insurance. Or I could return to a civil war as an HIV-infected outcast.

"The congregation of Sweet Holy Spirit didn't know the details of our relationship or my illness. They were excited when we announced our engagement. The congregation gave us a beautiful wedding. In those days I thought I wouldn't live very long, but then came all the new drugs to treat HIV. I finished my master's degree and applied to work with Yale's AIDS Care Program. I felt healthy. Rather than a handicap, I thought I had an extra qualification to work with AIDS patients.

"At church I watched the ladies keep an eye on my waistline. They hoped the Reverend and I would have a baby. But for the ten years of our marriage, we kept our vow to live like sister and brother." Mariama smiled gently. "Life isn't always logical, and neither is love. When I came back to Sierra Leone, I felt in constant danger. And in a way, I think Paul knew he wouldn't leave Africa alive."

Luke knew Mariama was right. How many times had he heard Paul refer to death in his sermons? Luke thought he had been preoccupied with the reality of life in Sierra Leone. He never dreamed how close the message came to reality.

Luke had heard enough. It was time to persuade her to come home.

"If you're pregnant, Mariama, that's all the more reason you should come home with us. You know the risks to yourself and your baby. Please come home."

Mariama smiled softly and shook her head. Frustrated, Luke turned to Marta. "You try to reason with her!"

Marta shook her head. "I'm staying here with Mariama. No, Luke, don't plead. The children you freed are heading this way. Brima and Lazaro will need all the help they can get when they go into narcotic withdrawal. And Sammy will only believe in Papa God's forgiveness if we're here to kill the fatted calf for our long-lost son." She took Luke's arm. "Go home and tell our story. We'll let you know what medicines we need. The work of Bethany House must continue."

At first Luke reached out to shake Brima's hand, but then he put his arms around him. "Mi nurse."

"Mi docta."

The two men stood back and measured each other for the last time. Luke was the first to speak. "I've heard patients call their nurses 'angels.' I always thought that was like calling a nurse a servant. Now I think I know what they mean."

Brima flashed one of the smiles Luke had come to treasure. "The Bible says to be careful with your fellow mortalman, Dr. Luke. You never know when you might meet angels unaware."

"Write to me," Luke ordered.

Brima laughed. "Our postal service might get it to you in a year."

"Then e-mail."

"I may be able to get down to Freetown every three months or so and look for an Internet café."

Luke paused. After all this time he still hadn't fathomed how different life was in Sierra Leone. "I'll come back someday," he told Brima.

"Mi docta, you have made me a promise I intend for you to keep."

Luke looked toward Mariama. "Take care of her, broda. You're the only hands I have here." This was the doctor's final order to his nurse.

"Do you understand why she's staying?" Brima asked.

Luke bowed his head. "For the same reason you hoped I came. For love of the people."

Brima nodded. "That kind of love doesn't come through the head, mi docta. It comes from the heart. Saint Paul called it a gift from the sweet Holy Spirit—the best gift, even greater than the gifts of faith and hope."

Luke blinked away tears. "Her baby is going to need all three."

From the comfort of Nassour's SUV, Luke watched Bethany House grow smaller. For the first time since his long journey began, the doctor began to cry.

EPILOGUE

De two man beena taak bout all dem ting wa jes
happen.... Jedus esef come nigh ta um an waak long
side um.

—LUKE 24:14,15, *De Good Nyews Bout Jedus
Christ Wa Luke Write* (Gullah)

Pursued by Captain Cut Hands, Luke raced through the jungle.
Emerging into a clearing, he staggered down rows of crosses in
Flanders field. Giles was waiting there for him.

"Hi there," his grandfather said. "Are you going my way?"

Luke looked behind him to see if he had escaped his pursuer. "I'm
trying to go home."

"Sounds good to me," Giles said as he picked up his pace to keep up
with his grandson.

They slowed to a gentle jog when they heard music. Giles pulled up
beside a man on the path.

"Do you know what's been happening around here?" he asked.
"Back on the trail we overheard people talking."

The man laughed. "You've got to be a stranger around here not to
have heard. Nobody's talking about anything else these days."

Luke stopped jogging and walked back to join his grandfather. "I
can tell you what happened," he told his grandfather, "but I can't say I
understand what it means."

Starting with his discovery of *The Deaths of Lucas Tayspill,* he re-
counted the events since the previous Thanksgiving and ended with
Mariama's and Marta's decisions to stay at Bethany House.

Giles didn't look confused, but Luke felt disoriented. How could he start out in Sierra Leone, turn up in Flanders, and pop out into the woods in America? Where was that music coming from? African drums and voices filled the early evening sky.

I have seen the victory of Jesus
Satan has fallen, hallelujah
Jesus has conquered!

Luke watched the sun start its descent toward the horizon. "Come on, Grandpa."

Giles broke into a sprint. "I'll race you home."

"Finally we're going home! The music is coming from our house."

But where, Luke wondered, *is my home?*

Luke awoke in the dark, disoriented as to time and place. The bed he had slept in was as unfamiliar as the starlit window on the other side of the room. As he slipped out of bed and stepped on a pile of clothes, he remembered the last words in his dream—"Where is my home?"

Luke had a home in Yellow Springs—the house where he grew up, the parental home to which he often returned. He had unfinished business there, the burial of his father. But that must wait. He remembered a story he had read in the Gullah gospel about a man who had taken the first step to follow Jesus. He turned on a lamp on the bedside stand next to him and saw the battered copy of the gospel that had followed him on his journey. He found the dog-eared page he had marked and began reading. "Bot de man ansa um say, 'Sah, fus leh me go an bury me papa.'" That man turned back from following Christ.

Luke had a home in Connecticut. Soon he would take Theo back there to resume their lives and wait for their new baby. That, too, must wait. Between sleep and wakefulness, words from Giles's manuscript came to him as he struggled between his father's burial and his own need for resurrection. *If you have no cause worth dying for, do you really have a reason to live?*

He thought about his third home—Sierra Leone. For much of the trip, he had focused on himself—the dangers he faced, the risks to which he was exposed. That was before he met poor women and dying children, mutilated men and patients who, like Mr. Emmons, said "thank you."

He heard voices coming from another part of the house, his fourth home. He followed the voices to the kitchen. Although the sun had not yet begun to rise, the kitchen was alive with activity.

Eula May waved at him with a mixing spoon and pointed to a large leg of lamb on the kitchen counter.

"Docta Luke, you white folk sho can turn an Easter dinner inta a project an a haf. I could jes have fried us up some chicken."

Theo bellied up to the counter and put her arm around Eula May's shoulder. "When I was a little girl in Greece, my papa used to roast a whole lamb on a spit over a wood fire for Easter."

Luke laughed. "We tried that once in Connecticut. Moose stood under the lamb right next to the fire with his mouth open, hoping for juice to drop. I was afraid he was going to burn his paws."

"Dat dawg got mo courage dan sense," Cedric said. In a corner of the kitchen, Moose was romancing a very large lady hound.

Eula May motioned to Luke. "Now that you awake, come over here an preside."

The doctor lifted a scalpel and brought it down on tender flesh. With deliberate strokes, he incised the skin in a dozen places. Then he used the blade to slice a clove of garlic. Eula May picked up the garlic slices and stuffed them into the pockets Luke had scored into the side of the lamb.

Edith Tayspill emerged from the guest room where she had been sleeping. "Is it time for me to peel the potatoes?"

Luke smiled when he saw his mother. What was it Rabbi Hilkiah had quoted from the prophet? *The people shall build up the ancient ruins and raise up the former devastations.* Miss Eula May was a builder upper.

Eula May made room for Edith in the small kitchen by shooing Cedric and Luke out. "We oomans can take care of all de fixins."

"Shoo, now!" Theo echoed.

Cedric called to Luke from the front door, "Les go down to de dock."

Luke smiled, happy that Eula May had brought the family together. Right now St. Helena Island was the home where he needed to be.

Moose and his new girlfriend followed Luke and Cedric out the door.

Luke sat on the edge of the dock and swatted at a mosquito that zeroed in for the kill on his forearm. "More skeeters here than in Sierra Leone," he said. "Sundown and day clean. Those are the times of day they like best."

Moose sat with his chin on Luke's lap as his master looked across the salt marshes and the bay that led to the open sea. Luke scratched his head and pointed to the salt marsh.

"Cedric, the shoreline here is just like Sierra Leone."

Cedric and his hound girl sat down beside them. "Which way it be to Yale?" he asked.

Luke oriented himself and looked for a star. "Yale seems such a long way from here."

"I wanna go to Yale someday."

Luke smiled and nodded.

"Will they understan me at Yale?" Cedric asked. Carefully, the boy was leaving behind the Gullah dialect Luke had learned to love.

"They'll understand you in Sierra Leone," Luke answered. Luke wanted to hold on to the precious link to Bishop Paul and Sierra Leone. "There's enough time for Yale."

They lapsed into silence again, which Luke was the first to break.

"I'm so sorry about the journal. I don't know what got into my dad." In his mind's eye, he pictured Giles's manuscript and Lucas's journal going up in flames.

Cedric didn't answer right away. He got up and shook out his legs. With the first rays of sunrise, Luke could see sadness in the young man's face.

"I be sad bout de journal, but I be sorrier bout Bishop Paul."

Luke turned to face the old bungalow across the road that Paul and Miss Maggie had once called home. Silence seemed to be the day's best answer, and Luke's gaze drifted to a patch of marsh grass that resembled the blades he had painted on his grandfather's canvas so many years ago.

Cedric saw a copy of *De Good Nyews Bout Jedus Christ Wa Luke Write* in Luke's back pocket. "You ever read de end of de book?" he asked.

Luke shook his head. "I never got that far."

"Man, dat be de bes part."

As the sun continued its lazy ascent, Cedric read aloud the story of a risen Jesus who was hidden from the eyes of the very ones who were seeking him. With Gullah gusto he gesticulated the actions of the disciples walking on the road to Emmaus. They didn't recognize the stranger they met along the way, but they couldn't let him go. Cedric, who knew the story by heart, put down the book. He folded his hands, pleading with the stranger to come home for a meal. "Comin home wid Jedus," he told Luke, "dat be de bes part."

Cedric sat down on the broken planks of the dock and crossed his legs. He mimed the breaking and passing of the bread. Then he changed places, becoming a disciple and inviting Luke to join him at the imaginary table. His eyes widened with surprise, and he motioned to Luke. "Dat be Jedus."

Luke joined in the drama. He, too, finally recognized their companion.

Cedric sprang to his feet and reached out a hand to help Luke up.

He slapped Luke on the shoulder as he recited the end of the story. "Dat be like a fire in we heart, ainty?"

Luke laughed and nodded. "Fire in we heart, eh?"

"Yessir, dat be jes de way it feel."

Luke rolled his shoulders to work out the tension in his muscles and started walking toward the beach. Cedric followed him, and they took off their shoes at the water's edge. The wet sand between Luke's toes felt cold but inviting. He reached down and picked up a broken stick the tide had washed up on the beach. In the sand he wrote "WHERE ARE YOU?"

"You still lookin fa Grandpa Giles?" Cedric asked as the water lapped up and tickled his feet.

Luke looked out toward the sunrise where a marsh hawk was circling. "Always. I'll look for him my entire life, even if I'm not a Tayspill."

"Lucas, man, you be a Tayspill fa sure. An we be cousins."

Luke laughed. "We be better dan cousins. We be brodas."

Cedric rolled up his pants. He slapped Luke on the shoulder and ran toward the tide. "Come on, broda. Les go wadin in de water."

Luke raced after him but stopped when the shock of cold water went through his whole being.

"What you waitin fa?" Cedric called to him.

As Luke waded in, he called to Cedric, "Fire in we heart, indeed!"

Lyric Acknowledgments

Song lyrics have been taken from the following sources:

    Billy Crockett and Milton Brasher-Cunningham, "Let Us Be Thankful Boys and Girls," copyright © 1994, Radar Days Music.

    Mark Knopfler, "The Bug," copyright © 1991, Chariscourt Ltd.

    Marlena Smalls, "Praise Him," copyright © 2000.

    John Rutter, *Requiem,* copyright © 1985.

    Graham Kendrick, "We Believe," copyright © 1986 by Make Way Music.

The following hymns, spirituals, and African songs are in the public domain: "I Have Seen the Downfall of Satan"; "In the River Jordan"; "I So Glad I Here"; "Let Everything That Hath Breath" (traditional praise song based on Psalm 150); "O When I Come to Die"; "Send the Light"; "Sheep Know His Shepherd's Voice"; "Wade in the Water."